D0773047

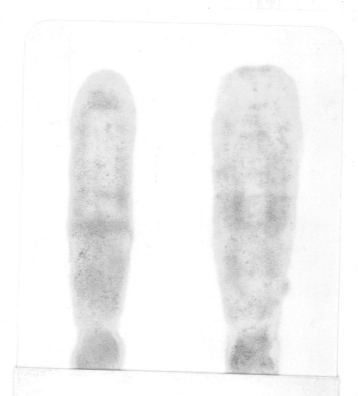

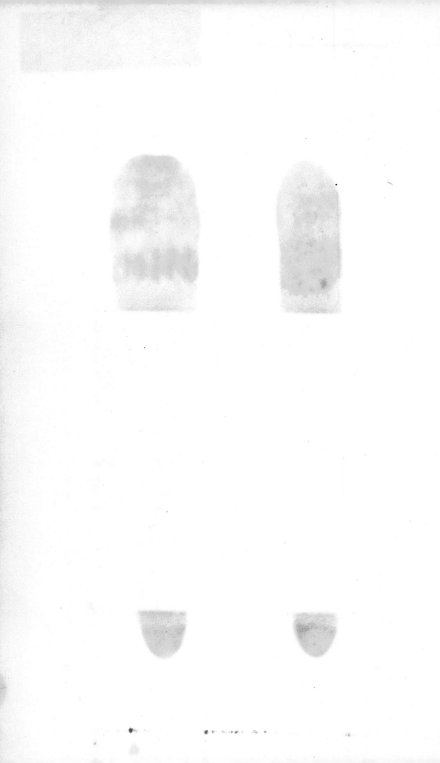

WATER HOLE

WATER HOLE

by
Julian Savarin

St. Martin's Press
New York

$f\!c$

Library of Congress Cataloging in Publication Data

Savarin, Julian Jay.
  Water hole.

  I. Title.
PR6069.A937W3   1984   813   83-27444
ISBN 0-312-85768-3

First Published in Great Britain in 1982 by Allison and Busby Limited

First U.S. Edition

10 9 8 7 6 5 4 3 2 1

For
Julia

WATER HOLE

Prologue

THE END of the gangway rested on a pier in Taormina, Sicily. A man left a gleaming ocean-going yacht, walked down unhurriedly. He looked at peace with the world. The yacht belonged to him.

A small plastic bag of rubbish lay directly in his path at the foot of the gangway, spoiling the air of bright cleanliness that seemed to hang about the ship. The man paused, scowled in annoyance.

He raised a foot to step over the obstruction. Just as he was directly above it, a small charge buried in the rubbish exploded. It took his entire crotch with it.

He died a few hours later, in terrible pain.

A year passed.

An eight-foot band of gold moved sinuously across the hot surface of the red outback soil of an Australian desert region, as it slid between the sparse tufts of porcupine-like spinifex in the fierce heat of the late November day. The golden snake would normally have sat it out in the dubious shade of a sun-bleached clump of shrubs, waiting for night before doing its hunting. But it had sensed an unexpected meal.

A tawny frogmouth, having flown too far from its roost, lay gasping on the red earth some distance away. Probably disturbed from its daytime nap by some predator, it had panicked. Now its mottled, muddy-brown and white form flapped listlessly in the heat, its oversized beak opening and closing slowly. The golden rings of its dark eyes gave it an air of quiet desperation. A nocturnal creature, the furnace-like sun was its deadly enemy.

Another enemy was fast approaching. The bird lay on a patch of ground that had been cleared of all obstruction. The huge snake, its body gleaming, moved swiftly towards its prey, reared its head and struck, seemingly all in one incredible motion. The frogmouth's first indication of its danger was also its last as the fangs bit deep into its body and the toxins began to attack its central nervous system. In fleeting seconds, it was dead.

The snake rolled, twisted and coiled as it sought to ingest its catch.

High up in the naked sky, a soft whine began to intrude upon this scene of death. The whine grew louder as a speck came into view and gradually took on recognizable shape.

The Cessna Citation III lowered its wheels and began a straight run-in for the landing, its twin rear-mounted jets throttled back, easing it down to earth.

Nine tonnes of aircraft, crew and passengers landed on the snake as one of the main wheels slammed into it. The wheel spun red dust and the golden snake into the air. Writhing as if in reflex, the already dead reptile struck the tail of the Cessna, caromed off it to land off the strip, the frogmouth still gripped in its jaws. Its body twitched momentarily.

The Cessna rolled to a stop. It had been a good touch-down.

"Jesus! The heat of this place!"

Eight people had got off the aircraft — five men and three women — all carrying automatic weapons, from rifles to submachine guns. They also had with them boxes of various sizes which held ammunition and more weapons. The boxes lay on the red earth at their feet.

"You ever see a place like this?" the man who had spoken asked of no one in particular. He stared at the limitless, arid horizon. "Jesus!" he repeated. "This red stuff is going to be fun in my hair."

The Cessna had turned, and was lining itself up for take-off. Everyone watched interestedly as the engines were opened up. The executive jet rolled forward, gathering speed quickly. It hurled itself into the air in a flurry of dust, banking sharply to the left and climbing at the same time.

Roasting in the heat, its erstwhile passengers watched its departure until silence once more descended upon the emptiness about them.

Someone said: "We'd better get all this ammo out of the goddam sun." Another man. He consulted his watch. "The others should be arriving in about sixteen hours or so and we've got work to do. Things should be happening just about now. Let's move it."

They picked up the boxes and began walking towards a long and exceptionally low-lying building.

The sandy beach blazed whitely in the sun and stretched for miles in three directions. In the forth, it was halted a mere few yards away by an expanse of calm, blue water which lapped ceaselessly at the sand. With a muted, continuous hiss, the sand drank unendingly.

He was alone, and quite naked; totally alone and naked, on the vast, white beach at the edge of the huge ocean; at the edge, it seemed to him, of the world. He looked about him.

Nothing had changed. There was no one in sight.

No one.

He could not remember how he'd got there. There was no boat drawn up at the water's edge; no ship riding at anchor. The ocean was empty, devoid of life it seemed, even beneath its surface.

He looked about him once more; slowly, carefully. He peered at the sand. There were no marks upon it, save for his own footprints. No aircraft had landed him.

He stared at the footprints. There were two sets: one leading to and one coming from the hole. Both sets went all the way to the water's edge. At each end of the journey, they merged.

He frowned, momentarily perplexed. What had he been doing?

Without first realizing it, he began walking towards the water. He stopped, letting the gentle wavelets caress his toes. Suddenly, he squatted, and scooped up some of the liquid with cupped hands. Very carefully, he straightened, walked back towards the hole, poured what was left of the water into it.

The water disappeared.

He made another trip, hurrying a little. The water disappeared just as swiftly. The hole was insatiable.

He ran. The hole drank.

He speeded up. The hole beat him to it every time.

He was rushing about now, trying to get as many scoops into the hole as he possibly could, so that he could fill it. It was extremely important that he should do so. He knew that; but he didn't know why.

The hole continued to beat him. The faster he worked, the faster it drank. Soon, he was panic-stricken, and at the end of each trip he would pause to stare desperately into the hole, searching, hoping for the slightest glisten that would show he was winning; or at least, beginning to.

He was still losing.

The hole was unbeatable. He was staring into it more and more now, losing precious time! He became obsessed, frenzied. He would dash to the water's edge, scoop some up, dash back to the hole, pour it in, stare longingly after it, dash to the water....

The sand was churned by his frantic hurrying.

Now, he was looking up at himself looking down into the hole, and the water was coming down ...

He screamed! And from within the scream....

9

Day One

I

"THIS IS not your captain speaking."

Gallagher's eyes snapped open. There were people screaming, but he was not one of them. The first-class airliner cabin he shared with them was suddenly full of balaclava-masked people. With horror, he saw four passengers – three men and a woman – rising almost simultaneously from different seats. Their manner told him what they hoped to do, just as surely as he knew they were bound to fail.

The reports, when they came, were four rapid coughs. Four previously living people jerked like marionettes and became four lifeless rag dolls. There were more screams. None had come from the four who were now sprawled untidily across the seats, and across those nearest to them. The still-living cringed in terror from the recently dead. Everybody else seemed frozen where they sat.

Gallagher himself remained absolutely still, his eyes taking in everything they could without his having to move his head. His mind was raging. *Good Christ. I use a complimentary ticket to get away from one piece of shit, and I get this. Why couldn't these bastards have picked on another bloody aeroplane?*

"Ladies and gentlemen," the English voice with a London accent was announcing over the muted sound of the jets. The voice had a sense of humour. "Ladies and gentlemen, your very sensible captain has kindly handed over the command of this plane to my good self and my colleagues."

There was a pause while the speaker allowed the news to sink in.

"If you're all very sensible," the male voice went on, "no one will get hurt. However, it seems that some people have been very, very stupid. There are now four corpses in the first-class cabin." The voice had lost all its apparent cheerfulness. "We do mean business. Make no mistake. So let's have no more of that, shall we?"

Gallagher could imagine the stifled screams in the economy-class. Not a sound came from the first-class. Death had come too close.

From where he sat, Gallagher could see the stunning girl with the chestnut hair. He wondered how she was taking it. At Heathrow, her eyes had passed over him as if he'd been an ornamental fixture. Next to her, nearest the window, sat an old man, and across the aisle from them Gallagher could see the top of a sleek head of black hair.

The owner of the head must have moved forward sometime during the flight, for Gallagher had not seen him before. *Must have happened while I was asleep. Christ, that nightmare.* He shivered involuntarily, remembering.

The head was attempting to talk to the girl, who did not seem particularly interested. A balaclava mask shifted menacingly, and the man stopped his attempts at conversation.

In front of the old man and the girl, Gallagher could see the shape of a bulky African in the outer seat; while behind them, also in an outer seat, was a solidly built man whose Roman-cut hair was so blond, it was almost white. Gallagher had seen the man's face in the airport lounge. He'd thought it was the meanest face he'd seen in a long time.

The blond man was well over six feet, taller than Gallagher himself who was one inch over the six. The man had a wispy blond moustache, and his eyes stared like pebbles from so deep inside his head, they looked as if they were trying to get back in.

Without moving his head, Gallagher could see no more. *And I'm not going to give you trigger-happy bastards the excuse either.*

The hijackers' spokesman was still talking. "In a few hours, we'll be landing at an airport of our choice where a transfer will take place. For economy-class passengers, this is your lucky day. We're taking first-class only.

"You'll be pleased to know," the announcement went on, "that we're releasing the crew, unharmed. Hope you enjoy the flight." The cheerfulness was back and, for Gallagher, that seemed like an ill omen. "Refreshments will be brought to you from time to time. We'd advise you to accept them. Thank you for flying with us." *Click.*

Gallagher fumed at himself. One ticket and a moment of despair had landed him in this.

His eyes caught sudden movement. Sleek Hair had stood up and was trying to say something. A balaclava mask was pointing an automatic pistol at his face. Another hijacker came up, pistol ready, and dragged Sleek Hair unceremoniously past Gallagher. People tried to look.

"Don't move until we tell you!" a hijacker yelled in a muffled snarl through the mask. A woman's voice.

Heads snapped back quickly. Gallagher was barely able to see Sleek Hair's face, but what he saw struck a chord in his memory. That face, he knew, was familiar to many people. It was a face the media knew very well indeed. The face also seemed to know the girl well, for as the man was hustled out, Gallagher had caught a glimpse of his smile at her. It had been the shaky smile of someone who was intensely worried.

Oddly, the girl didn't seem to care. She'd caught Gallagher's glance,

11

but her astonishing eyes had held no friendliness, and no reaction to what was going on about her.

The promised refreshments were brought, and after them Gallagher fell asleep again. The nightmare returned in all its awful entirety.

Gallagher's eyes flashed open with the horror of it. They were the only parts of his body to move. The rest of him remained absolutely still. It was a skill he had learned, had been made to learn, years before.

Had his scream escaped? Had it sneaked, treacherously, out of the dream? Who else was awake? Were they all, even now, staring in horror at him? *Christ*, he thought wearily.

He still hadn't moved. He continued to stare at what had greeted the return of vision: a stretch of bare, earthen floor, less than an inch from his right eye. Further vision was blocked by a pair of unstockinged female legs.

He was lying on his side, in an almost foetal position.

He didn't move. He enjoyed the view instead. They were truly beautiful legs. Too much flesh on them to belong to a model; but they were long, and strong. Beautiful.

He remembered whom they belonged to. Had she heard his scream? He'd not had that dream for ages; not since .... Now, it had come to him twice in succession. It must be the drug; the bloody stuff they'd pumped into him.

The legs were not moving. So she was still out. She too was lying on the floor, turned away from him.

I'd better move.

It was very quiet. No; a low hum was coming from somewhere.

Come on, Gallagher. Move.

He stayed where he was, deriving great pleasure from the sight of the fantastic legs. The floor was warm. His eyes grew heavy-lidded, closed. He fell into a deep sleep.

The dream did not return.

He resurfaced in the midst of a jumble of noises. The others were snuffling, shuffling, moaning themselves awake.

"Where are we ...?"

"What the hell's going on ...?"

"Hey! The guy they dragged out is not here. They've killed him!"

"No way. That was Alex Harding. He's worth more to them alive."

"My fucking cigarettes! *Where are my fucking cigarettes*?"

There were counterparts in other languages too. Exclamations, of anger, outraged puzzlement, rent the air. Those who didn't utter a sound had been made mute by the horror of their predicament; and a very real sense of fear.

There were three exceptions to this: Gallagher, the young woman and the old man.

Gallagher had been placed in a corner, so he leaned comfortably into it and watched his fellow captives struggle awake. He remembered the girl's disdain during the hijack. Despite his preoccupation with her legs, her manner had caused him to feel an instant dislike for her. They had not spoken a word to each other. Neither knew the other's name. They couldn't have been more complete strangers.

Like everyone else, he was now looking about him. *Where the hell are we?* Unlike everyone else, nothing of his thoughts showed on his face. He listened unmoved while they jabbered at each other.

Their prison was a peculiar room: very large — almost square — no windows, with a single door at the end furthest from him, which was shut and undoubtedly locked. The walls and low ceiling were panelled with a pale yellowish wood. In the wall with the door was a long grille about a foot wide and two feet above the floor. The low hum was coming from there. Air-conditioning, Gallagher decided.

There was not a piece of furniture to be seen. Deeply recessed lights shone brightly down from the ceiling. There were no guards in the room.

Harding, he thought musingly. *The big man of Harding International himself. And he knows her.*

Gallagher watched the young woman. She was not looking in his direction. She had propped herself in a sitting position against a wall opposite. He was quite certain she knew she was showing yards of bare leg and thigh to all comers. The front-buttoned faded denim skirt could not in a million years have been chosen for the purpose of concealment. As he remembered it, the hem had barely reached her knees when she'd been standing. Her feet were pushed into a pair of rope-soled shoes that had plain denim uppers and low wedge heels. Her legs were close together, the knees drawn up; and despite the apparent leg-show her posture sent out its message clearly: Keep off. Do not touch.

You've got a hope, Gallagher thought sarcastically, secure in the knowledge that he had no designs upon her.

There was no doubt that she came from a wealthy background; in spite of the casual appearance of her attire, everything he'd observed about her so far betrayed that fact. The plain blouse, which shivered every time her breasts gently vibrated in response to a body movement, had not come from any ready-to-wear shop. The apparently careless way in which her long, chestnut hair was gathered up so that strands of it wisped rebelliously about her face only served to accentuate the patrician cast of her features. The wide-apart grey eyes gazed out upon the world from a position of inherited privilege. Her nose was sharp and small; but the lips, as if in perverse contradiction, were full and sensual. Despite what had happened, she looked ravishing.

She had been inspecting the room, her gaze slowly tracking round like a radar scanner, the eyes showing as little emotion. Her cold gaze swept over Gallagher as if he did not exist. He ignored the apparent slight. He'd expected it.

His mind wandered, tired of his little game.

"Gareth Gordon Gallagher, do you take this woman ...."

Oh, Christ! Shut up. Shut up. Shut up.

Oh, Celia .... He killed the thought savagely; but he was not quick enough to prevent a spasm of pain from flitting across his face. He was back in control swiftly, unaware that anyone had seen the brief disturbance upon the surface he presented to the world.

Once more in the present, he began thinking about the old man and his young companion. He knew that everyone — at least the men — seemed to think she was travelling with her sugar-daddy. Long before there had been the slightest inkling of what had been about to descend upon them, he'd heard two male passengers grossly discussing the possibility in the airport bar. He'd thought then that the men had been wrong in their assumption. He thought so now.

The old man was so completely different from her, they could only be relatives. While she seemed the epitome of a thoroughbred, his peasant background screamed out of him, notwithstanding his tasteful but now crumpled suit. He was dark in comparison to the fairness of her complexion. There was a lumpishness to his features that contrasted with the precise etching of hers. He was short and stumpy, to her tall elegance. In Gallagher's reasoning, the sheer diversity merely served to convince. Her grandfather, he decided.

He gave a small yawn, settled himself more comfortably into his corner and closed his eyes. Damn. Whatever they'd pumped into him was still making him sleepy. He fought it for a while, then gave in. The sounds of everyone talking at once, trying to work out where they were, what had happened, what was about to happen, mercifully faded.

The old man watched Gallagher's sleeping form for some moments, before saying: "If we are to leave this place alive, Lauren, this is the man who will help us."

The grey eyes she turned upon the oblivious Gallagher held no expression. The old man knew what was going on in her mind; he made a noise that sounded like a cross between a chuckle and a sigh of despair.

"Your upbringing betrays your reason, child." His words, lacking the tone of rebuke, were spoken with a precision that lent an air of mystery to his North American accent.

"That man? You can't be serious, Jake." Her voice was well modulated, mellow, with the high breeding of rich Massachusetts blood in it.

"What can a child of twenty-two know?" The old man asked the question both of himself and of his young companion. "I'll tell you: nothing. You see only the surface. Sometimes I feel like crying over all the money that was spent on your education. All those expensive schools!" He sighed, as if the thought of the outlay pained him. "I suppose —" he smiled — "you are not too stupid."

"Why, thank you, Gramps." Lauren took it all with good grace. Teasing each other was a game they had played since her childhood. Now it helped her to ignore temporarily the realities of their predicament. "I do believe I've even got a degree."

"That does not prove anything."

Lauren saw that the old man was no longer smiling. "You are serious," she accused uncertainly.

"You are being stupid, and that is not like you. That is not like the granddaughter I know who is hidden behind that silly girl at the cocktail parties in Boston. You are not on a private beach in the South of France. You are not at an *après ski* in Gstaad. You are *here* and it is a matter of life and death — *your* life, *your* death. That man over there may be your ticket to life."

Stunned by his vehemence, she remained silent.

"If you want that ticket," he continued, "you must forget all the nonsense your background has taught you. You know how I feel about some of the ways in which you have been brought up. I have tried, ever since you were a little girl, to explain things to you, and sometimes I believe you have listened. I have no complaints, except one. We both know what it is. Today, I ask you to forget that part of your conditioning. I ask it not for my sake, but for yours." The old man stopped, his eyes pleading with her. "The rules have changed, Lauren."

At last, after a long silence, she asked: "But how do you know, Gramps?" Her eyes were now on Gallagher's drooping form. "How can you be sure? You don't even know who he is."

"I know the type. I recognize something in him. I have had my eye on him since the airport. I like watching people. I've done it all my life. You can learn much, before you have even spoken to the subject. He is also a watcher. I recognize his kind. I wonder," Jake Smallson added mildly, "what happened to Harding."

Gallagher came awake for a third time, to find people still babbling at each other. Panic had not yet had time to set in. Disbelief still held control.

Then he saw that the girl's unsmiling grey eyes were upon him. He stared right back, assuming what he hoped was a quizzical expression. The grey eyes were singularly unimpressed. They held the stare, stubbornly refusing to give ground for some moments, before losing interest and slowly turning to look elsewhere.

If you weren't such a spoilt brat, Gallagher thought, *I could like you.*

Someone else was looking at him. The old man had a tiny smile on his face and nodded slightly. The indication were clear.

Gallagher levered himself off the floor and walked over, curious. There was a perceptible hush as he did so and he could imagine all eyes following each step he took. The effects of the drug had still not worn off completely and he had to make an effort to avoid staggering. Suddenly the distance across the earthen floor seemed unendingly long. He was relieved when at last he got to where the old man and the girl were sitting by themselves, some distance from the rest of the group. When conversation finally resumed, it was more subdued, speculative; watchful.

"We have given them something else to think about for a while," the old man said to Gallagher, half-amused. His smile transformed him into a very likeable person. "Allow me to introduce ourselves. I am Jake Smallson and this is my granddaughter, Lauren Tanner, who can sometimes be very stubborn. I'm afraid she inherited that from me."

So I was right after all. Gallagher felt pleased.

The strange inflection in the old man's voice teased at Gallagher as the girl's grey eyes continued their remote appraisal. Gallagher kept his own eyes on Smallson.

He said: "Gordon Gallagher."

"Gallagher!" The old man seemed amused. "A fine Irish name. Please sit down, Mr Gallagher. May we call you Gordon?"

"Mr Gareth Gordon Gallagher!"

"Sergeant!"

O'Keefe. Gallagher had on occasion found himself working with O'Keefe. By the time he had left the Air Force, Gallagher had become a Squadron Leader, while O'Keefe ....

II

"Gordon?"

Gallagher came back to his surroundings, looking sheepish. "Mr Smallson ...."

"Jake. This is hardly the time and place for ceremony."

"Er ... Jake. Sorry."

"For a couple of seconds, you really weren't here at all. More memories? I've been watching you," Smallson announced quite shamelessly into Gallagher's silence, "since Heathrow. I've watched you disappear into your memories for minutes at a time. A few of them, I think, were painful."

Gallagher felt himself bridle.

"You're angry." The old man was smiling. "You keep it well under control. That takes training, and a special ability. Like you, Gordon, I am a watcher. I know the kind of man you are."

"You know nothing about me."

"Nothing and everything."

"You called me over here to play word games?" Gallagher began to rise.

Smallson touched him briefly. "Please sit down." The words came mildly, but the voice had a steely firmness to it. "You have only just got here. The others will begin to wonder if you leave so suddenly."

"They're already wondering." Nevertheless, Gallagher settled down again.

He turned briefly from the old man to look directly into the girl's unflinching eyes. There was something in them he could not quite fathom. Despite all she'd been through so far, Lauren Tanner was still able to maintain her poise, was still able to look beautiful. Gallagher's skin prickled from being so close to her. He felt irresistibly drawn, yet something within him remained detached. It was all rather academic, for she was still holding up her KEEP OFF, DO NOT TOUCH signs for everyone to see. *Don't worry*, he thought grimly, *you're quite safe from me.*

An American voice bawled into his thoughts. "Those fucking bastards!" A female voice, loud, petulant. It went on, with emphatic enunciation: "They've taken my fucking cigarettes. I need a *fucking* smoke, god*dammit.*"

Gallagher recognized the voice as the one that had risen above the babble when he'd come awake for the second time. He smiled as he turned to look in the direction of the complaining woman.

"She said something funny?" Smallson asked.

"I was just thinking how enlightening it is to hear the jet-setting rich use the language of the streets."

"If you want the genuine article," the old man said, "go to the right shop. I have heard language among the so-called jet-set that would make a doughboy blush. A doughboy is ..."

"An infantryman."

"You understand American slang?" Smallson appeared surprised.

"A bit."

The old man gave him a speculative look. "How old are you?"

17

"Thirty-four," Gallagher replied before he could stop himself. He looked annoyed.

The old man actually grinned. "Gotcha. You are a little out of practice, I think."

"I don't know what you're talking about."

Smallson bypassed the protest. "What exactly did you mean when you said the jet-setting rich? You were, as I remember it, travelling first-class."

"A mad impulse. An indulgence. I'm not rich. I don't belong to this party. I blundered into it."

Smallson looked interested. "What happened?"

Gallagher made a dismissive movement with his hand. "It's a rather long, sordid story. Let's just say I talked myself into this mess." *While the balance of my mind was disturbed.*

"Talked yourself into it?" Smallson surveyed him keenly. "The painful memories. You must excuse me being so direct. It is sometimes a good thing to be direct."

Gallagher made no comment.

"So you're not rich," the old man went on. It almost sounded as if he wanted to add: *We all have our problems.* "What do you do for a living, Gordon? Are you in business? Or perhaps an academic?"

"Why all the questions?" Gallagher finally asked.

"We have little time for fencing," Smallson remarked. "We can go on with this dance of words forever and it will get us nowhere. I want to know in the shortest possible time if I am right about you. At the airport, it was an amusing exercise. Here, it is a matter of life and death. I believe you can help us."

"Help you? Help you to do what?"

"We need your expertise."

"What expertise?"

"No games, Gordon. Please."

Gallagher appeared to think about that. "I'm still puzzled by your request, but I'm assuming you're after a bodyguard of some kind. You've got the wrong person. I've never been a bodyguard." *Liar*, his mind accused. "And besides, it's open season on bodyguards. Remember what happened to the four who were travelling with those regal-looking people?" He recalled in graphic detail how swiftly and efficiently the unfortunate men and the woman had been killed in the plane. There had not even been time for them to reach their weapons. "Three bodyguards and an armed nanny. The way people travel these days. Yours on holiday? Lucky for him."

Smallson made a scornful sound. "I've never had a bodyguard, and I don't need one now. A bodyguard makes you dependent." He jerked his head in the direction of a man, a woman and a child who were sitting in a dejected group, barely speaking to each other. The child

18

was unnaturally still and wide-eyed. "Those people – the regal-looking ones, as you call them – are members of an ancient German aristocratic house. Just look at them. They are lost. The bodyguards are gone. Now, they have no idea how to fend for themselves. All their money is useless. You have a much better chance of surviving than they could ever have. So have I. I can look after myself, old as I am."

Gallagher grudgingly admitted to himself that Smallson looked a tough old sod indeed. "Money can buy health, it seems."

The old man's scornful sound came again. "Money did not give me my health. I come from a very tough line." Smallson's faded grey eyes blazed fiercely, daring Gallagher to contradict him.

"Your granddaughter," Gallagher began, retreating diplomatically, "has inherited your eyes."

"Ah. You have noticed. That's not all she's inherited. Well? Will you answer my question?"

"I'm still the wrong man. I'm not your hero. I'm just a photographer trying to make a living."

Even as she contributed her first words to the conversation, Lauren Tanner knew she was saying the wrong thing: "Kind of unusual. Er ... occupation, I mean."

"What's so unusual about my being a photographer, Miss Tanner?" His voice froze her out. He knew exactly what she was getting at. "Would you find it easier to accept if I were a blues singer, or a tap dancer, perhaps? Or maybe even a reggae singer? You do know about reggae where you come from, I take it?" He was smiling now, and that made it far worse.

Lauren stared at him, hot with embarrassment and anger. Her cheeks burned.

"You are rude, pompous and stuffy," she said coldly. Hugging her knees, she rested her forehead on her crossed arms, dismissed him completely.

Oh, boy! Gallagher thought ruefully. *Rude, stuffy, pompous. That sorts me out.* He shifted his gaze to Smallson, who was unperturbed by the exchange.

"You did ask for that, Gordon," the old man said mildly. "That's not the way to make friends, especially with someone to whom I have just given a lecture on social responsibility."

Though unrepentant, Gallagher kept his peace.

The cigarette woman was yelling again, above the low murmur of conversation: "*Goddammit it, you bastards! Can you hear me? I want my fucking cigarettes! Goddam thieves!*"

There was a sudden welter of "SHHH's" from all around her.

"Jesus Christ!" an aggrieved male voice exclaimed. "Are you trying to get us all killed? Don't you know you don't provoke these kind of people? You keep a low profile, that's what you do."

"Don't you yell at me, buster! Go screw your profiles! What the hell were you doing when they killed those four people? Wetting your fucking pants, that's what, creep!"

"Don't you call *me* a creep, you cheap broad!"

"*Cheap?*" she shrieked, not at all worried by being called a broad. "*Cheap?* Who the hell do you think you are?" She glared outraged round the room. "I could buy the whole fucking lot of you, with change to spare!" She reserved her most poisonous look for the man who had dared call her cheap.

"A mild exaggeration," Smallson remarked to Gallagher. "But she is extremely wealthy."

"Well, she could buy me and still have her fortune intact. Who is she, anyway?"

"Our floor show is none other than six-times-married Mrs Paula Cavendish Browne; with an 'e', of course. Each husband, having had the foresight to accumulate considerable wealth before marrying her, left vast sums of money and/or properties in her capable hands, before departure; either running from her or quitting this life altogether. The score so far is three divorces and three deaths. Don't you read the papers?"

"Never the society pages."

"Ach. She is a page-one headliner, that one."

Smallson's quirky phrasing revealed the mysterious tinge to his accent that had been worrying away at the back of Gallagher's mind. It was Germanic.

"I know of the name, of course, but I'd never have recognized her."

The yelling continued in the background.

"Paula Browne," Smallson informed them, "is making it harder for all of us. She'll find she won't be able to buy herself out of this one. None of us will."

Gallagher stared at him. "I can do without the nightmares. You're not trying to tell us there'll be no demands for ransom?"

"I'm not *trying* to tell you anything. I'm stating a cold fact. They intend to kill us; all of us, without exception."

Gallagher found he'd suddenly become hoarse. "And that child over there?"

"Without exception," Smallson repeated.

Gallagher tracked his gaze round the room slowly. "If what you say is true," he said at last, his eyes now on Smallson, "we really have no chance at all. They will have thought about people attempting to escape and will have made *that* virtually impossible."

"Exactly. So, we must attempt it."

"Jake. Did you hear what I just said?"

"Loud and clear. All the more reason for us to attempt something.

20

We don't know the set up, but it's bound to be so good they'll think a person would have to be crazy to try anything."

"The unexpected?"

"You've got it. That will work in our favour."

Gallagher found himself smiling, if reluctantly. "You're a stubborn old man; and more than a little crazy."

"You'd better believe it."

They had become so accustomed to the noise made by Paula Browne and her yelling partner that it was almost a shock when it stopped. They were truly shocked, however, by what followed: the keening wail lacerated their senses. Lauren noticeably trembled.

Before he realized what he was doing, Gallagher had reached out to take her gently by the upper arm. Lauren tensed immediately. Her warm, bare arm remained within his grip.

"It's OK," he said in a quiet voice as the awful wail lashed at them once more. If, God forbid, he should ever hear the cry of a lost soul on a dark and lonely night, he was certain this was how it would sound.

The terrible wailing was beginning for a third time when it was cut off abruptly by a sharp slap that cracked like a pistol shot in the room. Several people jumped in response. Now only a low sobbing could be heard. All conversation had ceased.

At last Lauren said, very softly: "I'm fine now. Thank you. I'm not normally like this."

"You don't have to apologize," he said. "It scared me too."

It seemed a long while before Gallagher realized he was still holding her arm. He released her, disguising his reluctance to do so by smiling sheepishly, as if to say: *I forgot.*

Jake Smallson watched them, a satisfied expression on his face. If there was the slightest chance of Lauren getting out of this alive, he knew it would be because of Gallagher. He was not particularly worried about his own survival. Seventy-seven years was a good enough run by anyone's standards. He'd done plenty in that time, more than most people could cram into ten lifetimes. But Lauren. Lauren had to get out.

Paula Browne's sobs were becoming less and less audible.

Turning to Smallson, Gallagher said, "I've never heard anyone scream like that." *But I've heard worse*, he didn't say. *Much, much worse.*

"She was screaming from her soul," the old man said, remembering the Teutonic myths and superstitions of his peasant childhood. "Mrs Paula Cavendish Browne does not contemplate dying at forty-five."

Gallagher was aware that Lauren had again found great interest in her knees. He was at once relieved and disappointed. He had liked the feel of her eyes upon him; and her skin had been so smooth, so silky to the touch. He remembered another whose skin had been smooth and silky to the touch. *Oh, Celia.*

"What does the room tell you, Gordon?" the old man was asking.

Gallagher wrenched his mind back. "The air-conditioner tells us we're somewhere quite warm. Since we were on our way to Africa escaping an English winter — at least, I was — we could be anywhere in the general area." *Like the Middle East?*

"Suppose we've been asleep for days?" Smallson wanted to see it from all angles.

"The body needs sustenance. Are you hungry? Are there puncture marks on your arms? Are there sore areas where they may have fed you intravenously?"

"No to all questions."

"The same applies to me. Are you hungry, Miss Tanner?"

She raised her eyes to his. "No. And the name is Lauren."

He acknowledged this with a brief smile. "We'd have been hungry," he continued to Smallson, "and you and I would have rough chins by now."

"They could have shaved us."

"Every man here? We can't have been out for more than the equivalent of a good night's sleep. It seems a lot of trouble for them to put themselves to. For whose benefit? Not ours, surely. We'll be feeling hungry pretty soon, which would be normal after a long sleep."

Lauren asked: "But how far could they have taken us in that time?"

He made rough calculations. "Using the eight-hour yardstick, and allowing some time wastage for transfers by truck, boat or maybe even another aeroplane, I'd say somewhere in North Africa. They could have taken us to some Mediterranean country, but somehow I doubt it. None of those places would need an air-conditioner at this time of the year."

"As long as it's not the Middle East." This time the shiver was in her voice.

Gallagher could imagine what she was thinking.

"You took much longer than I expected," Smallson put in, "to come awake."

"They gave me an extra dose. Needle." Gallagher rubbed his forearm reflectively. "That's why I asked you about punctures. The one I got has nothing to do with food."

"Why did they give you the extra dose?" Lauren asked.

"The stuff in the food didn't work so well on me. I remember waking up during the transfer."

The old man's eyes burned with sudden excitement. "Did you see anything that could be of use to us? Did you hear much?"

"No," Gallagher lied easily, wondering why he had. "I must have moved. I was barely conscious when I felt the needle going in."

He had come out of the drugged sleep without movement, mind

fully alert, eyes remaining shut. He had lain there, conscious among the other drugged bodies, listening to his captors talking. Nothing had so far been said to give him any indication of the ultimate destination. The conversation was of the immediate problems of preparing the sleeping people for the next stage of the journey. However, someone had in passing made mention of "the burrow" and had been instantly hushed.

Gallagher had remained perfectly still for what had seemed an interminably long time. No new information had been forthcoming for the simple reason that there had been no further talk. He had not considered escape, knowing without opening his eyes that he would not have stood a chance. He had also known it was not the best time to be discovered awake and had done the only thing he could in the circumstances. He had whimpered in a convincing imitation of someone fighting to emerge from an enforced sleep.

Footsteps had raced towards where he lay, and two people had studied him closely. He had whimpered again for good measure, as if totally oblivious to what was going on.

Footsteps receding; the sense of being peered at still very strong. Footsteps returning; more than those which had receded. A needle entering his arm. Gallagher had steeled himself against even the slightest reaction to the sharp prick of its point. The woman had been far from gentle, and he had wanted to clobber her. The drug-induced sleep had begun to claim him once more as he wondered what the hell he was going to do with the snippets of information he had gathered. He had also identified the speakers' accents. The woman was French; another voice was English, the Londoner; and the third voice had been the stuff of Lauren's nightmares. It had belonged to the Middle East.

Gallagher now looked at Lauren, knowing he would say nothing to her about it.

"You've been having one of your thinking sessions," the old man said. "Any conclusions?"

"I'm trying to narrow the possible choices open to them within the time they had available," he said. "I have some ideas."

"You don't sound too sure."

"There really isn't much to go on, is there?" Gallagher's next words were tentative: "I still feel it's somewhere in North Africa. It would certainly be hot enough for the air-conditioner. They wouldn't have risked going west; not unless this place is at the bottom of the Atlantic." The attempted joke fell flat.

There was an eager look, however, in the old man's eyes. "But?" he prompted.

Gallagher shrugged, glanced at Lauren. "There are no buts." He sighed, as if in exasperation. "I haven't quite worked it out. As I've said, there's very little to go on at the moment. Besides, my mind's still fighting that bloody drug."

Jake Smallson had not travelled so far in life, so successfully, without being able to sniff out nuances where most people would have steamrollered past them. He understood, as clearly as if Gallagher had told him, that the Middle East was the most likely candidate. He also knew why Gallagher had omitted to say so, and felt a sudden warmth for the strangely self-contained young man.

"And about this room?" he asked, casually easing the troublesome subject out of the way.

"The lack of windows," Gallagher began calmly, "and the earthen floor make it obvious we're in some sort of basement or cellar. Most practical place to keep hostages. A couple of armed people outside that door could finish us off before any rescuers could get in here."

"Rescuers," the old man scoffed.

"People do these things for a reason, Jake. They usually require something in return."

"Ah, yes. You want to believe they are after ransom money, or some kind of exchange."

"Take a look at the people in this room," Gallagher reasoned. "Paula Browne alone is worth a few million to them. What would they get for the whole bunch? What would they get for you two? There's more wealth trapped in here than the gross national product of quite a few countries. I can't believe they'd pass up a chance like this." *And after all this time, no mention of Harding. Why?*

As if to support that line of reasoning, someone at the far end of the room was saying: "... and the world press, radio and television must be full of it by now; ransom demands or political swaps. You name it. There are many different nationalities here. I *cannot* believe that our respective countries haven't already been in some form of communication with the kidnappers, or are working together on a rescue mission. The United Nations...."

A harsh laugh cut into the speaker's words. Paula Browne. "United Nations? What fucking United Nations? That bunch of fucking creeps?"

"You know," Gallagher said, "I think I like that woman."

Smallson raised an eyebrow. "You do not like the UN?"

"She said it all. What United Nations?"

"Ah. The glib condemnation of youth."

"It's a bit more than that, Jake."

The old man made no comment, because just then the door at the end of the room opened.

III

It slammed wide with sudden violence, and six people came charging in, as if propelled from behind: four men and two women. They were all armed.

A stunned silence had swooped down upon the room, and people were frozen in whatever attitude it had found them.

The newcomers fanned out – swiftly and professionally – and took up watchful stances about the room. The way they pointed their weapons removed any doubts that they would use them.

Gallagher let his breath out very, very slowly. He could not remember the instant he had begun to hold it. He had recognized all the weapons immediately. The men carried the ubiquitous AK-47; the women, a pair of Ingrams with which they seemed thoroughly at ease. Unlike the deadly long-range AK, the Ingram's rapid rate of fire made it a powerhouse at close range. The women were positioned to lay down a murderous crossfire, should the occasion demand it. The place would be a slaughterhouse in seconds. He hoped no one would do anything stupid.

Both women were black. The men were two Europeans and two Arabs. All six wore casual dress in which denim jeans were the prime ingredient.

Gallagher stole a slow glance at Lauren and saw a haunted fear in her grey eyes. He sensed her valiant struggle to contain it; but she could do nothing about the quick look she darted at the two Arabs. Her terrified gaze turned to Gallagher. He had the strangest feeling that the other armed people did not matter to her; only the Arabs seemed to have triggered this pathological response. He got no information from Smallson's totally inscrutable face.

Gallagher returned his attention to the open door, slowly relaxing his own denim-clad legs as he did so.

"*Don't move!*" one of the men snarled. A white.

Gallagher found himself staring into the gaping mouth of an AK. His blood congealed; he stopped moving. A hungry-looking rictus of a grin scarred the man's mouth.

Jesus! Gallagher thought shakily. *They really are crazy.*

But now something else was happening. A man had appeared in the doorway. He was tall, slim and expensively dressed, as if for a yachting trip on the French Riviera. The vivid paleness of his countenance was in sharp contrast to the sleek blackness of his neck-length hair. He was also extremely handsome and looked as if he knew it, while pretending he didn't. He was a man in his late thirties, by name Sir Philip Michael Alexander Harding, Baronet, the sole inheritor of one of the largest fortunes in England.

Looking at him, Gallagher felt his nostrils twitch involuntarily in a primeval scenting of danger. It was at that moment that he gave full credence to Jake Smallson's theory that the captives were all to be executed.

A collective gasp had staccatoed round the room, and now everyone was staring. Alexander Harding was well known, if not personally, to all; even Gallagher. His face had graced magazine covers, newspaper front pages and television screens so often, it made prominent film stars envious. It was inevitable that Paula Browne would know him personally.

Gallagher was prepared for that. He was not, however, prepared for Harding's first words to Lauren Tanner.

"Hello, darling," Harding said conversationally to her. "Again."

Gallagher turned to look at her. She was staring at Harding as if mesmerized, though he had already switched his attention to Paula Browne who was rising to her feet before anyone knew it was happening.

The lifting snout of an AK was halted by a brief wave from Harding.

"Alex H.!" she shouted happily, blind to the terrible reality.

"Well," Harding said to Paula Browne; and waited.

The distinct coolness of the greeting stopped her in her tracks. She had been moving excitedly towards him, a smile on her face. At last, pennies began to drop with ominous regularity. The smile shuddered uncertainly, slipped out of existence.

"Alex?" Her voice was at once puzzled and questioning. "Are you responsible for *this*?" She ended on a disbelieving squeak.

Gallagher swept a swift glance round the room.

"*Don't move!*" the maniac with the AK bawled.

Against all the tenets of his training, Gallagher made a protest. "I didn't move."

"Your eyes!" the man yelled. "Your fucking eyes moved!"

Harding seemed amused by the whole thing. He did not even glance at the rabid man.

The room was very tense. People were trying to divide their attention between the two explosions they could see coming: between Gallagher and the barely restrained killer, and between Paula Browne and Harding. In the event, it was Paula Browne who flipped. Her great wealth had removed from her any passing acquaintance with caution, if indeed it ever existed. At the levels where she'd operated she'd apparently had no need for it. She made the mistake of believing nothing had changed. Her desperate need of a cigarette, on top of all that had already occurred, caused her remaining shreds of wisdom to desert her.

26

"*You two-faced shit!*" she screamed. "*You fink! Goddam you!* What the hell are you playing at? You were on the plane with us. I thought they'd killed you too. Goddammit, Alex, what is this?"

She paused for breath, while Harding simply stood there smiling at her. She should have been warned. Instead, his silence goaded her to new heights of indiscretion.

"*What the fuck are you smiling at? Answer me, you bastard!* Did you really do this? Are you in with them on this, you motherfucking shit?"

Shut up, woman, Gallagher thought, horrified. *For your sake, for all our sakes, shut up!*

Paula Browne, however, would not shut up. She had a good head of steam going. An ugly twist came to her mouth as she prepared to commit her greatest folly. She began to address the room.

"Shall I tell you what this tailor's dummy's like in bed? He's afraid of eating bush. D'you know that? A friend told me."

Christ! Gallagher thought, marvelling at her suicidal drive. *Stop stop stop stop!*

"He...."

The sickening thud when it came – though partially expected by everyone – was terrible to hear. No one had seen Harding's signal. Each person in the room, however, saw in vivid detail the butt of an AK slamming viciously into Paula Browne's back. The blow was delivered in the region of her kidneys.

She pitched forward, crashing to the floor, where she rolled, arched her back, fighting to scream the pain out of her. Arteries in her temple, neck and arms seemed to be trying to burst out of her skin. She lay there, struggling for a sound that would not come.

"Oh, my God!" Gallagher heard Lauren say softly.

The man with whom Paula Browne had previously enjoyed the yelling match leapt to his feet and advanced upon Harding.

"You yellow sonofabitch!" he shouted. "Try someone your size!"

Gallagher watched in weary resignation. He knew what would happen, knew he was watching a man throw his life away quite needlessly. But the man was trapped within a distorted sense of chivalry, trapped by something he had no doubt learned as a child.

The captives, shocked by what had happened to Paula Browne, were barely able to cope with what next took place. The same AK was used. This time it barked; just once. The foolishly brave man was back-pedalled across the entire width of the room by the force of the heavy bullet slamming into his chest from a range of less than six feet. He cannoned into a wall, smearing his lifeblood over the hole that the bullet which entered and ploughed through him had made in the thick wood panelling. He died of shock before he hit the ground.

Screams erupted in the room. The sharp smell of gunshot stung the

27

nostrils. The AK belonged to one of the Arabs who held it menacingly, ready for further action.

"Shut up, you snivelling shits!" roared the man who had bawled at Gallagher.

The screams died immediately, but the horror remained in all eyes. Everyone stared with appalled fascination at the dead man. The people with the child tried to shield the youngster's eyes. The child resisted. He wanted to look. It was exciting; for now.

No one spoke for a very long time. Paula Browne's wheezing gasps of pain could now be clearly heard. No one dared move to help her.

Poor bastard, Gallagher thought. He could make out what seemed to be a short, bare passageway beyond where Harding stood. He wondered where it led.

Harding was speaking. "The late Mr Bannion was rather stupid." The callousness with which this was said made the epitaph doubly obscene. Harding's eyes, a pair of gleaming coals full of reptilian menace, raked the room.

"I trust," the cold voice went on, "there will be no more examples of such stupidity." He turned to the armed men and addressed his next words to the two whites: "Take Mr Bannion away, and tell the caterers to include cigarettes with Mrs Browne's tray. She'll be needing them."

They complied silently, grabbing the corpse by the armpits and dragging it out like a side of beef.

Gallagher was wryly aware of the practicality of the earthen floor. It soaked up the blood. *Like a sodding abattoir.* His mind refused to be further horrified. He needed it in top working order if he were to find a way out of the nightmare. *I must be crazy*, his mind insisted. *There is no way out.*

But he was determined to find one. No bastard was going to shoot him down like some poor bloody animal.

Harding's emotionless voice cut through his thoughts. "You must all be quite hungry. I originally came in here to announce that food is being brought to you. The unfortunate occurrences sidetracked me."

Gallagher's pulse shot up briefly. The gleaming coals were fastened upon him. "Mr Gallagher?"

All eyes turned upon him, already seeing him as Harding's next victim.

Taking his life in his hands, Gallagher slowly got to his feet. Nobody yelled and nobody shot at him; but the armed group watched him hungrily. One of the women had crazy, feverish eyes.

"I'm not one of them," Gallagher said hesitantly. "I was travelling on a complimentary ticket. I'm not rich...." He allowed his voice to fade into a self-conscious squeak. He cleared his throat, as if embarrassed.

28

Despite the danger in which they found themselves, his fellow captives were still able to summon up strong feelings of contempt for him. Gallagher felt the silent, raw distaste come at him like a wave of nausea.

Harding was smiling again. "Do stop bleating, Mr Gallagher. You intrigue me. Care for a walk?"

Never respond with the emotions, sir. Let the mind do it. O'Keefe.

Gallagher let Harding's calculated insult wash over him. "Yes. Of course," he said eagerly. He stood waiting, not wanting to do anything to alarm the guards, particularly the primed Arab and the two women. Those three could turn him into mincemeat in seconds. An Ingram could be triggered by a sneeze. He'd seen it happen.

He presented a deliberate picture of abject surrender.

"Come along then," Harding said, as if to a recalcitrant child.

Gallagher walked gingerly towards him without glancing back at Lauren or the old man. There was a tiny smile on Harding's incongruously sensitive lips as he stood aside for Gallagher to pass. The smile was now directed at Lauren.

"See you later," he said in the same conversational tone he'd used when he first entered. He turned and left without waiting for, nor expecting a reaction from her. He had totally ignored Smallson.

Gallagher did not even glance back to see how Lauren had responded. He was too busy thinking up a plausible story to tell Harding.

The guards followed them out, and the door closed on silence.

"*Merde!*" a male French voice finally exploded into the hushed room. It belonged to Marcel Parguineau, once a paratroop colonel in Algeria, now chairman of a highly successful import/export business — importing and exporting "anything", as he was wont to say. He had been on his way to Réunion.

Parguineau was a squat, tough-looking man in his early fifties. His face, its skin made leathery by years in the naked sun, bore a tiny scar on the right cheek where an Algerian guerrilla had been unfortunate enough to miss scoring a bull on his target during a face-to-face shoot-out. The bad shooting had been fatal to the Algerian.

"*Espèce de fils de pute!*" Parguineau continued. "He thinks we can *eat* after this?"

No one passed comment, and he muttered into his own angry silence.

Lauren turned to her grandfather. "Well, Gramps, still think he's your man?" Her contempt for Gallagher had returned with a vengeance.

Smallson gave an exasperated sigh. "Lauren, Lauren! You are like the English weather. You change so much. First, you do not like him. Then you begin to like him a little. Yes, yes. Don't deny it.... Now you do not like him again."

"Didn't you see what he did?" she queried in a low, furious voice.

The old man was unperturbed. "I saw. And if you don't understand why, then you are very foolish."

"He was faking? My God. What will happen if they find out?"

"They will kill him, of course," Smallson said philosophically. He smiled knowingly at the concern on her face. "And now, you like him again."

"Oh, Jake. You're putting too much into it."

"Yes? It took me thirty seconds to fall in love with your grandmother," he remarked serenely. "Thirty seconds was all."

"Jake!" Lauren dragged the name out admonishingly.

He patted her knee lightly. "You need to give your love to someone." He saw her expression freeze. "You find something wrong with him?"

"No. It isn't what you're thinking," she answered after a while. "It's ... it's what happened in New York."

"Then I cannot think of a better reason. Gordon is a fine young man, and you're both going to need each other before this thing is finished. Your father, of course, would not approve. But what do I care about his approval?" The old man smiled impishly.

"I think he thought I was a bitch at first. A spoiled, rich little bitch."

"He does not know the reasons for the face you show the world. You cannot blame him. It matters to you what he thinks?"

"Before, it didn't."

"Ah," the old man said wisely.

"Excuse me?"

They looked up. A fat, piggish man with a smooth baby face was standing before them.

"I'm Ethan Sumner," he introduced himself, adding unnecessarily, since his accent had already betrayed him: "from Atlanta, Georgia."

They nodded politely at him and waited. Sumner was one of the men Gallagher had overheard discussing Lauren in the airport bar.

"I've been doing some talking with Piet Villiger over there." Sumner indicated the big blond man with the mean face. "We reckon we should try and make a break for it."

Villiger was looking back at them enigmatically. Jake Smallson's instincts made him strongly doubt whether Villiger had actually said that.

"How do you propose to do that, Mr Sumner?" Smallson did not ask him to sit down. Something about the man was repellent.

"First, we ought to stick together. We white folks, I mean, now that yellow-bellied nigger's gone." Sumner had conveniently forgotten Nbwale, the huge black African.

Smallson kept his voice polite. "Mr Sumner, we are all in serious danger here. We should *all* stick together. We don't know where we are, and we don't know how many people we face. Didn't you see those weapons?"

"Of course, we must plan," Sumner began lamely, "but first we must build our team. We're asking you two to join with us."

"And what about that big man over there?"

"The other nigger?" Sumner was dismissive. "We leave him. They've probably already shot the one they took." He glanced at Lauren as he said that. He had seen Gallagher's hand on her arm.

Lauren was pointedly ignoring him.

Trash, his mind raged.

Six months earlier, Sumner had passed his fortieth birthday. It had been a very special occasion for him. His accountants had given him the satisfying news on that day that, apart from company assets, his personal wealth was over one and a half million dollars. By the age of fifty, he expected to be worth at least five million. He'd got where he was, he was fond of telling himself, by not taking shit from anybody. He was not accustomed to having his ideas treated with anything but the greatest respect. Why, even his chief executives jumped when he sneezed. For instance, he liked travelling alone on business. Why should he take a bunch of freeloaders with him? Now these goddam commies were keeping him from an important deal with some coon government.

Despite his feelings, Sumner paid lip-service to southern courtesy by not letting his annoyance show; but it did not prevent him from taking a surreptitious glance at Lauren's bare legs.

She knew he'd done it, and not for the first time since the hijack Lauren regretted her choice of clothing. But after what she had gone through in New York, she'd felt like brazening herself into cheerfulness. It hadn't worked, of course. The looks she'd received from men, as a result, had only served to make her hostile. Now, it appeared that Gallagher was responsible for a subtle change going on within her. She prayed for his safety, while wishing Sumner would get the hell away.

Sumner, however, was far from finished. The cool reception he had so far had was no deterrent. He glanced again at Lauren's legs. No goddam nigger was going to feel them. Not if Ethan Sumner had anything to do with it.

"I reckon," he said to Smallson, "We can use Harding to help us get out of here."

Smallson was intrigued by this novel idea. "How?"

"I don't figure he's one of that gang. I reckon this whole thing is because they wanted to kidnap *him*. They snatched him from somewhere, drugged him, then brought him on the airplane in disguise. They hijack the plane to take them somewhere else. We just

31

got caught in the net."

Smallson wanted to see just how far Sumner was going to pursue this train of thought. "How do you explain Bannion? And Paula Browne?"

"Hell. They've got something on him. Blackmail, or maybe bombs down one of his oilwells. He's got to do what they say, or else. Look how they stopped him trying to talk to you on the plane. Maybe they were still afraid he'd give them away.'"

"Why would they want him?"

"C'mon, now. I'm worth nearly two million. Harding makes me look like a man on welfare. He can bring down governments. Maybe one of them wants to stop some plan he's got." Sumner warmed to his theme. "I see it this way. Those people who came in here with guns were a couple of white commie hippies, two ayrabs and a couple of nigger bitches. There's no way you're going to make me believe Harding's thrown in with them. The guy's a duke or a lord or something." The possibility was incredible to Sumner.

Smallson was incredulous for his part, finding it hard to credit the man's reasoning. He wanted to smile. "Mr Sumner," he began, "I agree with you that we must get out. Wait. Wait. Let me finish. I believe we are in a greater danger than you think. No ransoms will be asked for. Your two million dollars, your whole company or companies will be of no value to you here. So. I agree with you that we must escape. It is all I accept."

Sumner did not like having his opinions swept unceremoniously aside, but was prepared to take half a loaf. At least the old man had accepted the need for escape. Where Smallson went, the girl would go.

"Leave it to us," he said confidently. Not wanting to make it a total surrender, he went on: "I still think you're wrong about Harding. All the time he was in here he had on that weird smile, like a man under drugs. And did you see his eyes? Just like those I used to see on hippies — kind of crazy. The warning he gave after Bannion I reckon was from those deviants, not him. We'll talk again." With a last look at Lauren, Sumner went back to his place.

"A man who always likes the last word," Smallson observed drily to Lauren. "A fool and, I think, dangerous because of it." He gave a grim little smile as he considered Sumner's bizarre appreciation of their circumstances. *Harding is not the target, Mr Sumner. I am.*

Lauren made a sound of disgust. "All the time he was here, he was undressing me with his mind."

"I know. We must hope Gordon makes it. Otherwise I think we might have trouble handling both Alex Harding and Mr Sumner." He put an arm about her shoulders. "Do not worry, my child. Have faith. I am not wrong about your Gordon."

In spite of her fears, Lauren had to smile. "*My* Gordon?"

Smallson's own answering smile was impish. "But, yes. I know it."

While Sumner had been casting his pearls of non-wisdom, Gallagher had discovered, on being thrust out of the room, that the short passageway turned left at right angles into a long corridor. The floor here was also of hard-packed, smooth, reddish earth. There were several doors set into each wall.

As he walked along with Harding at his side, the two Arab guards following closely – the two women with the Ingrams having remained on guard in the passage – Gallagher's mind worked furiously. He knew it would be like taking a stroll in a minefield once he began to tell Harding his story. One moment of carelessness, and the whole thing would blow up in his face. He was very mindful of Bannion's fate.

But Harding seemed to want to talk. "Showers," he announced. He pointed at each wall alternately: "Bedroom, bedroom, small dormitory, lavatory, lavatory, communications, dining (staff) ... er ... storage, kitchen, foodstore, this one is of no importance, games room...."

Why is he telling me all this? Gallagher's expression continued to feign the right amount of interest. Too much would arouse suspicion; too little might cause offence. He had no intention of offending Alex H. just yet.

Gallagher's mind began to wander. He thought of Celia and of the last time they had made love.... *Celia....*

He shuddered.

"Not cold, are you, Mr Gallagher?"

Sod off, you bastard! Gallagher's mind snarled. Harding's smooth voice, encroaching upon the memory of that wonderful time, was an obscenity.

"No. Just a slight shiver. It was nothing."

Harding inevitably misunderstood completely. "Of course. That unpleasant incident in the room. A stupid man, Bannion. Imagine throwing your life away for someone like Paula Browne." He shook his head. "Unbelievably stupid."

Gallagher made no comment. Harding would not have liked what he really wanted to say.

"Well, Mr Gallagher," Harding said eventually. "Exactly what is your story?"

The gleaming black eyes seemed to attain a new luminosity. Gallagher could not dispel the horrible feeling that he was being mesmerized by a deadly snake. He now knew how a trapped rabbit felt. This suppressed terror helped to put the right amount of apprehension into his voice when he spoke. He cleared his throat nervously. It was not all play-acting. One mistake and he was as good as dead.

"I'm not rich ..." he began.

"So we've already heard from you," Harding interrupted in his smooth voice. He looked away, much to Gallagher's relief, keeping in step as they walked.

"I was travelling on a complimentary ticket." *Not too hastily, Gallagher. Don't push it!* "I couldn't normally afford a first-class ticket, especially on this route."

"What can you afford, Mr Gallagher?"

Gallagher laughed nervously. "You won't get much for me. There's no one to pay a ransom."

Harding stopped. "You don't seriously believe I went to all this effort for mere money? Do you really believe I would be so crude as to hijack people for money?" Harding looked quite dangerous.

Gallagher allowed fearful comprehension to dawn upon his face.

"Yes, Mr. Gallagher," Harding said emotionlessly. "You've got it. Now tell me why you, of all the others, should live. You now know wealth has nothing to do with it."

"But it was an accident," Gallagher said pleadingly. "I only got the seat because it was spare. OK, so it's not wealth; but whatever your reasons for taking these people, it has nothing to do with me. They're all rich or powerful in some way; anyone can see that. What do I have in common with them?"

Harding continued to walk in silence.

Gallagher put the right amount of desperation into his voice. "Look. I can't even begin to understand why you took them. All I can come up with is their wealth – I know, I know...." Hastily, at Harding's cold glance. "Then it's because of their power...."

Harding was actually laughing. It was not a pleasant sound. It was at such variance with the body from which it was being expelled, it sounded unspeakably vile: the rasping, phlegm-ridden noise one might expect for a hundred-a-day smoker. Harding had never touched a cigarette in his life.

The laughter stopped abruptly, as if a switch had been pressed. "Mr Gallagher, I'm still waiting for your story."

"I was on this flight because of a personal problem." *Get it right, Gallagher, get it right!* "My wife ... my wife...." Again Gallagher cleared his throat. "I ... found her in bed with ... with another man." But that had not been all of it.

It was the most terrible thing he could remember ever having happened to him. He had not thought it possible to experience such total devastation of the spirit.

That day, he had come home unexpectedly, fully believing Celia would still be at her office. Seeing her little silver-grey Renault G5 Gordini had caused a surge of excitement in him, and he'd begun looking forward to the sheer abandon of an afternoon with her. Four years of marriage had not diminished the intensity of their love-making; their "wrestling matches", as they'd liked to call the furious, no-holds barred bouts. The bed was like a combat area, and when they had finished it would be soaked with the moisture of their exertions. Clean, dry sheets would always be needed afterwards. With this anticipation pounding in his brain, he had entered the pleasant house they'd jointly bought in London's Highgate. He had done so quietly, hoping to surprise her, vowing to make love with her in whatever room she was found.

She had not been downstairs. He had begun to make his way upwards, heading for the main bedroom, when he'd heard a sound he'd never hoped to hear as a non-participating listener: the high, wailing sound of Celia approaching climax.

It was as if the weight of the entire world suddenly lodged itself in his stomach. He'd forced himself to continue, dreading what he knew he was about to see; dreading the death of everything that had meant so much to him.

The door of the bedroom was wide open, and what he saw was even worse than he had expected. On his bed, their bed, was a strange man, naked, with Celia astride him in a manner that Gallagher knew so well. Eyes tightly shut as she approached the extremity of her passion, Celia was bouncing frantically up and down, her wonderful, naked, gleaming body rippling and squirming as she squealed.

Gallagher had been unable to see the man's face. A naked woman whom he had never seen before had been sitting on it, doing her own fair share of squirming. Gallagher had watched the scene numbly, everything dying within him, and instead of exploding into atavistic rage as most men would have done, he had simply wanted to get out of there.

As he'd been turning to go, the strange woman had seen him.

"*Oh, my God!*" she'd shrieked, and everything had suddenly stopped.

As he'd bounded down the stairs, shame and humiliation pouring over him, Gallagher had retained a vivid picture of the three on the bed all moving at once; trying to extricate themselves from each other. The most vivid image of all had been Celia raising herself off the man; seeing the man come out of her.

Sickened, Gallagher had slammed out of the house, Celia's forlorn, ashamed cry of "*Gordon! Wait!*" ringing in his ears.

He'd climbed into his blue BMW, driven dangerously to a nearby park where he'd stopped and sat shaking, hurting, feeling personally violated.

Gallagher told the whole story to Harding, with the exception of a few minor details which he felt might have prejudiced the image he was trying to build. He chose not to mention the type of car he owned, for instance, though it was secondhand.

He felt no shame giving such personal information to Harding. A man pleading for his life could not afford the luxury of pride.

"Some women can be such bitches," Harding commented with a vehemence that startled Gallagher and set him wondering. "So you took this flight to get away?"

"Sort of. I used to be a soldier, you see ... squaddie," Gallagher added hastily at another of Harding's cold glances, "and I thought maybe I could find a little war somewhere...."

"Your version of the Foreign Legion syndrome." Harding sounded as if he wanted to laugh. The man's quick changes of mood warned Gallagher to be even more careful with his story.

"If you like."

"You look and sound like a well-educated man. I'd have thought you would have done better than squaddie. A commission, perhaps."

Gallagher felt his heart lurch, but he made his voice, and his expression, sour. "I was not considered officer material."

Harding got the message Gallagher had hoped for. "Do I detect a note of bitterness? Are you saying the colour of your skin barred you from further advancement?"

Gallagher shrugged, the epitome of a man bitterly disappointed by certain things in life. "Who knows?"

"Who indeed," Harding said, sounding bored as they turned a corner.

"Perhaps I can be of some use to you."

"What would I want with a disaffected ex-soldier?" Coldly.

In apparent final desperation, Gallagher said lamely: "I'm a photographer."

"What a man of parts you are, Mr Gallagher." Uninterestedly. Then Harding stopped walking, so suddenly that Gallagher went on a few steps ahead before turning round.

Harding's eyes burned at him. "Are you the Gallagher who won that award last year?"

"Yes." Eagerly. "For a series of studies I called 'Drunks in the Night'." *Anything. Anything that pleases you is fine with me.*

"I'm impressed." Harding came up to Gallagher, and they resumed walking. "I saw them in a magazine, and was struck by your eye for detail. You are indeed a man of parts. Don't be too disheartened by not having gained a commission. If my knowledge of commissioning boards is anything to go by, you should take it as a compliment."

Gallagher permitted himself a cautious smile.

"Care to eat?" Harding threw in unexpectedly as the corridor along which they'd been walking ended abruptly at a door. "Ah. Here we are." He opened the door, flung it wide. "I do hope you're hungry."

36

IV

Gallagher could hardly believe his eyes. The large windowless room, ventilated by the ubiquitous air-conditioning unit, would not have been out of place in a luxury flat. The Persian wall-to-wall carpet would have paid most people's rent for a few years, and there was nothing about the rest of the furnishings that spoke of utility; but it was the table in the very centre of the room that held his eye. It was laden with an appetizing array of dishes, and set for two.

Harding was ostensibly amused by the expression on Gallagher's face. "Please go in, Mr Gallagher. I certainly hope you enjoy a good lobster. Even when roughing it, I like a decent meal."

If this is roughing it, Gallagher thought drily, *I've been living in a slum all these years.*

He entered the room, wondering if he'd ever leave it alive. He was very conscious of the fact that the two guards had taken up alert positions in the corridor. Did they seriously believe he would be mad enough to attack Harding in the heart of this heavily protected warren? He was trapped in an elaborate and well secured maze. While walking down the various corridors, his apparently disinterested eyes had not missed the strategically sited closed-circuit TV cameras. He could only wonder at the purpose of this underground complex run by Harding.

He successfully hid the despair he felt as he walked towards the table. Escape seemed an impossible lunacy, for it was obvious that Harding had been expecting him. Gallagher could not understand why, refusing to believe that he'd been singled out because Harding knew about his past. Rather than treat him to an expensive meal, Harding would have long since fed him to the Arab guards waiting silently outside.

"This is roughing it?" Gallagher at last asked as he heard his host enter and shut the door.

Harding was pleased by the reaction. "My office, dining-room and bedroom. You should see the ancestral pile in Gloucestershire. Here, space is rather at a premium. Please sit down." He gestured with a pale hand.

Gallagher eased himself into a chair that was upholstered in rich quilted leather. All the furniture in the wood-panelled room was black and greeted the eye with a subdued sheen. He allowed his gaze to wander curiously, as would be expected of him; and the overriding impression he gained from his scrutiny was that, barring the absence of portholes, he was in the master's cabin of a luxury yacht.

Harding took a seat opposite. "You can, I trust, cope with a whole lobster? Rather massive fellows, these. Local, of course, and rather good." He chose to keep the whereabouts of "local" to himself.

Gallagher's emotional responses urged him to refuse the food, but reason and hunger gave him little chance. Apart from the fact that he would be courting danger to reject Harding's hospitality, bizarre as it was, he had not realized how truly hungry he was. "I can cope," he said.

Harding's bottomless dark eyes watched as, with detached amusement, he filled two cut-glass goblets with wine from a chilled bottle.

"Hunger, I see, has won over conscience. Good. I like to see pragmatism."

"You make it sound like greed."

"Do I? That was not my intention, I assure you." Harding raised his glass in salute. "Let us toast prudence, then."

Gallagher raised his own glass. "You were expecting me," he said as he set the glass down.

Harding lowered his own slowly. "Yes, Mr Gallagher. I must confess to a mild form of subterfuge, in your case. Now you're looking frightened again. Just when I thought you were starting to relax."

"What do you expect?" Gallagher asked, feeling he could push his luck just a little. "You're playing a cat and mouse game with me."

"And the cornered mouse is beginning to show signs of fight." Harding was not smiling.

Discretion returning, Gallagher said, "I've told you how I came to be on the flight. I got the impression that you ... sympathized...."

"Oh, I did. I did. But that was not the reason I brought you here. You see, Mr Gallagher, fortune appears to have smiled upon you. The leader of my little band of desperadoes – perhaps I should not say *my* band, since they work strictly by contract – the leader seems to have a taken a fancy to you." Harding gave his peculiar laugh at the expression forming on Gallagher's face. "Come now, not a closet chauvinist, are you? Why must the leader be a man? This is the far end of the twentieth century. I suppose by the conventional patterns of your thinking, Lauren Tanner would be the most likely candidate for such attention. That may yet follow. I'm certain one or more of the men will be only too pleased to accommodate her."

There was an odd quality to Harding's voice that caught Gallagher's attention. It only appeared when Harding talked about Lauren.

"Had you not stood up when you did," Harding was saying, "you would still have been brought here. Did you not wonder why no one shot at you when you moved?"

"I knew I was taking my life in my hands," Gallagher admitted. "But what choice did I have?"

"None," Harding answered shortly. "But I was interested enough to listen to what you had to say."

"So this was just to check me out?"

"Precisely."

"But what's the point? You can do what you want with me anyway."

"Certainly. But Marika – she's the leader – has a soft centre, so to speak; though I'd strongly advise you against mistaking that for soft-headedness. She is a very tough nut indeed and would not think twice about killing you if she wanted to. You see, Mr Gallagher, we already know all about you. The story about your wife merely helped to clarify the picture. Now, let us not keep this excellent table waiting a moment longer."

So saying, Harding tore a foreleg off the lobster on his plate, broke it, and bit into the exposed, sweet, white meat. Gallagher, feeling very much like a condemned man having his last meal, did the same to his own lobster. Harding watched him from time to time as he ate.

"I can't," Lauren said.

The old man gave her shoulder a squeeze. "You must," he insisted.

There were no lobsters and no wine; but the cold ham and salad, with a cup of fairly decent coffee, was infinitely better than nothing.

"You need to build up all the strength you can," Smallson reasoned, "or later you'll wish you had. Look over there. Even the others are eating."

From across the room. Sumner's voice came to them. "Well, they brought us food. That's got to mean something." The voice died as Sumner concentrated on his eating.

"Pigs," Lauren said to the old man contemptuously.

"Am I also a pig? I'm eating."

"Oh, Gramps, you know I don't mean you. The next oldest person here must be at least twenty years younger than you are."

"And in worse health."

Lauren had to smile. "You're not going to give up, are you?"

"You'd better believe it. We must keep eating. We must ... because we're getting out."

Lauren tightened her lips and shook her head slowly, exasperated and saddened by his blind faith. It was hard to believe there was the slightest chance of their escaping. From what she knew of Harding, she could not see how Gallagher could possibly prevail against him. She sighed.

"He is all right," Smallson said, accurately gauging what was uppermost in her mind. "They'll not kill him yet. I understand the Alex Hardings of this world. They need to display their power, sometimes secretly for personal satisfaction, sometimes they need an audience. This is one of those times. We shall all be made to watch each other's death if he is allowed his way." He added gently: "But for the moment, I feel Gordon is safe."

She said nothing, and Smallson studied her wisely.

"What are you looking at?" she queried at last.

"I believe I am looking at you." He smiled at the soft staining of her cheeks. "So. I am correct. You are very worried about him. For the moment, as I have said, you have no cause. Gordon is a man of certain skills; skills that Harding will not expect him to possess. Those skills are going to help us. Have faith. Now, please eat. You will need the strength for when Gordon makes his move. Harding cannot kill us all as quickly as he did Bannion. He will need time. It is far more difficult to dispose of so many bodies, even for a man like Harding. Go on, my child. Eat."

Reluctantly, Lauren started on the food she'd been given.

"Please eat as much as you like," Harding urged Gallagher convivially. "Can't allow a good lobster to go to waste, can we?"

"I'll do it justice," Gallagher said. "I just like to eat slowly."

"A man who likes to savour good food; and, no doubt, good wine and good women. I like that."

Harding seemed to enjoy picking at a conversation from all angles, discarding bits of it as and when it pleased him, much as he did with the dismembered crustacean on his plate.

"As a photographer," Harding went on, "you must have come across a plentiful supply of all three."

"Don't believe everything you hear," Gallagher said lightly.

"I seldom do."

A tense silence fell between them, and Gallagher began to wonder if he had slipped up somewhere. Was all this yet more game-playing? Harding was sowing a minefield. The trouble was he kept returning to change its pattern so that you never knew where to expect a mine.

"It's the only sensible way," Gallagher said calmly. "Unfortunately, I can sometimes be quite gullible." As he had hoped, Harding was deflected.

"A reference to your wife, I take it," he said with his odd smile. "You must have loved her deeply."

"I did."

Harding began to replenish the glasses. "You are a strange contradiction, Mr Gallagher," he said, while pouring. "What was a man of your obvious sensitivity doing in the Army in the first place? I would have thought the life of a squaddie rather beneath you." The glasses filled, he lowered the empty bottle to the table.

"I was hoping for a commission," Gallagher said. "In my innocence, I'd expected it to be a simple matter. After all, I'd had a fair education. Now I know education was not enough. Still, they made me a photographer. That's something. At least I can earn a reasonably decent living."

"But when your wife betrayed you, you wanted to go out and kill something. Is that it?"

It was not like that at all, but Gallagher said: "Perhaps." It was all helping to fit into the image he hoped he was successfully building in Harding's mind. He needed that image to stick, if he were ever going to make it out of this place.

"Killing your wife and her lovers was out of the question, so you went looking for a war where you could exorcize your pain and rage with impunity; and Africa, of course, was your logical choice."

Gallagher risked a jibe. "Until you stepped in."

Harding didn't seem to mind. "These things happen. I believe you're quite a romantic. Man is betrayed by wife. Man runs away to war. Has it occurred to you that you were not going out to kill but be killed? God knows, there are plenty of little wars in Africa to accommodate you."

Gallagher sat back in his chair. "What do you mean by 'to be killed'?"

"Soldiering in Africa requires considerable skill if one is to survive. I take it you wanted to survive?"

"Of course." Gallagher went back to his food.

Harding maintained a silence long enough to cause Gallagher to look up at him again.

"I think you wanted to die, Mr Gallagher," he remarked quietly. "I happen to know that you were a poor soldier. Perhaps that's really why you never got a commission. Although, as I said, I know some appalling examples of the commissioning boards' creations, so perhaps you should indeed be comforted by your failure. You did, after all, gain by it. I wouldn't be surprised if you now earn far more than, say ... a major?"

"I don't know what a major earns these days. Anyway, what did you mean when you said you happen to know I was a poor soldier? Earlier, you said you knew all about me, but I never imagined you knew my service record." Gallagher's astonishment was very real.

Harding smiled. "I have unlimited resources. I have the ear of governments, and therefore of government departments. Sometimes I am able to learn quite astonishing things in a manner that leaves no one the wiser as to the identity of the enquirer."

Gallagher hoped his face did not betray him. What, he wondered, had Harding dug up about him?

"Have you finished?" Harding asked, indicating Gallagher's plate.

"Yes. Thank you. It was excellent." He was pleased by the steadiness of his own voice. "Whoever prepared it is a chef."

41

"Thank *you*," Harding said, looking pleased. "I did. When ... er, roughing it, I like to prepare my own meals." He laughed briefly at Gallagher's expression. "I am many, many things, Mr Gallagher. Even a good cook. My father always hated the idea. My dear father," he added thoughtfully. "Let me tell you about him," he went on. "More wine?"

"No, thanks. I'm fine."

"My father. Now there was a bastard for you."

Gallagher waited to see where this new tack in the conversation would lead.

"I killed him, you know, for destroying my sister." Harding said this so calmly, Gallagher could only stare at him. "It was simply and very efficiently done." Harding's smile came and went. "Care to know how?"

"Why not?"

"A safe reply from a captive audience," Harding commented drily. He toyed with his glass, his eyes remembering. "My father was a singularly unpleasant man: in demeanour, in habits, in ideas. He was successful, supremely so, and he used his vast power to stamp on everyone, even his own flesh and blood. My sister committed suicide because of something he did to her. That was when I decided to kill him."

Gallagher listened in silence to the amazing tale. He could not understand why such information was being divulged to him, unless it was because Harding knew Gallagher would never be in a position to do anything about it....

"He had a stallion," Harding went on, "a beautiful Arabian beast, given to him by some sheik he'd managed to con into buying obsolete weaponry at an extortionate price. He hated Arabs, you know. They were right next to the Jews on his hate list. They were all wogs to him, and being rich wogs made it the absolute limit. He used to exercise the stallion every day, at precisely the same time, over the same route. At a certain point on the route, he'd charge at an old oak that had a low branch spread squarely across his path.

"Just before it appeared that the branch was about to decapitate him, he would duck, clearing it by inches at full gallop. It gave him a thrill to survive day after day. Perhaps he imagined himself a cavalry officer at full charge. God knows what went through his mind. After my sister's death, I watched him for two weeks. His routine never varied. He always arrived at the oak at precisely the same time, and horse and rider were always in perfect rhythm. It was as if every day they went through an elemental gate of some kind. If they went through, there would be life. If not....

"The experience would leave him keyed up for the rest of the day, and he would be in top form when conducting business. He loved those rides so much, he would be almost reluctant to travel abroad, choosing instead to send representatives. If his presence was vital, he would chafe until he could return home. I think that horse became part of him, and I knew that if I could disturb that special rhythm, the oak would finish him off. So I watched him closely for those two weeks. Then I knew how to do it.

"Harding International has very wide pharmaceutical interests. We have produced drugs that no one outside those particular firms will hear of for at least another five years. I used one of them on the stallion in minute doses over a period of five weeks. The animal became dependent upon it. My father used to comment on how superbly he ran, how perfect his rhythm, how acute his senses. Then I stopped giving the drug.

"The horse ran perfectly for three successive runs. On the fourth day, the lack of the stimulant had its effect. As luck would have it, my father chose to push him too hard that day. At the crucial moment, the stallion missed his footing and the rhythm disintegrated. My father had not time to duck. The oak finally got him.

"I was abroad when it happened. Cannes, as a matter of fact. I had gone there as soon as I stopped the drug, knowing it would take at least four days for the desired result. They said my father's head was practically torn off by that old oak, the skin of his neck ripping open like rotten cloth."

Harding's cold-blooded recital of the manner in which he had murdered his own father chilled Gallagher.

"You seem shocked," Harding said mildly. "My sister was a beautiful young woman, very much in love and very happy. My father had no right to do what he did to her." The luminous eyes seemed on fire. "No trace of the drug was found, of course. Even by present standards it is undetectable. Officially, my father's death was misadventure. Apart from myself, you are the only one who knows the truth." His smile came on. "Do you know know why I told you?"

"No," Gallagher answered truthfully.

But Harding merely continued to smile, and that made Gallagher very apprehensive.

Harding left the table to go to a streamlined wall-telephone. He lifted the receiver from its recess, punched two buttons on its underside.

"Ah, Marika. Would you care to join us? Good." Replacing the receiver, Harding returned to the table and sat down. "You will see that Marika is quite a stunning young woman. Interesting history. Mother Rumanian, father Greek, but she was born in Rumania and brought up in Alsace. She is fiercely French, yet speaks German as well as any native. Both parents are dead. She was once trained to be a concert cellist. Now, you'd be hard put to find a better exponent of the art of using an M16. In her delicate hands, it becomes a quite devastating weapon. From cello to rifle. I've always found that rather fascinating.

"I think it only fair," Harding went on, "to let you understand one other thing about Marika. Men do not pick her. She picks them. When she first started her group, some of the laddies tried the old machismo on her. One brave soul pushed his luck too far. She shot him ... in the groin. Had to finish the poor fellow off. No use to himself or to anyone after that, I'm afraid. So do watch your step."

Gallagher had no time to make comment, for that was when Marika entered the room. He found he was staring. Harding had not exaggerated. If anything, he had understated her physical attributes.

Marika Angelou was a tall, Junoesque beauty. She had long, golden-blonde hair that contrasted startlingly with dark eyebrows. Her eyes were a vivid sea-green – Gallagher could not remember seeing such green eyes on anyone except Celia. The close-fitting combat jumpsuit did everything to accentuate the magnificence of her body. She was a shade bigger than Lauren, Gallagher thought, but the two women, while sharing great beauty, possessed an individuality of physical presence that was not interchangeable. Lauren's patrician features were far removed from the powerful slavic strength of Marika's. Her hands, he noted, were indeed delicate, being well shaped, with long, expressive fingers. She had a proud chin and a wide, sensuous mouth. Despite the obvious strength she radiated, Gallagher found it difficult to equate her with the murderous skills that Harding had credited her with; but he knew through bitter experience how suicidally dangerous such thinking could be.

"She's quite real, I assure you," Harding was saying, amusement in his voice.

Gallagher realized he'd been staring at her. Already, the seeds of a plan were germinating within his mind. He did not disguise the open admiration in his eyes. Harding had intimated that Marika was attracted to him. If that were truly the case, then that attraction must be put to good use.

Mindful of Harding's warning, Gallagher said: "I was just catching my breath." He wondered what reaction his words would produce in Marika.

She smiled, pleased. It was an amazing thing, that smile.

"Marika, this is Mr Gallagher," Harding said.

Gallagher stood up. "Gordon," he said to Marika.

Harding raised an eyebrow. " 'Gordon', is it? Well. I think you please him, my dear."

"Hello," she said. "I'm sorry."

Gallagher frowned, puzzled. "Sorry? What for?"

"The needle."

Danger! Gallagher smelled it immediately. The moment Marika had spoken, something had nagged at his mind. Now it began to take shape. He recalled the French-accented voice of the woman who had injected him. He also remembered one of the unseen men's reference to "our leading lady". Marika.

Gallagher kept the look of puzzlement firmly fixed on his face. "Needle?" He'd said that quite well, he thought.

"You fought the drug," Marika informed him casually. "We had to use a needle. I was not very gentle at the time. I had to move for someone to get past and, as I am sure you understand, we were in a hurry. The interruption annoyed me."

"Didn't feel a thing, but I was wondering about the slight soreness in my arm."

"I am sorry about that too. It will not last. Am I forgiven?"

"Of course," Gallagher assured her pleasantly, not relaxing his guard for an instant.

The radiant smile came on again. "Good. These are for you."

For the first time, Gallagher paid attention to the things she was carrying. He took the floppy hat and sunglasses from her, staring at them, baffled. Now Harding was smiling, enjoying a secret joke.

"I'll see you on top," Marika said to Gallagher. Another radiant beam, and she was gone.

Harding wore a look of satisfaction. "It appears that you two will be getting on rather well; but do remember not to become too blinded by her obvious charms. She can be a trifle deadly when crossed."

"Can anyone be a *trifle* deadly?" Gallagher asked, apparently worried. "What are these for, anyway?" He indicated the hat and sunglasses.

"A surprise," Harding said enigmatically. He returned to the theme he seemed determined to pursue. "There seems to be the promise of barely controllable fire in Marika, wouldn't you say? Rather more than in Lauren Tanner, I'd have thought."

More danger. "I have no experience by which to compare them," Gallagher said lightly, making a joke of it. He knew Harding was probing.

"Of course. Silly me." Harding stood up. "Come. Time for your surprise." He pointed to the hat and sunglasses. "You'll be needing those. I'll pick mine up on the way."

V

"*My ... God!*"

Both Harding and Marika realized at once that Gallagher was not faking. He had reeled with shock.

The heat slammed at him with all the delicacy of a sledgehammer. Despite the sunglasses, the fierce sun made him squint until his eyes became accustomed to the glare. Perhaps, he thought, it was because of the sudden transition from the coolness of the underground complex.

"Where is this place?" he said softly, as if the vista before him had awed him into whispering. He did a slow three-hundred-and-sixty-degree turn while Marika and Harding watched him keenly.

Three things relieved the ghastly monotony of the landscape: a stretch of land cleared of stunted, parched scrub that could only be an airstrip; a large dish aerial that rocked to and fro; and a long, low, dun-coloured building bristling with antennae. The building was obviously mainly underground, for its roof barely cleared the surface by about two feet. Unless one knew precisely where to look, there was little chance of spotting it unaided from the air.

And that was it. In every direction, the horizon stretched unendingly, running from this flat, arid land with its lack of visible life, its polka-dot pattern of sun-punished scrub, its reddish earth.

But upon its barren face Gallagher could see a terrible majesty in it. Its sheer immensity filled him with a sense of wonder from within which he could actually appreciate its dread beauty. Without his realizing it, his mouth had hung open. That was a mistake. The heat seemed to claw at his throat. He shut his mouth quickly, swallowing at saliva that was suddenly no longer there. In seconds, he was thirsty.

Harding watched Gallagher's hasty swallowings. "Should have warned you about that. Personally, I find it rather daunting out here. But Marika. Ah. Healthy outdoor type. She seems to find it inspiring. Don't you, my dear?"

"I think it is beautiful."

"Where are we?" Gallagher asked. No one appeared in a hurry to tell him. He looked at Marika. A tiny smile hovered about her lips. He noted that her mouth was strangely similar to Lauren's, though a little wider.

"Do you like what you see?" she asked. It was not said archly, for which Gallagher was very grateful.

"Very much."

She seemed pleased by his reply.

"Tell him where we are, Marika," Harding prompted at last. "Then let's go in. I'm cooking out here." To Gallagher he added: "I tan atrociously. Sensitive skin and all that."

"We're in Australia," Marika said casually.

The news left Gallagher benumbed. He tried to dredge up all he knew of the island continent from memory stretching back to his schooldays. He realized with despair that his knowledge was pitifully inadequate for the task ahead, if he were forced to cross this unforgiving land.

"You're not serious," he said. He didn't want to believe it.

He looked about him once more. Dear God. It must be true. But how had they done it? How had they lifted passengers from an Africa-bound flight and ferried them all the way to an Australian desert without having half the world's police forces, and the rest, on their tails? And why had they shown him this baking land?

"There's no changing reality, I'm afraid," Harding said. "This is Australia. Absolutely awful place to get lost in. One does not perspire. Moisture simply evaporates off you. For how long do you think a man could last out here without water?"

"God knows." The prospect horrified Gallagher. He began to feel thirsty again.

"Without finding a waterhole, not very long. Some people give it as little as twenty-four hours. There aren't any waterholes in this area for mile upon mile. We know. We have surveyed it extensively. Here, however, we're all right. Our own artesian well, right beneath our feet. The whole area abounds with underground water, of course; but you've got to dig. Can't see a man getting very far with his bare hands, can you?"

A warning? Gallagher wondered.

"Why are you telling me all this?" he asked, looking from one to the other. "I'm not going anywhere."

"No one said you were," Harding told him. "Now let's go in. All this talk of water has made me quite thirsty."

They returned the way they had come, through a double door in the main housing of the dish aerial, and descending a long spiral staircase that rang metallically beneath their feet. The staircase passed through a wide concrete tube that rose chimney-like from the nine-foot-high ceiling of the corridor below. The drop from the top was thirty feet.

At the bottom, Harding said to Gallagher: "You don't have to tell the menagerie where they are, if you don't wish to."

"You're sending me back there?" Gallagher looked horrified.

Without the barrier of sunglasses, the cobra eyes seemed uncomfortably menacing. "It won't be for very long. Now. I'm sure you would like some water before you return. Will you see to him please, Marika?" Harding said. "Then take him back." To Gallagher, he went on: "You can tell that menagerie in there that the situation is hopeless."

"Does it really matter?" Gallagher queried boldly. "They're going to die, anyway."

"Desperate people will try anything. There may be some heroes among them."

"They can't get out of that room." Gallagher pushing it.

The black eyes stared coldly. "Tell them," Harding insisted. "I have no intention of allowing them to kill themselves by their stupidity. They'll die when I want them to, and not before."

A loony. A real loony.

"As you wish," Gallagher said accommodatingly.

"Good. Marika will take good care of you." Harding seemed to have reverted to his earlier, less menacing manner. "Ask her anything you like, within reason, of course." The twisting smile did not quite become a leer, but the suggestive meaning was there. "I'll see you in a little while, Marika."

He left them and disappeared down another corridor.

Gallagher took a chance. "He told me you hated clumsy advances. Didn't you mind what he was suggesting?"

The green eyes surveyed him. "Alex is all right. No one else would have got away with it. We have a kind of brother/sister relationship."

"I see," Gallagher said, remembering the story of Penelope.

"What else did he tell you about me?"

Gallagher chose to be prudent. "He told me you were quite something. He was right."

"Not so many compliments at once. I might not believe you." The lips were smiling, but the eyes held an unnatural stillness.

He took his courage in his hands. "I meant it."

The eyes warmed a little. "*Bon.* Now, I must take you back."

"Er ... the water?"

"Oh, yes. First, I will take you to the water."

"What if the people in the room get ugly when you put me back?" Gallagher asked as they walked down the corridor Harding had taken.

"The guards will be instructed to stop anything. Do not worry. We shall come back for you." Marika smiled her radiant smile, promising him much.

"Well?" Harding asked.

"First, you tell me," Marika said. "Then I shall tell you."

They were sitting at the table in Harding's room. All signs of the meal he'd had with Gallagher were gone. A glass of clear water was set before him. Marika sipped pure orange juice from a whisky glass.

"I think he is who he says he is," Harding said and gave her a brief résumé of the story of Gallagher's wife. "That was no fake. He was hurting even as he told it. And he is the one who won that photographic award; the title of the work came out easily. We know his army record. We know he was an awful soldier, which was why they made him Clerk/Photographer. He is bitter about not having been given a commission. The reasons may well have been those he believes them to be. He is reasonably intelligent, so could have made a good officer. Not being made one may have turned him into a bad soldier. What do you think?"

"It is possible," she agreed. "All that you've said makes sense. He was so unlike the others, it was only sensible that you should have

48

checked on him. He could have been a special policeman, like the Afrikaner."

"Yes. But Villiger is not after us. He is after the big African, even though his passport says he is a businessman. My contacts tell me differently. The African must have ANC connections. Not that it matters in this case. They're all going the same way."

Marika was silent.

"Say it," Harding urged mildly.

"We are both agreed that Gallagher is just someone with the bad luck to have taken that plane. He is not like the others, who people will believe were hijacked for ransom. But Gallagher?"

"We cannot let him go. He would talk to the first policeman who would listen."

"There may be a way," Marika insisted.

"I hope, Marika, you're not letting your attraction for this man cloud your reason. Your team has worked for me twice before, and I've always been impressed by your efficiency."

"I am still being efficient. I find him very attractive, yes. But that is not my reason. He is not an important person, and people would expect him to be released. Not releasing him might start someone, somewhere, wondering. You would not like that. Did we not let the ordinary passengers and crew go? So why keep Gallagher?"

"And how would you propose to keep his mouth shut? The charade we played with him was not a preliminary to letting him go, but to find out who he really was. It's bad luck he is who he professes to be."

"It is very simple to stop him from talking. We simply say we will kill not only him but his wife, his friends, their families and so on." She spoke as calmly as if she were discussing a piece of music about to be played. "Someone would follow him all the time. We would let him know this, though he would never see that person. He would live in fear of being responsible for the death of an innocent person, perhaps a child. Anyone he spoke to would be at risk. He could not take such pressure. He would never know when and where we would strike. It might be days, weeks, months, hours. You tell me, Alex: what could a man like Gallagher do in such circumstances?"

Harding knew she meant every word. The slaughter would mean nothing to her.

"He would go mad," he answered. "But I have a better idea. One that avoids tying you down to keeping watch on him. We keep him with us for the time being, and involve him. He told me he was looking for some soldiering. Perhaps we'll supply him with that." Harding grinned. "It won't be what he expects, but he'll hardly be able to shoot his mouth off afterwards. We'll set him free in Europe. If he's stupid enough to talk, who's going to believe his wild allegations against me?"

"He will not talk," Marika promised evenly. "He will still be followed."

"For how long?"

"As long as is needed. You have much to lose, Alex. Killing him here with the others is untidy. If it is to happen, it must be done well away from here, after he is seen to have been freed." She took a long drink of her orange juice.

"Perhaps Gallagher won't want to leave," Harding said. "You seem to have enthralled him." He smiled at her. "A new team member?"

She gave her most ravishing smile. "It would make his life much easier."

The door had been flung open and Gallagher pushed into the room. He had stumbled, fallen, hands shooting out to cushion the impact. He had taken the blow on a shoulder, rolled on to his back. The door had slammed shut.

After giving him some water, Marika had handed him over to a black American she'd called Cyrus, with instructions to return him to the room.

Gallagher lay panting in the disbelieving silence. Then Sumner's voice broke it loudly, in far from friendly tones.

"Well, I'll be goddammed. Look who's here. The nigger's back."

Gallagher felt a surge of anger, but he remained where he was. He already had enough to think about without adding a fool like that to the list.

Pandemonium broke out now. In seconds he was surrounded as everyone rushed up, demanding to know what had transpired.

"We thought you were dead!" A man he would later know as Lamoutier, and whom he would remember with great sadness.

"What happened?"

"Why did they let you go?"

"Are we being rescued?"

"Do you know where the hell we are?" Paula Browne.

Everyone was speaking at once. Gallagher lay there unmoving, listening to the babble of voices, savouring the memory of the fleeting glance he'd caught of the look on Lauren Tanner's face when she'd seen he was still alive. The grey eyes had fairly sparkled. It made him feel good.

"Give him room, you people!" A strong, commanding voice. "Why don't you help him up? He could be hurt." People were shoved aside.

The big blond man with the mean face was looking down at him. Gallagher was intrigued. He'd know an Afrikaner accent anywhere.

"You all right, man?" Villiger queried with apparently genuine concern.

50

"I'm fine, thanks. Roughed up a bit, but otherwise OK."

Everyone was now quiet and listening.

Villiger stuck out a massive hand. "Grab this."

Gallagher did not need help but he had no intention of offending the blond man by refusing. Though opposed to everything the Afrikaner stood for, he was pragmatic enough to realize that they would probably have to depend upon each other for survival. It was obvious that the man had come to the same conclusion and the helping hand was his way of saying so.

Taking the proffered hand, Gallagher levered himself up. "Thanks."

The big man introduced himself. "Piet Villiger. What happened back there?"

Gallagher found he could not help it. The accent grated on his nerves, and Villiger's piggy, suspicious eyes did nothing to dispel the media caricature of an Afrikaner from his mind.

"They questioned me," he answered.

"And what else, boy?" another voice asked. The voice that had called him nigger.

Gallagher turned to look at the fat, baby-faced man. "Who are you?" His voice was cold. He was aware that Villiger was looking keenly at him.

"Ethan Sumner." Sumner's manner suggested that Gallagher should bow, or at least touch his forehead in respect at the mention of the name.

"Mr Sumner," he said quietly, "I am not your boy. Please remember that."

Sumner did not like that at all. "Now, look here, b...."

"Say it, and you'll get one right in the mouth."

Sumner grew red and began to shout. "Why, you yellow-bellied —"

"Stop it!" Villiger snapped.

Sumner looked to him for support. "You going to let him talk to me like that?" In Sumner's eyes, he and Villiger had much in common when it came to niggers.

"It is stupid to fight among ourselves," Villiger said evenly. "We have a greater problem outside that door."

"But you saw what he did!" Sumner was still outraged. "You all saw how he tried to save his skin. How do we know he's not one of them? How come he's not dead?"

The piggy eyes stared at Gallagher. "Well, Mr Gallagher? Are you one of them? Like Harding?"

Gallagher glanced at the faces about him. Only Jake Smallson's and Lauren's bore any friendliness, Villiger's was watchful. The others varied from coldness to Sumner's open hostility. With the exception of Sumner, for whom Gallagher was caring less and less, he didn't blame them

"No," he answered. "I am not, and never have been."

"They questioned you, you said."

"Yes."

"You look all right to me."

The police-like manner of the Afrikaner irritated Gallagher. *You're not in South Africa now, you big shit. Bet you're some kind of policeman. You'd know all about how people should look after interrogation.*

Gallagher's reply was quite civil. "They just shoved me around for a while. No beating." He wondered if Harding were listening to all this.

"So you were just out to save your own skin."

"Yes," Gallagher admitted shamelessly.

Villiger did not seem unduly perturbed. The others, however, made varying noises of disgust. Some began to move away, as if wanting to distance themselves from someone as low as Gallagher.

Villiger went on: "What did they want to know?"

"Nothing of interest. They already know all they want to. I think they were just playing with me and wanted to show me how difficult it would be for us to try to escape."

"Escape?" Paula Browne gave a harsh laugh? "How the fuck do they think we're going to get out of here with those two po-faced bitches outside the door?"

"They've been changed," Gallagher said. "Two men are there now."

"That makes it easier?" Sarcastically.

"No, and there are many more of them around. You might as well know the worst. We're in an underground complex of some kind. I don't know what its purpose is, but I've seen lots of antennae and a large dish aerial." Gallagher looked at them all in turn. "Brace yourselves. We're in Australia."

"My God! *Australia!*" Paula Browne exclaimed.

"Impossible!"

"I don't believe it!" Sumner.

"It can't be ...!"

And everyone was speaking again, yelling, shouting.

Villiger had said nothing. Now he roared: "*Be quiet, all of you!* Let him finish."

It brought instant silence.

Gallagher could not prevent a feeling of unease as he looked at the heavy features, the deep-set eyes, the solid body. He imagined, vividly, what it would be like to be locked in a police cell with this man. *But I'm going to need him. He's the only one here who might have the kind of talent I'm looking for.*

"I know we're in Australia," he said to the staring faces. "They took me outside to show me; and if it's not Australia, I can only tell you that we're stuck in the middle of the biggest, hottest stretch of desolate land I ever thought I'd see. It's a bloody desert out there, with *nothing* on the horizon, in any direction. So if it's really Australia, the nearest inhabited place could be hundreds of miles away. And there's no water. Harding was very careful to point that out to me. Without shelter or water, he says a person could expect to last about twenty-four hours. You'd bake to death."

Someone began to weep softly. The faces before Gallagher stared back disbelievingly, despair creeping into them. Villiger's was neutral.

"Are you sure, man?" Villiger did not want to believe it either.

Gallagher had grown tired of the man's questioning. He said impatiently: "Bang on the door and ask the guards, if you don't believe me. Maybe they'll tell you." He wanted to talk to Lauren, away from these people.

The weeping person, a man, kept saying: "O God O God O God...."

"Was there any talk of ransom?" someone asked half-heartedly. The big African.

"No." Gallagher gave it to them short and sharp.

"This is crazy!" Paula Browne said loudly. "What is that creep Harding after?"

"Perhaps it's not really a hijack at all," a German-sounding voice put in. "This may be a government exercise of some kind, an anti-hijack exercise to find out how people behave in these circumstances. It helps them to plan rescues."

"You nuts or something?" Paula Browne said. "A *government* exercise? They're playing it so much for real," she went on scornfully, "they shoot people too? They may do crazy things like that in Germany, buster −"

"Last April in the United States," the German interrupted quietly, "they deliberately contaminated a wide area and put people in there, just to find out what it would be like in a nuclear accident. The place would be safe again in one hundred days ... they said." The man clearly did not put much store by that statement.

Paula Browne shut up. Gallagher could almost see the waves of panic coming, rippling from person to person.

Villiger sensed it too. "*Hold it!*" The harsh accent stopped them again. To Gallagher he addressed a mild question: "What do you have in mind?"

Gallagher stared at him, then looked past Paula Browne to where Jake Smallson and Lauren were still sitting in their old positions.

"I'm going to talk to some friends," Gallagher said, and eased his way through, leaving the crowded people standing about aimlessly.

"Well, how d'you like that?" Sumner grumbled to no one in particular.

People moved numbly away, to lower themselves slowly to the floor. Villiger and Sumner were left standing together.

"Goddam nigger," Sumner said loudly enough for those immediately nearby to hear. He glared defiantly at the big African, who stared ferally back at him. Hate sizzled between them.

Villiger moved away without saying anything.

We've got to have transport, Gallagher was thinking as he walked towards Lauren and the old man. *Without wheels, we've had it. Gallagher, me old son, are you in a mess!* He still had no concrete plan. All he had were fluid ideas that continuously adjusted themselves to various inputs as he went along. That, he decided, was how he was going to play it.

Lauren had been watching him all the way, but she was on guard once more. Gallagher felt deflated.

"Well," he said, "I'm back." He lowered himself to the floor, facing them.

Smallson said: "We had given you up for dead. You were gone so long." The old man turned to his granddaughter. "Are you not going to tell him how glad you are to see him safe and well?"

Lauren's cheeks grew red as Gallagher regarded her with a ghost of a smile on his lips. She looked away in confusion.

Smallson snorted in mock disgust. "She will not talk for a while. So. Tell me. Is it really Australia?"

"Yes. I don't think Harding would bother to make that up."

"So how do we get out?"

"Without transport, we don't. But I believe Harding must have vehicles — jeeps, Landrovers or whatever — somewhere. All I've got to do is find them."

He began to tell them what had happened. He left out everything about Celia and mentioned Marika only briefly. He said nothing about her apparent attraction to him.

Watching the three in deep conversation, Sumner said, in a low snarl: "Will you just look at that?" He had contrived to sit near Villiger, his adopted soul-mate.

"Look at what?" Villiger did not sound interested.

"That nigra over there. Ever since we've been here, he's been after that white girl. Where I come from, we don't look kindly on that. No, sir. Down in South Africa you people have got it right. It's illegal in your country isn't it? We don't have the laws, but there are other ways."

Villiger said nothing. Sumner bored him.

"And that's about it," Gallagher said, coming to the end of the abridged version of his encounter with Harding.

It had been a mostly one-sided conversation, with Lauren and Smallson seemingly content just to listen; but Gallagher had not failed to notice the intensity with which their eyes remained upon him.

Smallson was the first to speak. "Do you believe they will return for you?"

Gallagher shrugged. "It's anyone's guess. They said they would; but what they say and what they actually do...."

"How could they have found out about your Army career?" Lauren asked.

Gallagher looked at her, knowing that she was hiding a great deal. Well, that was her business. All he wanted to know was enough to give him an edge on Harding. Already he'd had one good stroke of fortune. Despite Harding's connections in high places, the man had been unable to penetrate the cover he'd been given on leaving the service. It had not been expected that anyone would want to check, but the precaution had nonetheless been taken. An obscure file, buried somewhere in the depths of a filing cabinet. Yet Harding had gained access to it in such a short time. So much for security. The fact that it was the wrong information was immaterial. Gallagher thanked his ex-boss for the insight. Harding would have had him killed by now had that not been the case.

"Harding is a very powerful man," Gallagher answered Lauren. "As, I'm certain, is your grandfather, in other ways. Harding can gain access to very privileged information, I wouldn't doubt." He looked at Smallson. "How about you, Jake? Don't tell me you haven't got your little channels of information."

Smallson gave the ghost of a smile. "Some city councils, maybe...."

"And the rest."

"But nothing like Harding. He is an aristocrat. Half the people in power in your country must know his family."

"The other half probably owe him something. Well, I've got to get to understand him so that I can out-think him. It's the only way we're going to get out of here alive." Gallagher looked at them in turn. "I have a strong feeling that both of you might be able to help me. For the life of me I cannot pinpoint the reason for this hijack. I have some ideas, but they don't make sense. At least, not at the moment. But you may know something that could throw a little light on the subject. It's obvious that you both know him fairly well." Gallagher hesitated, not wanting to press Lauren.

"What you really mean," began the old man shrewdly, "is that Lauren knows him very well. No, no. Do not protest. You have been diplomatic, and in the circumstances we thank you."

Lauren was looking away from them. Gallagher saw how pale her

55

face was. He decided not to push the matter, but he couldn't help wondering how far the relationship had got before it was overtaken by whatever disaster had struck.

"What about his father?" Gallagher asked Smallson. He saw the gratitude for the question in the old man's eyes. *Have we been hijacked because of a broken love affair?* he thought incredulously. *Impossible. Even a man like Harding wouldn't go to such lengths.* Aloud he added: "Could what happened have sent him round the bend?"

Smallson was about to say something, when an unnatural quiet descended upon the room. Gallagher saw that both Lauren and the old man were staring past him. He turned to look.

Marika had entered the room. She had done so quietly.

Her incredible beauty had stunned everyone. He realized that the green eyes were looking directly at him, then they raked Lauren before returning to settle on him. Something sparkled briefly, dangerously in them; then she gave him her most radiant smile. He knew the others were staring at her in awe. She was, he saw, completely unarmed, but the two guards had entered behind her.

She looked away from Gallagher, the smile going as she did so. The green eyes settled on the German couple and their child. "Take them," she ordered the guards.

The woman came out of her trance. "No!" she screamed. "Please!" She hugged the child.

"Don't be alarmed," Marika said kindly. "We're not going to harm you. We're setting you free."

"Free!" The woman's husband repeated uncertainly. "*Free?*" He was grinning now.

"Yes." Marika's smile impaled him with its radiance.

Gallagher felt a deep sense of foreboding; but all around the room, the word "free" was being echoed in hushed, hopeful whispers.

The German turned to his wife. "Lisl, you see?" he said in German. "The ransom has been paid! I knew Ueuerbach would have seen to it. If I can't depend on the chairman of my own company, on whom can I depend?" He raised his voice to speak in English. "We are leaving, my friends. I hope that soon you will be joining us. My name, for those of you who do not know it, is Von Dietlinger. When you are free, please do not hesitate to contact me. We shall have a banquet at my home in Baden-Baden to celebrate. My wife and I will be delighted to have you as our guests." He was smiling happily as he turned his attention to Gallagher. "I am very glad to see that you were mistaken, Mr Gallagher. You must have misunderstood what was said to you."

A still-smiling Marika held out her hand to the child. "May I?" she asked von Dietlinger.

"Certainly," he said eagerly. In his state, he would have agreed to anything. Besides, he did not want to offend his captors, with freedom so close.

Marika took the child's hand and, with a last smile at Gallagher, went out. Von Dietlinger followed with his wife, the guards bringing up the rear.

The door was shut quietly behind them.

VI

"Such a beautiful woman!" Parguineau exclaimed to the room at large. "And so terrible that she should be involved in this." His Gallic soul sighed with regret at the thought. "What a waste."

"Yeah," came Sumner's voice, full of appreciation. "She's some woman, all right. Looks as if we might get out of here now the first ransom's been paid. My people must be working on that right now. Hey, smartass!" he yelled at Gallagher. "Australia, is it? And desert too?" His voice was bitingly derisive. "The Germans got ransomed. What do you say to that?"

Gallagher ignored him.

"Hey! I'm talking to you. I think they made a fool out of you. What do you think now, hey?"

Gallagher did not even turn to look at him.

"What about Bannion?" Paula Browne asked, loudly enough for the room to hear. "They killed him, didn't they? Why do that if we're to be ransomed?"

Sumner had an answer to that. "Bannion got killed because of his own stupid fault. He should have known better. I wouldn't have gotten myself killed for some dumb broad," he finished nastily.

But Paula Browne did not take up the challenge. She simply glared at him with all the contempt she could muster.

"A very stupid man," Smallson said to Gallagher. "It happens that I agree with you — you don't believe there was any ransom, do you? Neither do I. I know Alex Harding. They must have taken those people out to be killed, hmm, Gordon?"

"I'm afraid so, Jake."

"But the child!" Lauren said in horror.

"The child too."

"Oh, my God!" she said softly. She lowered her head and placed a hand over her eyes. After a while, she looked up at him. "She is very beautiful, isn't she? You never told us that. She looked at you very strangely."

"She's a strange woman. You saw that."

The grey eyes focused on him with all their power, making Gallagher feel engulfed. He saw all sorts of questions in them and for a brief moment the room seemed to fade as a mad thought entered his mind.

He wanted to kiss her.

Before he realized what he was doing, he had given in to the impulse, had leaned forward to touch the full, sensuous lips with his.

Lauren's eyes widened, surprised by what was happening. But she did not pull away, and the lips, surprised themselves, responded fleetingly. He pulled away slowly, amazed by what he had just done. The eyes stared at him.

Ethan Sumner was the kind of man with a set of conditioned responses that went into gear wherever he might be and whatever the circumstances. He saw everything that happened, and his own desire for Lauren drove him to the response he made to what his eyes had shown him.

"Goddam!" he snarled. "I'm not going to take this!" And he was up and moving towards Gallagher before anyone realized it. He grabbed Gallagher's shoulder in an attempt to turn him around. "Now see here, boy...."

But that was as far as Sumner got. Gallagher had risen and was spinning all in one motion. He hit Sumner very hard with a flattened fist, just below the sternum. It was a blow O'Keefe had taught him.

To Sumner, the pain was excruciating. He slammed down gasping, barely able to take breath. The whole room was silent.

Sumner began to get his breath back. "Jee ... *Jeezus!*"

"Mr Sumner," Gallagher said in a chill voice. "You will never lay hands on me again."

Sumner was trying to get up. Finally, he made it and stood before Gallagher swaying, hands across his middle.

"When ... when we get out ... of here ... I'll ... I'll see to it that you get ... get...." Sumner staggered back to where Villiger sat, his words unfinished.

Villiger had not moved a muscle throughout, but his eyes were pensive.

Sumner sat down next to him. "I'm ... I'm going to ... get me that ... goddam nigger. You see if I ... don't. Jesus! The bastard ... hurt me, you know that? Why didn't you ... help?"

Villiger was looking at Gallagher, who turned again and was in the act of sitting down. "I never do anything hastily," he said. "You are very short on patience, Mr Sumner. That fault has just earned you a very painful blow. I would recommend very highly, man, that you leave him alone. For your sake."

"I'll leave him, if you ... get him."

Villiger's face strongly suggested that he wanted to sigh.

On the other side of the room, Gallagher was saying to Lauren and Smallson: "He'll be all right."

Lauren was wide-eyed. "Where did you learn to hit like that? In the army?"

"I think perhaps not, my child," Smallson put in. "You were very, very quick, Gordon. They do not teach such things to an ordinary soldier." He raised a restraining hand. "All right, I will not ask, and you do not have to tell me. It is enough that I have seen."

Gallagher shrugged. He looked at Lauren, remembering the brief taste of her lips and the fresh smell of her, despite her having had no access to water since the hijack. He was pleased to see the twin spots of colour blooming on her cheeks. He knew she was remembering.

The door was again opened, and everyone tensed, waiting. An hour had passed since the von Dietlingers had been taken away. An Arab guard had entered the room; the man who had shot Bannion.

He pointed his AK at Gallagher. "You will come."

Gallagher felt Lauren's hand reach for his suddenly and grip it tightly. Then she let go.

"Don't worry," he said quietly to her as he stood up. "You too, Jake. I'll see you."

"Do not talk!" the guard shouted.

Gallagher turned without another word and began walking towards him. Lauren stared after Gallagher, trying to keep the fear from her eyes and only just succeeding. Smallson, with his unerring instinct for these things, reached out to touch her hand and to give comfort. She gave him a weak, grateful smile.

Just as Gallagher reached the guard, Paula Browne's voice loudly broke the silence:

"I want to go to the john. I've been holding on since we got to this dump. Now I can't any more. I feel nauseous. You people got a john in this place?"

The room held its breath. She apparently had not recognized the Arab as the one who had shot Bannion; but then she had been on the earthen floor, writhing in pain at the time. The man glared at her hotly. The AK was pointing at her.

"She means a toilet," Gallagher said quickly. "A toilet," he repeated with some urgency. He felt certain the man was about to shoot.

The Arab still glared at Paula Browne who, to her credit, stared right back at him. Gallagher felt a surge of admiration for her.

"I will ask," the guard said finally. He looked at Gallagher. "We will go now."

The door closed behind them. The entire room let out a collective sigh of relief.

It was Sumner who spoke first. "I hope they shoot the bastard," he said.

59

"Sumner," Paula Browne began, her mouth turning down in practised contempt, "you're a real shithead. You know that?"

"Can you see anything?" Marika said.

"It would help," Gallagher said, "if I knew what I was looking for, and where to look."

She had handed him a massive pair of powerful Zeiss binoculars, similar to the kind naval commanders used. Their specially coated lenses cut down the glare of the savage early afternoon sun. The Arab had given him a hat and sunglasses and had brought him up through the concrete tube to Marika before departing, leaving him alone with her. She stood close to him, and Gallagher was very conscious of her strong magnetism. She was holding his sunglasses for him.

"It would spoil the fun," she said.

He continued to scan the expanse of empty land. Even through the binoculars, the horizon seemed to stretch for ever. The prospect of escape looked even more daunting.

"Where's Harding?" he asked casually, the binoculars still to his eyes. He turned slowly, sweeping the emptiness before him.

"He's gone on a little trip," she answered without hesitation, seemingly unmoved by the question.

Gallagher wondered how Harding had travelled. The binoculars passed over the airstrip at that point. Gallagher did not pause, but he had not missed the furrows in the light coating of surface dust. There was no place in which to hide an aircraft, therefore one must have come to pick Harding up. Gallagher continued sweeping the desert landscape. The heat was pounding on him; the horizon appeared to dance briefly.

"A trip?" He was still casual about it.

"He'll be back by the time it's all over."

What the hell was she on about now? "What do you mean?" he queried.

"Keep looking," was all she would say.

Soon afterwards, he saw it: a small puff of dust. He had already swung past it, eyes having received the information and passed it on to the brain. The brain had registered the input and demanded a second look. Through the binoculars, Gallagher saw movement. He hadn't known what to expect, but it was not what he now saw.

The figures seemed at first to have been foreshortened by the distance, even through the powerful lenses, until he realized that they were not walking upright but were stumbling and sometimes moving forward on all-fours. With a sickening horror, he knew the figures were the von Dietlingers. Gallagher's eyes were riveted by the sight of the small figure of the child being helped along by his parents, and there was a strong taste of bile in his mouth.

60

"Why?" he got out at last in a croaky voice. He couldn't take the glasses away. "I thought you were setting them free."

"They are free."

He couldn't believe it. "Out *here*?"

He took the binoculars away at last and looked at her. The fierce sun hurt his eyes and forced him to squint, but he didn't ask her for the sunglasses. His pupils adjusted themselves and the pain went.

"Of course," she said.

He couldn't see her eyes behind her sunglasses. He couldn't fathom what she was thinking, or even gauge the expression she was presenting to him.

"But they'll die!" *And* you'll *die if you keep this up*, Gallagher admonished himself. But he could not help it. Nothing could have prepared him for this.

"It will be a merciful death."

"Dying of thirst?" he asked in disbelief.

"It is not finished yet. We have the Abo Run to come."

He had not the faintest idea of what she was talking about. "Could I have my sunglasses, please?"

She gave them to him, while he handed her the binoculars. Putting on the glasses, he stared at her beautiful face.

"Tell me about the Abo Run," he said.

He saw the beginnings of her radiant smile. Then she said: "Kiss me."

Gallagher did not hesitate. Remembering Lauren and inwardly begging her forgiveness, he did so. Marika's lips were voracious as they attacked his mouth; but he was not unmoved. That pleased her.

"Hmm," she said.

At that moment Gallagher heard an engine. It startled him, for he could see nothing that would make the sound: nothing in the air and certainly nothing in sight on the ground. Yet the noise was drowning the subdued hum of the dish aerial. Then he pinpointed it. The sound was coming from the long, low building. It was the sound of a car motor, and since it was hardly likely that Alex Harding would have a car out here, Gallagher assumed it to be a desert-going vehicle of some kind. He had found the means of escape. Implementation would be another matter altogether.

The sound grew progressively louder. The vehicle was moving and, by the note of its engine, it was climbing. Even as he watched, it appeared to pop out of the ground. Marika noted the astonishment upon Gallagher's face.

"Come," she said. "I'll show you how it's done." She began walking towards what turned out to be a canvas-topped, short-wheelbased Landrover, kitted out for desert travel. The vehicle had stopped, its engine running.

Wondering at its purpose, Gallagher looked towards the spot in the distance where the von Dietlingers were fighting a losing battle against the sun and the land, before he set off after Marika. When he reached the Landrover, he saw what he had been unable to from where he'd been standing, and even when he'd been brought to the surface the first time. A long, shallow slope descended from the desert floor to end in wide doors painted to blend with the surrounding scenery. The doors belonged to the low building, which went a further thirty feet into the ground, its base being where the ramp ended. Only this frontal view gave the true dimensions of the building. The rest of it was dug into the earth and was no doubt connected via one of the corridors to the underground complex proper.

"Ingenious," Gallagher said.

"Practical," Marika corrected. "The Rovers would bake otherwise."

Gallagher made a mental note of the use of the plural. More than one vehicle was a boon not to be overlooked.

The walk to the Landrover could not have been more than a hundred yards, yet Gallagher felt the effect of the heat upon him. God alone knew what the von Dietlingers were going through out there.

The black American, Cyrus, was in the driving seat.

Marika said: "It is all right, Cyrus. We shall take it."

"Right," Cyrus said good-humouredly, and hopped out. "See you soon." He gave Gallagher a speculative glance and set off back down the long earthen ramp.

"Can you drive these things?" Marika asked.

"I learned in the army," Gallagher answered. "Anyway, it's no different from driving a car."

"There is a slight difference," she said, her sunglasses gleaming at him. "There are no roads, and you will use four-wheel drive all the time. Please get in."

Gallagher did as he was told and climbed behind the wheel as she got into the passenger seat. She was still wearing the combat jump-suit, which tightened about the swell of her thighs as she sat down.

"Let's see you drive," she said.

"Where are we going?"

"Where I tell you."

He started the Landrover forward. It jerked a little until he got the hang of it. Then he got it going as smoothly as was possible over such a terrain. There was not much he could do about avoiding the scattered clumps of withered grass. It was already quite hot in the cab, although the vehicle had been out in the sun for only a few minutes.

He wondered if they were going to pick up the three suffering people out in the desert. He kept driving, waiting for directions from Marika. The Landrover was not pointing towards the Germans.

After a long silence, Marika said: "You are worried about them?"

He gauged his reply carefully. "About the child, I suppose."

"You knew they were all going to die."

"I thought your plans had changed. When you said what you did in the room...."

"Oh, come, come, Gordon. You did not really believe we would let anyone go. They have seen Alex. Now they have seen me."

"People have seen their hijackers before and have been set free."

"Yes, but this is not an ordinary hijack."

Gallagher thrust out of his mind the horrendous thought of von Dietlinger and his wife and child, slowly dehydrating to death.... He glanced at Marika's beautiful profile, trying to work out what such a woman was doing in this place, pursuing such a murderous career.

"Stop!" she called.

Gallagher halted the Landrover. They were nowhere near the German family.

"Let us get out." She was already climbing out of her seat.

He turned off the engine and followed suit. He walked round the front of the vehicle to join her. The heat slammed at him. She handed him the binoculars.

"See if you can see anything." She pointed into the empty wastes. He removed his sunglasses, tucked them into his denims and raised the binoculars to his eyes. He focused on the spot towards which Marika appeared to be pointing.

"Do you see it?" she asked.

See what? "No," he answered.

"They are sometimes very difficult to spot. They are very clever."

Gallagher kept the glasses on the target area, feeling like an idiot. What was he looking for?

"Anything?"

"No."

"Keep looking. It is there."

Gallagher kept looking. And then he saw something: a sluggish movement. He could not believe it.

A lizard. He must have been looking at it all the time. The eighteen-inch reptile, sand-coloured with paler stripes across its body, was perfectly camouflaged where it lay among a scattering of small stones as sand-coloured as its own body. How had Marika been able to spot it from the moving vehicle?

"You've got phenomenal eyesight," he said to her, still watching the lizard.

"Ah! You have seen it."

"Yes."

"They call it a blue-tongued skink, these Australians. Funny name. Keep watching it."

Wondering what was so fascinating about a skink, he kept

watching, hearing Marika rummaging about in the Landrover.

"How far away would you say it is?" she called at him. "Keep looking! I want to know where it goes."

"It hasn't moved. Distance? I'd say about ... a hundred and fifty ... yes. A hundred and fifty yards." He didn't think he was giving anything away by showing he could judge distances.

"One hundred and thirty-seven metres," she said, going metric.

"Yes. I thought so too. You are good with distances."

Was there a sharpened interest in her voice? Gallagher hoped he hadn't overdone it.

"Are you watching?"

"I am. It hasn't moved. How the hell it can take this heat so calmly, I don't know."

"It is accustomed."

"I suppose so." What was she doing?

"Still there?"

"Yes."

"Good."

The sharp report going off unexpectedly next to his left ear startled him so completely that he flinched; but not before he had seen the contentedly basking skink suddenly become airborne, as its shattered body was thrown over a clump of desert grass.

Gallagher brought the binoculars off his eyes as if they had burned him. He stared at Marika, then at the still-smoking M16 in her hands. She held the lightweight weapon – under six and a half pounds of it – with the assurance of an expert. Harding had not exaggerated. The demise of the skink had been caused by an exceptional shot, by any standard. The M16, he noted, had open sights.

Marika was looking at him now, and he knew with a terrible certainty what was going to happen to the von Dietlingers.

"That was a fantastic shot," he said. He did not have to pretend he was impressed.

"Thank you. Another kiss?"

He forced himself to smile. "Of course."

She pointed the rifle at the ground as she came up to him and pressed her body against his. He felt her nipples hardening through the combat suit, through his shirt, against his chest. He wondered if this new rush of passion was due to his presence or to the anticipation of the killing to come.

She was breathing quite heavily when they parted.

"Hmm," she said, just like the last time. She put the rifle behind the seats and re-entered the Landrover.

Gallagher took his place behind the wheel. The Abo Run. Someone had a sense of humour. Early Australian settlers used to hunt the indigenous aborigines on horseback, chasing them like so many wild animals across the Australian landscape and shooting them down for sport. Harding and his crew had brought the sport into the twentieth century, with refinements. The quarry was different, as was the transport and the weaponry; but the end result would be the same for the unfortunate victims.

Good Christ, he though grimly as he started the engine, *I'm taking part in a human hunt!*

Marika was looking at him. "You know what is next, do you not?"

"Yes." The Landrover began to move.

"You are disturbed by it?"

"Are you surprised?"

"I would be very suspicious if you were not." She pointed to the left, out of the window. "Go this way. That is where they are headed."

Feeling inwardly miserable, Gallagher complied. The Landrover bounced across the red earth.

Von Dietlinger urged his family on. "Come, Lisl, *liebchen*. Come, Rüdi. Help your mother."

They were barely able to move, the child least of all. The intense heat sapped them, sucking them dry.

Von Dietlinger's mind was unable to appreciate the full horror of what had befallen him and his family. He clung to the impossible belief that salvation would come; that they'd make it, without water, without food, across the terrifying landscape.

The child began to cry. It was not the first time; but now he had little strength with which to make the sound. Instead, he made strange, wheezing noises. He fell.

Von Dietlinger stooped to pick up his son. As he did so, he happened to look up and saw the black speck of the approaching Landrover.

"*Gott se dank!*" he whispered feverishly. "We are saved." In his excitement, he let go of the boy. "Lisl!" he cried. She had continued walking. She stopped to look at him wearily.

"Lisl! We are saved! Look!" And he pointed to the approaching vehicle. "They have seen us!" He began to jump up and down, waving his arms above his head frantically, squandering what reserves of energy he had left.

His wife simply stood where she was, watching the Landrover. The boy still lay where he had fallen, curled on the hot earth.

Then von Dietlinger knew real terror as he heard his wife give a strangled gasp and back-pedal grotesquely, already dying as a 5.56-millimetre bullet, travelling at 3,250 feet per second, tore into her left breast and exited through her back. The report came when she hit the ground.

"*Liiislll!*" he screamed, rushing futilely to her. He held the blood-soaked body to him. "Lisl, Lisl, Lisl, Lisl...."

He heard a ghastly crunching sound, followed by the sharp report. He turned to look. The top of his son's head had disappeared. The boy's foetal position had been barely disturbed.

A maddened bull now, von Dietlinger ran towards the source of his torment. The Landrover had stopped, broadside-on.

The last, sharp image he carried into death was of the rifle muzzle pointing at him and of the exceptionally beautiful face behind it, before three bullets punctured his chest in a neat, close triangle.

"I'm sorry about the boy," Marika said. "But his position made it difficult. I had hoped for a cleaner shot. He was a beautiful child." She sounded truly regretful.

Gallagher hung on to the wheel, fearing that if he let go he would throw up.

It had been a most efficient execution, he was forced to admit. Marika's marksmanship was nothing short of miraculous. Where had she learned to shoot like that? He discarded the question. No one could be taught to shoot at that level. She was a natural. Marika, he knew, was going to be a formidable enemy.

She was putting the rifle away. "I must clean this thing when we get back," she said calmly. She had removed her sunglasses, and her green eyes were shining. "It is a very good weapon, but I have to clean it regularly. Are you all right?"

"Yes. Yes. I'm OK. What are you going to do about the ... bodies?"

"They will be buried. Let us go back. I'll show you the way." She smiled at him, lips sensuously promising.

Don't ask me to kiss you, he pleaded in his mind.

"Kiss me," she demanded.

Choking down his revulsion, he did.

They arrived back at the low building just as the executive jet was coming in for a landing. Gallagher recognized it as a Cessna Citation III.

"Alex," Marika said.

Gallagher wondered if it normally remained on the site. He doubted it, however. Harding would never leave such an aircraft exposed to the desert sun and wind. More than likely, the Cessna would be left at a proper airfield, to be called upon when needed.

Gallagher tried to remember whether he ever knew the Cessna's range, and to guess the distance to such an airfield. The jet would be a perfect way out if he could get to it. He felt sure he could fly it off. Then he killed the thought. It would be virtually impossible to get all the survivors into the aircraft undetected, then familiarize himself with the cockpit, then take off, still hoping no one had seen.

Impossible. But he did not close the door completely. He might be able to get Harding to show him around. After all, Harding did not know he'd once been a pilot. The more Gallagher thought about it, the less feasible it became. The Cessna was hardly likely to remain long enough to give him such a chance.

Cyrus was waiting for them at the top of the ramp. The Landrover carried a radio and Marika had used it to warn of their return.

"Good hunt?" Cyrus asked as they climbed out.

"Perfect," Marika replied, "but too simple, I think. We must improve it." She turned to look as the jet rounded off and touched down lightly in a cloud of red dust.

The pilot knew his job, Gallagher noted. "That's a lovely looking plane," he remarked.

"Know much about them?" Cyrus asked. "That's a Citation."

"All I know about those machines is that they take you from A to B faster than other forms of transport. Why do you ask?"

"Seems you were looking at it kind of hungrily."

Gallagher's answer was casual. "You shouldn't be surprised by that. I was just wondering what it would be like to own such a machine. I have an eye for beautiful things." He deliberately glanced at Marika.

The jet was whining itself to a stop.

Marika turned from it to look at Gallagher. She had not missed his glance.

"We are going in now, Cyrus. Will you take the Rover down?"

"Surely."

They left him, and entered via the spiral staircase. Gallagher did not see Cyrus staring after him.

"This will be your room," Marika said. "It is next to mine."

It was about half the size of Harding's, but well-appointed. The walls and ceiling were pale blue, and there was a full-width, thick red carpet. There was a wide fitted wardrobe, a small table with two chairs, and a pale blue sink in one corner, with a good-sized mirror above it. The single bed look comfortable, set against one of the longer walls. It had been recently made. There was a single, recessed light in the ceiling, and a small wall-lamp above the mirror. There was even a shaving-point. All the furniture was of good quality. Finally there was the ever-present grille for the air-conditioning unit.

"Nice," Gallagher commented, trying hard to put the von Dietlingers out of his mind and making a poor job of it.

He wondered who ran the complex, who made it work. Quarters like these were obviously for scientific staff of some kind, but he had seen no one who remotely fitted that description; only the armed members of Marika's group.

Deciding to chance it, he asked: "Where are the people who run this place?" He glanced at the white wall-telephone near the bed, wondering if there were a bug in it.

"It runs itself," Marika answered readily. "People only come here sometimes. Alex comes any time he likes. We do not come often, but when we do, we arrive at different times as his guests, or employees. No one outside notices."

So much for the vague hope that activity in the area might have attracted some attention. There was still the pilot of the Cessna.

"What about the pilot?"

"He's Alex's man. He used to be with the British Air Force and is very good."

Gallagher hoped he showed no reaction. It was unlikely that the man would know him, but it put paid to any thoughts he'd entertained of going anywhere near the executive jet.

"He is well paid to keep his mouth shut," Marika was saying. "He also knows he would be killed very quickly if he even thought about doing anything." There was a gleam in her eyes. "Talking is for later."

She began to unzip the combat suit. It came open like the skin of a ripened banana, revealing silkily smooth flesh the colour of the palest honey. She had been wearing nothing underneath.

As the suit fell away, she stepped out of it. Hers was a glorious body, and Gallagher was forced to look upon it in dumbfounded admiration. It was a powerful-looking body, well structured; in perfect shape.

She came towards him. "I will help you with these," she said, her voice tense and eager as she started on his shirt.

I've got to do this, Gallagher persuaded himself. *If I don't, people will die ... including me.*

They fell struggling to the bed, and Gallagher realized with a mixture of horror and relief that he had become greatly aroused. Marika was scrabbling at him, trying, it seemed, to devour him with her mouth and body. She thrust at him, powerful legs opening and scissoring across his back. Thus she held him as they rolled and thumped.

Then he felt a great rage in him and was suddenly determined to. punish her. He slammed at her brutally. She screamed, but it was not in pain. A paroxysm of ecstasy seemed to have taken hold of her.

"Oui! Oui! Oui ouiouiouioui!" she frantically urged him on. Then she began whispering in another language, then shouting, then whispering, urgently gasping, shouting, whispering, crying with pleasure, all in that language. He assumed it to be Rumanian. Then the Greek started. Soon, it became mixed in with the French and the Rumanian.

They rolled off the bed, and enough of Gallagher's sense of reality remained for him to be grateful for the carpet. He was underneath. He rolled again and their bodies continued to fight each other.

Then she was gripping him tightly between those powerful thighs, and Gallagher felt a great explosion within him, pouring out of him, rushing into her.

She screamed.

Cyrus was at an intersection of corridors, walking with a white man named Johnson, the man who had snarled at Gallagher in the room of captives when Harding had paid his visit.

"Hear something?" Cyrus asked.

Johnson too had caught the faint tail-end of Marika's scream and knew it for what it was. Such a sound was unmistakable. He nodded. "Yes. Sounds as if Marika's got what she wanted."

"Yeah."

They walked on.

"Gordon," Marika said at last. They lay spent on the carpet. The way she said his name spoke of her intense satisfaction.

He wondered whether that bode ill for the future. A too well-pleasured Marika might be as dangerous as a rejected one.

She rolled over to lay her moist, heated body upon him. She kissed him, surprisingly gently. "That was good, very good."

"I know." It was the right choice of words, for his smile had paid her the compliment.

Pleased, she kissed him again lightly and stood up. "I must go." She put on the jumpsuit and her sand-coloured basketball-type boots.

Then she left him lying on the carpet, with a backward glance, a radiant smile.

Gallagher did not remember dozing off, but when he awoke he got up quickly, washed himself in the sink, looked for and found a towel with which to dry himself. He dressed.

He would attempt to persuade Marika to show him around, hopefully without arousing her suspicions. There was a lot to do if he were to get out of this warren alive.

Then he rushed to the sink and vomited.

VII

Gallagher worked assiduously on the sink, cleaning it out and trying to disguise the stench of his vomit with liberal quantities of lather from a bar of sweet-smelling soap he had found. Marika would not be particularly pleased if she were to find that their recent bout of love-making had made him sick.

As he worked, he wondered about self-disgust. He continued to force the murdered von Dietlingers out of his mind, particularly the child. He wanted no clutter at the moment. Escape plans were all that mattered. First, he needed a map. He had to find out exactly where this complex was. There were bound to be maps of some kind about the place. But where, and how to get his hands on one?

Another thought nagged like a pain that refused to go away. The pilot of the Cessna jet was on his mind. Gallagher didn't want the man to get a look at him in any circumstances. He'd have to be particularly careful about that.

But the memory of the Citation III taunted him. The beautifully sleek, swept-winged, T-tailed aircraft represented the fastest way out; and the most difficult. His mind, however, would not leave the concept alone, and he was beginning to wish he had never set eyes on the little jet.

He gave the sink a final rinse, wiped his hands, then left the room. At Marika's door, he knocked.

"Come in, Gordon."

In a brief moment of panic, he wondered if she'd been able to see him somehow, then he realized that she must have heard him leave his room. He opened the door.

She was totally nude and was sitting on one of the chairs, her magnificent legs spread carelessly open. Her body seemed to be glowing.

The room was an exact replica of Gallagher's, but she's made it very homely. She stood up and stretched, greatly reminding him of a contented cat. Her raw sensuality flaunted itself, but Gallagher felt no responsive stirring in his loins. He kept an appreciative smile upon his face, relieved that he was able to maintain his self-control with ease.

"You're beautiful," he said. It was the right thing to say.

She approached him with long, slow strides, placed her arms about her neck and pressed that powerfully sensuous body to him. Gallagher fought for his self-control as she began to kiss him in that attacking way of hers. He was saved, literally, by the telephone.

Marika made a little sound of annoyance deep in her throat as she continued to kiss him.

The telephone buzzed again, then did so continuously.

She swore in what must have been Rumanian, went to the offending instrument and practically ripped it off the wall.

"*Yes.*" Testily. "Oh. It is you, Alex." She didn't sound any less. testy, but what Harding said apparently mollified her. "This is the worst time, but all right, I shall send him." She hung up, turned to Gallagher. "Alex wants to see you. Cyrus is coming to take you." She began to slip into the jumpsuit. "You can zip me up if you like."

He went up to her to do so. The zipping-up operation took much longer than was necessary as she kissed him again.

At last, she moved away and began putting her long hair into a single bunch at the back, fixing it with a clasp. He kissed the back of her neck.

She smiled, pleased by this. "You will spoil me," she told him.

Then Cyrus knocked.

Gallagher found Harding waiting for him at the door of his opulent quarters. The dark eyes were giving nothing away, though the strange, twisting smile was there. He wondered what Harding wanted of him this time. Cyrus, who had remained silent all the way there, gave him a sidelong glance before turning away, still silent, having made his delivery.

"Thank you, Cyrus," Harding said to the retreating back. "That man is not all there," he said conversationally to Gallagher. "Vietnam, you know. The Americans have truly reaped their harvest. Do come in, Gordon, and sit down." He stood aside for Gallagher to enter. "Join me in a drink?"

Gallagher took a seat. "Nothing alcoholic, thanks." His stomach was still tender from the vomiting. "But I'll have an orange juice, if you keep things like that here."

"As a matter of fact, I do. It's Marika's favourite drink."

"Oh." Gallagher didn't know what else to say.

While Harding got a pitcher full of pulped oranges from the fridge, Gallagher tried to work out how long Harding might have been away, and guessed five hours. In that time, the Cessna would have flown a round trip of at least twenty-seven hundred miles. He remembered from the specifications he'd seen for it at the home of a civil pilot friend that the executive jet had a cruising speed of something like five hundred and forty; but he still couldn't remember the range. In any case, with twenty-seven hundred miles to play with, Harding could have gone anywhere in Australia. He must have extensive industrial and mining interests on the island continent, in addition to this complex, which could be anything from a climatic research to a scientific tracking station.

Harding passed him his drink and sat down. Gallagher nodded his thanks and waited.

"Marika seems to have settled you in quite nicely." Harding laughed shortly at Gallagher's expression. "Oh, Gordon. Not a prude, are you? Let me spare your blushes," Harding went on good-humouredly. "No one was listening. Marika herself told me while you were on the way here. We had another little chat on the telephone. Naturally, she was most discreet, but the euphoria in her voice was quite unmistakable, not to mention the annoyance that came over the line when I first called." He smiled knowingly. "I am rather pleased for her. She needed someone to release all that tension in her. You would do well not to disappoint her in other ways."

"In other ways?"

"Today's Abo Run, for instance."

"You can hardly blame me for my reaction. I've never experienced anything like it. It was a far cry from being an ordinary soldier."

"As a mercenary you would have seen far worse," Harding countered, "and I certainly would not have called being an Army clerk/photographer ordinary soldiering. The death of the child? Children are being killed every day by soldiers all over the globe, in the name of some government or cause. Perhaps you are not disturbed by the deaths but by the hunt itself."

"It was a shock. That's all. A first-time experience."

Harding seemed to accept the explanation. "Shed no tears for any of the people in that room. Though they are a random crop, their histories are quite interesting. I'll give you some idea of the monsters that have inherited this earth. Von Dietlinger. On his way with his family to the Seychelles for a holiday. Four bodyguards. Why? Von Dietlinger's father and mine had much in common. The difference was that he was actually able to pursue his ideals during the Hitler era. Von Dietlinger inherited wealth that was soaked in blood.

"Piet Villiger. Afrikaner, secret policeman. People have been known to discover the principles of flight in his custody. Jefferson Nbwale. The big black African. Though possibly with the ANC, his government is not noted for its record on human rights. Marcel Parguineau. Was in Algeria during the revolution. 'Herod', they called him. He was once know for butchering children.

"Paula Browne. From the gutters of New York to the international set via dead and divorced husbands. Do you see? You never know who you could be travelling with. And what about Sumner? Burning crosses are probably the high spots of his life. Sumner is involved in international commerce and I know quite a bit about him."

Gallagher noted that Harding stopped short of mentioning Jake Smallson and Lauren.

"And what about Alex Harding?" he went on mildly. "I know exactly what I am. The difference between those people and myself is

72

that they do not admit it to themselves."

The telephone buzzed. Harding was sitting close to it. He reached out and plucked it off the wall.

"Yes?" He listened, then: "Very well. Thank you." He replaced the receiver. "My pilot, on his way to take-off. Cyrus says you find the Cessna interesting." It was casually said.

Gallagher went on full alert. "I found it very beautiful," he said easily.

"You know the Cessna?"

"No," Gallagher lied as he had to Cyrus, "but I couldn't help admiring it. The way you'd look at something like a Ferrari, never really expecting to own one." He glanced round the room. "Or a yacht, or whatever."

"Most people see an aeroplane as a fast way from one point to another."

"I must admit, so do I. But your ... Cessna, did you say?" And when Harding had nodded: "Your Cessna demands admiration."

"Then I really must show you around," Harding said, to Gallagher's mounting apprehension. "You'll find Crofton as excited by it as I am."

"Crofton?" Gallagher queried, already knowing the answer.

"My pilot. Very good man. Ex-RAF, of course."

"Of course," Gallagher echoed. "I'd like that," he added, wishing for anything else instead. He'd never heard of Crofton, but Crofton might have heard of him.

"Pity we can't do it today. No time."

Gallagher was relieved. He hoped Harding would forget the subject in time.

"I've got one of the first batch," Harding went on, glad to talk about the aircraft he was so clearly proud of having. "They're still very rare. This one's a Citation III. Set me back over six million. Dollars, of course. Perhaps you'd like to see it take off." He was like a child with a new toy.

"Why not?" Gallagher hoped the pilot was already aboard.

"Let's go." Harding rose. "She's really meant for a crew of two, but I do much of the flying myself, so there's no co-pilot as such. But I'll have to get one eventually."

Gallagher took in this piece of information with a surge of optimism. One pilot meant one person to immobilize and less time wasted. It still didn't mean he'd succeed in getting at the Cessna; but he decided to leave that option open. Perhaps he could corner Crofton privately and plead air-force solidarity.... No. Crofton was making too much money to throw it all away; and there was always the threat to his life.

Gallagher followed Harding out.

The Citation III lined itself up for take-off from the red Outback strip. From where he stood with Harding, Gallagher could see the registration: G-LAUR. Lauren again. She must surely be the reason for the hijack, he thought.

He was pleased he had accepted Harding's invitation to watch the take-off, for a very practical reason. The sun was performing a glorious sunset; but more important to him than the stunning display by nature was the fact that he now knew which way was west and thus that, like a compass needle, the long, low building was pointing due north. If he could find out which state they were held in, he would at least have a vague idea of how far the escapees would have to travel to find salvation. He glanced about him. Which direction was the shortest route? Despite the beauty of the sunset, the land looked as horrendously daunting as ever.

The soft whine rose as the Cessna's twin Garrett turbofans began to wind themselves up to take-off thrust; then G-LAUR was rolling, towing a billow of red dust. The take-off was clean. Developing thirty-seven hundred pounds of thrust each, the Garretts hurled the fifty-five-and-a-half-foot lightweight jet into the air. It leapt on slender swept wings towards the heavens, soaring to freedom.

Gallagher's heart went with it. He had to stop himself from miming the stick motions that Crofton was carrying out. The Cessna tore upwards, and his practised eye appreciated the astonishing rate of climb. They watched it until it became a speck in the immensity of the outback sky.

"I could never do a take-off like that," Harding said with regret. "Crofton still thinks he's in the air force from time to time. The Citation allows him to pander to that whim. He used to fly Phantoms, you know."

Christ. "Phantoms?"

"Of course, you wouldn't know. I forget the Army does not have Phantoms. Big brutes of aeroplanes, but Crofton swears by them. He misses them, rather; but I do pay him somewhat more than Her Majesty's government. Shall we go in?"

They found Marika waiting in Harding's quarters. She took Gallagher back to his own room where a salad meal had been laid. There was also a glass of wine.

"Is that good?" she asked him, indicating the generous salad.

"It looks very good."

"I made it."

"Thank you."

"Tomorrow you will eat with the rest of us in the Mess — Alex likes to call it that, although he was never in the army."

"He comes from a long line of military people. It's to be expected, I suppose."

74

"I must go now. *Bon appetit*." She gave him one of her gentler kisses. "I will see you later."

Gallagher sat down to eat, wondering whether Crofton, from the pilot's seat, had been kept sufficiently busy by the take-off to prevent him from glancing to the left. Gallagher had seen him briefly but clearly enough. Crofton would have had the same clear view, had he looked.

Nine and a half hours away, in a London office overlooking a secluded, sleepy square, two smartly dressed men – one young, the other not so young – were holding conversation.

"This hijack thing," the younger man said. "I've gone through everything. Thoroughly."

The older man got up from behind his inlaid pedestal desk, walked to a window, looked down on the square. A couple had braved the cold sunshine of the November day and were having a quick grope on a bench.

The man surveyed them dispassionately. "And?" He did not look around.

"A name jogged my memory. One of the passengers. I looked it up."

Silence.

The younger man continued: "Gallagher. Seems he used to be one of ours ... sort of."

"Sort of."

"Was he good?"

"Very. Once."

"Will he do anything?"

"He's probably dead by now," the older man said in a matter-of-fact tone. "If he isn't, I strongly doubt that he'll have the chance to do much. These people have not followed the usual pattern of the average hijack ... assuming one can call any hijack average. They have shown a singular lack of interest in publicity; no political rhetoric, no ransom demands, no call for exchanges. That makes them a rather special and dangerous new group, and we are still no nearer sorting out this mess than when it first started. The police forces of nine countries, working round the clock, have not had a whiff of the scent. But the ball's in our court. It was, after all, a British aircraft they hit. The Germans, the Americans, the French – to name but a few – all with nationals among the captives, are breathing down our necks as a result."

"But why take Gallagher? With his exception, this list is made up of very wealthy or powerful people."

"He must have blundered into it. With prices the way they are these days, he must need his head seeing to, travelling first-class. If he's still alive, he'll have his work cut out." The older man did not sound too hopeful about Gallagher's prospects.

"I thought you said he was good," the younger man said after a while.

"He was; but that was before he lost O'Keefe. He left us at the end of that mission, to become a photographer, of all things."

"Ha, ha, ha, ha," the young man spoke, punctuating each "ha". Someone must once have told him it was a smart way to laugh. "A photographer. One of those people who take pictures of frilly dresses for glossy mags?"

The older man had still not turned from the window, preferring to give his companion a full view of his back. The absurd laugh had caused his lips to twitch in distaste. The couple on the bench were getting heated in the cold air. Passers-by pretended not to notice.

"He's a good photographer by all accounts. Won an award; not for frilly pictures."

"From our mob to commercial photography. Interesting switch."

"I once met an American special services bod with more kills than flies up a cow's behind; he became a padre. Who can tell what motivates people?"

"These hijackers have done their homework. They could find out about him."

"He's well covered. He's never been with us, according to the background he now has. We hold the only copy of the real background."

A policeman was walking towards the couple on the bench. They ignored him. He ignored them.

"His wife – shouldn't we contact her? *They* might...."

The older man finally turned. "We do nothing. If she is being watched, and Gallagher is not yet dead, our contacting her could prove fatal to him. Standard contact with the near-relatives of a hijack victim has already been carried out by the relevant authorities. We do not meddle there at this stage."

"They weren't exactly on best terms, anyway," the callow young man said dismissively. "She did him a bit of a dirty, I see."

His superior stared at him coldly, but the young man looked quite unrepentant.

He turned to go. "Smart idea, using a darkie on those jobs. Gallagher...." He shook his head slowly, smiling a little. "That name threw me for a while. I was surprised to learn he wasn't white; but then, he was before my time."

"Boyle!"

The young man was surprised by the vehemence in the voice.

"You will not use that term in my presence *ever* again! Well?"

"No." Then seeing that more was required of him, Boyle added sheepishly: "No, sir."

76

"Now get the hell out."

Boyle left, chastened. What had got into the old man? Gallagher *was* a darkie, wasn't he?

The older man turned back to the window as Boyle left. What with the spending cuts, all you could get these days were cut-price personnel. The first-class ones were either dead, like O'Keefe, or out of the mob, like Gallagher.

The girl on the bench was having her inner thigh stroked and liking it. Some people would do it anywhere, the man thought, viewing the exercise with almost scientific detachment.

"I hope you make it," he said quietly. He was not thinking of the overheated youth on the bench but of Gallagher. He had once commanded a squadron that Gallagher had served in. The squadron had flown Phantoms.

Gallagher finished his meal, rinsed the dishes then stacked them at one end of the sink. He had decided to have a look around the complex. He would do so openly, for the benefit of the closed-circuit cameras, until someone stopped him.

He opened the door, stepped out into the corridor and began walking. He didn't get far. Cyrus came round a corner, a big US Army Colt .45 in a green canvas holster at his hip.

"Going for a walk?" Cyrus had a thin curving moustache that joined a tiny goatee which seemed to twitch as he smiled fleetingly.

"What does it look like?" Gallagher was quite sure Cyrus wouldn't dare do anything. "You can come with me if you want." He continued walking.

Cyrus's hand went to his hip, unsnapping the holster. "You go nowhere, brother."

Gallagher kept walking.

The .45 came sliding out, centred on Gallagher's back. "Hold it right there!"

Gallagher kept on. He heard the ominously loud click of the hammer going back. He felt his whole body tense. At this range, the big .45 would rip a terrible hole in him. His legs kept moving him on. He fought the urge to break into a run. That would, of course, be futile. Where could he run to in a corridor? None of the doors he passed were open. If he tried a dash to force one open and found it locked, he would have achieved nothing, except a display of fear. He cursed himself for his bravado. He uncomfortably remembered Cyrus's sidelong glances at him, and Harding's passing hint about the man's instability. A loony in a group of loonies.

Then Cyrus was laughing loudly. The expected shot did not come. Gallagher felt a weakness in his muscles as he relaxed, stopped and turned. The slab-sided automatic was back in its holster, and Cyrus came up to him, grinning.

"Heyyy, man. That was real cool." Cyrus sounded impressed.

So as not to spoil the image he had so carefully cultivated, Gallagher said: "Not really. I knew you wouldn't shoot. Marika would not have let you."

"Have I got news for you. She told me to keep watch and to stop you if you got too nosey." Cyrus's grin widened at the shock in Gallagher's eyes. "Yeah," he continued. "You're not dead because I didn't feel like it. A hard lady, our Marika."

"Christ!" Gallagher was shaken, appalled by the magnitude of the risk he had just exposed himself to.

"You can say that again," Cyrus said, misunderstanding.

"But I'm one of you now." Gallagher put reproach into his voice, playing his role.

"Because she kind of likes you? Forget it, brother. No one joins us that easy. We're kind of exclusive." Cyrus clapped him on the shoulder. "Don't take it too hard. Shit, man, maybe I didn't shoot you because I knew she wouldn't like it, anyway. Got to be very careful with our lady boss." He grinned again.

Gallagher responded to this overt display of friendliness. "Look. Why don't you take me around? I can't stay cooped up in that room. What harm can I possibly do? And, besides, you'll be with me all the time."

Cyrus appeared to consider this. "All right. But you stay close, and you don't go where I don't take you. Right?"

"Right."

They continued walking.

From the monitoring room, Harding and Marika had watched it all. They'd heard what had been said too.

"Cyrus did that very well," Harding said. "And Gallagher displayed rather more courage than I would have expected, walking away from a loaded automatic like that."

Marika was not so sure. "You heard him. He did not think I would allow anyone to shoot him."

"Granted. But I distinctly remember hinting to him that Cyrus was finely balanced. Even with the security of his belief that you would protect him, he had no way of knowing whether Cyrus would choose that moment to go off the rails."

"What are you saying, Alex?"

"Perhaps our friend has more backbone than we credit him with."

"Oh, Alex." Marika was dismissive of the idea. "You saw the shock in his eyes. Perhaps he forgot what you had told him about Cyrus. Why should he remember?"

She wanted to stop discussing Gallagher in those terms. She felt a twinge of anticipation between her thighs. It was a long time since she'd met anyone like him. Now Alex, normally so calm under pressure, was twitching with needless suspicions.

"You are too nervous," she told him. "We are safe. Everything was well planned. Remember Sicily. Do you not trust our capabilities?"

"I have every faith in them." Harding smiled fleetingly. "But don't let a little lusting stand in your way if the need for action against him becomes apparent."

"He wants to join us."

"You have always chosen your team. I am not about to give you advice on that. I only suggest that you remember that physical attraction, or love, if you prefer, can sometimes be very bad for one's good judgement. Gallagher's found this out. So have I ... and so have you."

Marika did not like this reference to Serge. "Leave him out of it, Alex. I made a mistake and I corrected it. There was no need to bring it up. I was not afraid to face up to my responsibility."

"I never suggested you were."

"Then end the matter now."

"Very well." He smiled again, to take away the tension. "You'll be pleased to know that the outside world still has no idea where the passengers have got to. At the moment, all efforts are being concentrated on North and East Africa and the Middle East."

Marika was prepared to forget their slight disagreement. "Did I not tell you it was well planned?"

"I never doubted it. My recent remarks were said in a spirit of concern for you, and not as an expression of censure."

"I am glad. I would not like us to quarrel." She gave him her most radiant of smiles.

In the office in London, Boyle was again with his boss. He had just entered.

"Well?" the older man enquired.

"Reports coming in from the Mid-East are all negative. But that's not all. The Americans are restive." Boyle sometimes came up with phrases like that. "Oh, they're worried about the man – er ... let's see...." He consulted notes. "Smallson ... but they're absolutely frantic about his granddaughter. That's the girl Lauren Tanner. She's the daughter of...."

"Myron Tanner IV, friend and fund-donator to senators. Yes, yes, Boyle. I know all that."

"Well, sir. What do we do?"

"Do, Boyle?"

"It's the minister, sir. He's quite agitated. Thinks we should make some response."

The older man smiled. There was an air of sudden mischief about him. "Agitated, is he? Tell him, Boyle, we're looking. Perhaps Timbuctoo?"

Boyle retreated in confusion. The old man was obviously cracking up. Where the hell was Timbuctoo?

The old man rose from behind his desk and went to the window. The bench was empty, awaiting new clients. A solitary policeman strolled past. The man wondered if he were the same one who'd passed the groping couple earlier; but his mind was not really in it.

Come on, Gallagher, he urged mentally. *Let's be having you. You can't have forgotten all we taught you, surely.*

VIII

Gallagher was back in his room. His mind was buzzing. What he'd seen and learned on his tour of the complex had convinced him that the break-out would have to be made very soon. Most importantly, he'd found the means of escape.

Cyrus had first taken him to the computer room – the complex was indeed a weather-research station – and Gallagher had been astonished to find the large room totally devoid of human occupation, despite what Marika had previously told him about the automatic workings of the place. The machines hummed to themselves in eerie sterility. Next, Cyrus took him to the dining area that Marika had said Harding liked to call the Mess. It was comfortably appointed, and Gallagher had been drily introduced to some of Marika's group they'd found there.

"This is Pinkus Lipschitz," Cyrus had said with a straight face. "But we call him Flyboy."

Lipschitz looked like a time-transplanted hippie, complete with streaky blond hair tied in a bunch at the back, beads, faded denim waistcoat over jungle-green short-sleeved T-shirt, and a short beard. His washed-out blue eyes seemed a little mad and he was, like Cyrus, an ex-Vietnam vet. The dust got in his hair, he'd said.

Next had come Johnson – the man who had snarled at Gallagher in the captive-room, eager to shoot. It was Johnson who had led the hijack. He was ex-SAS.

"Done Northern Ireland?" Gallagher had asked casually.

"Would I tell you?" Johnson had countered, smiling thinly with a distinct lack of humour. "What about you?"

"Would I tell?" Gallagher had replied.

Johnson's thin, humourless smile had remained in place. He was a short, muscular man with a severe crew-cut. Gallagher had not forgotten Johnson's hungry rictus of a grin in the captive-room. The thin smile was its first cousin.

The introductions had continued.

Inge. Bonily thin, mousey hair, weak-looking eyes and a vicious mouth. German, from Geissen.

The two African women. Ngoma, the one with the hot eyes. According to Cyrus, her children and husband had been murdered by police agents in her country; and Selini Makanza, tall and haughty, about whom Cyrus had given no information.

The Arabs. Cyrus had introduced them simply as the Libyan and the Jordanian, though he'd seen fit to point out that the Jordanian had served with the Arab Legion.

Throughout, Gallagher felt that some sort of show had been put on for him. Cyrus next took him to the long, low building which had turned out to be the home of three Landrovers, two Range Rovers, all kitted out for desert travel ... and a helicopter. Gallagher knew a Huey gunship when he saw one, even without its guns mounted; but he'd been content simply to stare in amazement at the sand-coloured machine with its civilian registration.

"How does it get out?" he'd finally asked.

"The roof opens," Cyrus had answered adding, none to convincingly: "Harding uses it for surveys."

And the rest, Gallagher had thought grimly, knowing what Flyboy's job was, and what the man used to do in Vietnam.

"Those Range Rovers," Cyrus had gone on without prompting, "are for the eggheads. They'll be coming here soon to do the kind of fooling around this place was built for. We got to be out of here long before then. After everyone in that room's been taken care of," he had finished casually.

He had then continued the conducted tour, showing Gallagher a number of other rooms, none of which had been a communications room, or a weapons store; hardly surprising in the circumstances.

As he now lay on the bed in his room, mentally reliving everything he'd seen and heard, Gallagher kept coming back to the major discrepancy he'd found on his accompanied tour. Nowhere had he seen a single map; a highly unlikely omission in a scientific establishment. The walls of such places were usually decorated with maps of every conceivable type. The maps had therefore been painstakingly removed.

"Which means," Gallagher said aloud to himself, "my little expedition was set up from the moment I stepped out of this room. Well played, Cyrus. You never intended to shoot me, you bastard."

He knew he would have to be even more careful with the game he himself was playing. Love-making had not yet put Marika sufficiently off-guard. He was still being tested.

In the earthen-floored room, Lauren was trying to settle herself down

81

for the night, using her arms as a pillow. The general lumpiness of the ground didn't help; she shifted this way and that in an attempt to find a comfortable position.

Everyone had been fed again, and since being given access – under guard – to toilet and washing facilities, the all-pervading acrid perfume of body odour had lessened, though its presence had not bothered her. What sat on her mind was another smell that was beginning to tease her nostrils. She tried not to think of it, but the smell invaded her senses. It came from Bannion's dried blood.

She squeezed her eyes shut and prayed for sleep; then she thought of Gallagher, hoping he was still alive. She touched her lips with a gentle finger, remembering his sudden kiss....

She kept her eyes shut, and, for the moment, the smell of Bannion's blood left her in peace.

It was now mid-afternoon in London. The intercom buzzed on the desk of Gallagher's old boss.

"Yes?"

"It's the Minister, sir," a woman's voice answered. "He said he'd hang on, even if you're busy."

The man had a blissful vision of the Minister hanging by his feet above Whitehall, sighed, and said: "Put him through on the green." He picked up the telephone.

"Come up and see me," the Minister's petulant voice commanded; then he hung up.

Twat, the man thought, descending briefly and enjoyably into soldier's language.

He waited for half an hour before buzzing his secretary. "Get me a car," he told her.

"Decided to go, have we?"

The man smiled. Delphine Arundel, widow of a colonel killed in Armagh, who liked to mother him. "Who's boss here?"

"Why you, of course."

He smiled again at the intercom. "My car, Mrs Arundel." Sternly.

"Waiting, sir."

He could hear the smile in her voice. Sometimes they called each other by their first names.

"I expected you sooner," was the first thing the Minister said. "Take a seat." He hated to be kept waiting by those he considered his underlings; which, at a push, could mean the entire nation.

The man sat. "We are kept pretty busy, sir," he offered in excuse, civilly.

"Hardly seems like it." The Minister was not going to be fobbed off. "You have absolutely nothing to show for your display of effort."

"You have our up-to-date reports, sir."

"I'm more interested in what they don't say."

"There's nothing more to tell at this stage." Though he didn't feel like repeating himself, the man decided to put into words what had already been said on paper; if only to get back to his own office quickly.

"We know," he went on, "that the 747 landed at night, at Nairobi. We know the hijackers demanded and got two Datsun passenger vans. We know they threatened to kill the captives if they were followed. We know one van was eventually found in Muhoru on Lake Victoria, near the Tanzanian border. The other was found inside Tanzania itself at a place called Usa, within convenient distance of no less than three airfields. Both were abandoned, with no sign of either captives or hijackers. No one saw anything unusual at the airfields in Tanzania, though the locals at Muhoru claim to have heard an aircraft, or possibly a high-powered boat, on the lake."

The Minister's petulant mouth twisted in contempt. "Damned Africans. Can't trust them to do anything right." In his younger days he had served in the colonial service in Africa, and it still showed.

The man looked at his superior dispassionately, seeing before him the type of person who had truly, he felt, lost the Empire, who had indolently played God at the expense of the indigenes, resulting in the eventual loss of fat territories with fat resources, the loss of fat potential markets, the loss of potentially vast international political clout. His regret was due more to national self-interest than for humanitarian reasons; but the criminal shortsightedness of colonial policies still left him breathless. He remembered discussing them with Gallagher, who had more brains in his little finger than the Minister would have had in a hundred bodies. Cut-price ministers in a cut-price nation.

"What about ... er ..." the Minister was saying, "that dark horse of yours." He gave a weak smile at his weak joke.

His smile was not returned. The man remained silent, forcing the Minister to continue.

"Gallagher," the Minister said reluctantly.

"What about him, sir?"

"Good God, man! Can't he do anything?"

"He's no longer with us, sir. Before your time."

"Quite. But people don't really leave, do they?"

"Gallagher has. I sanctioned it. To have kept him on would have eventually caused his death."

"An occupational hazard. What was so special about him? You were not molly-coddling, I hope, because he's...."

"Gallagher," the man interrupted his superior unceremoniously,

83

"was unique. He did very well for us. It is department policy not to waste good men. We don't waste any personnel." *The way you wasted the Empire.*

"Why wasn't I told of his existence before? I had to get it from your man Boyle. He'll go far, that young man."

The man said nothing. He'd have a word with Boyle. Everything was cut-price these days; even departmental loyalty.

"Well?" the Minister prompted. "What about Gallagher?"

"If anything can be done, Gallagher will do it. I —"

"The Americans...."

The man stood up. He'd had enough. "With respect, Minister, I don't give a damn what the Americans, the Germans, the French or any others think, unless they come up with constructive ideas. We're doing all we can, co-ordinating with various international security forces. I would like to be left to get on with the job." He walked to the door and let himself out.

"I have not forgotten Timbuctoo," the petulant voice called after him savagely.

Marika came into the room just as Gallagher was about to doze off. The place was in darkness, and he heard the soft rush of her clothes as she took them off; then the magnificent body was rubbing itself against his.

"You're not asleep, I hope," she whispered hungrily as she searched for his mouth.

"Nommff," he said, just as she found it and began to eat at him. He thrust all disturbing thoughts into a far corner of his mind and began to work on her. It was necessary that he wore her guard down, no matter what it took to achieve this.

"Oh, Gordon, Gordon!" she said in a low voice. "Mmmm! *Mmmmm!*"

They fought, joined, off the bed, and once more on to the floor. She begged, moaned pleaded. She rolled on top of him, pressed her full breasts against his face. He rolled, she whimpered. He squeezed, she gasped. He thrust, she came back at him sighing with pleasure. He pounded, she locked him fast with her strong legs.

Then came her long, drawn-out scream.

"Oh, oh, oh," she said after a while. "*Oooh!*" It was a sigh of great contentment. She kissed him, gently. "You're not sleepy?"

"No," he answered truthfully. Sleep was far from his mind now.

"Good," she said, drawing out the word. "Good."

They made love a second and third time. Each time, Marika became more and more abandoned. The last time, she tossed her head from side to side, crying: "My Gordon! My Gordon!"

For his part, Gallagher could no longer deny to himself that making

84

love to her was becoming dangerously enjoyable. While that served to give authenticity to his performance, he had to keep in mind that each had seduced the other for specific reasons. Gallagher intended to make sure that his reasons won the day.

Mercifully, Marika seemed to want a break. She lay on her back, purring deep in her throat and stroking his inner thigh languorously.

"What are you doing to me?" she whispered, her voice thick with satiation.

"He inspected the question for traps, decided it was sincere. "Exactly what you want me to," he answered.

She gave a chuckle of pleasure. "Yes. Yes. It is what I want you to do." She stretched the marvellous body, arching her back off the floor. Thus tautened, she rolled on to him, then let herself relax. "I like it. I like it."

He felt the wetness of her lower body slither against his. She kissed him lightly, and rolled off again.

"You are making me forget Serge," she said. "That is good."

"Serge?" he queried, wondering at this new aspect.

"I was once in love with him. For five years."

"What happened?"

"I will tell you from the beginning. We met in Paris. I was studying the cello for a career. I am not French, but I have lived from childhood in Alsace. My mother came from Caracal in lower Wallachia, in Rumania, and my father from Volos, in Greece. They met in Bucharest. My father was a Party member, so he stayed in Rumania to be with my mother. After I was born, they both wanted to leave. There were many things they did not like. My mother had relatives in Alsace that she had not seen since the last war. She wrote to them saying she wanted to come out. By then, I had the age of ten.

"My parents sent me first, saying I was going on holiday. They said they would follow me soon. What I did not know was that they had been doing things the Party did not like. They never came out. They were killed. The relatives brought me up. When I went to Paris, I met Serge. I told him about my parents. His had died in the war. He was much older than myself. We talked revolution, and about Bakunin. For me, it was exciting to talk about these things, but I was not seriously interested. Serge was everything. At that time, I believed he was not truly serious himself because he had plenty of money. He told me he had been in the street-fighting in 1968. I listened, but still without much interest."

Gallagher listened to the unravelling of the story. The insight it was giving him into Marika was going to help him understand her motivations, and, perhaps, enable him to out-think her.

"Are you listening?" she asked, seemingly anxious that he should.

"I am."

"You were so quiet, I thought perhaps you had gone to sleep."

"I am too interested," he assured her truthfully.

She leaned over to kiss him hungrily.

"How do you know where my mouth is in this darkness?" His hand caressed her.

She gave a sharp little gasp of pleasure. "How do *you* know where *that* is?"

"Ah," he said.

She squirmed some more, then stayed his hand with hers. "Let me finish."

She lay back again, and continued her narrative.

"Before Serge, I had not known many men. One, two, maybe three. Not very satisfactory affairs. They were clumsy men; but Serge ... ah! He was very good, very patient, very gentle with me." She paused. "You are jealous?"

Gallagher knew what was expected of him. "Yes."

Her hand slid down his stomach, rested between his legs. "Do not be. You are very good too ... better than Serge. You are —" her body trembled with recent memory — "powerful." She caressed him, taking her time about it. "Ah!" she said, pleased with the result. Then she stopped. "Later."

"Serge took me to a big place in the country," she continued, "and showed me how to shoot. I learned very quickly. I became very good. He said I had an instinct. I had learned faster than anyone he had known, man or woman. He said it was a pity that such talent should be wasted in the conservertoire. I did not understand then.

"One day, he told me that the people who had killed my parents were still alive. At that time, I did not know of all the strange people he knew. I was surprised he was able to get such information. I had once told him that, when I was a child, I had made a vow to find the people who had killed my parents and to kill them myself. He asked me if I still meant my vow. I do not know why, but I said yes. Perhaps I did not really believe he was serious.

"I could carry out my vow, he said. He knew people who could train me and take me into Rumania. I said I would do it. It was crazy; but he was challenging me. What could I do? I trained for three months, and with two men I went in. I found the people and killed them just as I had said I would. My two companions were killed by guards. I did not realize at the time that there were more guards than should have been normal. Later, I found out that we should have all been killed. Somebody inside had wanted those people killed, but it had to look like an action by foreigners. The foreigners then had to be killed too. I was too quick for them. I got away.

"When I got back to France, Serge had a strange look on his face when he saw me, but I thought it was from worry. He *was* worried about me, but not for the reasons I believed. For months afterwards, he would seem nervous in my company. It was a long time before I knew the truth, you understand, and he was never certain about my having this knowledge.

"Then another time, he said to me that certain people had heard about what I had done, were impressed, and would I like to do a small job for them. I was still studying, but as I was doing well, I said yes, and took a short holiday. It was an easy job. Then Serge suggested that I make a team. I was not sure about that, so I did not answer him for many months. When I finished my studies, I told him to suggest some people, and I would pick them myself. I would not approach them until I knew I wanted them. I also said no one must know of our existence outside the people we would work for. Selini was the first one. Then Serge introduced me to Alex. By that time, there were ten of us. Now, we are twenty. That is the maximum."

Twenty! Gallagher thought. *Christ. And they're all here.*

"Before Alex," Marika was saying, "our ... clients never knew us personally — we have worked for governments, sometimes — but with Alex, something special happened. He took over from Serge as our ... agent."

Gallagher did not ask what had happened to Serge.

"I found out," her voice, now tense, went on in the darkness, "the truth about what had taken place all those months ago. During all the time after I came back, he made love to *me.*" She stressed the last word through gritted teeth, as if Serge's love-making had soiled her. "But he had been so sure that I would have been killed, he had already taken another woman.

"We came here for one of Alex's jobs. I shot Serge. He went down on his knees to me when he realized that I knew. It was disgusting! He even started to cry. I shot him while he was still crying. He was stupid to believe that I who had gone through so much to destroy my parents' killers would spare a treacherous man who had schemed for my death, betrayed me with another woman and then still took me to his bed."

Gallagher let out his breath slowly. Marika's body was rigid with the anger of remembrance. She remained silent for a long while, allowing the emotion to subside.

"What happened to the woman?" he asked quietly.

"I think she fell under a Metro train."

Another long silence. Then Marika said: "Gordon? Would you mind if we did not make love tonight?"

Gallagher hid his profound relief. He'd been wondering how to screw up the enthusiasm for a further bout of love-making after what he had just listened to.

"It's all right," he said. "I understand."

Her body relaxed and she moved closer to him. She put her head on his chest. "You were betrayed once, were you not?" She sounded almost like a little child, pleading sleepily to be reassured.

She snuggled against him and soon her breathing took on a regular, soft beat. As he lay there, her gentle breath sighing against his flesh, Gallagher could not dispel the uncomfortable feeling that a cobra had climbed into bed with him.

In the morning, she was gone. He had not heard or felt her leave. He was annoyed with himself for sleeping so deeply. He got up washed, and had just finished dressing when she entered, looking bright and glowing in her jumpsuit. She smiled widely.

"You were very tired, I think."

He gave her a rueful grin. "I must have been. I didn't feel a thing when you got up."

She came to him, arched her body against him and placed her arms about his neck. His own arms went about her waist.

"You're beautiful," she said.

"So are you," he told her.

"Come. You will join us for breakfast." She kissed him.

Day Two

I

LAUREN CAME slowly awake. Her whole body ached. She had slept fitfully, after a night of unsuccessfully trying to make herself comfortable. The lights had been dimmed, but now they brightened again. Her grandfather was watching her as she sat up painfully, yawned.

"Did you sleep well, Gramps?"

"Better than you, it would seem." There was a flash of humour in his eyes.

"What do you think will happen today?" She brushed bits of earth off her clothes, then stared disinterestedly at little indentations in the skin of her legs, made by the tiny stones in the earthen floor.

"We can only wait and see," the old man answered her.

"I hope Gordon is all right." She examined her feelings closely, testing them for a sense of reality. She had not thought herself capable of feeling anything for a man so soon after what had happened in New York, and certainly not for someone like Gallagher. It was inconceivable that their paths would have crossed had it not been for the hijack.

"He is very much in your thoughts, I see. Do not worry. He can look after himself."

"Jake ... that woman. She's very beautiful. You saw the way she looked at Gordon...." The words died lamely as she saw the shrewd look in her grandfather's eyes. "I hate jealousy in anybody," she went on quickly, "and I have no right –"

"Remember just one thing," Smallson interrupted her gently. "That woman is very dangerous. Gordon is playing with his own life to help us. Remember that. Hmm?" He smiled at her fondly.

Some of the others were moaning and groaning themselves awake. Nbwale appeared not to have slept at all and was sitting with his back against a wall. Paula Browne was lighting up her first cigarette of the day. Parguineau was trying to talk to her, through her smoke. The Lamoutiers still lay huddled together. Sumner was saying something to Villiger, who appeared not to be listening.

The door opened and Cyrus poked his head through.

"Wash up time!" he called cheerily.

"How many of them are there?" Lauren whispered to Smallson in

89

despair. "We've not seen him before. Oh, Gramps, there are too many. Gordon will not...."

"Shhh!" the old man said softly. "You must not think it."

"Well?" Cyrus grinned at them. "No one wants to go?" He caught Sumner's eye and the grin went. Centuries of hatred flashed between them. "C'mon, move it!" he snarled. The cheeriness had fizzled out like a snowflake on a hotplate. "You get nothing to eat, else."

Paula Browne was the first to go.

"I want that goddam redneck in there," Cyrus said. He was sharing a table with Gallagher and Marika in the Mess.

"You can have him," Marika said.

"OK." He finished his meal and left them.

"He is from the South," Marika explained to Gallagher.

"Oh." Gallagher was running through his mind the amazing story she had told him during the night. He wanted to think he had been told it because Marika was beginning to relax her guard and not because of any ulterior motive. "What's happening today?" he asked casually.

"Today, you go with Cyrus."

They walked along the corridor leading to the captive-room. Gallagher was quite glad to have been sent with Cyrus. It would help him begin escape preparations. Cyrus carried the big Colt at his hip. Behind them, Johnson followed with an Uzi. Gallagher had not been given a weapon.

"I want to have a go at the Afrikaner," he said to Cyrus, hoping this would be received sympathetically. "Rough him up a little."

"He's a big motherfucker."

"So?" Gallagher prompted. "You two have the guns."

"I'm promising nothing."

They walked on.

"Who's going today?" Gallagher asked as they arrived.

"Wait and see." Cyrus nodded to Flyboy and Selini, who were standing guard, and slammed the door open.

It was ten o'clock; above their heads, the late morning sun scorched the Australian earth.

The people in the room stared at Gallagher, at Cyrus, at Johnson. Their eyes said they believed Gallagher had joined their captors.

Cyrus stared round the room, feet planted apart, hands on hips. At last he said, "Some more of you people have been ransomed." He grinned at their dawning hope. To Gallagher he said: "Go on. Have your fun. We'll cover you." He took out the Colt.

Gallagher marched up to Villiger. "I've always wanted to do this to one of you." He kicked Villiger. It was expertly done, and made more noise than the effect warranted. His eyes signalled to the Afrikaner's.

90

Villiger came at him like a bull and they went down heavily. In the ensuing gasps and screams from the captives who had stood up instinctively, Gallagher tried to talk to Villiger as they ~~they~~ rolled in combat.

"Don't break my bloody neck!" he whispered fiercely. "This is not for real."

"Think I'd let you kick me if I didn't know that, man?" Villiger's own whisper came. He slammed Gallagher's head.

Gallagher could have sworn he heard bells.

"Stop them!" Lauren screamed.

"Find out if computers can work ... in isolated ... places," he gasped into Villiger's ear, "without ... staff, and where the power source is." He kneed Villiger close to the groin, causing some pain but no damage.

The Afrikaner grunted, relaxed a hold that in a real fight would have been crippling, and seemed to prepare for another attack.

"Hold it!" There was the click of the .45's hammer.

Gallagher and Villiger separated, stood up, glared at each other. Villiger's glare looked very real, Gallagher thought.

"Rough him up a little," Cyrus said with a derisive smile, while Johnson laughed silently. "Yeah. You sure did that."

Gallagher was satisfied, though he showed only chagrin. He could have severely damaged Villiger with the first blow, had the fight been in earnest; but then, Villiger would not have stayed put to receive it.

Shaking his head slowly, Cyrus turned to the Lamoutiers. "It's your lucky day. Let's go."

The middle-aged couple went out eagerly, after wishing everyone luck. Gallagher followed, looking at no one. Cyrus and Johnson came after, still amused by his less than commendable display.

Villiger waited for some moments after the door closed on their laughter, then he went over to Smallson and Lauren. Everyone watched him but said nothing. Sumner looked puzzled.

"I did not hurt him," Villiger said to Lauren.

"You banged his head," she accused. "I saw you."

"I could have cracked his skull if I'd wanted to."

"And he could have done you great damage with his first blow," Smallson put in mildly.

Villiger gave a thin smile. "If I'd waited for it."

"So. We are agreed it was an act. Why?"

"You know why. He is getting ready to make a break for it. This was our warning. He chose me because those terrorists would never suspect him of working with an Afrikaner. Agreed?"

Smallson nodded slowly. "But I think it is also because he feels you can be relied upon to do what is required later."

The thin smile lived briefly. "Perhaps."

"What did he want?"

"He asked some questions about a computer. Sumner knows about computers. I'll ask him."

II

The fleeing vehicle was now a speck on the distant horizon. Only the faint dust cloud continued to mark its progress.

"We move when the dust is gone," Cyrus said quietly.

Gallagher looked at him in surprise. Gone was the wisecracking, hip-talking street brother. In his place was a coldly efficient hunter. There was a new tenseness, an alert edge to this man who before had seemed nothing more than yet another piece of human flotsam out to get his kicks wherever he could find them. To Gallagher this sudden transformation was profoundly disturbing. It meant adding Cyrus to the ever-lengthening list of those he'd have to watch out for. Marika and Harding were quite enough by themselves; and if when he made the break Sumner and Nbwale were still alive, he'd have to take those two bastards along too. They were bound to be trouble. Already impossible odds were drifting into the realms of lunacy. Perhaps Villiger would be alive. He needed Villiger. The man would be an asset. *Who'd ever have thought I'd one day be counting on the help of an Afrikaner like Villiger?* he thought wryly.

Now, he stared through the baking windscreen of the Landrover, across miles and miles of the empty, arid plain of the Outback. The dust cloud that marked the trail of the fleeing Landrover was still there. There was no wind to disperse it. Brief glances showed him the other two Landrovers, still at their silent station, one on either side. The predators, waiting.

"How did you get into this, Cyrus?" he asked calmly, as if the human hunt that was about to start meant nothing to him. Deep inside he felt sick.

There was a moment of tense silence during which a side panel flexed itself loudly in the fierce heat.

Then Cyrus said: "That sounds like someone being nosy to me."

Gallagher pretended to take offence. "Look. I'm just interested to know what made you join up with Marika. *She* told me how she started. You don't have to tell me anything. Forget I asked."

Always try to find out, if you have the opportunity and can afford the time, the psychological make-up of your opponent. You may learn something that may later save your life.

"Oh, don't get huffy," Cyrus finally said. "You want to know how a nice boy like me came to be in a place like this? That it?"

"Oh, never mind, Cyrus."

92

"It's all right, brother. I'll tell you." Cyrus was grinning. "Wha, Ah wuz born," he began in an exaggerated Southern drawl, "in that lovely state of the South, Alabama. Yeah."

At the wheel, Johnson's shoulders shook in silent mirth. Gallagher ignored him, and watched the dust instead. It was still hanging there, a temporary shield for Lamoutier and his wife; a temporary extension of their lease on life. But where could they go? He had been unable to help them. They had no map and, he was certain, not enough fuel for the hundreds of miles they would need to travel to find safety.

"My parents moved north," Cyrus was saying, "to get away from the redneck racists. They didn't think it was such a hot idea to get shot at just because some white trash felt like it. I was five at the time." A surge of suppressed anger entered the narration. "They left one hell-hole for another. My mother scrubbed other people's floors, and my father emptied their garbage. Come Vietnam, I find myself shooting Gooks in the fucking jungle. I was pretty good. Collected enough cheap metal on my chest to make a four-star general sick with envy. Even got me a field commission. Made lootenant, would you believe. Me, the nigger boy from down south with the floor-scrubbing mammy and the garbage-collector pappy makes it to officer grade in the man's army. Can you dig it?"

"That was good, wasn't it?"

A sniff of derision. "Are you green or what? It was no big deal. I thought I was someone special getting that commission. I get back to the States and find there is nothing going. Lootenants from Nam are a dime a dozen. You ever hear of the Point?"

"You mean the record?"

"Jesus! *West* Point!"

"Is that some sort of club?" Gallagher being ingenuous.

"Very good!" Drily. "Yeah. You could say that. A club. A club for rich white kids who want to be officers, usually generals' sons."

"It can't be all like that. There must be other kids too, some black."

"Yeah, but you'd have to look for those niggers." The last word used pointedly at Gallagher like a weapon. "Fucking Uncle Toms."

"The dust is gone," Johnson said.

"Right," Cyrus said firmly. "Discussion of my past ends right now." Into the radio: "Start engines!" He grinned happily. "Nice of Marika to give me command of this hunt."

The three engines started as one. Marika and Ngoma were in the left and right Landrover respectively.

"Go!" Cyrus shouted.

The three vehicles hurtled forward, the two outriders setting off diagonally until they grew small with the distance, before coming into station with the lead Landrover, in a wide arrowhead formation. They tore across the arid plain in pursuit of their prey, red dust billowing like monstrous plumes behind them.

"Ever see one of these?" Cyrus had to raise his voice over the roaring of the engine and the bucketing noise of the Landrover as it bounced across the uneven plain.

Gallagher looked, and his heart lurched. "No," he answered. "What is it? Looks like an overgrown sawn-off shotgun."

But he knew. He'd never seen one in the flesh, so to speak, but he had seen the manuals. And O'Keefe had known all about them.

What would I give for a blooker now, sir.

A what, Mr O'Keefe?

Grenade launcher, M79. American job, and just what we need.

But why "blooker"?

That's what it says when it goes off. The Yanks gave it the nickname in Vietnam....

O'Keefe had had all sorts of crazy information like that.

Gallagher stared at the blooker, his mind running over the specifications. M79 grenade launcher, 40mm shotgun type. Weight loaded, 6.45 pounds; length, 28.78 inches; muzzle velocity, 250 feet per second. A murderous weapon in the right hands; and Cyrus's hands looked very capable indeed. Lamoutier and his wife would be blown to pieces. *And I can't do a single thing to help them.*

"It is like a shotgun," Cyrus was saying, "but just a little more powerful."

Johnson went through his silent laughter routine again at Cyrus's words.

"This, my friend," Cyrus went on, "is a blooker. You load it like this. Push this lever ... fully to the right ... so." He showed Gallagher. "Break the weapon open, just like a shotgun. See? Then you put this forty-millimetre round in, shut the weapon, move the lever back. Your blooker is now ready for firing. Nothing to it."

"My blooker?" Gallagher echoed, not wanting to believe what he knew was coming.

"Sure. You and I are going to lay down a barrage. See?" Cyrus held up the twin to the launcher he was already holding.

"But I don't know how to use one of these things."

"I'm a pretty good teacher."

The Landrover swerved briefly before going back on course.

"Hey!" Cyrus yelled. "What what you're doing, you white crazy."

"Sorry, Cyrus," Johnson said. His silent laughter went on.

"Don't mind Johnson," Cyrus said to Gallagher. "He finds humour in the weirdest things."

"I can see that." *What the fuck am I going to do?*

Gallagher glanced out to where the distant Landrover on the left wing was keeping station. Suddenly, it seemed to pivot on its front wheels.

94

"I think something's happened to Marika," he called before he could stop himself.

Cyrus poked his head through the canvas hood to have a look. He ducked back in to grab the radio.

"Marika! What's wrong?"

"We're all right. Tyre gone. We'll join you when we have fixed a new one."

"Sure you don't want help?"

"No, no! Go on. We shall catch up." She sounded furious.

"She really hates missing a kill," Cyrus informed Gallagher as he broke transmission. He grinned. "Looks like it's gonna be all for us." He spoke to the radio again. "Ngoma, you heard?"

"Yes. We'll stay with you."

"Fine." Cyrus released the transmit button. "Johnson, what's our speed?"

"Sixty."

"How much do you reckon those Frenchies have been doing?"

"Not more than forty. They couldn't hold more on this terrain."

"They're Swiss," Gallagher said, as if in some sort of defence of the doomed couple. "From Geneva."

"Same difference," Cyrus said disinterestedly. To Johnson, he went on: "So what does that give us?"

"Well, we gave them an hour, and we've been going for half that again. If they're doing forty, they've gone sixty miles by now. Nearly a hundred klicks, if you prefer." Johnson had picked up the American slang for kilometres.

"Let's stick to miles. So what have we got? Go on."

"Another hour and a half and we'll catch up with them. But we'll see them long before that."

"That's if Harding and his goddam gunship don't find them first. What do you reckon on that guy? A motherfucking gunship out here in this asshole of Creation." Cyrus shook his head in wonder.

Gallagher wanted to shake his own head in wonder. It was like listening to a madman pronounce another madman insane. *What do I mean "Like" ...? He* is *mad.*

"He won't do anything unless we lose them," Johnson said.

"But we're not going to do that, are we, Johnson baby?"

Another hour passed, but there was no telltale dust cloud.

"Shit," Cyrus said, so quietly that Gallagher almost missed it above the noise of the bouncing Landrover.

Gallagher's spirits lifted, remembering that all male Swiss were citizen soldiers. Perhaps Lamoutier had undergone a rough terrain course and was even now driving much faster than his pursuers gave him credit for. The tracks they'd been following had taken them into perceptibly rougher country and Johnson had slowed on occasion to much less than his claimed sixty miles an hour.

"I think they're going towards the Centre," Johnson announced equably. "They've had it. They'll be running out of juice in another hour anyway. Besides, we didn't give them enough water."

Gallagher sat quietly in the baking, jolting vehicle, his mind urging the Lamoutiers on while continuing its information-gathering tasks. He had unobtrusively scanned the landscape, memorizing as much of it as he could. Johnson's remark about the fugitives turning towards the Centre had given him an idea. The late morning sun was coming from behind, and the Lamoutiers had turned right, towards the north. If the Centre were truly northwards, it followed that Harding's research station was somewhere in the southern half of this vast island continent. Going south, therefore, would be the best bet. He had already decided to take the Range Rovers when he made the break. They were higher off the ground than the Landrovers, and their bigger wheels and engines would serve to outstrip ground pursuit. The gunship was another matter altogether. The break should be made while Harding was away on one of his trips.

"Dust!" Johnson sang out.

Gallagher felt his spirits plummet as he looked. There it was, a faint haze in the distance, but unmistakable.

"All riiight!" Cyrus had gone back to street talk. "Heyyy, man. Those Frenchies are pretty good, Johnson. Must've been doin' nearer sixty, man."

"Better than I thought," Johnson admitted without rancour.

"Reckon you can catch 'em before they run out o' gas?"

"Any time of the day or night." As if to prove his word good, Johnson put his foot down. The Landrover lurcher alarmingly.

"Heyyy, baby, take it easy. Don't kill us, now."

"What's up, Cyrus? Scared?"

"When you drive like that, baby, I sure am. Ease up. They ain't goin' nowhere."

If Johnson eased up, Gallagher didn't notice it. The mad pace continued, but Cyrus appeared satisfied. Those two understood each other.

So I'll have to watch out for Johnson too. If I kill Cyrus, Johnson won't be any easier to take. They'll have to go together.

The radio buzzed. It was Marika.

"You on your way?" Cyrus asked.

"We have been for some time. We can see your dust."

"Christ!" Cyrus exclaimed, releasing the transmit button. "Must've been a desert record for wheel changing. All right, Johnson. Do what you want with this thing. I want this kill." The hunter was back. To the radio he said: "See you at the kill."

"We shall be there." Marika sounded positive.

"She will too," Cyrus commented, "if we don't haul ass."

Trudi Lamoutier glanced at the wing mirror at that particular moment and what she saw caused her heart to freeze.

"*Henri!*"

His name, called softly on a rising note of terror, told Lamoutier all he didn't want to know. He looked in his own mirror, and saw the plumes of death. So it had all been a terrible game. Well, they would not take him and his Trudi easily. Perhaps he could still save her.

"Think they've seen us?" Cyrus asked.

"Must have," Johnson answered. "We can see the Landrover."

"Why isn't he doing anything? He's just driving straight."

"Perhaps he's waiting." Johnson laughed at a joke that was obvious to him only.

Another half-hour. It was two o'clock now and the sun was beating upon the hard earth of the plain with a vengeance. Dust swirled about and inside the Landrover. Cyrus had rolled back and secured a section of the canvas hood and was standing up, his upper body exposed to the hot slipstream and the ever-present dust.

"Come up here, Mr Gallagher!" he bent down briefly to call.

Gallagher scrambled into the back to join him.

"Take a look."

Gallagher looked. The horizon danced in front of his eyes, before settling down to where it should be. Then it danced again, and he realized that the bouncing of the landrover was responsible.

The fugitive vehicle seemed quite close.

"How far away are they?" he asked.

"Still too far for what I have in mind."

Cyrus reached down to pick up a blooker. "Here."

Gallagher took it, wishing it anywhere else but in his hands.

"Why do you call it a blooker?" *Say anything; anything to take your mind off what's going to happen.*

Cyrus grinned. "Blow gooks. Blook. Get it?"

So much for O'Keefe's information.

"There are some folks who say," Cyrus went on, "that this baby goes *blook* when it fires. Some people will say anything."

"Yes. Yes, I suppose so."

A strange smile was now on Cyrus's face. "Time for some practice. Break the weapon open."

Gallagher did so.

"Good." Approvingly. "Now here's the round. Put it in."

Gallagher took the forty-millimetre explosive shell and slid it home. He snapped the weapon shut, locked it.

"Good," Cyrus said again. "Now. A target. How about that one?"

97

He was pointing at Ngoma's Landrover, hurtling and bouncing on the right flank.

Gallagher stared at him.

Cyrus's grin was back. "It's not as close as you think. The dust makes it look nearer than it actually is. It's well out of range."

Gallagher was well aware of that. He kept up his air of ignorance. "But what if I do hit them?"

"No chance. It takes plenty to hit a moving vehicle, especially one that's moving upwards, downwards, sideways and forwards all at the same time. I want to see how you use this thing. C'mon. Shoot!"

After some hesitation, Gallagher gingerly pointed the blooker in the vague direction of Ngoma's Landrover and fired. The weapon jerked in his hands like a live creature, and he could almost swear it did go *blook*.

Cyrus shut his eyes in despair at the performance. The round exploded well away from Ngoma's Landrover.

The radio buzzed. "What are you doing, Cyrus?"

"Not me, Ngoma," he answered, laughing as he straightened from picking up the radio. "I'm trying to teach our friend Gallagher how to shoot."

A wild laugh pealed over the airwaves. "He's just a pictureman."

"He used to be a soldier ... once," Cyrus said disbelievingly.

"Well, be careful. He might miss, and hit me." More laughter ended the transmission.

Cyrus put the radio down. "OK. Here's another round. Try again."

If anything, the second performance was worse. Gallagher fired just as the Landrover hit a particularly hard clump of dead spinifex. The shell went sailing upwards. It exploded far behind in their wake.

"Never mind," Cyrus said soothingly. "Maybe you'll do better when the target is closer. Johnson! Pour it on. Marika's catching up."

Gallagher could clearly see the lines of her Landrover.

Suddenly Cyrus broke into his street lilt. "Heyy! We gots action! Look what's goin' down, man."

The Lamoutiers' Landrover was weaving; skilfully, too.

"Hey!" Cyrus said again, the laughter going out of his voice.

Gallagher watched the well-executed zigzags with growing comprehension. Lamoutier had indeed done a rough-terrain course. A lot of dust was being thrown up. The other Landrover could hardly be seen, though it was now quite close. A brave try, but it could only end one way.

"Know what I think?" Cyrus said. "I think that guy's been playing with us. He can drive."

"But it's not going to do him much good, is it?"

"Nope. Load your blooker. Here." Cyrus gave Gallagher a pouch full of shells.

Gallagher loaded. He watched in only partially feigned awe as Cyrus loaded and fired his own weapon in an apparently single, fluid motion. The round exploded ahead of the Lamoutier Landrover just as it was beginning another swing. This had the effect of frightening Lamoutier completely, causing him to zig-zag frantically and confusedly.

Cyrus laughed. "Just getting the range. Would I have loved to see his face! Bet he didn't expect that. Not a blooker round right up his nose. You try."

Gallagher loaded and fired, making a production of it. The shell exploded nowhere near the target.

"Jesus! Look, Gallagher. I don't expect you to be as good as me. No one is. But even you can do better than that. Try again." There was a new grimness in Cyrus's voice.

Gallagher's latest effort was no better.

"Shit, man. You're not trying."

"I am bloody well trying!" Gallagher yelled. "What do you fucking expect on this crazy, bouncing roller-coaster?"

Cyrus was taken aback by the outburst, and because Gallagher was scared both for himself and the Lamoutiers it had the ring of sincerity.

"OK. OK. You load them, I'll shoot."

Raging inwardly at his helplessness, Gallagher did as he was told. Cyrus fired the two blookers so swiftly and so accurately, he bracketed the target. Gallagher waited in heavy resignation as he watched Cyrus lining up for his third shot. Gallagher knew it was going to be a direct hit. Johnson was using the wheel skilfully, and despite Lamoutier's undoubted expertise, he was no match for Johnson. The range remained stable. Johnson was riding herd on Lamoutier.

Cyrus fired. The effect was not what Gallagher had expected. The round exploded against the left rear wheel of Lamoutier's Landrover, blowing it to smithereens and sending the vehicle careering into the air.

The Landrover danced upwards and sideways, while continuing to move forward on its front wheels. Its rear underbelly was exposed, its engine screaming as Lamoutier uselessly pressed his foot on the accelerator in frenzy.

Cyrus grabbed the second, newly-loaded blooker from Gallagher, while handing him the used one. "Load it!" he ordered.

He fired. The round tore into the Landrover's underside while it was coming down. It went up again, great chunks flying off it. The dust swirled, as if churned by a maddened animal.

Numbly, Gallagher loaded, trying to keep his mind off the carnage going on inside the stricken vehicle. He lifted the loaded blooker to Cyrus who handed him the one he'd just fired.

You are a dead man, Cyrus, Gallagher's mind raged. He smiled at the man before him. "Nice shooting."

Cyrus's blood was up, his face shining. "*Nice*? Listen, man. In the Nam. I was *it*. I could lay down a barrage that would have the gooks shitting their pants." He fired while still speaking.

The shell blew the Landrover cab, and the Lamoutiers, apart. The vehicle rolled over and over, exploding in sheets of flame as it went. It was all over.

The hunters stopped their vehicles. Marika's came hurtling up, towing a high tail of red dust, to slide expertly to a halt close to Cyrus's Landrover. She climbed out.

"I saw most of that, Cyrus. It was magnificent."

"I agree with you." No false modesty for Cyrus.

She looked at Gallagher who was leaning gingerly against the hot side of the vehicle, walked up to him.

"Gordon? What did you think?"

Gallagher smiled. "Bloody brilliant." He meant it. *And a fucking murdering bastard*, he didn't add.

She took his arm. "Walk with me a little."

Cyrus watched them go. "Some guys have all the luck. That's one juicy bit of poontang."

Johnson climbed down to join him. "Me, I'd rather fuck a black widow."

"Don't let her hear you say that."

"Don't let her hear *you* call her poontang."

"Yeah," Cyrus agreed. He knew how far he could go. "Let's go see what's left of our game."

In the distance, Harding's gunship thrummed into view, a metallic vulture coming in after the kill.

"Well, we beat him to it, Cyrus," Johnson said.

"Yeah. We sure as hell did."

Standing a little way from the others with Marika, watching the gunship prepare for landing, Gallagher took a swig from the hip flask of water he had carried with him on the hunt. It was the first drink he'd had since the whole thing had started well over three hours earlier. The water was warm, but it tasted good. Johnson and Cyrus, secure in the knowledge that they were never going to be left adrift in this arid hell, had drunk quite freely from their own supplies during that time. Gallagher considered himself in training for what was to come. Three hours out here in the relative comfort of a Landrover would be nothing compared to a possible walk. He had to assume the worst.

He offered the flask to Marika. She declined with a shake of the head. She was looking at the now descending helicopter. Its whirling

100

blades created a huge funnel of dust through which it lowered itself with slow care.

Gallagher took another swig of the sun-heated water, then secured the flask to his belt. He would not touch another drop until he returned to Harding's burrow.

The gunship landed and, even before the blades ceased turning, Ngoma's Landrover was speeding towards it, stopping just as Harding climbed out of the aircraft.

As Harding entered the Landrover, Gallagher tried to put the sickening murder of the Lamoutiers out of his mind. It would not do to let his thoughts be betrayed upon his face. He watched unconcernedly as the Landrover sped towards where the Lamoutiers' remains were being cooked by the flames from their destroyed vehicle. Lamoutier may have been taught the skills of rough terrain driving; but he had been no match for Johnson, and no terrain he had learned on was a match for the Outback.

Marika was now studying Gallagher. Her flawless skin, darkened only slightly by the sun, gleamed smoothly; yet there was not a bead of perspiration to be seen upon it. Gallagher felt globules dotting his own face. He wiped at them with the back of his hand.

"Why are you so thoughtful?" she queried. "Is it the Lamoutiers?"

He took his time answering, like a man at ease with himself. A quick denial would only arouse suspicion.

"No. I wasn't thinking of them but of you."

"Me?" She appeared surprised.

"Yes. I don't care what the others do, but I've just seen what killing turns Cyrus into. I don't want it to happen to you." He felt the globules of sweat running into each other across the planes of his face as she stared keenly at him for some moments. Had he misjudged it?

"Cyrus," she began carefully, "is one of my best people. He is very skilled."

"I don't deny it, any more than I can deny I worry about you."

"Because you care?"

"Yes. What will happen to you if something ever goes wrong? I care about that."

"Nothing will go wrong." She waved an arm, indicating the empty landscape. "We have hundreds of thousands of square kilometres to play in. What can go wrong?"

"Well, you can't stop me worrying," he said stubbornly.

She smiled at him, pleased by his concern. She brought her lips momentarily against his. "You look very hot. Let us get some shade."

She held his arm lightly as they walked back to her Landrover. The two Arabs, who had travelled with her, were standing next to it. As Marika and Gallagher reached the vehicle, a single pistol shot rang out.

The Arabs exchanged silent looks, while Marika and Gallagher stared in the direction of the Lamoutiers' Landrover. Ngoma and her crew, together with Cyrus and Johnson, stood in a group near the still-smoking wreckage. To one side stood Harding, a pistol in his hand.

"I wouldn't have thought anybody could have lived through that," Gallagher said. "Cyrus was good with that thing of his."

They continued to watch as everyone piled into Ngoma's Landrover. It came slowly towards them, stopped. Harding was the first to get out.

"Mrs Lamoutier," he said calmly, by way of explanation. "Poor woman. Lower body completely gone. Had to finish her off. Cruel not to."

Gallagher felt his gorge rise. He let it show in his expression, knowing it was what would be expected of him; but, more importantly, it acted as a screen for the anger boiling within him.

"You seem a bit peaked, Gordon," Hardin said solicitously. "Perhaps you should ride back with me."

"Well ..." Gallagher began hesitantly, though there was nothing he wanted more than an opportunity to see the terrain from the air.

"Don't worry. It will be a reasonably smooth flight. You won't feel sick. I guarantee it. Besides, it will give you a new perspective on things. Pity about your camera. Remarkable views up there."

"I suppose so," Gallagher said unwillingly, glancing at Marika.

"It is all right, Gordon," Marika said. "I will see you later. Yes?" The last word held a wealth of promise.

"All right," Gallagher agreed, though still reluctantly.

She kissed him beneath Harding's amused gaze, then Gallagher climbed into Ngoma's Landrover with him. Marika watched it head for the gunship, before going to where Cyrus and Johnson were getting ready for the return trip.

"Cyrus."

"Yeah?"

"Did you notice how much water Gallagher drank when he was with you?"

Cyrus stared wonderingly at the question. "As much as we did, I guess. Didn't pay much attention."

"You, David?"

"I was busy driving," Johnson answered, "but I suppose Cyrus is right. About the same as us."

"But neither of you is sure?"

"Well, no ..." they both began at once.

Marika cut across their reply. "You should be sure! There will be no excuses for slackness." The vivid green eyes blazed at them. "It takes me a very long time to be sure of anybody. Please make sure you both understand it."

102

Cyrus waited until she had started her Landrover. "Now what the hell's biting her?"

"Give me a black widow any day," Johnson said with feeling. "Gallagher can have that crazy bitch with my blessings. As for you, Cyrus, I've seen you eyeing her bum. Take a tip from a friend: leave it out, mate. Unless you want your balls blown to bits."

III

Flyboy lifted the Huey off the ground with a flourish. The gunship rose like an express lift. Gallagher shut his eyes, as if too afraid to look.

"Come now, Gordon," Harding's voice shouted in amusement over the clatter of the rotors. "It's not as bad as all that, surely? Flyboy's rather proud of his piloting skills."

Flyboy turned his baseball-capped head briefly to grin at Gallagher who had now opened his eyes, as the helicopter stopped ascending to rush forwards in a nose-down attitude.

"That may be so," Gallagher shouted in return. "But if that thing about our heads stops turning, what's going to keep us up?"

From the seat next to the pilot, Harding merely smiled. Gallagher turned his attention to the thing he'd seen as soon as he'd approached the helicopter on the ground. It was a door-mounted General Electric M.134 Minigun, a six-barrelled monster that could fire 7.62 millimetre rounds at four different speeds, from sixteen hundred to four thousand rounds per minute. It had not been on the helicopter when Gallagher had first seen the Huey. That meant that Harding's people could put it on and take it off at will.

"What the hell's this thing?" he had asked, staring.

Harding had answered with an amused smile, giving Gallagher specifications of the weapon that he was already well familiar with.

Gallagher had asked the question expected of him: "But how could you have lain your hands on something like that?"

"I can get anything," Harding had replied. It had not been a boast.

Gallagher now reflected ruefully that this was probably no exaggeration. Harding had power, money, the ear of governments, companies by the dozen and a position of great privilege. He could probably blow up the bloody world, Gallagher decided sourly.

He let his eyes wander over the unfolding landscape beneath as the Huey clatter-cruised at a steady hundred miles an hour. Flyboy held the machine at a thousand feet.

The vista was as bad as Gallagher had feared. The parched red earth seemed to extend for ever, dotted here and there with hardy desert growth. Once or twice, he thought he could make out what seemed like tracks, only to realize they were dried water-courses that began nowhere and ended nowhere. Now and then, the uniform redness was broken by outcrops of rock and low hills; but that was all. He saw no animals, no waterholes.

"Frightening, isn't it?" Harding said loudly from his seat.

"I wouldn't like to try and walk it."

Harding laughed easily. "I should think not!"

Gallagher surveyed the daunting landscape. How many people would be buried out there before this was all over?

Suddenly, the helicopter swooped low. Had he not been familiar with the air, Gallagher would have been made ill by the violent manoeuvre; but he acted the part for good measure, without actually being sick.

Harding was struggling out of his seat. "Sorry about that," he shouted cheerfully at Gallagher's queasy-looking face. "We've just seen some targets." He took up position behind the Minigun.

"Dingoes!" Flyboy called in explanation.

Gallagher knew about the Australian wild dogs. He looked out. A pack of six were running away from the swooping machine. He marvelled at the tenacity of the yellowish dogs. How could they live in such a landscape?

"They're fair game," Harding was shouting. "The authorities actually pay bounties for each dog destroyed. They're a menace to livestock and other protected animals. Some people make a living hunting dingoes. Doggers, they call them. All right, Flyboy!"

Flyboy went into the attack with the practised ease of a combat veteran. The Huey swooped in a tight circle, herding the dogs.

Harding set the gun at maximum, and fired. A sharp roar like a monstrous sewing-machine cut across the clatter of the gunship. Three dogs were minced as a hundred and thirty-three rounds ripped into them in the space of two seconds. Their blood disappeared into the already red earth. Fur and flesh had turned into brief mist.

The gunship rose and swooped again. The remaining dogs ran in confused circles.

The gun spat, very briefly. Gallagher's trained mind judged it to be for less than a second. Harding was good with that thing. Another dog had disintegrated.

"I want the other two in one go!" Harding called.

"Right!" Flyboy agreed. On full rudder and opposite cyclic, he slid the gunship down in a heart-stopping sideslip, nearly to ground level.

The last two dogs were now running in tandem. Gallagher wondered if one was a bitch, because they seemed inseparable. Where one turned, the other followed. Now, they were running side by side. He wanted them to escape, though he knew it to be hopeless. There was no cover, no escape from bullets that could come at you at the rate of sixty-seven per second. Gallagher paid particular attention to that. The minigun would rip the Range Rover apart like a tin opener.

The dingoes made a mistake. Confused by the Huey's constant harrying, they ran into each other. At that moment, Harding fired. He gave them three seconds of it. That was two too many. The dogs had died in the hail of the first second.

"Lovely!" Harding crowed as he made his way back to his seat. "More fun than big-game hunting, this."

Flyboy kept the Huey scooting low all the way back, making Gallagher wonder if he were playing at flying under the radar.

Both Harding and Flyboy were flushed with excitement.

Gallagher felt sorry for the dead dogs and hoped his fate would not be theirs. He tried not to think of the Lamoutiers whose remains were still cooking in a petrol fire, under the Outback sun. He tried not to think of the von Dietlingers, already buried beneath the hot, red earth. He tried not to think of brave but foolish Bannion, expiring by a brass-jacketed AK-47 bullet in a windowless underground room. He tried not to think of Serge. He tried not to think of having to make love to Marika later. He tried not to think of what would happen to Lauren if he did not succeed in the escape attempt.

While all this was going on in his mind, Flyboy danced the gunship round the site of the complex in an extravagant circuit before landing it with precision through the slowly opening roof of the long, low building, and with all the delicacy of a feather kissing the earth. The noise reverberated within the hangar-like structure before Flyboy cut the engine. The roof was already closing above them. Whatever he was in this community of homicidal maniacs, Flyboy certainly knew how to fly.

Harding left almost immediately, and Gallagher found himself sharing a table with Flyboy in the Mess. Flyboy ate mightily, while Gallagher, unable to stomach the thought of meat, chose a salad. He wondered if Flyboy were meant to keep an eye on him until either Cyrus or Marika returned.

"You handle that chopper well," Gallagher said casually, "even if you did turn my stomach inside out."

Flyboy grinned. "Hey, that was nothing. Back in the Nam I used to pole Loaches and Snakes with the Air Cav, and the things we did with those ships would have your eyeballs on stalks."

"Loaches?" Gallagher queried. "Snakes?" He knew what the military jargon really meant, but reasoned that an ordinary squaddie would not.

"Uh, yeah. You wouldn't know. A Loach was like that ship back in the hangar. A Huey. A Snake was the Cobra. Man, that was some ship." Flyboy warmed to his theme. "Hey, you should have seen us, man. We'd roll on to our backs and half-loop down to ten feet. Or the spiral. Rudder and cyclic hard right together, and down we'd go, chasing our tails."

Gallagher listened, as if in awe. "You could really do that?"

"Sure. Still can."

Gallagher did not doubt it, especially after the display he'd recently experienced. He would not enjoy the prospect of having Flyboy hunting him in that gunship. He wondered whether there would be an opportunity to disable the Huey before the escape.

"Well, Gordon? Did you enjoy your flight?" It was Marika.

He looked up, smiled. "Flyboy does things with helicopters that they weren't meant to."

"Ah. He is good, is Pinkus." She sat down next to him. "Alex says you saw some dingoes."

"Yes. He got them all."

"He said. He enjoyed it. He is good with that gun."

Flyboy stood up. "See you guys later."

"OK," Marika said.

Gallagher nodded. "See you."

They watched him leave.

I was right, Gallagher thought. *Someone to watch me all the time. They still don't quite trust me.* He'd have to do some more work on Marika, but he could not see how he'd be able to face up to making love to her later that day.

In the event, he would be spared the necessity.

"I was thinking," he said to her. "Don't you ever worry about transmissions when you go on a hunt? From what little I know of it, Australia's supposed to have the biggest concentration of private radio sets for the size of population. What if someone picks you up?"

Marika was unperturbed. "Unlikely. We never say anything that would give us away; and if anyone did hear our transmissions, they would think we were hunting dingoes." She smiled. "And everyone is glad when dingoes are killed. Is that not good?"

Gallagher spent the rest of the day on his own in his room. Marika did not come that night, for which he was very thankful.

Day Three

I

SHE CLIMBED into his bed the next morning. They made love, and wound up on the floor, inevitably.

"Ayayayeee," she breathed when it was over. "Ah, Gordon, Gordon." She kissed him. "I missed not being with you last night, but Alex and I had much talking to do. He has gone away."

Gallagher stemmed the rise of excitement within him. "Gone? Are there problems?"

"Oh, no," she answered, dashing his hopes. "Remember Alex has many companies to run all over the world. He must leave for a few days. That is all."

Gallagher knew also that Harding wanted to keep in the public eye as much as possible. His many friends and acquaintances would know of his past relationship with Lauren, and he would want to be seen being suitably anxious, even though the relationship had ended.

"We shall have plenty of time together before he returns," Marika said. "There will be no more hunts until he gets back. I made him a promise."

A few days. Gallagher wondered how long that actually meant. He had to assume he would have as little as two days, possibly four. His thoughts were interrupted.

Marika was caressing him.

The Cessna landed at four o'clock that afternoon with fresh food. Crofton and Gallagher passed each other at the entrance to the Mess. Crofton was on his way back to the aircraft. A frown appeared on his brow, then he shook his head as if dismissing a sudden thought.

In one of the corridors Crofton met Cyrus and said in passing, "I see you've got a new man."

"A new ... oh, you mean Gallagher. Kind of. Not much of a shootist, but Marika's got the real hots for him."

Crofton grinned. "Ah, yes. The lovely Marika. I could have the hots for her myself."

And Crofton knew he had overstepped the mark. He was tolerated by these dangerous people because he was Harding's pilot, but they never truly took him into their circle. His remark about Marika had not been appreciated, he saw from Cyrus's expression, and he felt a slight quake of fear.

"I'd not say that again," Cyrus warned, "if I were you. Not in our hearing."

Crofton smiled his relief. "It was just a joke."

"Yeah." Cyrus went on his way.

Crofton went weak at the knees. God. These people. Mad, the lot of them. He hurried to the world he felt safe in. His aircraft.

As he went swiftly through his pre-takeoff checks, the nagging thought returned to him. Gallagher. No. Impossible. It could hardly be the same man. Yet.... Oh, to hell with it. He could be wrong, and the last thing he wanted was to tangle with that mad gang out there. The new man was one of them and he, Crofton, the outsider.

He started the Garretts, wound them up, rolled the Citation III into its take-off run and lifted it cleanly into the hot desert sky.

He worried all the way to Adelaide.

Gallagher lay staring into the night with a well satisfied Marika sleeping peacefully, her head against his bare chest. The shock of running into Crofton still lingered. He had not missed the sudden, brief widening of the other's eyes. Mercifully, Marika had not been there at the time.

It was obvious that Crofton had as yet said nothing, or Marika would not have given herself with such wild abandon. She was more and more transported with ecstasy each time they made love. Gallagher hoped all this would help him when the crucial time came.

Would Crofton do anything before the time was right for the escape?

Day Four

I

IN ADELAIDE Crofton picked up three senior Harding International executives and flew them to Perth for a conference. The Citation was normally for Harding's express use, but he'd left instructions sanctioning the flight. He himself was in London, having flown there by commercial carrier.

Crofton worried all the way to Perth.

"Is that girl anything to you?" Marika asked suddenly, casually.

Now that she had at last asked the question he'd been awaiting so long, Gallagher found he could answer "No" quite easily.

"I'm glad you did not say, 'What girl?' It is so false when men do that. Serge tried to fool me with it. 'What women, chérie?' he said, and I could see the lie in his eyes." Her green eyes searched Gallagher's. "But you are not lying. I am glad."

He knew she would have killed Lauren without compunction, irrespective of Harding's absence. He was thankful for his past training; thankful to O'Keefe.

They were alone in the deserted Mess.

"Where's everybody?" he asked.

"With Alex away, we are relaxing a little. Some have gone out hunting the dogs, others are lying about somewhere, and Flyboy is playing in the hangar with his beloved helicopter."

Shit. "Oh. In that case, what shall we do?"

She stood up, her eyes opaque. "Come, and I'll show you."

Gallagher looked at Marika's sleeping form. They'd had another frantic bout of lovemaking in her room. Now, he eased himself slowly and cautiously away from her. She did not come awake.

He stood up. It should not be more than about three o'clock now, he guessed. Which meant plenty of daylight left for what he'd decided to do. He looked down at Marika. *I should kill her now.* But he couldn't bring himself to. He chose his target area carefully, and hit her. The recumbent form relaxed into something deeper than ordinary sleep. She'd be out of commission long enough for his purposes.

He dressed quickly and walked boldy into the corridor, heading towards the captive-room. No one stopped him.

"Have a heart, Cyrus," Johnson pleaded. "Haven't we dug far enough? This bloody heat is killing." He brushed angrily at his face.

"No," Cyrus answered. "You ought to know that."

"And these bloody flies. How can flies live in this place?"

Cyrus grinned. "Where's the tough SAS man?" He glanced round at the work they'd been doing and was pleased. He'd chosen the spot well. It was perfect.

Johnson had been about to make a suitable retort when he froze.

Cyrus and the Libyan saw it too.

"Don't move!" Cyrus commanded his two companions in a sharp whisper.

"Oh ... my ... God!" Johnson's voice was shaky.

"And don't talk!"

Acanthophis antarcticus slid down the incline towards Johnson, five feet of bluey-grey viper-like body, topped by a wide, nasty-looking triangular head. The Death Adder, one of the most vicious and widely feared snakes in all of Australia. It was a well-developed specimen and its bite would certainly kill.

Johnson felt as if his blood, despite the pounding heat, had suddenly turned to ice.

"Do something, for God's sake!"

"Shut up, goddammit!" came Cyrus's harsh whisper. He had slowly removed the big .45 from its holster.

Click!

The snake stopped at the sound of the Colt's hammer. It had sensed the vibrations that had travelled down through Cyrus's body to the ground, where its acutely tuned sensors had picked them up.

The snake moved, more slowly this time, concentrating on the target before it. Although the target was still, there were vibrations coming from it, strong enough to ascertain that it was alive. Johnson could not prevent himself from trembling.

Cyrus fired just as the snake reared to strike. The heavy .45 slug tore through the snake's already opening mouth, ripping its way out of the back of the reptile's head. The snake was flung backwards up the incline, coiling and uncoiling as it went. Venom spurted uselessly from its fangs.

Cyrus fired twice more into the body; then twice again for good measure. He holstered the Colt.

"I've seen cottonmouths, copperheads, moccasins and rattlers," he said. "Even kraits in the Nam. But I've never seen a motherfucker like that sonofabitch. Look at that venom! Johnson, that big bastard would have killed you, man."

Johnson was trembling violently from reaction. "Where ... where did it come from?" His eyes scanned nervously about him for more.

110

"Our digging must've disturbed it in its hole. Even snakes keep away from this heat."

"I have seen something like it," the Libyan said in careful English, "in Africa. You Western people call it the Gaboon Viper. It has horns. Very, very bad. Flies are better," he added, poker-faced.

"Thanks," Johnson said sarcastically. "No more digging Cyrus, until we make sure that thing doesn't have relatives."

"OK."

They hunted for an hour, poking about the place and making a lot of noise. A dangerous enough occupation; but there were no more snakes.

They continued their digging, until Cyrus was quite satisfied. They made their preparations, then climbed into the landrover to wait. It was relatively cool in the vehicle now, despite the brilliant sun beating down.

"Yeah," Cyrus said with satisfaction. "Perfect."

Gallagher approached the door. Selini and the Jordanian were on guard. He smiled at them, and looked as if he wanted to talk.

They regarded him curiously, without the tense alertness of someone expecting an enemy. Their weapons remained pointing downwards. Selini carried her Ingram, while the Jordanian had an M62 Valmet, the Finnish all-metal-and-plastic derivative of the AK-47.

"Hello," Gallagher said as he came up close. His boldness had left them momentarily nonplussed.

He hit the Jordanian first, using the same blow that he had on Sumner, only this time it was meant to immobilize. The Jordanian doubled up, and Gallagher hit again on the back of the neck, taking the assault rifle off him in almost the same motion. The Jordanian died as he fell, and Gallagher was pointing the Valmet at Selini.

The attack had taken her by such surprise, she had not moved.

"Don't force me to kill you, Selini. Give me the Ingram. No sudden moves."

Eyes glaring hotly, she complied.

"Good. Now open the door. Easily!"

He pushed her through and followed quickly. Everyone in the room goggled.

"Shhh!" he hissed at them before they could start a clamour. "No noise!"

Villiger was first on his feet, tensed for attack. Gallagher tossed the Ingram at him. He caught it easily, the weapon seeming to shrink in his big hands.

"I'll get you something more substantial later," Gallagher said.

111

"There's a dead man out there. Drag him in."

Without a word, Villiger went to haul the body into the room. He pulled the slight Jordanian with barely any effort. He inspected the body professionally, pursed his lips, nodded as if impressed by the way Gallagher had done his killing.

Lauren had come across to Gallagher and had laid her hand on his arm. The look in her eyes warmed him.

Everyone had got to their feet now, and for once Sumner seemed at a loss for words. But not for long.

"Shoot her," he ordered Gallagher, glaring at Selini. "Shoot the goddammed bitch!"

"And bring the rest down on us?"

"You've just shown there're other ways."

Gallagher looked away from him to say to Selini: "I don't know if you've killed anybody. I've never seen you do it. I'm going to ask you just once. Where are the weapons kept? If you don't answer, I'm going to turn you over to our civilized friend over there." He jerked a thumb at Sumner.

Sumner was pleased to be considered an object of fear, but he did not like the way Gallagher had put it. Both feelings struggled for supremacy in his expression. At any other time, it would have been comical to look upon.

Selini readily told Gallagher, perhaps because he had not killed her when he'd had the opportunity. He did not think it was because she feared Sumner. Perhaps she believed Gallagher would really kill her this time. She had witnessed his ruthless speed in despatching her companion.

He hit her suddenly. She crumpled. There were many gasps from the captives.

Lauren's eyes widened at this new Gallagher. "Is ... is she dead?"

"No. But she'll be out of action long enough." He looked at Villiger. "Did you find out?"

Villiger's button eyes showed professional respect. "Sumner knows about electronics. Tell him, Sumner. Make it quick."

Responding to Villiger's no-nonsense tone, Sumner said: "Computers can't work in isolation. They have to be linked. The one here would have to be patched to another one, if there's no one here to work it."

"I see. And what would happen if we cut the power?"

"The people at the other end would know immediately if ... it's an important link. They may not check it for some time."

"Well, we'll just have to hope. Where's the power source?"

"Usually in the floor somewhere."

"What's the reason?" Villiger asked.

"There's a weapons research establishment in a place called

Salisbury, near Adelaide in South Australia. Harding's into many things. Maybe this place is more than just a weather-research station. I don't know. Maybe this computer is linked to the one in Salisbury, and cutting it off may set them wondering down there. It's just a hope. Anything that may tie up the pursuit is a bonus. Let's go, everybody. We've been standing around long enough."

They filed out cautiously. No one stopped them.

Gallagher made for the weapons store, the others trailing behind him. He recognized the door as one that Cyrus had not allowed him to enter. It was locked.

"Let me," Villiger said. He put a massive shoulder against the door and began to strain at it. It was not substantial. There had been no foreseen need to build a door to stronger specifications. It began to move away from the jamb. Gallagher made to lend his weight in support.

"No!" Villiger hissed. "I don't want it to fly open."

The lock was a simple one, and no doubt guarded nothing more dangerous than stationery or bed linen. It creaked under Villiger's relentless pressure. The gap between the door and jamb grew progressively wider. Villiger's face was red with the effort. Suddenly there was a popping sound. Villiger held on to the door to prevent it slamming open. The whole operation had taken only a few seconds.

Gallagher could not help wondering how many doors Villiger had broken open like that during the course of his duties.

"Grab everything you can carry," he whispered to the others. "Don't forget ammunition." He did not like the idea of giving Sumner a weapon. He was not too sure of Nbwale, either, who might want to shoot Villiger, something Gallagher would rather not have occur during the escape. Those two could go back to Africa to shoot it out if they wanted.

Gallagher knew the particular weapons he himself was looking for and, when he'd found them, passed two to Lauren. He took as much ammunition as he could carry without being encumbered, picked up an M16 and what looked like a West German army-issue Walther P1 automatic pistol in a canvas holster. He strapped on the pistol.

"All right! Let's go!"

There was still enough stuff in there to equip a good-sized assault force and he wished he could have blown it up before leaving. But apart from the fact that the noise would have raised the alarm, there were no grenades handy.

Villiger was the last out. He shut the door behind him. Gallagher stared in amazement. Villiger grinned, looking incongruously boyish.

"Magic," he said.

"Let me take some of that," Smallson said to Gallagher, indicating an ammunition pouch.

Gallagher gave him two pouches and refrained from telling him to be careful.

They moved on.

Food! Gallagher suddenly thought. *We need food! Damn*! Was there time to dump the weapons in the Range Rovers and return for a raid on the Mess? He wondered about the people that Marika had said were still in the complex. Where were they? Was Flyboy still in the hangar? And what about the closed-circuit TV?

No one came at them.

Gallagher was confident that both Marika and Selini would remain out for some time. He had dealt the blows well. The group hurried round a corner, after he and Villiger had first swiftly checked it, working smoothly as a team.

"Someone trained you well," Villiger whispered at him drily.

Gallagher smiled but said nothing. He was amused to see that Villiger had given the Ingram to Paula Browne, having selected for personal use the Ak-47.

Villiger noticed the look. "You won't find me denying that this is a bloody fine weapon, man, just because the Communists make it."

Gallagher had given the tubular-butted Valmet to Parguineau, who had elected to keep it. Of the three men with special combat experience, he was the only one to choose a Western arm. Gallagher glanced back to see if the others were all right. Paula Browne carried the Ingram as if it were about to bite her; he hoped she would not trigger it off accidentally. Sumner had picked up two Uzis, while Nbwale carried yet another AK-47. Villiger had also strapped a Browning High Power thirteen-shot automatic to his waist.

"I hate to ask at this time," Villiger whispered as they paused at another turning, "but how are we going to get away?"

"We've got transport. Two Range Rovers, desert-ready for some scientists who are supposed to be coming here. They're in a big hangar dug deep into the ground. Wait till you see what's in there with them." He looked back. "Sumner!"

"Yeah?" the whisper came back.

"The computer room is just ahead. Come with us."

Sumner came forward. Villiger and Gallagher moved swiftly to the door, checked inside, covering each other. No one.

"Right, Sumner," Gallagher whispered. "Get in there and pull the plug."

As Sumner made to move past, the Uzis clunked against each other.

"Christ. Give me one of those things." Gallagher snatched one of the Uzis before Sumner could object. Smallson had come up. "Can you carry this as well, Jake?"

"Of course." Taking the Uzi, Smallson slung it across his back.

114

Sumner came out. "Done."

"Good. Let's go."

"What about my other gun?"

"*Your* gun, Sumner? For God's sake!" Gallagher turned away impatiently.

The others followed.

Where was everybody? Gallagher continued to wonder. More people must have gone on that dog hunt than Marika had thought.

They came to the entrance to the hangar.

"Someone's supposed to be in here," Gallagher warned Villiger. "Cover me." He glanced at a worried looking Lauren. "You all right with those things?"

She gave him a weak smile, nodded.

He turned back to Villiger. "Here we go." Opening the hangar door slowly, quietly, he slipped inside.

Villiger followed. He stared disbelievingly at the gunship, but his surprise did not affect his capabilities. With Gallagher, he rapidly checked the entire hangar. It was empty.

"Jesus, man," Villiger said, staring at the gunship, "I don't believe it."

The others were filing in. They too stared.

"You'd better. That's the *pièce de résistance* of the hunt."

"Hunt? What hunt?"

Gallagher said evenly: "We were meant to be the game." He reached inside the machine to pick up a pair of binoculars he had noticed. "Might need those."

Villiger's small eyes widened. "Those other people...."

"Dead. Hunted down."

"With that thing?"

"I've only seen it in action once, but it was too late for the Lamoutiers. Cyrus, the man who took them out, got them first."

"Jesus. How does it get out?"

"I'll tell you about it on the way. Let's get these people in the Rovers."

"We should blow it up."

"We'd waste time doing it, and we'd be warning them. Harding is not here. It doesn't fly without him. Come on, everybody. In!"

They hurried. The keys were in the Range Rovers.

"You take one," Gallagher said to the Afrikaner, "I'll take the other."

"Right."

Lauren, Smallson and Nbwale climbed into the one Gallagher would be driving. Sumner, Parguineau and Paula Browne boarded the other. Gallagher went over to Villiger.

"We've got to get some food," he said. "Those jerrycans on the

115

Rovers will have water as well as petrol, so we don't have to worry about that; but it means going back in there."

"Let's do it then."

II

"I'm coming with you." Lauren had climbed down from the Range Rover. "The two of you won't be able to carry enough," she reasoned into Gallagher's silence. "I'll have both my hands free."

He had been about to turn her down flatly, to tell her how dangerous going back could be; then he realized that if they did get into trouble, it would be all over anyway. He would prefer having her with him.

"All right. Come on." The decision had only taken split seconds.

He left Parguineau in charge, and they hurried out of the hangar. He wondered what had happened to Flyboy.

Had Flyboy been in the hangar, they would have killed him, saving themselves a lot of grief later on. Unfortunately, Flyboy had decided to pay a long visit to the lavatory – which was well away from the hangar – where he'd fallen asleep. It was a habit of his, stemming from his Vietnam days, when he'd wanted to dodge a mission. He used to cite battle fatigue as the reason, while everyone knew he was smashed out of his skull. He didn't touch the stuff any more – Marika would not have tolerated that – but old habits died hard.

Gallagher and Villiger flitted along the corridor, Lauren hurrying between them. They sniffed for trouble at the turnings, covering each other with practised skill while protecting Lauren at the same time.

"Where the hell are they?" Villiger asked at one point.

"Dog hunting."

"What?"

"Dingoes. That's why all the other vehicles are gone. They're practising on the animals before it's time for human game."

They came to the turning that led to the Mess, and someone literally walked into them. For fleeting moments that seemed to stretch for years, each person paused, as if balancing precariously at the edge of a yawning precipice.

Gallagher recognized the man as the other white who had partnered Johnson when they and four other members of Marika's group had burst into the captive-room while accompanying Harding. The man's momentary shock at seeing Gallagher armed now gave Villiger all the time he needed. The edge of one of his massive hands slashed at the other's throat with all the savagery of a medieval axe.

Blood erupted out of the man's mouth, spraying itself darkly on to the nearest wall. Lauren gave a stifled scream as a couple of droplets

116

spotted her face. She wiped them off frantically, then hid her face in her hands as the man crumpled gurgling to the floor, drowning in a place without water.

Gallagher gripped her shoulder briefly. "Come on," he told her gently.

She uncovered her face. "I'll be all right."

"Sure?" And when she nodded: "Good for you."

Villiger put the choking man out of his misery by administering a silent *coup de grace* to the back of the neck before they hurried on.

There were no further incidents and, finding a couple of plastic bags and a small cardboard box in the food store, they gave themselves no more than half a minute to grab anything they could within that period. Lauren had the presence of mind to include a tin opener. They hurried back, meeting no one on the way.

In the hangar, Gallagher said: "Just dump the stuff in. We'll sort it out when we're well away from here." He added to Villiger, who had lost no time in getting behind the wheel of his designated vehicle: "Don't start until I've got back from opening the doors."

He ran to the doors and found that they were operated by a push-button, each folding swiftly and silently upon itself. While they were still opening, he ran back to his Range Rover and got in.

For some frustrating seconds, neither vehicle would start; then the engines caught. Gallagher shifted first gear home, slammed out the clutch and hurtled through the open doors and up the ramp, with Villiger's Range Rover practically sitting on his rear nudge bars. The doors were already beginning to close automatically as the two vehicles, trailing billowing plumes of red dust like contrails from a high-flying jet, tore across the empty, baking land.

Gallagher fervently hoped they didn't run into any of Marika's dingo-hunting crew; but if it did happen, he wanted it to occur as far away from the complex as possible. He put his foot down. Villiger stayed almost glued to him.

"You reckon that nigger knows what he's doing?" Sumner called. He shared the back of Villiger's Range Rover with Paula Browne, while Parguineau sat in the front with Villiger.

Sitting as far away from Sumner as she could, Paula stared at him disgustedly. "You'll never change, will you? Come hell or high water, the superior, asshole racist goes marching on. That man just risked his ass for you."

"I wasn't talking to you," Sumner told her sharply. "Anyway, he risked nothing for me. He came back because of the woman. A nigger will do anything to get his hands on a white woman."

She looked at him in stunned disbelief. "My God. You must spend most of your life sitting on your brains. Villiger? Do you hear this bullshit?"

Villiger stared through Gallagher's dust storm. "Please allow me to concentrate on what I'm doing," was all he said.

In the back, Paula Browne and Sumner journeyed in hostile silence.

Lauren sat in the front with Gallagher in the lead Range Rover. In the back, Smallson and the huge Nbwale lolled, Nbwale taking up most of the available room because of his bulk. Smallson's eyes were closed in blessed relief.

"Thank you, Gordon," he said.

"For what? I saved my own life too ... for the moment, at any rate." He scanned the horizon, searching for the tell-tale sign of another dust cloud.

"Why will you not accept gratitude?"

"We're not out of the woods yet. Rest yourself, Jake. We have a long way to go."

The old man smiled to himself. "So. Gratitude embarrasses you."

Gallagher said nothing.

Smallson opened his eyes to look at his granddaughter. She was sitting turned partly inwards, and every so often she would glance from the desert landscape to Gallagher. The old man thought he saw a kind of pride in the grey eyes. He knew what that meant. A woman takes pride in the man she loves. He shut his eyes again, pleased that, from the very beginning, he had judged Gallagher correctly.

With each glance Lauren gave Gallagher, her eyes lingered on parts of his body: his strong, dark arms fighting the wheel effortlessly; his profile, his eyes ceaselessly scanning the horizon; his chest through his opened shirt; his hair.... She smiled at the thought of what her Boston friends would say if they knew what was taking place within her. *How I've changed.* New York was fast becoming just a bad memory.

Gallagher was not unaware of her glances, but he forced himself to concentrate on the task ahead. God alone knew what distance they'd have to travel to find safety, and what kind of terrain they'd have to cope with. He'd have to stop soon to have a quick check of all supplies. The Rover's tank was full, and he assumed or hoped that Villiger's was in the same state; but it was just what the jerrycans held that would determine their eventual range. He did not discount the idea of abandoning one vehicle and utilizing whatever quantity of its supplies the remaining Rover would be able to carry. That would extend the distance the fugitives could travel.

But would a single admittedly specially strengthened Range Rover carry all eight people and extra water and petrol cans, on the desert sands?

They'd been travelling for what he judged to be about an hour when he stuck his arm out of the window and waved it up and down. Villiger slowed.

"What's going on?" Sumner called. "Why are we slowing down?"

118

"Gallagher wants us to," Villiger answered him neutrally. "I suspect he wants to check our supplies. We didn't exactly have the time to do so before."

"But why now? We're still too close to those people back there."

"I think we can spare a few minutes for a vital check," Villiger said patiently. "The desert can kill us as easily as that gang."

He stopped the Rover, climbed out. Sumner and Parguineau joined him in the sweltering heat.

"God Almighty!" Sumner exclaimed. "It's hotter'n hell out here." He stared dauntedly about him. "God, will we make it?" he added quietly.

"With luck, and if we don't act stupidly, we should," Villiger said.

Gallagher came up to them. "Well, let's see what we've got. Oh, Mrs Browne," he called.

"Paula," she said from within the Rover.

He smiled at her. "Paula it is. Will you have a good look round and see if you can find a map of some kind anywhere? I'd have thought it highly likely that the people for whom these wheels were meant would have at least one stowed somewhere," he went on to the others. "The old man's having a good look in ours."

The others began checking the jerrycans mounted on the sides, roof, front and rear of the vehicle. There were ten in all, three mounted on the roof. Those three rang full when tapped. They were the sand-coloured petrol cans. The four pale blue ones, mounted two on each side, held water. There were two petrol cans in the front nudge bars, and one at the back. The two at the front were empty.

Villiger came down from the roof. "Probably had not got round to them yet," he said when Gallagher told him. "What about yours?"

At that moment, Lauren called from the roof of the other Rover: "All full!" She began to climb down.

Nbwale strode up with wrestler's gait. "Water cans full. Petrol can at the back empty. Two at the front full."

"The cans hold thirty litres," Gallagher said to Villiger. "That gives me, with the full tank, a range of about six hundred kilometres, give or take a kilometre or two. I'm assuming thirty litres to every hundred kays we do on this kind of terrain, if everything goes well."

"My tank was also full, but with two empty cans, I've got less range."

"We'll share. That should still give us close to six hundred kilometres together. We're going south, so even in country as big and empty as this, we're bound to find a homestead or something."

"If nothing goes wrong."

"There's always the chance that it will."

Sumner said: "So you're saying we can make about four hundred miles with the gas we've got?"

"Yes. And if it appears that we're using up more than expected, we may have to abandon one of the Rovers and use its petrol. Any luck?" he called to Paula Browne.

She poked her head out of a window. "Sorry. Nothing here."

"Well, there was always the possibility. Let's see what weapons you've got," he added to Villiger.

In addition to the Ingram, the Valmet, Sumner's Uzi and Villiger's AK-47, for all of which there was plenty of ammunition, they discovered some blooker rounds.

"I thought maybe they were grenades," Sumner said.

"They are," Gallagher told him.

"Never seen grenades like that before." There was almost a challenging note in Sumner's voice, as if he were reluctant to give credence to anything Gallagher said.

"If they are grenades," Parguineau began, "how can they be used?"

Gallagher smiled tightly. "I've got just the thing in my Rover. More rounds too."

They next checked the food. The combined stocks might just about make do for eight people if they were very careful, and if nothing went wrong.

"Which means we have no margin for error," Gallagher said.

Lauren said: "Well, we've got plenty of water at least."

Gallagher nodded without comment. Villiger drew him to one side.

"You don't seem particularly thrilled," the Afrikaner said quietly.

"It shows? Something's not quite right, but I don't know what it is."

Villiger's eyes were speculative. "I take it you would not like the others to know this."

"Absolutely."

Smallson had been searching in vain for a map, and almost in desperation, he lifted the material covering one of the spare wheels that were fixed upright in each rear corner of the Range Rover.

A folded map fell out.

"I have found one!" he shouted.

Everybody rushed forward. Paula Browne decided to brave the naked heat and joined them in the shade of the Range Rover.

Gallagher hung the map against the side of the vehicle. As it unfolded itself another, smaller map fell to the ground. Lauren picked it up.

The bigger map was to a scale of ten kilometres to the centimetre, and covered the western third of the state of South Australia, stretching from the Northern Territory border all the way down to the coastal cliffs of the Great Australian Bight.

They stared disbelievingly at the vast expanse of emptiness dominating the map. Two tracks came down from the north, one passing south of an elevation marked Bowden Hill, the other zigzagging southwards to join it at a T-junction from where it curved slightly towards the south-west. This track was in turn met at another T-junction by a third coming down from the north-west. This was marked Cheesman's Junction, the same name as a peak some ten kilometres away. From Cheesman's, the track ran crookedly south-eastwards, deep into the Great Victoria Desert for another two hundred and forty kilometres, before ending at another track that bisected the state in an east-west direction, to disappear off the map into Western Australia.

A hundred and ten kilometres west of that junction, a new track began, describing a shallow curve to the west as it headed southwards and across the even more featureless Nullarbor Plain, to the town of Cook that seemed to straddle the lone rail track that scoured the Plain. Cook was the only sign of human habitation marked along the entire route. On that last section, there were three wells marked at the top, close to the track. Further south, about eighty kilometres north of Cook and on the Nullarbor itself, was something called a rockhole. That was the extent of possible available water.

Sweet Jesus, Gallagher thought. The two Range Rovers would never make it to Cook. There just wasn't enough petrol; but all things being equal, one would with the extra fuel.

It was Paula Browne who finally put into words what they were all thinking. "My God!" she exclaimed. "We've got to cross *that*?"

"It's the only route we've got," Gallagher told her.

"Perhaps it is the wrong map," Nbwale suggested.

"I've a feeling it's the right one. Besides, the complex is marked on it."

Sumner peered. "There's nothing there."

Gallagher pointed to a crossed circle marked about fifty kilometres due north of Bowden Hill. "There."

"That could be anything. Could be another hill."

"Gallagher's right," Villiger said abruptly.

Gallagher said: "We're going to continue south, Mr Sumner, until we get past Bowden Hill. Soon after that, we should come upon that first track. If I'm wrong, you can have a good laugh."

"What's so funny about being lost?"

Gallagher said patiently: "If you glance to your left, Mr Sumner, I think you'll find a shape dancing on the horizon. That's Mount Crombie." He pointed at the map. "Here. We must be closer to it than this one to the north which is higher at a thousand and seventy metres, but which we can't see. Mount Kintore. Here."

"So you can read figures and names on a map."

Gallagher was still patient. "I'm fixing our position. We've been going for an hour or so, and the trip meter says we've done over thirty-five kilometres; which is not bad on this terrain." He was speaking to everybody now. "Bowden Hill should be only about fifteen kilometres away. A kilometre or so after that, we should hit the track. Once we're on tracks, if we can keep up an average of about twenty-five to thirty, we should make Cook, allowing for night stops...."

"Night stops!" Sumner was incredulous.

"Mr Sumner ... I don't know any more about this terrain than you do, and in normal circumstances I would not go near this desert with what we have. We haven't even got shovels. Suppose we strayed into sinking sand during the night? Or hit a half-buried rock, or a dead stump because we didn't see it in time? And suppose the following Rover did not get enough warning and ran into the other one? That's only a small example of the things that could go wrong. My God, it could happen during the day. At night we would simply be multiplying the risks."

"And what about those goddammed terrorists? Won't they be coming after us at night too? They'll know this route."

"The desert will be no kinder to them. We've got the faster vehicles. Besides, there's something else you seem to have overlooked. At night, our lights would give us away for miles."

Sumner shut up, and Paula Browne looked at him as though he were something crawling at her feet, before saying to Gallagher: "Isn't twenty-five kilometres a little slow?"

"Not as an average speed. You see, we'd need to do bursts of perhaps even as much as seventy or eighty, if the ground permitted it, to keep that up for the whole distance."

"So how long do we need to get to Cook?" Parguineau asked in his heavily accented English.

"With luck, and two night stops, about three days."

"But you're reckoning on nearer four," Paula Browne said.

"I hope we won't need four, because we've got to outrun any pursuit before Harding gets back. That will mean the gunship, otherwise; and there's no way we're going to outrun a helicopter. One other thing. At some stage, we're going to have to abandon one of the Rovers. There's not enough fuel for both of them to make it. But we've got to burn off some weight, so we might as well travel as comfortably and as far as we can to that time. Let's get back in."

As the others began to climb into the Rovers, Gallagher looked at Villiger. The Afrikaner paused, waiting, then followed as Gallagher walked a little distance from the vehicles.

"You are still worried," Villager said.

"Radios."

"What?"

"Radios," Gallagher repeated. "Do you have one in your Rover?"

"No."

122

"Neither have I. Those are supposed to be field research vehicles," Gallagher said. "In this country, you don't go for a piss in the bush without a radio of some kind, in case you get lost. Why aren't field research vehicles crawling with communications?"

"Like the empty cans, they hadn't got round to it." Villiger smiled tightly. "Man, they didn't expect the things to be out in the desert today."

"Perhaps. Perhaps. Keep a good look-out all the same."

Villiger nodded. He was enough of a professional to take Gallagher's feelings of uneasiness seriously.

From where he sat in the Rover, Sumner watched Villiger's nod. "That nigger sure likes to give orders."

From the front, Parguineau looked around. "Why do you hate the Negroes so much?" He had his own thing about Algerians and was interested.

"I've got nothing against them."

"As long as they know their place," Paula Browne commented sarcastically.

At that moment Villiger climbed in. Sumner said nothing more. Paula Browne rummaged for one of three crumpled half-smoked cigarettes she had saved.

"Mind if I smoke, anybody? I'll hang it out the window."

"Go ahead," Villiger said to her, and started the engine. The clock on the dashboard told him the stop had lasted fifteen minutes.

He saw the other Range Rover start to roll and pick up speed. He went into gear and followed suit.

In the computer room of a large building in Rostrevor, in east Adelaide, a man said to his woman colleague: "That's odd. Look at that. The HA 3600 at the Kintore Research Station's gone off."

She looked. "Is Sir Alex up there?"

"No. Crofton flew him down yesterday or the day before. He took off for London."

"Where's Crofton?"

"Perth. He took the MD and two of his boys there for some kind of conference. I know Sir Alex doesn't always let us know who he takes up to the Station, but you'd think they'd at least warn us if they're messing about with the computer. We do have to look after the bloody thing, after all."

"Do you want to check?"

The man thought for a moment. He sighed. "This is bloody awkward, you know that? If I contact them and there's nothing wrong, I'd look bloody silly."

"If, on the other hand," she added for him, "something is wrong and you don't get in contact....." She left the rest hanging.

123

He sighed again. "All right, Merien." He picked up a phone, pressed a series of buttons. "The HA 3600 at Kintore has gone off," he said into it. "Try and get them, will you? Call me back when you find out what the bloody hell's going on up there." He hung up, looked at Merien. "Dinner tonight at Maggie's? I thought you might like that, your just being back from England...."

She had just returned after three years with Harding International's main London office. "Hmm. A Victorian evening. I might be persuaded." She smiled at him.

He felt pleased with himself. It was the first time he'd asked her out and he had not really expected her to accept. The problem with the HA 3600 was already beginning to recede in his mind as the promise of the evening ahead gained ascendance.

Flyboy woke from a dream of strafing a VC village at nought feet. He stood up, flushed the lavatory, secured his trousers and stepped out. On the back of his T-shirt was printed a slavering vulture with the caption: "Patience my ass...." He put on his denim waistcoat as he walked.

For no particular reason, he wandered into the communications room and was in time to hear: "Adelaide calling Kintore. Who's crooked the HA 3600?"

Flyboy went to the transmitter. "Say again?"

"Who's pissing about with the computer? It's gone off."

Not knowing what the hell was going on, Flyboy said: "Hold."

He left the room in a rush, sprinted to the computer room. He saw the dead machines.

"*Shit!*" His heart began to beat faster. He knew just enough about computers to make hunting for the power source his first priority. It didn't take him long to find out what had happened.

"*Shit!*" he said again, agitated now as he reconnected the plugs. He ran back to the communications room. "It's all right now," he said calmly. "We were just doing a test." He broke transmission. "*Shit!*" he said for a third time and dashed out, heading for Marika's room.

He did not relish the idea of possibly disturbing her love-making but liked even less the chance that something serious had gone wrong without his informing her about it. He banged on her door.

"Marika!" Receiving no reply, he banged on Gallagher's. It jerked open under the pounding of his fist. He pushed it open, looked in at the empty room.

She must have taken him topside, Flyboy decided. He'd check the captives first, before looking. He ran along the corridors, wondering at the absence of people. His stomach tightened as he rounded the corner leading to the captive-room. No guards! And the door open.

Dreading what he would see, he entered. The room was empty, save for the bodies of Selini and the Jordanian. A thrill of fear went through him. He'd been asleep! Marika would tear into him.

"Holy shit!" he said softly.

He left the bodies where they were, assuming they were both dead. He ran, heading for the hangar. The horror of discovering the Range Rovers gone was only partially assuaged by the fact that his beloved gunship was not damaged. He inspected it carefully to make certain, all the while dreading the coming meeting with Marika.

This was disaster, completely upsetting the plans that had been made. The mass break-out had not been expected this soon. They had to be stopped, no matter what. Flyboy did not like the look of what the future held if they weren't. He wondered if there was the death penalty in Australia.

He could not even escape in the Huey. With its range of just four hundred miles, it was virtually useless in a country this big with the sea as its frontier. Besides, even if he were able to escape, Marika would come after him. He was an ace gunship pilot, but on the ground, against Marika, he'd have as much chance as a goat hunted by a tigress....

In the computer room in Adelaide, the phone rang. The man picked up the receiver.

"Yes," he said into it. "We're back in business. The monitors are going. What?" He laughed. "American, was he? Well, they always like fiddling with things." He laughed again at a joke the person at the other end had made. "Well, thanks. Good on you, mate."

"So everything's all right," Merien said as he hung up.

"Yes. Seems Sir Alex has another bunch of scientific guests up there that he hasn't told us about. Getting to be a habit with him."

"He pays the cheque. He can do what he likes."

"It's all the same to me. I'm just glad I didn't have to rush up there early tomorrow to find out what was wrong with HA3600, seeing I'm the resident expert on it." He grinned. "We might have been forced to give Maggie's a miss."

"But we won't, will we, now?" Her smile held the suggestion of promise.

The computer's temporary shut-down was soon forgotten.

Flyboy stomped back down the spiral staircase. Neither Marika nor Gallagher was topside. He hurried to the Mess, stared in shock at the dead man from whose mouth blood had congealed to the floor, and at the bespattered wall. This was beginning to look like a forward base after the Cong had hit it.

"*Marika!*" he shouted.

He went back to her room. She was just coming out of the door, zipping up her jumpsuit, as he approached. She looked sleepy. He hesitated. So they'd been in there, after all. They must have had a very long session of it and, worn out, gone into a deep sleep that even his hammering had been unable to disturb.

Marika yawned; grimaced, rubbing her neck. "Ooh, I must have slept in a bad position," she said drowsily. "Those beds were definitely not made for two. Flyboy, have you seen Gordon?"

And Flyboy felt the dread descend upon his mind.

III

She sat lovingly cleaning her M16, her face white, her nostrils pinched with rage and humiliation. The hands that attended to the bits and pieces of the weapon were, however, absolutely steady. She squinted down the bore. At least they hadn't taken her favourite.

The others stood or sat around the Mess, warily watching.

She had called them back from the dog hunt, saying nothing on the air to arouse the suspicions of any ears that might accidentally have broken in on the transmission. In a coldly enraged voice, she had told them what had taken place, when they had returned. She had not recalled Cyrus and the other two, wanting them to remain exactly where they were.

As she cleaned the weapon, she composed in her mind a message that would tell Cyrus that Gallagher had escaped with the rest of the captives, yet would sound innocuous to any unwanted listeners on the airways.

Flyboy was feeling greatly relieved. His nap in the toilet was a puny thing in comparison to what Marika had allowed to happen to her and as yet she had said nothing about it. That was no guarantee that he had escaped her wrath; but he was determined to improve his chances by carrying out whatever task he was set with total, professional efficiency. He could hardly wait to take the gunship up.

He knew that the others were all thinking that Marika had jeopardized everything because she'd allowed herself to be conned into getting laid. They also knew that had any of them been responsible for a similar incident, Marika would have been utterly ruthless with the person concerned. They knew, however, that she was fully aware of what was going on in their minds, and that a terrible vengeance would be wrought upon Gallagher. Most significant of all, they knew that their only chance of coming out of this alive was with Marika. No one would consider challenging her leadership, even supposing there was anyone who would dare do so.

Watching her meticulously cleaning the weapon with silent

concentration, Flyboy was glad not to be in Gallagher's shoes. He vividly remembered hearing from Selini what had happened to Serge — Marika had shot him five times in the balls out there in the desert, and had stood watching him while he'd crawled about on the hot ground, begging to be put out of his misery. She had waited a long time before finally shooting him between the eyes. Flyboy, without realizing it, covered his groin with his hands. Crossing Marika was suicidal folly.

She laid the rifle down and looked at the faces about her. Her eyes settled briefly on Selini, who was now completely recovered from Gallagher's blow.

He could have killed me, Marika thought, bemused, *yet chose not to*. But it made no difference. He had betrayed her. He would be made to pay. *So go, Gordon Gallagher. Run with your spoilt American girl, who is not as pure as you would believe.*

"They will not get far," she said finally. Her voice was controlled, the green eyes like deep, stagnant pools. "This is not exactly what we planned, but the Range Rovers were already prepared. Things will happen earlier than was intended, with some changes. That is all. We shall still have our hunt." She paused. "I make no excuses. I allowed my guard to relax. I am responsible for not having Gallagher killed. Now that he has chosen to go with them, he will die with them." She spoke quietly, lending even more deadliness to her words.

Selini, in an attempt to share some of the blame, said: "He fooled us all, Marika."

"But you did not all sleep with him, did you? *Did you?*" The heat of Marika's rage and the pain of her humiliation coalesced into a savage fury that glared out of the green eyes.

They stared back at her, none daring to pass comment.

"Alex would not want to miss the hunt," she continued, her voice once more calm after its momentary burst of passion. "We must send word to him."

"How?" Inge, the thin mouse with the vicious expression, queried. "We cannot reach him the normal way without telling every policeman in the world where we are."

"Crofton," Marika said. "Crofton will fly to England and get him. The jet is very fast. Three days should be enough. Crofton is due to be here tomorrow morning. I shall tell him then. Gallagher will still be out there when Alex gets back. He'll want the old man for himself, and that stupid girl. But Gallagher is mine, and I want you all to remember that. I shall shoot the person who shoots him; even Alex."

As her green eyes surveyed them, they knew she meant every word.

"Now go and prepare yourselves. We shall not go after them tonight. The morning is time enough. We know where they'll be."

"What about the weapons they've taken?" someone asked.

Marika actually smiled. "We did not expect them to take weapons.

But this makes it more exciting, no?" The tigress was ready for the hunt. "Flyboy, you will wait for Alex."

Picking up her M16, she went to the communications room to contact Cyrus.

"Station calling Cy."

"I'm here."

"We've lost the dingoes."

An exclamation came over the air. "What?" Cyrus was canny enough not to say more.

"The two bitches, and all the males. The leader is with the pack. We want you to intercept but not destroy them. We want the leader alive for study. But be careful. Dingoes have sharp teeth." She ended the transmission.

She went to her room, removed her clothes, got out the cello. The long, drawn-out note followed by the triplets and crotchet of the opening measures of "Death and the Maiden" echoed along the corridors as she began to play. She put a lot of feeling into it.

"First time I've ever heard her play before a kill," Flyboy said musingly to himself. It seemed to him that the sound was reaching out, searching for Gallagher.

"Does that message mean what I think?" Johnson was the first to speak. "They've all hopped it?"

"Yep," Cyrus answered.

"Not what we had in mind, was it?"

"Nope. Not that it really matters. The more the merrier."

"What's she mean by 'leader', I wonder. The South African?"

"Think again. How did she sound to you?"

"Pretty bloody pissed off, I'd say." Johnson stared at him. "Not Gallagher!"

"Give the man a prize."

"I don't believe it! *Gallagher*? The marshmallow soldier. Never."

"He played one hell of a close game. Fooled Marika all to hell. That takes some doing. Shit. He ripped off Marika and is loose. That's some marshmallow."

The Libyan spoke softly. "She said: 'Dingoes have sharp teeth.' She means they have taken guns. Yes?"

Cyrus nodded. "She means that all right. She wants Gallagher, the old man and the girl kept alive. The rest...." Cyrus shrugged.

"But can they use the guns?"

Cyrus stared at the Libyan. "Hey ... not scared, are you?"

The Libyan felt insulted. His eyes grew hot. "No! I am afraid of no one."

"I used to hear guys say that in Vietnam. They're mostly dead now," Cyrus said casually.

128

Johnson stepped in, to prevent the Libyan's misplaced feelings of injured pride from taking things further. Being cooped up in the stationary Landrover wasn't helping.

"Villiger will be handy with a gun," he said quietly, "and the Frenchman ... Paragua-whatsisname. He's an ex-para. We'll just have to see about Gallagher. He didn't do too well with us that last time, Cyrus."

"I had my suspicions, but in the end he had me believing it. But it really doesn't matter." Cyrus grinned tightly. "They won't know what hit them. We'll wait here for them to come to us. There's no other way for them to go. They have their map." He laughed.

He reached behind him to pick up one of the three blookers he'd brought. He broke it open, loaded it. He replaced it and did the same with its twin. He repeated the performance with the third one.

"Don't forget," he said to the Libyan. "I want a loaded one in my hands until I tell you to stop. Just keep them coming nice and smooth."

The Libyan nodded, his eyes expressionless.

Johnson said evenly: "We had a nice thing going with Harding and Marika. It was better than being shot at in some banana republic that usually couldn't afford to pay you for the privilege."

"We'll still have it," Cyrus said determinedly. "I'm not going to throw away three of the best money-making years I've ever had. No, man. I'm not going to let any dude blow this deal for me. You can bet your sweet ass on it."

In Perth, Crofton looked out over the Swan River from the balcony of his very comfortable room on the twentieth floor of the hotel on Riverside Drive. Barely two years old, and tastefully designed, the hotel was owned by Harding International. The executives Crofton had flown over were still in the main conference room, heavily engaged with their talks on a proposal for increased investments in one of Harding's bauxite interests near Jarrahdale. They'd be at it well into the night, he knew.

Normally, this would be of little interest to him. The workings of Harding International meant nothing to him outside his piloting of the Cessna. But today, having to wait for the conference to end before he could fly again served to irritate him. Not for the first time, he wished Harding had left them to use another company aircraft in the normal way, instead of pressing the Citation into service because it happened to be available.

In the morning, Crofton had planned to fly up to Kintore with a load of marrons – the Western Australia freshwater lobsters – that had been ordered for those people up there. Harding certainly knew how to look after his own, and he, Crofton, had been no exception.

129

His hotels, always of good standard even where there were none owned by the parent company, were paid for. His salary, which would be the envy of many an airline captain, had enabled him to buy a large, sumptuous flat in London's St John's Wood. For the same money he could have bought himself a massive house in one of the home counties; but as a confirmed bachelor, the idea of settling down with a wife and two and a half kids did not appeal to him. He was doing quite nicely, thank you, with his varied and steady stream of transient ladies, and his red, three-litre Porsche Turbo.

Now all that was threatened by the presence of Gallagher. If he were wrong, Crofton would end up antagonizing those dangerous people at Kintore, something he had no relish for. Yet if he were correct and did nothing about it....

He sighed. He had supped with the Devil, and now it began to appear that payment of some kind was about to fall due. He had one choice open to him within which to resolve his dilemma. He would have to speak to Harding; and there was only one way to do that safely.

Gallagher said to Lauren: "That smaller map that dropped out when I opened the large one...."

"I've got it right here. Want to look at it?" She held it out.

"Yes. It might show us something missing on the other one. If you can hold it just about there," he indicated the centre of the dashboard, "I'll glance at it from time to time."

It was about foolscap size and was folded once across the middle. He waited as she shifted in her seat to lean across and spread the map open by its top edge with the forefinger and thumb of her left hand, against the dashboard. This leaning position served to accentuate the trembling of her breasts, in response to the motion of the Range Rover over the harsh ground. A wisp of hair had come away from the loose gather at the back of her head, to hang across her right cheek and rest on the top of her nose. She wrinkled her nose, shook her head. The wisp of hair came back. She reached for it with her free hand, tucked the hair behind her ear. Gallagher, glancing at her just then, found he wanted to see her do that again and again. The pleasant smell of her came tantalizingly to him.

"Thanks." He looked quickly at the map. He was going to find it difficult to ease his conscience, he knew, after what had happened with Marika.

He didn't see the widening of Lauren's smile as he concentrated on driving the Rover across the hardy, ubiquitous clumps of spinifex. A few glances later, he was able to pick out the salient features easily.

It was a photo-relief representation of the entire northern part of South Australia, from Hawker, moving northwards to beyond the

130

borders of Queensland in the top right-hand corner, with the rest covered by that of the Northern Territory. Roads and tracks had been etched upon it, and some of the larger towns had also been printed on, but they were all within the range areas of the eastern part of the state. Gallagher's eye flitted over the strange-looking names, reading them off in his mind: Marree, Andamooka, Oodnadatta. Then he saw Woomera, a little to the south-west of Andamooka. He remembered from his air-force days that this was the rocket town.

His eyes took in the western section of the map and saw duplicated there the route on the larger map. He could not know, however, that where the track from Cheesman's Junction ended, instead of turning right, he could turn left where, only eighty-nine kilometres later, he would find people at Emu. From Emu, a track went south to Maralinga, another going east to Mabel Creek. He could not know about them because those tracks had been carefully painted out with mapping ink.

"There's the whole picture," he said to everyone. Smallson and Nbwale had also been looking. "It looks as if we picked the correct route, after all. There's nothing going east and nothing going south except this one." He pointed to the track going towards Cook.

Far to the east, and well out of reach across too much desert, the Stuart Highway came down from the north, running through the middle of the state, all the way south to Port Augusta.

Gallagher looked at it wistfully. People and safety. It might as well have been on the moon.

Lauren said: "Both maps say we're in an Aboriginal Reserve. Maybe we'll see some. Don't they know a lot about the desert? They may know places that are not on the maps."

"They've got too much sense to go wandering about a place like this, even with their skills. Much as I'd like their help, I don't want them killed. Marika's people would certainly do that if they caught them with us." Gallagher stared out at the forbidding landscape. "Some reserve. OK, Lauren. Thanks." He nodded for her to put the map away.

"You should not be surprised, Mr Gallagher," Nbwale said. "It is historically inevitable." Nbwale spoke perfect Oxford-accented English. "As with the Indians in America, and the recent charade of the Homelands in South Africa, so here. You should not be surprised."

"It's not surprise that I feel. Sadness, perhaps."

"Ah."

This had the effect of bringing down a silence that lasted for a good half-hour, before Lauren spoke again.

"There's a section marked Commonwealth Prohibited Area," she began. "Why is that?"

"They test weapons there," Gallagher answered. "Or used to."

"You seem to know about these things," Nbwale remarked. "Among others," he added drily.

"Ah, well."

Nbwale smiled to himself. "Nevertheless, I am most grateful for what you have done, though it's most unfortunate about some of the company we must share this ordeal with."

Gallagher knew he was talking about Sumner and Villiger.

"If we're going to get out of this alive," Gallagher said, "we're going to need each other."

"Marriages of convenience."

"Look. In normal circumstances, none of us would be seen dead together." Out of the corner of his eye, Gallagher saw Lauren bite her lower lip and look out of the window. He hadn't wanted to make it such a bald statement, so he added: "We just didn't move in the same orbit." He knew she was remembering her original aloofness.

"It was a shrewd move, choosing Villiger to act as your second-in-command, so to speak."

"Not really. He was the logical choice."

"Ah, yes. Logical. In his own country, and I use the term advisedly...."

"You mean South Africa is not his country?"

"He happens to share it with just a few other people," Nbwale said mildly. "In his own country," he repeated, "he has quite a reputation."

Gallagher did not doubt that Nbwale was well aware of Villiger's purpose on the plane.

"You can't bring another war here. We've already got one. I repeat: we need each other."

"Do you seriously believe Villiger will call a truce?"

"It's a funny thing, but I do."

Lauren turned from her scrutiny of the desert. She said to Nbwale: "Why should you need a truce with Villiger?"

Nbwale gave a world-weary sigh. "Ah! The innocence of the well-insulated North American. My dear young lady, Villiger was on that plane for one purpose ... to kill me." He chuckled at her widening eyes. "You may believe me."

"Are you South African?" she asked Nbwale.

"No ... but I am one of those in my country who has made no secret of his sympathies for certain elements down there. Those sympathies have earned me a death warrant. Mr Villiger is a secret policeman, and mine own executioner." Nbwale was theatrical about it. He even grinned.

She turned to look at the desert again. "My God," she said softly. "Haven't we got enough trouble?"

"This is the real world, Miss Tanner." Nbwale's words were

132

softened slightly by the gentle way in which he spoke. "It is never pleasant to find out, wherever you may be at the time."

"I've already seen the real world," she said with surprising intensity.

Smallson, who had remained silent throughout, knew what was going on in her mind and watched her anxiously.

Silence descended once more upon them. Not long afterwards, they saw Bowden Hill.

In the second Range Rover, Paula Browne said: "Looks like we found that hill. Seems he knows what he's doing, wouldn't you say, Sumner?"

Sumner glared at her. She laughed, and struck one of the crumpled cigarette stubs between her lips. She flicked the lighter she'd had returned to her in the captive-room. It was solidly plated in gold and had been a birthday gift from her third husband. She lit the stub, shut the lighter with a snap. She stared at it thoughtfully, turning it over in her hand; then she gripped it briefly before putting it down on the seat next to her. She took a couple of puffs, then pinched the stub out.

"Never know how long they'll have to last," she said to no one in particular.

As the vehicles approached the hill, the ground changed perceptibly. The low clumps of spinifex had become more sparsely distributed, and within those spaces the ground was littered with small red, brown and black stones and pieces of translucent quartz, all polished smooth by centuries of wind-blown sand. The Range Rovers rumbled over them as they glinted in the sun.

"Look at that!" Lauren exclaimed. "Aren't they pretty?"

"Gibber," Nbwale said.

"Pardon?"

"Stony sections of desert are called gibber."

"You know about deserts, then?" Gallagher asked.

"My country borders on one, but I'm no expert. However, the closely spaced striations on the map seem to indicate we'll be going into dunefields."

"Well, as long as the tracks are passable we should be all right."

They passed Bowden Hill, rising to their right. Two kilometres later, they hit the track. Everyone gave a little cheer as Gallagher turned the Range Rover right, and on to it. In the following vehicle, Villiger pursed his lips, nodded to himself as if in approval.

Paula Browne said: "You're kind of silent, Sumner."

"We're a long way from home base," Sumner remarked indifferently.

"Now what made me think I'd hear anything better?" she asked herself sarcastically.

They'd travelled along the track for about fifteen kilometres when Gallagher suddenly understood what had been nagging at him.

"Ambush!" he mouthed softly.

He pumped the brakes to warn Villiger, then brought the Range Rover to a halt.

"Wait here," he said to the others, taking the bigger map as he left.

"Now what?" Sumner began as he watched Gallagher approach.

Paula Browne cut him off. "Don't say anything, Sumner," she pleaded wearily. "Please."

Gallagher had reached them. "See you a moment?" he asked.

Villiger climbed out, followed him to the shaded side of the Rover. Gallagher hung the map against the side, the way he'd done previously.

"I know what's been worrying me," he said. "Too easy. It was too easy a getaway. I don't mean they stood around and watched us go. I think something went wrong. We went at the wrong time. The Range Rovers were for a definite purpose."

He went on to tell the Afrikaner about the Von Dietlingers, the Lamoutiers and the gunship.

Villiger swore in Afrikaans when Gallagher had finished; the brutal-sounding language jarred Gallagher's psyche.

"So you think they were planning to send some people off, just like the Lamoutiers and the German family?"

"Yes. Marika told me there would be no more hunts until Harding returned. But I'm not so sure now. It's likely they would have had a small one, to amuse themselves until he came back for the grand finale, gunship and all. It sounds mad, but that's what I think. I also think the map was deliberately planted."

"I'm listening," Villiger said.

"Then there's Cyrus." Gallagher looked about him. "I feel that he's out there somewhere. Marika will have woken up by now. She may or may not have called the others in. But Cyrus?" He paused. "I don't know. It's a feeling." He pointed a finger at the first junction on the map. "In six or seven kilometres, we come to this junction near Dry Hill; then there's Cheesman. Two good places for ambushes."

Villiger said nothing for a while. He peered closely at the junctions. At last he said:

"According to this, there should be a plain of sorts at Cheesman, about fifteen kilometres across; and one at Dry Hill, about a kilometre. Open country's not much good for an ambush."

"But you don't think the idea is crazy."

"After what has happened, nothing would seem crazy to me; but I still don't see how anyone's going to mount a bloody ambush when we may see them for miles."

"We don't know there isn't cover. I'm not sure I trust the map now, but it's all we've got. One thing is certain: they'll come after us. I know Cyrus is waiting out there. We've got to get past him if we're to get beyond range of that gunship."

"They might have fitted extra tanks."

"Thanks for cheering me up."

"We must consider that."

Gallagher knew the South African was talking sense. "Of course."

He looked up and down the track, its loosely mixed surface of small stones and red earth seeming to turn ochre in the lowering, still hot sun of the late afternoon. The only things distinguishing it from the surrounding terrain were the furrows along its sides and the absence of spinifex.

"They could also extend the range," Gallagher went on, "by carrying the extra fuel in one of the Landrovers. I only saw four of those, one of which was destroyed with the Lamoutiers. Because I didn't see any more doesn't necessarily mean there aren't any. Pity we couldn't have blown the place up. We might have got their fuel supply."

The Huey, with normal tanks, would cross the point of no return at two hundred miles, or three hundred and twenty kilometres. That was just about halfway to Cook. If Flyboy intended to indulge in his fancy for combat flying — which went without saying — then fuel consumption would rise sharply. It was most unlikely that Harding would risk stranding the Minigun-armed helicopter in the desert for want of fuel; he had not gained control of his vast and expanding global empire by making such fundamental errors.

Villiger stared at the Range Rovers in turn.

"Think they may have doctored them?" Gallagher asked.

"It's likely," Villiger replied thoughtfully.

"Let's see what we can find. Check yours. I'll do mine."

"What's wrong?" Lauren asked from the cab as Gallagher opened the bonnet.

"Just making sure we're all right."

He looked carefully, but found nothing to cause alarm. Villiger's was equally clean. Gallagher thought of something else.

"The supplies. They could have done something to the water, or the petrol," he said.

There was nothing wrong with the water.

He said to Lauren: "We're going to have to use one of the fruit tins. Take the top right off and share the contents between the three of you."

"What is it, Gordon?" she asked as Nbwale reached behind for a tin of peaches which he passed to her. Taking the opener from the glove compartment, she began working on the tin, anxiety in her eyes.

"Just covering our bets."

The opened tin was passed round and, when empty, handed to him.

"Thanks," Gallagher said. Opening one of the petrol cans, he poured some of its contents into the peach tin, rinsed it out, poured some more and looked for signs of opacity or the break-up of its surface consistency.

"What are you looking for?" she asked.

"Water," he answered. There was nothing wrong with the petrol. He checked every can, with the same results.

In Villiger's Rover, Sumner was chafing at the slow process. He kept looking expectantly through the rear window.

"Jesus!" he exclaimed in exasperation. "We're wasting time."

Villiger looked at him coldly. "Shut up."

Sumner was too surprised to say anything.

Gallagher came up, handed Villiger the empty tin. Without a word, the Afrikaner began to check his own supplies. He found nothing wrong.

"Well," Gallagher said. "It may be something else we haven't even imagined, or nothing at all. We'll just have to wait and see." He glanced up at the sky. Not a cloud in sight. "Plenty of daylight still left. We'd better try to get as far as we can before nightfall. I'll slow down just before the Dry Hill junction, to check for an ambush."

Villiger did not argue. "OK." He would have done the same in Gallagher's place.

Gallagher took the empty peach tin back with him. "Shouldn't litter the desert," he said jokingly as he handed it over to Nbwale to put behind the back seat.

He climbed in, started the engine, and the little convoy moved off at a good speed.

There was plenty of spinifex bordering the junction, but no ambush. The convoy turned left, heading south-west, towards Cheesman.

IV

Some three kilometres after the turn, the track began to slope sharply towards lower ground, eventually bottoming out five hundred metres lower, into an ever-widening plateau which at Cheesman Junction would be a good forty kilometres across, before continuing to widen into what would become the Great Victoria Desert itself. The track curved in an eastward vee for four kilometres before regaining its south-westerly direction, to hug the base of a five-hundred-metre escarpment that stood like a ruined hilltop settlement against the hot sky. A few skeletal mulge trees, looking for all the world like sprigs of emaciated broccoli in the distance, clung tenaciously to its battered flank.

With the sun sinking westwards, the Rovers were in shadow for a few minutes.

About a kilometre before the junction, Gallagher warned Villiger with a brief pump on the brakes before slewing the vehicle to a stop diagonally across the track. Villiger stopped parallel to it.

"Everybody out," Gallagher said, climbing down. "Except you, Jake." He went over to Villiger. "Will you all get out, please?"

Watching him questioningly, they got out, Sumner slowest of all.

Villiger said: "Well?" His eyes were lively with interest.

"I think it could be here." Gallagher felt certain. The tenseness within him must be like that felt by a destroyer captain who *knew* there was a submarine lurking beneath him, even though his instruments did not register its presence. "We're going to change a wheel."

"*What*?" from Paula Browne.

He smiled at her. "Not really. But we'll go through the motions. To Villiger: "Could you point your Rover more towards ours? I want to confuse vision, if anyone's watching."

Paula Browne's voice trembled. "My God! They're here already?"

"Mr Gallagher believes," Villiger told her, "that someone may have already been ahead of us. It just so happens that I agree with him." He climbed into the Range Rover, repositioned it the way Gallagher had asked.

Paula Browne gripped Gallagher's arm. "But how? They couldn't have known we were going to escape."

So he told them, watching the horror mount on their faces as they found out the truth about the Von Dietlingers, the Lamoutiers, the gunship.

Lauren put her hands to her face, trying not to think of the child. Paula rushed to the Rover for one of her cigarette stubs.

"The murdering bitch," Lauren then said, with quiet intensity. "And as for Alex...." She stopped, shook her head slowly.

Only Villiger appeared unmoved, because he had already been told about the hunts.

"If they are there," Nbwale said, "how are we going to get past?"

"First, we change our wheel," Gallagher said.

"All I can see is low scrub," Sumner began hopefully. "There's nowhere to hide a Landrover."

"One of the objectives of an ambush," Gallagher said evenly, moving to the back of his vehicle, "is to ensure that you cannot be seen by your prospective victims." He opened the tailgate and began to work at releasing one of the spare wheels.

Villiger came to help, and together they manhandled the big wheel to the ground.

"We'll go through the motions, without actually doing the change," Gallagher went on, reaching in for the jack. He put that to the ground, then went round the unexposed side of the Range Rover to reach inside for the binoculars.

Smallson, from where he'd remained in the back seat, said: "You think there is an ambush?"

"It's the best place, if they're out there."

"But where could they hide? At this distance, it would not be difficult to see their vehicle."

Gallagher tapped the binoculars with a forefinger. "We'll soon know if they're there."

"But there is nowhere to look."

"That's just it. I think I know just where." He gave the hint of a smile as he moved away.

The Range Rover was rising off the ground. Nbwale was working the jack.

"Stand around in a loose group," Gallagher told the others. "Your legs will give me cover."

They watched him puzzledly as they positioned themselves. Paula Browne seemed to have relaxed a little as she smoked one of her stubs into extinction. Only Villiger, as usual, appeared to realize what Gallagher was about to do.

Lowering himself to the hot ground, Gallagher lay flat on his stomach. He wriggled forward until he was lying in shadow, screened by the five pairs of legs and, in part, by Nbwale's bulk. He propped himself on his elbows, feeling the loose mixture of sand and stones digging into them. He quickly smoothed out the two offending areas, rested his elbows once more. It was more comfortable.

He put the binoculars to his eyes, secure within the knowledge that his position would not be betrayed by a chance glint on the lenses. The binoculars were even more powerful than the pair Marika had previously given him to use, and the distant clumps of spinifex seemed to jump at him, giving him incredibly sharp and detailed vision. He could understand why they had been chosen for use in the helicopter. He wondered whether Flyboy had already realized they were gone.

Gallagher tracked round slowly until the binoculars were sighted upon a particular colony of spinifex. He saw nothing; but he waited, staring at it, waiting for his eyes to pick out the anomalies.

"Why don't we hit them while they're changing the wheel?" Johnson suggested. "We'd be on them before they could do anything."

They had seen the approach of the convoy for some time, and had watched the sudden slewing of the leading Range Rover, followed by the hasty disembarkation.

Cyrus was watching the scene through his own binoculars. They were less powerful than the ones Gallagher held, but they were nonetheless on a par with the ones Marika normally used. His vision, however, was restricted by the hide they had made for the Landrover.

138

"No," he said casually in answer to Johnson's suggestion. "I want them to run for a while. Yeah. I want to see those chickens run." There was no reason at all for Cyrus to feel worried, from his point of view.

Johnson flicked a hand across his face in annoyance. "Bloody flies! Can I have a look?"

"Sure." Cyrus handed over the binoculars.

Johnson put them to his eyes, laughed without humour. "Bet those bastards are scared shitless." The spinifex obstructed his view, but he could see well enough. He returned the binoculars, and brushed a fly away from the tip of his nose.

"Want a look?" Cyrus asked of the Libyan who was sitting quietly in the back.

"There is no need," the Libyan declined. In the gloom his eyes seemed to have taken on a separate identity of their own.

Gallagher stiffened. He thought he'd seen something. He relaxed. No. Nothing yet. *Wait, Gallagher. Let the breath out. Easy, easy.* He felt his body turning into a statue as he relaxed further. Above him, the others moved and talked, as if on another plane. His eyes remained glued to the eye-pieces, the binoculars steady, unmoving in his hands.

Lauren took another of her glances at him, wondering how he could remain so still on that harsh ground. Villiger too had glanced from time to time at Gallagher, noting the other's rock-like stillness. As a hardened professional, he was very impressed with the way Gallagher had handled the situation so far. He was beginning to respect this strangely self-contained man; he who had never felt respect for any non-white before.

On the ground, Gallagher registered in his mind another stiffening of his muscles. He was positive he'd seen something. He waited. The seconds passed. He'd better pinpoint the ambush position soon. A wheel could not be changed forever.

There! No mistake this time. Something like the wave of a hand, between two clumps of spinifex. The movement was repeated, and he recognized it for what it was. Flies were no respecters of ambushes. Gallagher smiled tightly. Who would have thought it? Betrayed by flies. Now he knew what to look for and where to look, it was relatively easy to distinguish the dug-in Landrover from its cloak of concealing shrubbery. It had been expertly done; they must have worked hard and long at it.

"I've seen them," he said quietly, still searching for signs that the Landrover might be preparing to move. "No! Don't stop to look at me, and don't stare out there. Continue with the wheel change."

With the exception of Villiger, they had been about to drop

everything and stare down the track, something that would have given the ambushers all the warning they would have needed.

Gallagher took the binoculars away from his eyes, rolled over once to minimize any chance of being seen, and stood up. He brushed himself down, then looked into their tense faces.

Paula Browne was clearly frightened but she was trying hard not to show it. Lauren's eyes seemed to tell him she had absolute faith in him.

"They're out there," he said, "waiting. A hull-down job," he added to Villiger. "That's why we couldn't see them. Very cleverly done. I suspect Cyrus's hand. He would have learned all about good camouflage from watching the Vietcong."

"How do we take them?" Villiger went straight to the point.

"By surprise," Gallagher replied. "First," he went on, including everyone in the conversation, "we put the wheel back into the Rover as if we've completed the change. Then we rearrange passengers, doing that from this side, where they can't see too clearly what's going on."

"Why rearrange passengers?" Lauren wanted to know. She'd already sensed that Gallagher intended to move her. "Whatever you're planning, I'm staying."

"It's going to be dangerous and I need to lighten the Rover."

"How many people do you need?" She was not going to give up so easily.

"One driver and one person to load the weapons."

"Those funny-looking shotgun things I was carrying?"

"Yes."

"I'm your loader. I can handle shotguns. I used to go grouse-shooting in Scotland with...." She stopped in confusion as she realized what she'd been about to say, and saw at the same time the knowledge in Gallagher's eyes. She tried not to blush, failed.

Of course, he said in his mind. *With Alex Harding*. He saw again the very private something in her eyes and felt once more the certainty that she wanted to tell him about it.

"I'll be your loader," she repeated. "I'm lighter than all the men."

"And I'm lighter than she is." Paula Browne said, offering her services. It had been a brave effort. She was very scared.

"Thanks, Paula, but I think I will take Lauren up on her offer."

And why not? Nbwale was out of the question because of his size. Smallson's age precluded him while there were younger people about. Parguineau was whom Gallagher wanted to do the driving, and Villiger was needed for the second Range Rover. That would have left Sumner. Somehow, Gallagher did not relish the idea of putting his life in the hands of the diehard from Atlanta.

He saw gratitude come into Lauren's grey eyes.

"Mr Parguineau," he said to the Frenchman, "will you drive for me?" Parguineau would not have forgotten how to handle a vehicle in combat.

"Of course," Parguineau said.

"Thank you." To Villiger, he said: "I want you to go ahead of me, and keep straight down the track. They're right at the end of it. You'll be going down their throats initially, but they'll lose all interest in you once they see me break. They'll know then that their ambush has been spotted and will wonder what I'm up to. It will take them a few seconds to get out of that hole. I'm hoping that's all the time I'll need."

The piggy eyes looked at him. "Sure."

"Jake," Gallagher called. "Will you get into the other Range Rover, please?"

They put the wheel away, and everyone except Gallagher, climbed back in, according to the new arrangement. Nbwale found himself in the front seat with Villiger. Neither looked at the other. Villiger started the Rover and drove around the other vehicle, stopping again just ahead of it.

Gallagher walked up to it. "Villiger," he said, "if this thing goes wrong, I want you to...."

"It won't go wrong."

There was no expression on the Afrikaner's face, but Gallagher was pleasantly astonished to receive such a vote of confidence. He did not think Villiger was simply throwing out words. The man really meant what he had said.

Gallagher gave the door of the Range Rover a pat. "Right," he said, and went back to his own vehicle. He climbed into the passenger seat, turned to look at Lauren who was sitting in the back. "Let's see you load those things."

She sat in the middle with a blooker on either side of her, six rounds each lined up neatly. She picked one up, loaded it. She did the same with the other. It was done swiftly.

"Pretty good," he said, smiling at her.

"She has been practising while you were talking to Villiger," Parguineau said.

"I see." He kept looking at her. There was a tiny smile about her lips and he wanted to kiss them. He stayed the impulse.

She saw the intention in his eyes and was disappointed when he did not follow through. She told herself to be patient.

"Right, Monsieur Parguineau," Gallagher said. "Let's go."

Parguineau started the engine, having already familiarized himself with the controls. Ahead of them, Villiger began to move. They followed.

"They're moving," Cyrus said. "OK, Johnson, get ready to start the engine when I tell you." The little convoy was approaching fast. "I wonder why they changed places," he added thoughtfully.

"Maybe to check the wheels. Did we do anything to them?"

"Not that I know of; unless Marika had a little gag up her sleeve. You never know with that chick." Cyrus continued to look through his binoculars. "Soon, Johnson. Soon. They're nearly here." Then he saw the following Range Rover suddenly break to his left. "What the fuck ...? *Jesus! We've been made!*" he shouted. "*It was a con!*" He dropped the binoculars and grabbed a blooker. "Start the engine! Let's get the hell out of here!"

But the Landrover would not start.

Cyrus was screaming now. "*Start the fucking thing!*" He could recognize an attack in the making.

With stunned surprise and a feeling of dread, he heard a sound he had lived with for so long that he could never forget it. A blooker! And Cyrus knew with a terrible certainty just how well he had been fooled by Gallagher. Gallagher's shooting was not going to be anything like the pathetic performance put on for his benefit during the hunt of the Lamoutiers.

The round exploded, showering the trapped Landrover with dislodged earth. Part of Cyrus's mind, as if detached from the part that was screaming for survival, analysed the shot. As an exercise in ranging fire on a concealed position, it was incredibly good shooting. Cyrus knew he was facing someone who was as good as he was himself.

The round had landed close enough to make itself felt, without doing any damage to the vehicle. It did, however, draw blood.

Several waspish things had buzzed through the canvas panels, to buzz out again through the exits they had made. One, though, was stopped in its tracks by the Libyan's back. It ploughed in at an upward angle just below the right shoulderblade, ripping flesh, muscles, veins and an artery, finally lodging itself in his windpipe. The man made a strange coughing, choking sound, trying to inhale as the suddenly released blood flooded undammed within his body. He fell over backwards, fighting for air that was never going to come. His blood choked him to death.

The Landrover still wouldn't start.

Cyrus was screaming with rage, frustration and fear. "*Get this thing moving, you goddam honky dipshit!*" he raged at Johnson. "*Move it! Move it!*"

Johnson bawled back: "Who wanted to dig us into this fucking hole, you black bastard?"

Then the Landrover started. Like a pheasant flushed from hiding by beaters, it raced up the incline out of its lair, shedding dead spinifex like so many feathers. Cyrus was already poking his upper body through the opening in the canvas roof, blooker ready for action in his hands.

Gallagher was waiting. The Range Rover was stationary, waiting to the left of the Landrover's position, broadside on. The passenger door was open and Gallagher stood outside, gripping a freshly loaded blooker.

The Landrover came out of the hole, front wheels momentarily off the ground. Gallagher could see Cyrus's head turning, searching for the target. The Landrover came down jarringly, throwing up a cloud of dust and small stones and forcing Cyrus to brace himself.

Gallagher fired, allowing for deflection.

The Landrover kept going in a straight line. The blooker round exploded against Cyrus's neck, blowing his head completely off. It sailed in a rearward arc, a pulpy comet trailing a wake of red mist that seemed to glisten briefly in the westward-bound sun. The thing hit the ground. It did not even bounce but collapsed wetly upon itself.

Gallagher heard Lauren gag, even as he thrust his hand towards her for the other blooker. She stared numbly at Gallagher's dark, out-thrust hand, the instrument of the terrible death now spent and useless, in his grip. *I must give him the loaded one. I must give him the loaded one. O God! I must give him....*

She took the fired blooker, handed him the other.

He took it, seemed to come to a decision about something, leapt into the Rover and shouted, "Go!" to Parguineau. The Range Rover was moving even before he'd shut the door.

In the Landrover, Johnson felt the warm shower of Cyrus's blood upon him, bathing him. The body was still held upright by the transverse supports of the canvas hood. One hand on the wheel, Johnson reached to pick up his Ingram, fully loaded with thirty rounds, from the central seat of the Landrover. The weapon was already cocked, the skeletal frame of its retractable metal butt fully extended. He used his forefinger to flick forward the safety-catch near the trigger guard, to "fire".

He hauled the Landrover round one-handedly, heading back for the Range Rover. He poked the Ingram out of the window, the butt braced against his right shoulder, even one-handedly in the bouncing Landrover, he knew he could lay down a devastating barrage of .45s if he got close enough.

"Bastards!" he kept muttering. "Bastards!"

His dead companions looked in silent agreement.

He made another sharp turn, and Cyrus's headless body finally toppled and fell wetly across his back. The gaping neck slid downwards as the body at last came to rest with its trunk hanging over the backs of the unoccupied front seats, the neck leaking already congealing blood over the cushions.

"Bastards!" he said again. "this will be for you, Cyrus."

Gallagher watched the Landrover hurtling towards them, knowing what Johnson intended to do. He could see the foreshortened snout of the Ingram, knew what a blast of .45s could do. He'd once seen the effect at close range.

Lauren, he thought. Christ. Why had he agreed to take her?

"Get down, Lauren!" he yelled. "Get as far down as you can!"

She obeyed without thinking, trying to make herself shrink into the floor of the Range Rover.

Gallagher looked quickly at Parguineau. "We've got to get him before he lets loose with that thing. Spoil his aim."

The vehicles danced round each other at a distance. Johnson wanted just one chance for a single run-in. Gallagher wanted his blooker round inside the cab. Damaging the Landrover would not be enough. Johnson might get a burst in before he, Gallagher, could pick up the other blooker.

The vehicles continued to dance round each other, predators seeking an advantage, stirring up the dust with the violence of their passage, engines roaring like maddened beasts from the heart of time past. The desert listened, echoing to their sound.

Parguineau, even with two hands on the wheel, was having his work cut out. Gallagher knew only too well just how skilful Johnson was. The Range Rover, with its bigger engine, was like a bull being harried by a ferocious terrier.

Johnson fired. Emptying half the magazine.

Of the fifteen rounds, nine went wild. Of the remaining six, one went through the left rear panel to flatten itself against the spare wheel; one went through a left rear glass panel and out through the opposite one, describing a path that would have been interrupted by Lauren's head had she not been on the floor; one passed through Gallagher's open window and out through Parguineau's without touching either of them; one smashed a rear light; one came through the rear left panel at 545.45 miles an hour, just above the seat, travelling at a height that would have caused it to smash into Lauren's hip; and the last one grazed Parguineau's right shoulder on the way out.

He grunted, but did not pause in his driving.

"Lauren!" Gallagher screamed. "Are you all right?"

Scared as she was, it warmed her to learn of his anxiety for her safety. "Yes!" she called.

He closed his eyes momentarily in relief. "Parguineau?" he said. "I heard you make a sound."

"A scratch. Nothing more."

"OK. We've got to do it next time," he said.

"Yes. I believe I know how we can get him. You be ready with your mortar," Parguineau went on, referring to the blooker. "The moment will be very swift."

"Right."

Parguineau turned the Range Rover until it was heading directly for the Landrover. Every time Johnson jinked to break and give himself a field of fire, the Frenchman broke with him, going just out of range before swinging back on to the collision course. The vehicles sped suicidally towards each other.

Watching by the other Range Rover, Paula Browne said: "My Christ, why don't we *do* something? We've got guns."

"Too much dust," Villiger answered her. "The target is too unstable, and we might hit the wrong people. Even a sniper would have a job. He'll do it."

"Who? Gallagher or that mad bastard?"

Villiger looked at her unsmilingly. "Gallagher, of course."

No one else said anything. Nbwale, standing a little distance away, watched the combat intently. Sumner had a tiny smile on his lips. Jake Smallson sat in the Rover and prayed silently for the safety of both his granddaughter and Gallagher.

The two vehicles careered towards each other, using up acres of ground in their deadly waltzing, and boiling up the dust about them. Each time the Landrover jinked, the Range Rover would use its greater power to force itself back into the nose-on position. Johnson sometimes spun the Landrover complete to gain space.

On several occasions, Johnson could have tried head-on shots but he knew that, if he missed, he would not get a chance to reload. Driving one-handedly over the rough ground and trying to fire the Ingram accurately at the same time was no easy task. He did not want to waste his next fifteen shots like the first lot.

Suddenly, the Range Rover jinked, this time to the right, bringing itself against the left flank of the Landrover. Accustomed to having his jinks followed, Johnson was taken completely by surprise by the unexpected manoeuvre. He tried to bring the Ingram in, only to get it caught by the windscreen pillar, and he could only stare in terrible resignation at the fleeting glimpse of the gaping mouth of the blooker before it fired.

The round hit him squarely in the face, exploding his head as it detonated in a sheet of orange flame, cooking his disintegrating flesh. The Landrover, careering madly as the body swung the wheel with its weight, teetered on two wheels before finally completing the manoeuvre and rolling over to explode with a loud double crash of sound. It kept going, dragging along on its roof, towing a long tail of flame. Cyrus's blooker rounds exploded like a gun salute.

Parguineau brought the Range Rover to a stop and leaned wearily against the steering-wheel. The whole action had lasted just two minutes.

"You all right?" Gallagher asked.

The Frenchman nodded slowly. "Yes. Yes." He kept his head on the wheel, breathing deeply.

Gallagher looked into the back. "It's all over, Lauren."

She lifted herself gingerly, not daring to believe it. As her head came level with his, he did what he had wanted to do earlier. He kissed her.

He intended it to be a brief, gentle kiss; but she had other ideas. Her arms came up and wrapped themselves about his neck, pinning him to the back of his seat. She returned the kiss with interest. It was nothing like Marika's fierce mouth attack but was a full-blooded affair that sucked sweetly and gently at him.

She pulled back a little to gaze at him, then put her cheek against his. She held on to him tightly. There was nothing they needed to say to each other. They stayed like that for some time.

They parted to find Parguineau looking at them, his expression unreadable.

"I congratulate you," he said to Gallagher, "for an excellent action. You discovered the ambush, destroyed the ambushers and kept us all alive. We are not even hurt."

"You are."

Parguineau shrugged. "I think more damage was done to my shirt."

"Your driving was very good."

"Thank you. It appears I have not forgotten as much as I feared."

"You were afraid?" Lauren was surprised that anyone but she could have been.

"I was afraid I could not do what was expected of me."

"Where you afraid, Gordon?"

"Of so many things, I can't even begin to tell you. Let's have a look at that shoulder of yours," he added to Parguineau.

"It really is ..." the Frenchman began.

But Lauren interrupted him. "I'll look." She moved over to him before he could object.

He eased the shirt off his right shoulder and pulled his arm out of the sleeve. An ugly weal about six inches long tapered from just beneath his neck, gradually widening towards the shoulder before ending abruptly. It looked like an elongated teardrop. The skin had not been broken.

"This is going to be very sore," Gallagher said, "but you were lucky."

Parguineau made light of it. "I have been close to death before."

Leave the shirt off for a while," Lauren said. "Let the air get to it. Try not to break the skin or it might get infected. But you know all about that."

"Yes," Parguineau said, smiling slightly. "I know all about that."

"I'll drive," Gallagher said.

146

Parguineau nodded, and they changed places. The Range Rover had stopped on what was virtually a sandplain, having been taken about a kilometre away from the track by the battle. Gallagher noted the widely spaced dunes, more than a kilometre apart, disappearing into the distance. The dunes were themselves less than a metre high, with broad, flattened tops and dotted with the inevitable spinifex. He knew these were nothing to what would be found in the Great Victoria Desert itself, if what Nbwale had said about the dunefields were true. He hoped they would be able to travel on the tracks, all the way to Cook.

He started the engine.

"Stop!" Lauren called suddenly. "I've got to get out!"

He turned, saw her queasy expression and deduced what was about to happen. Quickly he helped her down.

She ran a short distance, bent over and was violently sick. Going up to her, Gallagher put an arm about her shoulders as she heaved. At last she was finished. She wiped her mouth with the back of her hand, and wiped that on her skirt.

"Ugh!" she said, straightening. "I suddenly had a vision of that head going off...."

"Shhh!" he interrupted gently, turning her round and holding her to him. She came willingly, resting her body against his. "Don't think about it." He kissed her on the forehead.

She laid her head against his chest and he stroked her hair.

She said: "Did it ever make you sick?"

"You'd be surprised how many times," he answered. He smiled at her. "Come on. Let's get back. The others will be wondering."

"I'd like to rinse my mouth," she said as they walked back to the Range Rover.

"Are you all right?" Parguineau called to her.

"Yes. Yes, I'm fine, thank you."

"It happens," he said.

Gallagher freed one of the water cans. "Cup your hands," he told her.

She squatted on her heels and put out her hands. Carefully, he poured just enough water to give her a generous mouthful.

"You'll have to make do with that, I'm afraid." He put the can away.

She scooped the water into her mouth, swirled it around, then spat it out and stood up. "OK."

They climbed into the Range Rover.

"They're taking a while," Paula Browne said. "Maybe they're hurt. We should go see."

"No. They're all right," Villiger said. "The other people never really had a chance to do much."

Nbwale, a short distance away, said loudly enough and with enough meaning for Villiger to hear and understand: "I know some people who could use a man like that." He kept his face turned in the direction of the distant vehicle.

Villiger looked at him but said nothing, turning away again.

"What do you mean?" said Paula Browne.

"Ask Mr Villiger," Nbwale answered, still without looking towards them. "He knows."

She turned puzzledly to Villiger.

Before she could speak, he said: "They're coming back."

V

"Station calling Cy. Station calling Cy."

Marika was in the communications room and Flyboy was with her. She had been calling at intervals for the past few minutes.

"They have got him," she said, her eyes opaque, withdrawn.

Flyboy was sceptical. "No one can take Cyrus. I never met that guy in the Nam but I'd heard about him. The Blooker King. No one can take him."

"Gallagher has." She was sure of it. Her tone left no room for further argument. "Two grenade launchers are missing. Gallagher has paid Cyrus for the Lamoutiers. I am going to tell the others what to expect when we go out after him. Those grenade launchers were the last ones."

Flyboy followed her out, deep in cautious thought. He was almost afraid she could see into his mind. He had noticed the absence of the powerful binoculars – a gift to Harding from an American general – but in the aftermath of the escape had paid scant attention, merely assuming that they must be around somewhere. That weapons had been taken seemed of far greater concern; anyway, had he chosen to inform Marika, there would have been precious little she could have done to inform Cyrus about the binoculars. Having searched for them later, Flyboy had come to the reluctant conclusion that Gallagher had taken them.

Goddam thief, he now thought angrily. He decided to say nothing to Marika about it. He'd tell Harding, by which time Marika would be well away on the hunt.

"Cyrus, Johnson and Kamal are all dead," she told the shocked members of her group without preamble. "Add Ibrahim and Jurgen, and we are already five less, while all of them are still alive."

"Is it Gallagher?" Selini asked.

"Yes. It must be."

148

"Cyrus was very good. Marika, is it possible Gallagher was planted on us?"

"No!" Marika's denial carried more than just a refusal to accept that any security agent could have got past her. "Gallagher was working for no one. I am sure of it. Our plans were too well made. He did come to us by accident. It was unlucky for us ... for *me* ... that he is a man who was trained in our business. Selini, you saw how he killed Ibrahim. Someone taught him how."

"So you believe he is no longer active?"

"I am sure he isn't. But that is not going to save him." Marika's eyes blazed with thoughts of the vengeance she would extract.

"Perhaps we should not go after them," someone suggested, "but wait until Alex Harding returns; then we simply wipe them out with the gunship. We know they won't be going anywhere. Or we can leave them to die in the desert while we disperse, perhaps for six months, a year. We are not in need of funds...." The words died.

"Are you finished, Roberto?" Marika looked dangerously at the Spaniard. "You are our newest member. Are you already too afraid? I picked you because I thought you were better than most. That is how I picked every one of you; for your skil!, for your bravery; for you ability to remain unknown, and untalkative." She had been carrying her M16. Now she lifted it and fired in a single motion. One shot.

Roberto was dead before he hit the floor of the Mess, having been flung across a table by the force ot the 5.56 millimetre bullet slamming into his chest at 2,215.9 miles an hour, at a range of ten feet. It had ravaged his heart on the way out. He took two tables and four chairs to the floor with him.

Everyone's ears were still ringing to the sudden sound of the shot within the room.

"Now there are six less," Marika said into the stunned silence. She looked at the weapon in annoyance. "I have recently cleaned this. Now I shall have to do it all over again. It must be clean for Gallagher." She nodded at the body. "Bury him." She lowered the M16, and walked slowly out.

They all watched her go. They had treated her before with respect and extreme caution. Now, they were truly frightened of her.

Flyboy said: "I never would have figured Roberto for a stupid man." He looked at them in turn. "We're all pretty good. Right? That's why the cops all over the world are picking up the other groups and not us. Now Marika ... Marika is better than all of us. She's a special, and *that's* the real reason why we're still running free. Just remember that no one's going to get us out of here except Marika. Don't even think of taking her out. None of you would live to do it."

Ngoma said, in her East African accent: "No one is thinking of it. But she has never shot one of us before. It is that man Gallagher who has turned her mind, just like the Frenchman Serge."

Flyboy grew impatient. "Aw, c'mon, will you? Roberto was dumb. If he'd done a little thinking, he'd have realized why we can't leave. We planned the hunt. Does anyone want out?"

No one seemed to.

"OK. Next, we don't know how Cyrus and the others died. Suppose Gallagher's got their Landrover? There was nothing wrong with it. Suppose he uses that when he finds out the Range Rovers are going nowhere? This is a new ball game. He's not going to sit there and wait for us to come to him. Before, we would have been hunting some scared people. Now, we've got a guy who seems to know as much as we do. That makes it more interesting." Flyboy grinned. "He wanted to see me fly. Well, he's going to. Yessir." The grin went. "I don't know about you, but I want to be goddam sure they're all dead. Leaving them to the desert is not enough. I want to see those bodies. If just one of them makes it, we're finished, and Harding International goes too; so the man himself is not going to want us out of here unless we do the job we came to do. Don't forget, he's got the plane. Now ... I suggest we get everything ready. Tomorrow's going to be a hard day."

Even as he stopped speaking, they heard the cello moaning along the corridors.

Gallagher drove the Range Rover back on to the track. He had paused briefly near the burning Landrover and had seen three charred bodies extending out of it, two of them headless. Lauren had averted her face, pinching her nose against the stench.

He had not lingered, for fear of more exploding ammunition. Villiger came up to the driver's door. The button eyes were speculative. "That was impressive stuff."

"But a little rusty," Gallagher said, succumbing to a touch of bravado.

Was there a hint of a smile near the Afrikaner's lips?

"If you say so," Villiger said. He looked at Parguineau who had climbed down and had moved round the Rover to join him. "Casualty?"

"A scratch." The Frenchman showed him.

"Lucky."

"We all are." Parguineau nodded at Gallagher. "He sensed the ambush and disposed of it. This is a good man to have. That is why I say we are lucky."

"Your star seems to be climbing ever higher," Villiger said to Gallagher, his expression giving nothing away.

Gallagher looked down at him. "It's a long way to Cook, and they will have checked and found that their Landrover does not answer.

Tell me about my star when we get there."

Everybody had been admiring the bullet holes. Now they came crowding round. Smallson was hugging Lauren, who had climbed down to see how he was.

Paula Browne poked her finger at two particular holes. "Where was Lauren when all this was happening?"

"On the floor, thank God," Gallagher answered.

"You tell her to get there?"

He nodded.

"Do you always think of everything?"

"Not always," Gallagher replied, resisting a smile.

"And I have the horrible feeling there's quite a lot I haven't thought of."

She reached up to pat the elbow he had rested on the door. "You're doing just fine." But she was looking at Sumner who was studying the other bullet holes. She knew he'd heard.

She gave Gallagher another pat and moved away. She was still very scared; by the pursuit she knew would still come, and by the immensity of the landscape they'd have to travel over to reach safety. But her faith in Gallagher was absolute.

Sumner followed her to the other vehicle. There was no one near or in it. She climbed in. He got in with her. She ignored him.

He said, quietly: "You think he's just about it, don't you?"

She looked at him, frowning. "Jesus, Sumner. What's eating you now?"

"Maybe his hair's not like peppercorns," Sumner went on in the same quiet voice, "and his nose is not squashed into his face. Maybe his lips don't look like innertubes, and his skin's not like he's been living in a coalmine, but he's still a goddam nigger to me."

Her eyes had widened progressively at his words. "You're sick. You're a goddam sick bastard. You hate it here so much, why don't you get out and walk?" She began to get out again. "I don't have to sit here and listen to this shit."

He watched her walk away to join the others.

"I don't take orders from niggers," he said to himself.

Villiger was heading back. He got in behind the wheel, turned to look at Sumner.

"Have you two been fighting, man?"

"What?"

"Paula Browne."

"Uh, no. No."

"Good. I think it's too small in here for arguments." The warning was explicit.

The others were returning now. Paula Browne got back in, stiff-faced. Parguineau took his seat in the front.

151

In Gallagher's Rover, everyone had taken their seats.

Nbwale said: "Good thing none of the bullets hit the cans."

"Yes," Gallagher said. "That was a bit of luck."

The three-and-a-half litre, all-alloy V8 rumbled into new life, and as he let in the clutch, Gallagher saw that Villiger was following close behind.

They turned left at the junction, picking up speed. This was a slightly wider track and though the surface appeared to be no better he put his foot down. The Range Rover moved easily along the track, riding the depressions with the aplomb it was designed to display.

Behind the little convoy, the still-smoking Landrover sent its funereal banner into the reddening sky. It was fitting, Gallagher felt, that Cyrus should have died in the same way as the Lamoutiers.

They travelled another sixty kilometres before he was forced to call a halt for the night. It was not quite dark but he felt that to press on till absolute darkness was exposing them needlessly to the possibility of an accident. They moved a few hundred metres off the track to park at the bottom of a low dune whose top barely reached above the Range Rovers. Along its base and midway up its slope, a scattering of low shrubs determinedly thrived.

Gallagher had chosen the site deliberately. He did not expect night pursuit, but anything could happen. Parking well off the track and behind cover would keep them hidden from ground pursuit, as well as giving them time to mount some form of defence.

He got out of the Range Rover, as did Nbwale who went up the dune and down the other slope to disappear into the gathering gloom.

"Don't go too far," Gallagher called. "We don't want to have to look for you in the morning."

The African's voice came back easily. "Nature," he explained.

Gallagher, amused by the demureness of the huge man, walked to the top of the dune. The ground was dark and the sun had long since vanished beneath the horizon; but a red-gold stain smeared the sky, as if the day refused to give in to the coming night without a struggle. There was still plenty of ground heat though there was a hint of coolness in the air. And the seemingly dead desert, Gallagher realized with an old astonishment, had come alive with subdued noises; scurryings, squeaks, rustlings; even the flutter of wings.

"Where did they all come from?" Paula Browne's voice floated up from below.

Someone answered her. Villiger, he thought.

Gallagher watched the shape of Nbwale returning, fascinated as first the man's head, then the rest of his body gradually became silhouetted against the dimming sky. Nbwale stopped, noticed that Gallagher was listening to the night.

"Most people think a desert is dead," Nbwale remarked, "but, as you can hear, it is very far from being so."

"Yes," Gallagher said. He knew enough from a past experience of sitting out with O'Keefe, a night pursuit among the rocks of another desert; but compared to this Australian vastness, that other desert had been a pipsqueak.

"They lie in their strongholds," Nbwale was saying, "beneath the shrubbery, in holes in the ground, waiting out the day. Come the night, they emerge to play."

"Hunt, you mean."

"Isn't that the same thing?"

Gallagher thought the African was smiling, but couldn't tell. "What do they eat?" he asked Nbwale. "You'd think there wasn't enough in this wilderness to feed a single fly."

"There's plenty of food. They eat each other." Nbwale chuckled suddenly. "Imagine. Right beneath our feet, a war is going on. Talking of feet, watch where you put them. Although you would not believe it, to see the terrain by day, there are snakes too. Sixty to seventy per cent of Australian snakes are elapid, that means venomous, of which there are no less than eighty-five species. Some of them are very nasty customers, and there are three especially which will kill you in minutes."

Gallagher controlled the urge to look down at his feet, now part-hidden in the gathering gloom. "How do you know about all this?"

He was sure Nbwale was smiling now.

"In my country," Nbwale said, "I am the Minister of Education. As is natural, but not always the case in many governments, I am a schoolmaster by profession."

"I see. Will we come across any of those monsters you've been talking about?"

"The two deadliest, certainly not. The taipan favours the north, tropical areas, while the tiger snake is mainly a swamp lover. There are still, of course, the mulga snake, the bushmaster and a particular fiendish customer, the death adder. But, as with all snakes, so long as you do not disturb them, they should do you no harm."

"I don't think every snake has read that book," Gallagher said. He had a healthy respect for that particular reptile.

Nbwale laughed as he began to move down the dune. "I'll tell the others to watch where they tread. Are you posting guards?"

"Yes. The five of us. The old man is obviously out of the question, and the women ... well, Paula Browne's still much too scared...."

"And the other?"

"I don't think it's really worth putting her on. We five can split the night into one-and-a-half-hour shifts. That's not too much for each man. We'll be leaving very early, with the dawn."

"May I have the third?"

"I was thinking of asking you anyway."

"That's convenient, then. Where are Sumner and Villiger?"

"Sumner's last, Villiger is second."

"Shrewd. Your weakest man last. He won't fall asleep after a night's rest." Nbwale went down the slope.

In Gallagher's Range Rover, Lauren had been watching Gallagher's silhouette on the dune for some time. He had not eaten, though everyone else, with the exception of Nbwale, had already done so. They had dined on cold, tinned meat, since no fires were to be lit; an apple each, and water drunk out of rinsed cans. No one was allowed more than half a can.

"What's he doing?" she asked of Jake Smallson, not really expecting an answer.

"Thinking, girl. Thinking of how to take us all that distance in one piece. He will do it. He was very good today. So were you. It was a brave thing that you did. I am quite proud."

"I was very scared."

"That is nothing to be ashamed of."

"He knows how to kill very well." She sounded perturbed.

"Lucky for us that he does, or we would all be joining Bannion, the von Dietlingers and the others."

"Oh, I know, Gramps, but...."

"Do not confuse him with those terror people."

"Oh, I don't! How could you think such a thing?"

"Then what is it that disturbs you?"

"I don't want him to like it."

"His kind never will. He walked away from it before. That says much for him. There are many people who have been taught to kill for their country and have not lost the taste for it."

"I want to tell him," she got out suddenly after a short silence.

Smallson knew what she meant. "About New York?"

She nodded. It was dark within the Range Rover, but the glow from the sky outlined her features. "It's important to me."

"Then tell him."

They heard Nbwale speaking, then Paula Browne's frightened "What!" and a sudden scramble into the other vehicle.

Nbwale came up to them. He eased himself behind the wheel.

"What scared Paula?" Lauren asked him.

"Snakes."

"That scares me too. There are snakes here?"

"They can be anywhere. In the desert, they come out at night to do their hunting. I merely told her to watch where she put her feet. There may well not be any within several square miles of us. I merely advise caution."

"Ugh!" she shuddered.

Gallagher came down from the dune. The sky was almost totally dark now. For some reason he'd suddenly thought of Celia; then the thought faded. There was a feeling of something lost but surprisingly little pain. The four days of the hijack had managed to do what eleven months of emotional festering had failed to achieve.

He told the others of the arrangements for keeping guard and was about to go to his own Range Rover when he heard Paula Browne flick her lighter. It did not catch.

"No!" he said sharply before she could try again. "Sorry, Paula. No lights whatsoever. You'll have to do without a smoke till morning."

"You're not serious?" she exclaimed, horrified by the prospect.

"I'm afraid I am. Even the glow of your cigarette or the flash of your lighter can show up for miles. We don't know what kinds of weapons they may have. You'd be giving a sniper with a nightscope a good aiming point."

She hastily put the lighter away. "You don't have to tell me twice."

"Now there's a good cure for smoking," Sumner remarked with nasty humour.

"Ooh, boy! I bet that made your day." Scathingly. "You don't think there's more of them out there already, do you?" she asked of Gallagher.

"I don't know; but I wouldn't like to sacrifice you while finding out."

"Me neither," she said with feeling.

He grinned in the dark. "Sleep well, Paula. You too, gentlemen." He moved away towards his Rover.

"I kind of like that guy, you know," he barely heard her say softly to the men.

He smiled to himself as he came up to the Range Rover. "I've got first guard," he told Lauren. He reached for his M16.

"Bet you haven't eaten. I've saved some of this meat and a little water for you. There's an apple too."

"I'll take them up the dune with me."

She began to get out. "I'll come with you."

"Don't you know about the snakes?"

"I'll walk behind you."

Gallagher doubted whether this would make any difference to any lurking snake, but he saw she was quite determined. "All right," he agreed reluctantly. "But bring the Uzi, just in case there's anybody out there."

She reached in for the weapon, slung it, then picked up the food. Nbwale climbed out.

"Where to?" Gallagher asked.

"Nowhere. I'm going to sleep."

"On the ground?" Lauren was astonished.

"There's no room inside for all of us." Nbwale chuckled. "There's hardly room for me. Whereas out here...." Then as Lauren started to protest he added: "The snakes? They won't trouble me if I don't trouble them."

"Will you know when to get up?" Gallagher asked. "The only clocks we have are in the Rovers."

"I'll know." Nbwale began to lower himself to the ground. Soon, his bulk disappeared.

"Go to sleep, Jake," Gallagher said to the old man, then began to walk up the dune with Lauren, where he showed her how to cock the Uzi.

From behind the other Range Rover, Sumner had watched their shapes move upwards. He seethed with quiet rage.

They sat down on the flattened crest of the dune. The ground was still very warm. There was no wind, but the air temperature felt considerably lower than it probably was. Gallagher knew this was because of the almost abrupt disappearance of the intense heat of the day. There was no high ground close by to trap some of it. It had felt appreciably warmer, for instance, at the base of the dune.

Lauren patted the dune, which was in fact a mound of hard-packed clay, cloaked by a non-shifting surface of coarse sand and grit. "This is comfortable," she said, as Gallagher began to eat. "It might be better to sleep up here."

The idea was attractive. The dune was long enough to give privacy from whoever was standing guard; but Gallagher was worried about spreading the group out. An infiltrator could cut out the exposed person without anyone knowing about it.

She watched him considering the pros and cons of it. She could see him clearly, because the stars were out in their millions now. Their combined glow made the vast landscape eerily beautiful. Lauren felt as if they were marooned on an island far above the earth, surrounded by the intangible gloom.

Somewhere in the night, a yelping wail sounded, to be answered by another, and another.

"What was that?" she asked.

"Dingoes, I expect," he replied. "Talking to each other." He looked up at the speckled sky. "They say there are satellites up there that could pick us out with ease. Any of those twinkling lights could be one of them."

He ran his tongue over his lips, feeling the light coating of dust upon them. The dust was upon his teeth, his face; even, he felt, beneath his eyelids. It was in his hair, and had insinuated itself beneath his clothes.

Lauren glanced up at the pinpoints of light. "Let's give them something to photograph," she said, turning her face towards his.

She kissed him lightly. "You're gritty," she said.

"So are you. I'm afraid we're going to remain like that until we can get a proper bath."

"I don't mind," she breathed against his mouth, kissing him once more.

Down in the hollow, Villiger and Parguineau lay on the ground a short distance from their Range Rover, talking quietly. Sumner stood against it, still looking at the two shapes on the dune. He made a soft, choking sound when he saw their heads merge.

Paula Browne poked her head out of the window. "What are you, Sumner?" she began in a low voice. "Some kind of peeping-tom now?"

"He's supposed to be on guard," he said from within his quiet rage. "Anybody could sneak up on him."

"Why don't you try it and see what happens?" she suggested hopefully. Gallagher would probably blow his head off before he got close enough.

But Sumner chose not to take up the challenge. Instead, he climbed into the Rover.

"Where do you think you're going?" She stared through the dark at him.

"To sleep. Where the hell else?"

"Go join the men." Indignantly. She was lying across the back seat.

He settled himself comfortably in the passenger seat. "Rest easy, woman. I've got no designs on you."

"Don't flatter yourself," she snapped. "But we know who you've got designs on, don't we?"

"Whom," he said.

"Don't get clever with me, smartass."

They subsided into a hostile silence.

On the dune, oblivious to the battle of words they had been the subjects of, Gallagher and Lauren sat close to each other, savouring the touch of their bodies.

"There's something I want to tell you," she said.

"You don't have to," he reassured her.

She linked her arm through his. "I want to."

He waited.

"Alex Harding and I went out together for a while," she began quietly. "There was nothing much in it. We were just friends, really. But Gramps never approved. There was something he didn't like about Alex. I don't know what exactly. Alex resented it. He resents being denied anything. He's got so much already, I think he feels no one should dare refuse him ... anything."

Gallagher stroked her arm, putting her at ease; but never once did he cease his scrutiny of the darkened landscape, nor allow his hearing

157

to be deflected by what she was saying. He could still pick out every sound the night made.

"My parents were quite pleased, of course," she continued. "Alex is titled," she added, and he could sense the downturn of her mouth. "He is also rich and powerful – just the right match for an American girl, herself from a rich family with a little bit of clout. Only Gramps didn't see wedding bells."

"And you?"

He felt her shrug. "There was this guy from MIT, from a good family. Well ... you know ... I wasn't serious about anybody yet. But Alex was determined to get me. Not because he was so madly in love with me, but I think because it would be one in the eye for my grandfather."

There was a sudden tenseness in Gallagher. *Smallson?* Was all this a vendetta against the old man, taken to the ultimate limit? He waited for her to continue.

"He took me everywhere: Cannes, on his huge yacht – which is called the *Lauren*; Scotland, for grouse-shooting; Gstaad for skiing.... We did it all. Don't think I didn't enjoy going around with him. He can be quite charming."

"I know," Gallagher said.

She gripped his hand. "Don't think badly of me."

"Don't be silly. How can I?"

"You might think I'm a stupid rich girl who got all she deserved. You did feel that about me when we first saw each other."

He said sheepishly: "I made a mistake. You were pretty hostile, you know."

"There was a reason." She took a deep breath and let the next words come out in a rush. "The fact is, I got pregnant. When I told Alex, he laughed. Then he said something very odd for a man about to become a father. He said: 'Now I've got him!' He was talking about Gramps!"

Smallson again. Gallagher tried to make the connection but came away with nothing. He'd have to find out some time, from the old man himself.

"It was then I realized," Lauren said, "that I had been used all along. I don't know what it is that makes him hate Jake so much."

"And you think that's the reason for the hijack?"

"Oh, I don't know. A week ago I wouldn't have believed Alex Harding knew any terrorists. Anyway, I had an abortion."

She'd said it without warning, without flourish. He felt her shake, remembering.

"It was awful," she said softly. "An illegal job in a New York back street. Oh, Gordon, you don't know how lonely and terrible that can be."

158

A great wave of tenderness swept over him and he put his arm about her, to hold her close. But he felt a great anger for Harding that was more intense, more personal than anything he'd felt previously.

She leaned against his shoulder. "That's why," she went on in a voice he could barely hear, "that's why I was so ... hostile. I saw all men as predators."

"I'm not surprised," Gallagher said with feeling. He held her closer, thinking of her in some poky backstreet room, frightened and alone among strangers, not having dared to tell anyone.... Then would have come the pain, and the misery, and the dreadful loneliness of her secret recuperation. "My poor, poor Lauren," he said gently. *You bastard*, he thought of Harding. It was another score he would take great pleasure in settling.

But first, they had to make it to Cook.

They remained close to each other atop the dune until Villiger said behind them: "I could have cut your throats."

"No, you couldn't," Gallagher said. "Look again."

Villiger looked down. The snout of the M16 was pointing directly at him, butt jammed into the sand. He could barely make it out.

"Very good," he said, impressed. "I never saw you do it."

"That was the whole point. I even heard you rise from where you were lying."

Gallagher and Lauren stood up together and began walking down the slope, having decided not to spend the night on the dune.

"Isn't the desert noisy?" Villiger murmured after them.

Next to him Villiger sensed rather than saw Nwale, who had come up to do his watch. African and Afrikaner, both natives of the same continent, stood silently together, staring into the Australian night.

Finally Villiger said: "A truce, Nbwale?"

The huge man laughed softly. "You talk truce with the kaffir? I am learning things. I am being instructed by a hijack. First, you work closely with and take orders from a kaffir...."

"Gallagher is not a kaffir." Shortly.

"Oh, yes, of course. I forgot. Down your way, you've got this strange designation, the 'honorary white'; like the Japanese. You've bestowed it in your mind upon Gallagher; for the duration, naturally. You could not work it, otherwise."

"Look, man, I'm trying...."

" '*Man!*' " Nbwale was vastly amused. "You acknowledge it! This is a departure. Not a munt or a kaffir, but a *man*. The world is full of wonders. I know, of course, why you have not attempted to kill me. Gallagher would have had something to say about it – or would you be forced to kill him as well? He is quite formidable for such an unassuming person. But the best ones are. He is also, I suspect, rather scrupulously fair-minded. He would not take kindly to my killing you."

"There you have it, man. It's a truce."

Villiger began walking back down to the vehicles.

Nbwale tightened his grip briefly on the AK-47 he held in his hands.

"For the time being," he said. He turned to look out over the darkened land. He didn't care if the Afrikaner had heard him.

Day Five

I

THE SUN, lifting smoothly, sent its blaze of red and ochre and gold stabbing across the dune towards the fleeing vehicles, to overtake and bathe them in a growing warmth that presaged the heat of the day to come.

They had broken camp in the pre-dawn, Gallagher wanting to use the very first light of the new day. A quick breakfast of judiciously divided shrimp and sweetcorn, a drink of water, and they set off, heading for the track. Now, thirty kilometres later, the track after a series of bends, was running west for about four kilometres. The dunes were growing progressively higher now and bordered the track on both sides. On one dune, about ten metres high, they saw a pack of three dingoes, about halfway up its slope.

The wild dogs paused to stare and, deciding they were no threat, continued up the slope to disappear over the crest.

They came into a wide bend that took the track eastwards once more, but all the time it was going south. They were making good progress, and there was a great deal of optimism that they were going to make it, after all.

"What do you think?" Lauren asked Gallagher. "We seem to be outstripping them."

"We still have a very long way to go." The Marika he'd come to know would be seething with the lust for revenge. In that respect, she was far more dangerous than Harding could ever be.

"It is wise not to celebrate our good luck too soon," Nbwale said. He was sitting in front with Gallagher, while Lauren had moved to the back with her grandfather who had complained of a mild headache upon waking. "The ambush was meant to stop us, rather than kill us all outright. They would have wanted to recapture most of us, for their entertainment. No evidence of pursuit does not necessarily mean they are far behind."

Gallagher found no fault with Nbwale's appraisal of the situation. "Which means we put as much distance between them and us as we can."

He had noticed a new razor-edged atmosphere between Nbwale and Villiger. African and Afrikaner. How insane that those two should be at each other's throats simply because, despite belonging to the same lands, they had been born into different skins. He had deliberately given them adjoining watches, wanting to bring them together to sort out their differences, or at least defer them until this whole business was over. He knew they had talked. He could only hope common sense had prevailed.

Sumner had been another deliberate placement. Gallagher had not relished the prospect of having him lurking around in the middle of the night with a loaded weapon and no one to keep an eye on him. As it had turned out, Gallagher, though he had not left the Range Rover, was awake at the time of Sumner's watch and indeed the whole camp was woken in the middle of it to prepare for the day's journey; which was exactly what Gallagher had intended when arranging the watches.

Parguineau's shoulder had been no cause for concern, but now the worry was Smallson's headache. Had the ordeal of the previous day taken its toll of the old man?

"Jake," Gallagher called over his shoulder, "how do you feel?"

"The head is passing," Smallson replied. His voice sounded as strong as ever. "It must have been the way I slept."

"Ah. But did you sleep as I suggested you should?"

Smallson chuckled. "When you're an old man, there is much to think about and sometimes the need for sleep is begrudged."

"You need all the sleep you can get, Jake." For the moment Gallagher chose not to follow up the matter of what it was that had served to disturb the old man's sleep.

Lauren had slid her window back to sniff better at a faint yet familiar smell that had been teasing at her nostrils for some time, without making her certain it was there at all. Now, with the window open further, all doubts were dispelled.

"*Gordon!* I can smell gas!"

He slowed down immediately, thinking that a fuel line had worked itself loose during the battle with the Landrover and had finally parted from its anchorage. He was more worried about the risk of fire than about the pint or two of fuel that might be lost before he could secure it again. He stopped the Range Rover. Villiger pulled up close behind.

The smell hit Gallagher almost before he touched the ground. It was stronger than he would have expected of a leaking fuel line. It was almost as if he had wandered into a filling station with its storage tanks open.

He heard a steady dripping sound. Fearing the worst, and that he had somehow holed the tank, he was about to look beneath the vehicle when he saw the streams coming from the petrol and water cans. Each one appeared to be leaking steadily from at least six points at the bottom.

He grew suddenly cold in the mounting heat of the day, as he understood the terrible trick that had been played on them all.

"Gordon?" Lauren called. "What is it?"

162

But he was already running to tell Villiger.

Crofton selected 120.5 on the Citation's number two VHF set, and called: "Perth Tower, Golf – Lima Alpha Uniform Romeo request time check, QFE, and airfield QNH."

"Golf – Lima Alpha Uniform Romeo, time oh-six-two-seven, QFE...."

Crofton reset his altimeter as the information came in; then he changed over to the number one VHF set to call for taxying instructions. He wanted to ensure that they both functioned properly. He had filed a flight plan for Darwin, with a brief stop at Kintore to deliver the marrons that had been loaded on an hour before. From Darwin, he would be flying solo to England, and he needed these two vital items of the aircraft's equipment to serve him unfailingly on the long flight.

Whatever happened from now on, his life would no longer be the same. He remembered the healthy, eager girl he'd left still asleep, in his hotel room. He sighed regretfully. Perhaps if he'd met her before all this.... No. No. It was all nonsense. Life, real life, was not made up of ifs and maybes and the rest. Life was what was facing him at this moment, what would face him in London, and what would face him when the whole thing was all over.

Many times during the night, with his temporarily satisfied companion sleeping half on and half off him snoring loudly, he had asked himself whether he should not have stayed on in the air force; but, almost immediately, he'd answered the question in his mind. Working for Harding had given him a life-style and salary the Ministry of Defence could never have afforded, no matter what rank he had achieved.

He reached the hold point and went through his power and pre-take-off checks. He got his take-off clearance, rolled the Cessna on its take-off run. The sleek, white jet with its gold and black sidestripes and Harding International insignia on its tail, climbed rapidly. Perth advised him to watch out for military aircraft on a training exercise crossing the first leg of his route. He would be heading north-east for the first thousand miles to Kintore, from where he would take off again for Darwin, due north and the next thousand miles. The Cessna's 3,500-mile range gave him no fuel problems. At Darwin, he would go to full tanks again for the first cross-water hop to Singapore.

With the Citation III virtually empty, it took him barely over twelve minutes to get to forty thousand feet, where the Cessna would be miserly with fuel. On the overseas legs, he intended to cruise at fifty thousand, just below its maximum ceiling. He would be well above all traffic and at that height would make good time to London.

As the desert began to unfold far, far beneath him, he had no way of knowing that the very subject of his inner turmoil was desperately trying to save rapidly dwindling stocks of precious fuel and water, in a dunefield directly below his track to the Kintore complex.

Military traffic did cross his path; but the four RAAF F-111Cs from Amberley in Queensland, streaking over the desert on a "Hi-Lo-Hi" mission, were nowhere near him. In the "Lo" phase of the mission, the Aardvarks, with their terrain-following radar, played suicidal chicken with the peaks of the Wilson Range in Western Australia at less than two hundred feet, at speeds of six hundred miles an hour. Like the desperate fight going on in the dunefield, Crofton did not know of them.

Similarly, Gallagher knew nothing of Crofton's impending presence high above him, nor of the heart-stopping antics of the four twin-jet swing-wing aircraft. The arbitrary nature of life had caused the mission planners to choose the Wilson Range for that particular task. Had they chosen the dunefields instead, an area that the terrain-following radar would have been well able to cope with, the aircraft would have seen Gallagher and his companions.

They had found that every can, on both Range Rovers, had been neatly punctured six times at the bottom.

"Turn them all upside down!" Gallagher had shouted, and they had hurriedly rushed to do so, but precious little of the supplies had been saved.

The cans had been leaking steadily, from minute trickles to full flow as the engineered holes had progressively widened, over a distance of some kilometres. Lauren had scented the leakage only after this had been going on for a while. No one in Villiger's Rover had smelled anything. Rapid evaporation had also played its part.

They had made bungs from sleeves ripped at the shoulder from the men's shirts and from the linings of their discarded jackets which had been piled in the luggage space of the Rovers.

With the exception of two cans on the roof, all of Villiger's petrol had leaked away. The two cans were themselves not quite full. Villiger had also lost two cans of water. Gallagher had two and a half cans of petrol remaining, and one and a half cans of water. The petrol, like Villiger's, were from the cans on the roof. All the empty cans were left to the desert, while the others were rearranged, upside down, along the sides and front of the Rovers.

"There may be some seepage through the caps," Gallagher said when they had finished, "and we're bound to lose something through slow evaporation through the bungs, and when we try to pour into the tank through one of these bloody holes."

They had filled Gallagher's tank, a painfully slow process, after having decided to run Villiger's tank dry and then pile everyone and everything on to the remaining Range Rover. They had discussed and discarded the idea of one vehicle, lightened to enabled it to make good time, going on ahead with the extra fuel to find help. The thought that if anything happened to that Rover they would all be at the mercy of the desert and their pursuers had dissuaded them.

Gallagher had also met stiff resistance from Lauren to his suggestion that she go with Villiger and Paula Browne. Lauren had said she would not leave her grandfather; Paula Browne refused to go if Lauren did not; and Villiger had said he preferred to stay. Gallagher liked to think it was not only because the Afrikaner had wanted to keep Nbwale under close observation.

He now picked up one of the cans, and poked his finger into a hole. It widened, and a small quantity of pastry-like substance came away on the finger. He rubbed at it with his thumb. It disappeared. The cans had been very carefully doctored. The holes had been made then sealed with the strange material, which had subsequently dissolved over a period of time. A very neat job of sabotage.

"Bastards!" Gallagher said with a quiet anger. He dropped the can and kicked it in his frustration.

He walked off the track to stand some distance away from them, staring in the rising heat of the morning at the now-ominous landscape before him. He no longer saw it as full of majesty and wonder. It had now become his implacable enemy. The dunefields were a daunting barrier ahead, between him and salvation. Behind, came an even more implacable enemy, bent on revenge, on death. Cook was a lifetime away.

Jake Smallson said to the others: "I know what that stuff is. Harding's chemical people have been experimenting with its manufacture. There are other firms who do, of course, but Harding's people had got their problems licked. There are different kinds, to dissolve in various liquids. It sets as hard as metal, then over a period of time disappears. Very good for sabotage, as you have seen."

"Very useful," Nbwale commented with interest. "Is this material on the market?" He chose to ignore Villiger's keen look.

"Not yet," Smallson answered. "Harding International call these two PN20WX and PN20PX. I don't know what PN20 means." He did, and Lauren glanced at him surreptitiously, because she knew this. "But the P at the end stands for Petrol and the W for Water. I guess for the States they would put a G for Gas. The X means it is still experimental. All the other liquid-dissolving agents have their respective code letters."

"Not only are we prey," Nbwale said, "we are also guinea pigs."

Villiger said: "You seem to know a lot about it, Mr Smallson."

"I am a businessman, Mr Villiger, like yourself." Villiger had the grace not to react. It was quite obvious that Smallson knew him for

165

what he really was. "I make it my business to know these things."

"Well," Sumner began, looking towards where Gallagher stood, "we'd better get our tails moving. It's helping us none to stay here talking." He paused. "He wasn't so smart, after all." They all knew he meant Gallagher.

The hard slap across his mouth took everyone by surprise. He stared at Paula Browne in shock and anger.

She was livid. "You little shit! Is that all you can say? Would you have known about that PN whatever-it-is? Would you?"

His eyes glared hate at her. "You do that again," he said through his teeth, "and so help me I'll whup you, but good."

"And I, Mr Sumner," Nbwale said calmly, "will break both your arms if you do."

No one doubted it, especially Sumner.

Paula Browne looked at Nbwale, surprised: "Why, thank you."

"It would be a pleasure. Believe me."

No one doubted that either.

The sound of the slap had caused Gallagher to turn round to look. He saw Paula Browne and Sumner squaring up to each other, and Nbwale saying something to Sumner, who backed down. Lauren was coming towards him.

"What happened?" he asked as she reached him.

"Sumner was uncomplimentary about you. Paula slapped him."

Gallagher smiled tiredly. "I seem to have got myself a champion."

"You have two," she said, the grey eyes engulfing him, "at the very least. And did you really think I would have gone off and left you?"

"You should have. It might have been wiser."

She guessed what he was thinking. "You mustn't blame yourself. No one in the world could possibly have worked that one out. You can't know everything. We're already so grateful —"

"Lauren," he interrupted her gently, "I don't want gratitude. I just want us all out of here."

"We'll make it." She smiled at him trustingly.

Warmed by this unshaken belief in him, he said: "No doubt about it."

They began walking back.

"Gramps knows what they used. It's called PN20. The PN standing for Penny, Harding's sister. The '20' stands for her age when their mother died," Lauren explained. "Alex does things like that. A lot of his projects are coded according to people or incidents in his life." She went on to repeat what Smallson had said about the PN20.

Gallagher felt a sudden twinge of alarm and broke into a run. He had a dreadful premonition. Lauren ran after him, not knowing what had caused his anxiety.

"The caps!" Gallagher shouted at the Afrikaner while he was still some distance away. "Check the caps!" There was the possibility that they had been doctored too.

Villiger did not waste time querying the instruction but was already following it. Nbwale, understanding the South African's actions, immediately went over to Gallagher's vehicle.

"Well?" Gallagher enquired as he arrived.

"Nothing here yet," Villiger answered. He'd checked two cans. "We'll see about the others."

But they could find nothing suspicious, despite careful scrutiny.

"It doesn't prove anything," Gallagher said. "We've come just over two hundred kilometres; it's taken all that time, plus however long the Range Rovers were in the hangar, for the material to dissolve."

"They don't all have the same dissolve rate," Jake Smallson said.

"That's what worries me."

"Wouldn't they have put holes in the sides too?" Paula asked.

"It's possible but not likely. Turning the cans on their sides would not be as effective in saving petrol or water as putting them upside down. They would still leak through the holes. The caps are the most likely places, because even with the bungs we would still have seepage and evaporation through the cloth. We've got a certain amount of evaporation already."

"So what can we do."

"Nothing. We'll have to risk it and press on to Waldana Well, which is the first one we'll come to, about two hundred and eighty-five kilometres from here."

Sumner opened his mouth to speak, but Villiger cut him off.

"Gallagher's right," he said firmly. Sumner closed his mouth. "I've got about enough juice for perhaps another two hundred," Villiger went on.

"That's when we'll shoehorn everyone into my vehicle. If those caps don't spring leaks on us, we'll still make it to Cook; but only just. Right. Let's go."

As the others got into the Range Rovers, Villiger paused to speak to Gallagher.

"Don't be hard on yourself," he said, face and eyes giving nothing away as usual. "No one could have known about that bloody PN20." Then he climbed into his vehicle.

Crofton did a circuit of the Kintore airstrip and brought the Cessna down. The flight had taken him just over two hours. He crossed the threshold at 117 knots, losing speed rapidly. The touch-down was smooth. As soon as the nose-wheel made contact, he hit the thrust-reversers. Red dust, already boiling up from the wheels, fanned out behind the high tail of the aircraft. The Cessna began to slow itself down. He touched the brakes gently, sparingly.

He'd had plenty of time to think about his decision on the way over. It had been with relief that he had received the message from the conference room in Perth that the twin turbo-prop Corsair had become available, and that he was no longer needed. He suspected that the executives, high up as they were in the Harding International hierarchy, had not relished the idea of keeping Harding's private pilot and aircraft hanging around. Even in his absence, Harding's power did not diminish.

Crofton brough the Citation III to an almost complete stop, turned it and began to taxi back towards the low-lying hangar. As soon as he saw the Landrovers, he knew something was wrong. Stomach pulsing with unease, he brought the aircraft to a halt.

He went to the door, opened it, climbed down the short flight of steps to the ground.

Marika and Flyboy were waiting for him. They were both armed: Marika with her M16 and a French MAB nine-millimetre automatic pistol holstered on her left hip; Flyboy with the same type of .45 auto that Cyrus used to wear.

Feeling queasy, Crofton said brightly: "I've brought you your marrons, all nice packed in ice."

Marika came straight to the point. "We want you to fly to England with a very special message for Alex."

Crofton's eyes widened in astonishment. He couldn't believe it. "What happened?"

"Gallagher has escaped, taking everyone with him."

Gallagher! Dear God, he had been right! And he had said nothing!

"You look white, Crofton. What is the matter?" Marika's green eyes stared at him with chilling menace.

Grudging every word he spoke, Crofton told them: "I was already on my way to England."

"What? Why?"

"It ... it's about Gallagher."

A stillness in which Crofton would swear he heard his own blood rushing through his entire body, descended upon them.

Crofton made three attempts to speak before the sound came. "The last time I was here, I bumped into him. His face seemed familiar." He went on quickly, as Marika's pupils appeared to dilate: "I asked one of your people – Cyrus, I think you call him...."

"Cyrus is dead. So are Johnson and Kamal, killed by Gallagher out in the desert. So are Jurgen and Ibrahim, killed also by Gallagher and his friends. Selini and I were also attacked and made unconscious. We do not as yet understand why we too were not killed; but that was his greatest error. Do you now tell me, Crofton, that you knew something about this man?" The M16 came up, and Marika's eyes had death in them.

"Marika," Flyboy took his courage in his hands to say cautiously, as if trying to placate a slavering she-wolf, "if you shoot him, he can't warn Harding."

The rifle did not move down, but there was no pressure on the trigger. "Go on, Crofton."

Crofton was certain his bowels had moved. He breathed a sigh of relief as unobtrusively as he dared. They were all mad. He felt a sudden rush of petulant anger. Why did Gallagher have to come and spoil his life in such a manner? It did not occur to him to consider that such risks went with the job. All the reasoning he'd done in the hotel in Perth seemed to have been thrown out of the window. It was as if he now knew he would be unable to escape unscathed. The die had been cast the day he had signed a contract of employment with Harding International.

"Go on, Crofton," Marika repeated dangerously.

"It ... it was in Germany," Crofton began quickly, "that I saw him. I was stationed there, on Phantoms. One day this off-station Phantom came in on a low, low pass, broke flashily to the left and landed like a feather. I watched, because it was very good flying indeed."

"Are you telling us," Flyboy began with great interest, "that Gallagher was a jet jockey on F4s?'"

Anything. Say anything you like. Just let me get out of here, please, Crofton prayed in his mind.

"I asked in the mess afterwards," he continued without further prompting. "When I had landed, the off-station Phantom was gone. Someone said he was a hush-hush bod. That's all I know."

"Hush-hush?" Marika asked. "You mean secret?"

"Yes."

"Christ," Flyboy said. "A fucking spook. We've got a goddam agent on our hands, Marika."

But Marika was looking at Crofton. Those in the past unfortunate enough to have experienced that look had found the condition a terminal one.

"Crofton," she said in a chilling voice, "I cannot believe you knew all this and said *nothing*. I am ... beyond words."

"But I thought he was one of you," Crofton protested. "I didn't want to interfere. I am not exactly privy to the workings of your team."

Marika seemed to think about that. She said: "Very well, Crofton. Now tell me: do you believe Gallagher to be still active?"

"To be quite honest, I don't know."

"I see. Well ... Crofton. You will go straight to England and tell Alex Harding everything."

"Yes."

Marika's eyes bored into his. "Crofton." Softly. "Let me tell you something about us. We do our work for money, and for pleasure. We are not politicos. We have found through individual experiences that each side is as bad as the other. Cyrus and Flyboy festered in Vietnam. When they came back, no one wanted to know. Flyboy is a Jew. Kamal and Ibrahim were Arabs, but they all worked well together.

"Johnson was with your British SAS, and once worked for the South Africans in Mozambique and Angola. He told Cyrus, but they were very good friends. Selini comes from a family whose wealth was taken by the revolution and who were all executed. Ngoma was a revolutionary in her own country; one night, on a drunken spree, revolutionary guards killed her husband and two young children. And as for myself...." Grimly. "I know all about the revolution. Do you understand what I am saying to you, Crofton?

"I am trying to tell you, Crofton, that the only allegiance we have is to our money, and we shall let nothing come between it and ourselves. Our money, our way of life. So, Crofton, you must go directly to England, and do not try to escape elsewhere; because if there is a single hole on this world where you can hide from Harding International, I ... will find it, even if they cannot."

The snout of the M16 came up slowly to rest against Crofton's throat. He swallowed in terror. The metal was warm, almost caressing.

"And, Crofton, it would be very, very bad to find me waiting there for you." Marika took the weapon slowly away.

Crofton had almost raised himself on tiptoe.

"You may go, Crofton."

"The ... the...." He was shivering. "The marrons," he got out at last.

She just looked at him.

"The weight," he said hesitantly. "The ice has taken the weight up to forty pounds. I want the Cessna as light as possible to save time and fuel."

"Forty pounds?" Sceptically. "That is less than twenty kilos."

Crofton stood his ground. "It's still weight."

"Oh, very well. Help him, Flyboy." She left them to off-load the marrons.

Crofton took some food back to the aircraft with him. He had no desire to remain among these people a second more than was absolutely necessary. Lunatics, all of them. He would eat in flight.

He went through his checks with lightning speed, started the Garretts and lifted the little jet cleanly into the bright sky.

II

Gallagher, had he been there, would have been dismayed to find that he had been correct about the supply of Landrovers. Three now stood outside the low hangar, with a six-cylinder long-wheelbase model still inside. This had an enclosed cab with an open rear body and was to be used to carry spare fuel for the gunship.

Two men, a New Yorker and a Belgian from Vollezele near Brussels, would stay behind to crew it. Marika had also left Inge behind to join Harding and Flyboy in the gunship. The remaining ten members of the group would begin the hunt in the three Landrovers.

Marika stood by her vehicle. Her green eyes shone like polished jade. There was no smile on her face.

"We all know," she said in a voice that carried the chill of death with it, "what Gallagher is, or used to be. Either way, we can expect combat; but remember, his escape means the end of us. This is the most important hunt we've ever had. We are fighting for our survival. I want Gallagher."

Memory of him brought an uncontrollable pulsing between her thighs, and she wanted to close her eyes and scream; instead she gripped the door of the Landrover until her knuckles whitened. The others seeing this interpreted it as rage and hatred. But beneath it all there was love, acting as a fertile ground from which the other emotions grew.

They boarded their vehicles, Marika getting behind the wheel of the one she shared with Selini and a Londoner called Charlie. She started the engine and the other two Landrovers followed suit, to trail in her wake as she set off at speed across the emptiness. Already, the sun was beginning to bake the land.

Ngoma commanded the second vehicle, and the third with its load of four was driven by a slim Italian girl called Giannetta, who raced the Landrover like a Ferrari on an autostrada. Several times she had to slow down so as not to pass Ngoma.

Between them, the pursuers carried a formidable array of weapons; but there were no blookers and no rocket launchers. The Landrovers sped, like hunting dogs off the leash, in a direct line from the complex to Cyrus's former ambush position. This would take nearly thirty kilometres off Gallagher's route.

Two and a half hours later, they came upon the scene of Cyrus's last battle. The Landrovers stopped nose-on to each other, surrounding the grisly scene. For a long time, no one climbed out, each person staring aghast at the evidence of the terrible fight, the smell of decomposing flesh already assailing their nostrils.

Then Marika got out. The stench hit her with force, and clouds of fat flies, gorged on the unexpected bounty, rose in their myriads to greet her. She brushed them away absently as she approached. She wanted to see, wanted to note what he had done. It would lend more fire to her vengeance.

The others climbed out, slowly, as if moving under water, staring about them. Marika heard someone retch. She turned to look. One of the men from Giannetta's Landrover. Giannetta herself approached, stopped, looking at something on the ground.

Cyrus's head, gnawed and picked almost clean by the denizens of the night, had during the course of their feeding been moved close to the burnt Landrover.

Giannetta's face crumpled briefly, for she had nursed a secret passion for Cyrus. Her pretty, plumpish face, which went incongruously with the slim body in khaki shirt and shorts, now hardened. If Marika wanted Gallagher, she would have to get to him first.

Marika saw Giannetta's expression and, reading it accurately, went up to her.

"Gianna, do not even think it. I don't want to have to go up against you as well. I meant it when I said I would shoot the person who got Gallagher. I want him, and nobody is going to take that from me. Not even you."

"He took off Cyrus's head!"

"Cyrus was a soldier. It could have happened to him in Vietnam. But I shall avenge him. You need not worry. I shall do it for both of us."

The Italian girl turned away and walked back to her Landrover without another word.

Marika stared after her. A squadron of flies performed chaotic loops in front of her face, but she ignored them, as if the power of her eyes could burn them into oblivion. At last she waved the flies away. *He is even destroying us*, she said to herself.

Selini had joined her.

"I would have given him anything, you know," she said to Selini, the only person to whom she felt she could make such an admission in the present circumstances. And Selini understood.

"Let's go after him. We have seen enough."

Marika took one last look. "Yes. And we shall catch him."

They went back to the Landrover, climbed in. Charlie was already in his seat.

"This Gallagher's got a lot of nerve," he said, as if to make conversation.

Both women ignored him.

172

Crofton landed at twelve-thirty, Darwin time. He refuelled, filed his new flight plan and was off again within the hour. He took the Cessna on a thirty-five-minute direct climb to forty-nine thousand feet, where he cruised for fifteen minutes before taking it a further thousand, up to fifty. At that height, the Citation III was giving him a less than eight-hundred-pounds-an-hour fuel burn.

He found the trim to his liking, switched on the auto pilot and relaxed in his comfortable seat. His eyes ran lovingly over the well appointed instrument panel, with its clearly marked and ergonomically assembled equipment. It was a pilot's dream; a dream he didn't want to leave.

He looked out. There was no cloud cover. Nine and a half miles below him, the Timor Sea and the southern group of the Indonesian Islands spread themselves in static repose.

He settled more comfortably in his seat, and picked an apple from the supplies he'd brought with him. He bit into it, and sighed.

He wished he could stay up here forever.

The three Landrovers came upon the discarded cans. They stopped long enough for Marika to inspect each of them. When she had climbed back into her own Landrover, Marika smiled.

Selini felt a great surge of relief. Marika was moving into top gear. She was getting primed for what was ahead.

It was Lauren's sharp eyes that warned them. When it happened, she didn't want to believe it. Nevertheless, that did not stop her cry of warning.

"*Gordon! Stop!*"

Gallagher did so immediately. Villiger slid to a halt behind him.

"One of the cans on the other Range Rover just came open!"

Gallagher jumped out, took in the disaster at a glance. He had been fooled again. The entire *cap* had been made of PN20. Now, it had simply melted away. No wonder they had found no evidence of tampering.

He made his decision quickly. He would fill Villiger's tank with what could be salvaged, since no petrol could be saved for later.

He told Villiger, and everyone got out to tip the remaining cans on their sides in an attempt to get as much as possible into Villiger's tank.

Lauren's warning had come just in time, for many of the caps were still intact. None of the water cans had so far been affected, but, taking no further chances, Gallagher decided to fix them horizontally in the spaces left by the unneeded cans. They removed the caps and replaced them with bungs.

"We're going to have a severe water problem," Villiger said when they'd finished. Enough petrol had gone into his tank to fill it, with

173

some left over for Gallagher's tank. The whole operation had taken a great deal of valuable time.

"I know," Gallagher agreed soberly. "We've each got a range of four hundred kilometres now, and that first well is now just a shade over two hundred away. At least we'll reach water."

"What about storing it?"

"We'll use the cans for as much as they'll hold, and all those tins we've saved. We'll just have to go sparingly. The next two wells are quite close, but after that, it's another hundred and thirty or forty to Muckera Rockhole. It's on that stretch we're going to have to watch it."

"We'll be almost out of juice by then."

"That's right."

Everyone had been listening quietly to the conversation, too numbed to feel dread. Now, Paula Browne spoke.

"What do we do then?"

"Walk," Gallagher told her, watching the shock spread over her face. "In normal circumstances, that would be the greatest of follies. You never leave cover in a desert, when you've broken down. But I don't think any of us would like to hang around for the others to catch up."

"How far is that town we're heading for, away from the rockhole?"

"Eighty kilometres. Four days." He was thinking of the old man.

"Oh, Gawd!" Paula Browne said in a trembly voice. "In this kind of heat, and this kind of country?" She did a slow, complete turn, staring at the dunes that rose frighteningly now from both sides of the track. "We'll never make it. They'll catch us!"

"Only if we let them," Gallagher interjected quietly, but firmly into what he could see was a rising panic that threatened the whole party. "We're not going to let them just take us, Paula. We'll make it very expensive. I don't pretend it's going to be easy. They've been playing their little game with us, but we can play our own game too."

Villiger looked at him. "What do you mean?"

"We'll do some hunting of our own. Who knows? We may even get ourselves a Landrover."

Villiger did not smile, but his piggy eyes looked lively. "That should be interesting. When?"

"Not as yet," was all Gallagher would answer.

While they'd been talking, a wind that had been teasing at them, as an intermittent, barely perceptible light breeze, had grown stronger. The sky had darkened too.

Gallagher looked up. "Rain would be nice."

"Dust storm," Nbwale said.

"What?" Gallagher looked at him.

The track at this stage was heading eastwards, and Nbwale was

174

pointing along it, in the direction they would be travelling. They all looked now at the gathering darkness of the whipped-up, loose earth, approaching them. It was still some distance away, but already it was beginning to blot out the sun. A reddish-grey pall was spreading across the horizon, acting as a backdrop for the crests of the dunes. Even as they watched, they could see the unstabilized sand-cover on the tops of the furthest dunes begin to rise and whirl like spumes of fine water from the crests of waves in a storm-tossed ocean. But these waves didn't move. They stood solidly, while they lost their heads and altered their shapes.

"In Queensland," Nbwale said, "They call these things the Bedourie. Perhaps it is the same here. Visibility can get down to half a mile; sometimes to thirty feet. The dust will get everywhere, and you can't outrun them."

"That's all we needed," Gallagher said with some unease. "Let's get back in and close everything down."

They hurried to the vehicles, accompanied by the low moan of the rising wind.

Gallagher heard Parguineau give a wheezing gasp and fall. He had instinctively reached to help the Frenchman up, when the three sharp cracks reached him. The others heard it too and were trying to work it out. The three closely spaced holes in Parguineau's chest were all the evidence Gallagher needed.

Marika!

"*Move!*" he yelled at them. "Get in! Get in!"

Villiger needed no urging, but the rest were a little slow.

She'd be lining up on another target now, despite the increasing opacity caused by the dust, sighting with deadly accuracy, letting out the breath, holding it there, pressure beginning on the trigger....

"*Move, for God's sake!*" He seemed to have swallowed a mouthful of dust. He spat. It didn't help much.

Sumner was pausing to grab at Parguineau.

Gallagher shoved him away. "Leave him! He's dead!"

Christ. She should be squeezing the trigger just about now....

But Sumner was baulking. "You can't leave ..."

Gallagher dragged him forcefully away. "Get into the bloody vehicle, you idiot!" Gallagher tried to bawl. The dust clawed at his throat, choking him. He hacked and tried to spit out of the wind. It helped, but not very much.

Where were the next shots? She wasn't so slow. The trigger should have been squeezed by now, and one or both of them should have been lying on this miserable, dust-whipped track, their life-blood soaking into the hungry ground.

Sumner was fighting at him. "Take ... your hands ... off me ... you...."

175

Then Villiger was out of his Range Rover, hauling at Sumner unceremoniously and bundling him into the vehicle.

Gallagher clambered into his own Rover, started the engine, slammed into gear and moved off almost in one motion, his mind asking over and over again why Marika hadn't shot a second time. She could not have missed, surely?

Marika hadn't missed. The crest of the dune upon which she had positioned herself had been suddenly whipped by the fringes of the storm and she'd had to shelter her head in her arms as she lay there with the wind and sand tugging at her body.

She swore mentally. She had not intended to shoot Gallagher; not just yet. It would have been too easy a fate for him; but she'd wanted the podgy American. Now, she'd have to clean the rifle before she could use it again.

In the Range Rover, Gallagher said: "Is everybody all right?" He peered ahead. There was no horizon. The wind and dust slammed at the big vehicle, rocking it.

"Yes," they each answered him.

Nbwale said: "They were very quick." His voice was neutral but there was a tenseness in him.

"Their whole intention was to slow us down and to restrict our range."

"They have done that admirably."

"True, but they hadn't planned for fugitives with weapons."

"But after what happened at the ambush, they'll be out even more for our blood, if that's possible."

Gallagher said: "We stand a far better chance if they're angry. Angry hunters make mistakes."

Visibility had now closed down to less than the half-mile Nbwale had predicted, and Gallagher was using the lights by which to see the track. He was pleased to note that Villiger had also switched on his. Almost nose-to-tail, they crept gingerly forward, careful not to go off the track. Once one of them did that, Gallagher knew, they'd never find each other again. It would also make each vehicle dangerously vulnerable to their hunters.

The Range Rover was a well-sealed vehicle but the dust managed to gain entry. A thin coating of it was on everything and on everyone. It hissed along the sides, against the glass panels. It flung itself dementedly against the windscreen, spreading outwards after its continuous impact, so that it performed a constant series of patterns against the glass.

Gallagher used the wipers. The dust was so dry, it was brushed off easily; but the wipers scraped at the glass as millions of particles remained on the blades. To use water would have been wasteful, and useless: the windscreen would have been coated a muddy red in

176

seconds. He stopped the wipers. The wind was doing all the wiping. Visibility dropped still further.

"How long do these things last for?" Gallagher asked Nbwale.

"As long as the wind lasts, by which time the dunefield will look markedly different."

"The dunes will have changed positions?"

"No, because there is a hardened base upon which the sand builds; but the shape of the dunes in the affected area will have changed according to the wind direction, particularly the crests."

Gallagher manoeuvred the Range Rover along the partly obliterated track. The sky had long since disappeared. Their only universe was the eerie twilight caused by the suffused glow of the lights within the dancing whirls of red dust..

Lauren stared at it, wondering if she or Jake would survive the hunt. Would Gallagher? She leaned back in her seat and looked across at her grandfather. The old man had closed his eyes. His face looked a little pinched. She wanted to ask him how he was, but decided against it. She returned her attention to the singing storm.

In the rear vehicle, Sumner, sitting next to Villiger much to Paula Browne's relief, was still fuming.

"We shouldn't have left that man back there."

"He was dead," Villiger said briefly.

"A white man needs a decent burial."

Paula Browne, despite the terror she felt, could not resist it. "What's this, Sumner? The Seventh Cavalry? A man is a man, white, black, green, yellow. They all need decent burials."

"I wasn't speaking to you. I haven't forgotten that slap."

"Don't wash your face," she snapped. "Then you can remember it forever."

Villiger's voice cut evenly across their argument. "It would have been stupid to try to pick up the Frenchman. We might have all been shot. Gallagher was right."

"You seem to support everything he does," Sumner accused with some petulance.

"So far he hasn't given me cause to doubt his ability."

Sumner chose to read that to mean that as soon as the Afrikaner found the necessary cause, he would stop his support of Gallagher and possibly take over himself. The idea pleased Sumner immensely. All he had to do was wait for Villiger to say the word.

The storm continued to rage, dashing its minute calcareous particles against the stubborn vehicles that insisted on travelling within it.

Gallagher said: "I've got an idea."

It had been forming in his mind for some time, and he decided to wait until the track again turned right and southwards, before taking the action he'd planned. Since there was not enough visibility to give him an indication of when the wide right-hand bend would come up, he was estimating the time to reach it by glancing now and then at the trip-meter. He gauged the distance as eight kilometres from where Parguineau had been shot. Two more to go now.

Marika had rolled herself down the dune before lack of visibility had closed the crest down completely. Now, she sat in her Landrover, waiting the storm out. The three vehicles were huddled in a hollow, and here the storm was lightest. Everyone had remained under cover.

As Marika studiously cleaned the M16, Selini watched her. "Were they shocked?" she asked finally. Marika had not said anything about the shots.

After a few more seconds, Marika began to reassemble the weapon.

"I couldn't see their faces," she replied without looking at her questioner, "but, by the way they moved, they certainly had not expected us so soon. Yes. I believe they were shocked."

Selini was almost afraid to ask. "And Gallagher?"

"I saw him." The assembly continued uninterruptedly.

"Is he...."

"No. There wasn't time for another shot. But I wanted the American. I want Gallagher to wait. I want him to know when I take him. I want him to see me when he dies."

She pushed a freshly loaded magazine home with a loud snap.

Gallagher flicked his left indicator on and off twice to let Villiger know he was going to turn off the track. Villiger's lights flashed twice to show he understood, and as the trip-meter counted off the second kilometre Gallagher thought he could see the bend in the track. A few moments later, he saw that was indeed so.

Half a kilometre later, he turned sharply off the track and into the dunefield. The storm seemed to be less furious, and he was sure it had begun to abate or was hurling itself past them. He drove between two high dunes whose tops had been made invisible by the storm. The dunes were about two hundred metres apart, and within this space the wind had lessened appreciably. Visibility was also greatly improved.

Gallagher turned off his lights. Behind him, Villiger did the same.

Gallagher switched off his engine, and turned to Lauren. "A blooker, please, and two rounds. Shouldn't need more, for what I have in mind."

"Which is?" she asked.

"A delaying action. I'm going to throw their ball back, but a little heavier."

No one wanted to talk about Parguineau. They had pushed the Frenchman's quick and sudden death to the back of their minds, to be thought about when they themselves were no longer under the same threat.

Nbwale said: "Your own ambush?"

Gallagher nodded. "Yes. The storm will have covered our tracks by the time it's passed us, and I'm hoping they'll think we've pressed on in an attempt to get away from them." He reached to take the blooker and its ammunition from Lauren. "Thanks." He loaded the first round, after blowing the dust off it.

Villiger was at his door. Gallagher opened it. The wind had lessened considerably. The storm was moving past, heading for Western Australia.

Villiger looked at the blooker, then back to Gallagher. "Reception committee?"

"Mm-hm. From one of those dunes, when the storm's gone. If I can hit the lead Landrover, it will block the rest for a while."

"They'll just bypass it."

"Not if I can get a second one to ram it first."

Villiger said: "Ah!"

"Then we'll have to get off the dune fast, because they'll be sending people after us."

"By 'we' and 'us', I take it you're including me."

"Yes. I need someone to take out a few while they're jumping out of their vehicles."

Villiger nodded. "Sensible. Right. I'll come."

"We'll go in about a minute."

Again Villiger nodded, then he went back to his Rover.

Gallagher said to Nbwale: "If we don't make it back, you get the hell out of here. You take charge."

Nbwale didn't waste time arguing about it. "OK."

"Can you handle Sumner? He won't like it, but he'd be useless at this."

"I can handle that half-wit."

Gallagher had no doubts about that. He looked at Lauren. "Don't worry."

"I'm not worried." Her eyes betrayed her. She leaned forwards to kiss him lightly.

"Jake ..." he began to Smallson.

But the old man interrupted him. "Sooner you're gone, sooner you'll be back. We'll be right here."

Gallagher smiled briefly. "One thing's certain. No one could call you a pessimist."

"Believe it."

Gallagher climbed out without further ado and went to join Villiger. As he walked, he tried to spit out some of the dust that still coated his tongue.

Lauren said: "Will he be all right, Gramps?"

"Of course he will."

Nbwale said, with a smile that seemed to bisect his face: "Believe it."

"There you go," Smallson remarked. "If Mr Nbwale can make a joke with my words, it must be OK."

Villiger was carrying his AK as Gallagher came up. "I've told Sumner that Nbwale will be leading if we ... ah ... blow it."

Gallagher was surprised. "You knew?"

"It was the only choice. I'd have done the same thing. Sumner could not lead shit out of his own backside."

"That's a nice turn of phrase." The wind had practically died. "How did he take it?"

"In his usual, generous way."

Gallagher suppressed a smile. "You surprise me, Mr Villiger."

"You're a constant source of surprise to me as well, Mr Gallagher. Which dune?"

Gallagher looked northwards. The sky seemed to have been split in half. To the west, the dust storm still hid the horizon while to the east, the sun was once more shining in its fierce glory. There was a strange filtered effect that marked the presence of invisibly suspended dust particles.

He pointed to the one nearest him. "The one beyond this."

"Right."

They hurried towards it, weapons at the port as they reached its base and began to climb swiftly up its freshly covered flank. The dune was only about six metres high and soon they were on its crest, feet sinking to the ankles in the newly deposited sand. They slid-ran down the other slope, then sprinted across the intervening three hundred metres to the next dune. This one was hardly twice as high. They flung themselves down on its rounded crest.

Gallagher turned to look back down at the prints they had left.

"Forty feet up, at least. We've got to run back down like bats out of hell, across that space up the other dune, down, and into the Rovers in half the time we took to get here."

Villiger smiled. "Out of condition?"

"Speak for yourself," Gallagher said, but he smiled back at the Afrikaner. He rolled on to his stomach, inched upwards to look beyond the crest.

The track wound its way in both directions, towards different horizons where it disappeared behind the dunes. There was nothing moving on it. He looked down the slope. A solitary mulga with frantic branches stood in skeletal splendour halfway up. It looked very lonely.

"Anything?" came Villiger's voice.

"No. They must be in the dunefield somewhere."

180

"Like us. Let's hope they're not behind."

Gallagher inched his way back below the skyline and turned on to his back. "That would not be very nice for us at all."

A silence descended between them.

Then Gallagher said: "I know about you and Nbwale."

Villiger too was on his back staring across at the other dune.

Getting no reply, Gallagher tried again. "I need hardly tell you that I detest what you people are doing to your own country. I just don't want any extra complications here."

"Look, man, we've got a good working relationship. Let's leave it at that, hey? I will do nothing to jeopardize it."

"OK," Gallagher agreed.

The silence descended once more. Some minutes passed, then they heard a soft sound. Motors.

They rolled quickly on to their stomachs, weapons ready. Gallagher moved upwards again, to look towards the sound. The bend in the track passed directly beneath him, at the base of the dune. Looking northwards, he saw in the distance first one, then two, then a third Landrover pull on to the track. Three of the bastards.

He began to count off in his mind the number of people he knew had been eliminated, then he allowed for Flyboy who would have been left behind to fly the gunship, and perhaps one more as crew member. He assumed the worst, feeling certain the gunship would have a fuel truck of some kind, which meant a further two people to crew it. He slid back.

"Three," he told Villiger. "Assume eleven people in all."

"We'll have to hit them hard."

"I intend to make sure we do."

They took up their positions and waited for their victims.

Giannetta had asked for and had received the lead from Marika.

"Why did you give it to her?" Selini asked. Their Landrover was third in the convoy.

"She wants to get at Gallagher before me," Marika said.

"Are you going to allow it?" Selini was very surprised.

"Selini," was all Marika said.

"Then why ...?"

"She wants to get at Gallagher? Then she shall."

The penny dropped. "You expect him to ambush *us*?"

"I certainly would in his place."

Selini looked anxiously at the dunes on either side. "But where?"

"About forty kilometres from here there is a sharp bend where the dunes are higher, longer and closer together. A dune can run for several kilometres. If they trapped us on one side, it would be a long time before we could catch up with them again. They must try to stop us, now that we are so close."

"But they have not much fuel."

"Which is why they must stop us," Marika said, "or try. They will be walking soon. The caps of their fuel cans will have melted by now."

Selini continued to look up at the dunes. If Gallagher did strike, Giannetta's Landrover could take the brunt of the attack.

Gallagher watched as the leading vehicle came within range. It was travelling fast, much faster than he would have dared on that track. It had outstripped the other two. He swore silently. He had wanted them much closer, so as to cause a collision. Well, too bad. Half a loaf was better than none. At least a damaged or knocked out vehicle would still slow them for a while.

Selini was still scrutinizing the dunes when she saw the shape on the skyline. She opened her mouth to shout a warning at the same time as the blooker fired.

Gallagher's aim was true. The round hit Giannetta's Landrover on the left front wheel and exploded. The vehicle was spun off the track, to the right, by the force of the detonation. Then, as its wheel shattered, it dipped its nose and tried to stand on its front bumper. The bonnet flew off and the Landrover slewed back on to the track, directly into the parth of the second in the convoy. The driver took avoiding action, but still caught a heavy glancing blow on the passenger side which knocked it sideways into the dunefield, where it stopped. People began to jump out, running for cover.

Villiger's AK-47 barked twice, and two of the runners fell. One lay perfectly still. The other squirmed, and the Afrikaner put another shot into him. All movement stopped. The third runner, Ngoma, made it to cover.

The first Landrover was still careering about the place. Just as Gallagher was about to fire another grenade into it, both doors were flung open and two people scrambled out. A man leapt out of the passenger door, risking life and limb; and a lithe form carrying a weapon jumped down from the driver's side and sprinted for cover.

Momentarily startled, Villiger missed his shot.

"Shit!" he said. "Did I just see female legs in shorts?"

"You did," Gallagher said grimly. "Now she'll live to fight another day."

"Sorry," Villiger said. He really was.

The Landrover was tipping on to its side. Gallagher fired. The grenade hit the sump. The nose blew itself apart. Two men were struggling to get out of the back. Villiger shot them. Then the Landrover exploded.

182

"Better than we had any right to expect!" Gallagher said happily. Something plunked into the sand like an angry wasp, inches from his nose. "*Move!*" he bawled.

Villiger needed no second bidding. They bob-sleighed down the slope on their behinds, hurtled across the distance to the other dune, raced up it and virtually leapt over the top.

Marika reached the top of the high dune just in time to see Villiger's head disappear. She did not bother to waste a shot. It was not she who had fired at Gallagher, but Selini, who had been trying for Villiger while jumping out of the Landrover before it had even stopped. Selini should have waited those vital seconds. There had been plenty of time.

Marika went back down the slope to inspect the carnage. Gallagher had paid them back for the trick with the petrol. She smiled. It was going to be a pleasure to get him.

Selini was waiting for her abjectly. "I should have waited."

"At least you know it," was all Marika said.

Villiger was actually laughing as they ran towards the Range Rovers. "Man! We really hit them. Four at least, one Landrover, possibly two." He clapped Gallagher on the shoulder. "I like the way you work." He was really high. "Whoever took that shot at us was quick, but not good enough."

Gallagher said: "It wasn't Marika. She never misses. She must have been driving that third Landrover. She was the one who got Parguineau."

"How can you be certain?"

"I'm certain. Remember the von Dietlingers, and the lizard."

They went to their respective vehicles, got in, started them, and were quickly rolling.

Everyone tried to talk to Gallagher at once.

"I'll tell you all about it in a while," he said as he turned the Range Rover about and headed into the dunefield.

Lauren was so pleased to see him safe, she kissed the back of his neck unashamedly as he manoeuvred round a cluster of big stones.

He drove deep into the dunefield, before finding what he'd been hoping for: a natural "road" running roughly parallel to the track between two colonies of dunes.

III

Marika counted the cost of the action. Four of the group dead, one Landrover destroyed and another damaged, though still usable. Gallagher had accounted for no less than nine of her people, to date. *He is destroying us, one by one.*

She thought of Gallagher's wife, an unknown face, but whose selfishness was directly responsible for what was happening now. The entire operation would have gone exactly to plan. Now, the existence of the group itself was in serious jeopardly, Harding International was at risk, her people were being killed and the years of careful work were in danger of coming to nothing. All because of a stupid empty-headed bitch.

Marika felt the fury rise within her. She had truly loved Gallagher, but that woman had poisoned him for ever. Then there was the equally stupid American girl. Did Gallagher really think that she, Marika, would allow herself to be spurned for that fluff-brained, spoilt, rich whore? Lauren Tanner, she decided, would die by the M16. And after it was all over, Marika intended to go to England and deal with Celia Gallagher too, the woman who had started it all.

Giannetta had planted herself in front of Marika, her slim, attractive legs spread. She was looking furious.

"You knew!" Giannetta accused. Her dark eyes burned with anger. "You knew it was going to happen. I could have been killed!" Her eastern Italian accent became more pronounced in her fury.

Strangely, Marika took no offence. "You wanted a try at Gallagher," she said evenly. "You got your chance, Gianna. You lost two good people instead."

Gianna opened her mouth to say something, thought better of it and remained silent.

Marika said: "You might as well speak your thoughts."

"It was nothing."

"You were going to say," Marika began with deadly emphasis, "that it is my fault nine of us are dead, that even Roberto's stupid outburst was because of what I allowed to happen. Yes?" The last word came like a whiplash.

Giannetta was cautious. "No."

"Did you, like Roberto, expect only the easy jobs? I admit my mistake. But even without Gallagher, there is the South African. He is not as good as Gallagher, but certainly as good as you are, Gianna. Whenever a plane is taken," she was addressing them all now, "all kinds of people are among the passengers. There can be wolves among the sheep. We found one who is very fierce. It is the risk we sometimes must take." But she knew she could never forgive herself for her mistake over Gallagher.

The faint sound of motors came to them.

"They're in the dunefield," Marika said, "but we shall clear up this mess before we go after them. They still cannot go far without fuel. Therefore they will try again. Gallagher is unpredictable. We shall be even more so."

"There's seven of them," Charlie said, "to six of us."

"You do not like the odds, Charlie? Of those seven, only two are worth consideration. Are those good enough odds for you?"

Charlie knew when not to push things. He kept his mouth shut.

Marika's expression showed neither contempt nor anger, but total indifference. "How is your Landrover?" she asked Ngoma.

"We'll have to change the wheel. But that is all."

"Good. Do it. Gianna, you ride with Ngoma. Max, you also."

Max nodded. He was the only other to escape from Giannetta's Landrover.

In ten minutes, they were ready to move again.

Marika said: "You follow the track, Ngoma. Let Gianna drive. She is crazy with motor cars, but this time we need her craziness. Do not destroy yourselves, Gianna. I shall want you all when the time comes."

Gianna smiled tentatively. Her being allowed to drive meant that Marika was not still angry with her, and Ngoma did not appear to mind.

"I shall go into the dunefields to chase them out. We must catch them before the next junction. Gallagher may decide to go east."

"They won't have the fuel to get that far," Selini began, "and in any case, we have removed the eastern track from the map."

"We assume nothing more about him," Marika said. "He may have more fuel than we believe. If he makes it to the junction, he may decide to go east, because it would not be expected of him. He would find that there *is* a track. We would need to split our forces, leaving one of us to travel a long way uselessly, possibly leaving the other dangerously exposed. It would take the one who had gone the wrong way a long time to make it back." She looked at Giannetta. "Suppose you, Ngoma, and Max found Gallagher first. Do you think you three could take him by yourselves?"

"We would try."

"That is not good enough. To try with Gallagher would get you dead. All three of you. Keep them in sight, and warn me on the radio, but do nothing until I tell you. Use the dingo code."

They climbed into the Landrovers, and Giannetta hurled Ngoma's vehicle round the wreck to tear off down the track as if she were driving in a rally. The fresh dust left by the storm billowed upwards behind her.

As Marika turned into the dunefield, she said to Selini: "I have not thanked you for seeing Gallagher in time. It might have been worse for us."

Selini felt pleased.

"Four kills, one Landrover, and possibly another badly damaged is a

185

good score," Nbwale said. "You are quite a formidable man, Mr Gallagher."

"Lucky," Gallagher corrected as he drove alongside a dune that was several kilometres long. It was now well after two o'clock, and the sun just above the cab told him he was heading westwards. Progress, however, was not as fast as he would wish. The surface was not as firm as he had hoped.

Nbwale was smiling. "And modest with it."

"We are still in deep trouble, Mr Nbwale...."

"Jefferson, please. We have been with each other for some time, after all." Nbwale was smiling again. "As long as it isn't Jeff. God, how I hate that! The English and Americans I sometimes meet insist on using it. I prefer the full name or simply Nbwale."

"I think I prefer that," Gallagher said. "Nbwale, I mean. It feels better."

Nbwale's eyes were hooded. "And what do I call you?"

"Gordon. Or Gallagher, if you prefer."

"I think I shall call you Gordon." Nbwale sounded as if he'd just won a victory of some kind.

They stopped soon after for a five-minute water break. The water was dusty, but it tasted good. They drank sparingly of it. Those who needed to relieved themselves; the women rushed over the lower crests, while the men did it where they stood.

"My Gawd I could use a bath," Paula Browne said as she returned, "and I feel like I've been eating sand for years." She looked haggard. "I look awful," she said to Gallagher. "Don't deny it. I can see it in your face, and I can feel it."

"I'm just worried about you. Are you all right?"

"It's nothing that escaping from those jokers won't cure. And this heat too." She wiped her wrist across her forehead. "I'm sweating myself away." She smiled crookedly. "Or don't ladies sweat? Don't answer that. I'm no lady." She looked at Lauren, who still managed to look fresh. "Not like you. Oh, the bloom of youth!" She wiped at her forehead again; twice.

Gallagher was distinctly worried. "Paula...."

"I need a cigarette."

"I thought you'd saved a few stubs."

"I need a *whole* cigarette."

"Not much chance of that out here."

"Don't I know it!" She went back to the Range Rover and got in.

Gallagher said quietly to the South African. "Keep an eye on her."

"Heat-stroke?"

"I hope not. Could be just the need for a long smoke."

They watched as Paula Browne lit up one of her stubs to draw the smoke luxuriously into her lungs.

"Dish out some food," Gallagher suggested. "Help keep her mind off it."

They ate on the move.

They came to the track again, some fifty kilometres later. Crossing the dunefield had taken so much time, it was now six o'clock.

Gallagher said: "We won't make that waterhole today by any stretch of the imagination, but I'd like to get to the junction before dark."

"Why the junction specifically?" Nbwale asked.

"It gives them a choice of directions. If the second Landrover can move, they'll be forced to split, to cover both routes...."

"But there's nothing going east on the map," Lauren interrupted.

"I'm not sure that I completely trust it," Gallagher said. "It was planted, after all. They could have done something to it. The big map covers only the western part of this state. There is not enough of it to show how far a track east goes, if at all. The little map is a photographic reproduction. You can do anything with photographs."

"Given that you may be correct," Nbwale said, "which way will you go?"

"I'll stick to our original route. If there is an eastern track, they'll know of it, while being secure in the knowledge that we don't. They'll expect me to do the unexpected. The route we know shows us where there's water, but we don't know if there's anything to the east. However, if there *is* a track, the reason the map was doctored was because there's a homestead or a station with, most importantly, a *radio*."

"Then it would be wise to go east."

Gallagher shook his head slowly. "No. That's where Marika will be. I'd rather meet up with the other bunch first. Once we take them out, we won't have to worry about a back-up force for Marika. We'll have more than enough on our plate dealing with her."

Gallagher urged the Range Rover along the track as fast as he dared. Villiger followed close behind.

Ngoma's voice came on the radio. "No trace of the pack." She was in fact ahead of the Range Rovers by ten kilometres.

Marika swore to herself. They should have run out of fuel by now. She had found tracks in the dunefield, but had driven into a wind, and by the time it had died down there were no tracks to be seen.

"How far are you from the junction?"

"About twenty kilometres."

Keep going. They may be on the track."

"What do I do at the junction?"

"Go to the west, unless I say differently."

The radio went dead. They could not be still in the dunefield, surely. "What do you think, Selini?" Marika asked as she came round yet another dune. "Could they still be here?"

Selini thought for a while before replying. "They'll be trying to get to the junction before dark, to force us to split up. We'll then waste the whole night."

"You believe them to be well ahead?"

Selini nodded.

"I am not sure," Marika murmured almost to herself. "Gianna drives like no one on earth. On proper roads, she is dangerous; but here.... It would surprise me if they are so far ahead that Ngoma cannot see them; yet.... Yet, yet, yet." She slapped impatiently at the wheel.

"I still believe he will try for the junction. It is the best chance for him to divide us."

"Perhaps you are right. We're wasting time in this dunefield." Marika began heading back towards the track and by seven o'clock she had reached it.

Now all four vehicles were on the track, with the Range Rovers in the middle of a fifty-kilometre sandwich. Because of the way the track meandered through the dunefield, neither was aware of the other. Because also of Gianetta's method of driving, she was continuingly pulling away. By eight o'clock, she was twenty kilometres ahead of Gallagher.

"We are coming to the junction." Ngoma's voice came over on the radio, broken intermittently by static.

"Anything?" Marika asked.

"No sign of the pack." The static was worse. "No fresh tracks."

"Go to the west. If we do not come upon them, we'll go eastwards."

"Understood."

The static was so bad now that Marika said when she had ended tranmission: "The dunes. They're breaking up reception."

Charlie said: "Perhaps we've passed them already. Perhaps they're still in the dunes."

"They must come out," Marika insisted. "They will need water. To be short of water is much, much worse than being without fuel. They will find none in the dunes; and if they get lost in there, then they'll be trapped for days, long enough for the gunship to find them. I do not believe Gallagher wants that. No. They will not stay in the dunes for long. I believe they are on the track."

Gallagher pulled off the track and headed for a particularly high dune. Villiger's Range Rover followed.

The vehicles stopped. Gallagher climbed out quickly, taking the binoculars with him. Telling the others to remain where they were, he ran over to the Afrikaner's Rover.

"I'm going up that dune to have a look around. We're about two kilometres from the junction. I want to see if anything's gone before us." Gallagher turned and started up the fifteen-metre incline.

"How much time are we going to waste now?" Sumner asked impatiently. "We want some more distance before nightfall."

It was a quarter to nine.

"You have a short memory," Paula Browne told him coldly.

"What do you mean?" He looked round at her.

Villiger said shortly: "The ambush."

Sumner faced front again. He said nothing. He couldn't understand why Villiger always took the nigger's side.

Gallagher reached the summit and lowered himself, stomach down, to the hot sand. He made himself comfortable, put the powerful glasses to his eyes. He had not told anyone, but for some time now he had been following wheel marks that he did not believe were more than a few hours old, if that. He knew that tracks could remain undisturbed for days, weeks, even months in desert climates; but this appeared to be a windy region. Tracks probably did not last here for very long. He was still too unsure, however, to mention it to anyone else. No need to worry them unnecessarily, in case he were proved wrong.

He could see the surface of the track clearly as it filed between the dunes, now and then broken by them, as if someone had dotted it across the terrain. From his position, he could quite clearly see the new track that headed westwards. The superb binoculars brought it remarkably close. He tracked along it, looking for what, he was not sure. Each time its zig-zags took it behind the dunes, he followed an imaginary course until he picked it up again.

He kept tracking further westwards. Finally, at a distance that he judged to be at least twenty kilometres, he was certain he saw movement. He tracked ahead and began slowly moving back towards where he'd thought he had seen the movement.

There! A scurrying across his field of vision. Something dark had vanished behind the flank of a dune. He waited, searching ahead. A longish stretch, and there it was.

A Landrover.

He waited no longer and hurried down the dune, his feet ploughing great imprints into the sand.

So one of them was searching to the west. Marika would most certainly be going east for the time being.

"A Landrover ahead," he told Villiger as soon as he reached the vehicles. "The other one could still be behind us." He told the Afrikaner about the tracks he'd seen.

"Why didn't you say anything before?"

"Didn't want to alarm you unnecessarily. I could have been wrong."

"What do we do now?" Paula Brown asked, her eyes wide with fear.

"We go to the west," Gallagher answered her, "then we'll pull into the dunefield for the night."

"Won't they be coming back to look for us when they find we're not ahead?"

"They'll have travelled a great distance before they come to that decision. It will be night by then. They'll have to sit it out, just as we're going to do. The same applies as last night. They won't want to show lights any more than we do. Tomorrow morning, I want to catch that Landrover before the other one comes from the east. If we can eliminate it, that will leave us with just Marika to deal with. Get her, and we might make it to Cook, with her fuel perhaps, if we're lucky. They are bound to have sent word to Harding by now. We don't want to be stuck out here for days and give that gunship time to hunt us down. So we must get those two."

But it was not going to be like that at all, and Gallagher could not know that as he hurried back to his own vehicle, clambered in, started it, and headed back to the track.

"It is getting too dark now," came the garbled, whistle-plagued message over the radio. "We shall have to stop for the night."

"Very well," Marika answered. "We have turned east towards Emu, but we shall also be stopping soon." It was already too dark to see the track properly without lights. "We shall go further in the morning. Call me before you start."

"Yes," Ngoma acknowledged, then switched off.

"In the morning," Marika told the others, "we'll go forty kilometres further towards Emu before turning back. Any closer and we may come across a travelling stockman. We cannot be too careful."

"So if they've gone east and we don't see them," Charlie began cautiously, mindful of Roberto's fate, "they'll have got away." He waited anxiously for her comment.

She was quite calm. "If we don't see them, they did not go that way. They need water and will go where they know there is water."

"So they'll have believed the map."

She frowned. "Possibly." She felt a slight unease, not liking the fact that Gallagher had managed to split her forces. She did not like to think of Ngoma isolated out there; yet if he had indeed gone east in the hope of finding salvation closer than he'd seen on the map, she had to find him and stop him. Permanently. There really was no choice. The possibly wasteful trip had to be undertaken.

190

She pulled off the track. "We'll spend the night here," she said.

Gallagher lay flat on the crest of the dune and looked out over the nightscape. It was a particularly high dune, towering above its nearest neighbours and giving him a superb vantage point. As on the previous night, stars lent their luminosity to the gloom. No vehicle would surprise him, but attackers on foot would use the darker patches afforded by the looming silhouettes of the mounds of sand. He watched those keenly, looking for anomalies; like an animal, sniffing for danger.

Somewhere in the distance a yelp-wail tore at the dark. There was no answering call. No pack, then; but a loner on a solitary hunt.

Some minutes passed, then the lone call came again. The sound had been much closer, it seemed. Did dingoes attack live humans for food? Gallagher brought the M16 up, just in case. He searched the slope beneath him. Nothing. There was no more for a long while. He relaxed minutely, allowing his senses to merge with the night, turning his body to the stirrings of the desert. When the sound came again, it was so close he almost jumped. It had come from directly below, fourteen metres down at the base of the five-kilometre-long dune that separated the dog from the camp.

What did it want? He kept the M16 ready. He could sense it down there watching him. It must be able to see him, flattened against the skyline. For what seemed a long time, the dog remained invisible to him, yet its presence registered itself upon him as clearly as if he could see it. Then he sensed it going away. He neither heard nor saw movement, but he knew it was leaving. Strange.

Some time later, the yelp-wail again tore into the night. It came from a long way away, as if the dog were saying goodbye.

Gallagher tried not to shiver. His acute senses picked up a soft sound behind him. He rolled swiftly, rifle seeking the source and aiming at it with deadly accuracy. The dog? Impossible.

"For God's sake, hold your fire!" Nbwale in a sharp, urgent whisper.

Gallagher watched him loom up the slope towards him.

"Your instincts are like that animal's out there," the African commented as he reached the top. He lowered himself to the sand, stretched out to stare into the night; then he looked towards Gallagher who had already resumed his former position. "The dog sounded close." Nbwale nestled his AK in the crooks of his arms.

"It was. Right below me. It stayed for a while, then just left."

"Perhaps it wanted company."

Gallagher was not sure whether Nbwale was laughing at him.

"Perhaps it sensed a kindred spirit for a brief moment," Nbwale went on, and Gallagher knew he was quite serious. "Perhaps it was even trying to tell you something. Who knows? The night has been known to do strange things to the senses."

Gallagher shrugged in the dark. The whole incident was a mystery to him. He continued to watch the night. What did Nbwale want?

"You must have loved her very much," Nbwale said after a while. "The woman who left you and was directly responsible for getting you into this," Nbwale persisted.

"I walked out," Gallagher said at last after a stubborn silence.

"You are not the kind of man who walks out on the woman he loves. She must have given terrible cause, in which case she had already left you, even if you still shared the same roof."

Gallagher said nothing.

"You had the look of a man trying to forget something, and running as far away as possible in the attempt. Was she white?"

Gallagher could not ignore that one. "What's that got to do with it?"

"Merely curious. So she was."

"I don't check a woman's ethnic credentials before falling for her."

"Perhaps you should."

"You're beginning to sound like Sumner." Gallagher wondered why Nbwale was trying to needle him.

"Please do not be angry, Gordon. I am indeed merely curious. You are an interesting man. I am fascinated by what motivates you."

"All sorts of things." Gallagher decided he would play Nbwale's game to see where it would lead. It was one way of passing the time.

"Ah, love!" the big African murmured, as if to himself. "Such a potent force. Have you been in love many times? I have."

"Twice," Gallagher answered. "Everything else was ships-in-the-night."

"What happened?"

"With the two? I got lacerated each time. I married the second one." It had taken him three aching years to get over Karin; then he'd met Celia, so different that everything was totally new. Then....

"There must be a moral there somewhere," Nbwale said amusedly. "Strange creatures, women. They hate being spurned but are ruthless with their own spurning. Deadly when rejected. In my country we are very aware of this inherent ruthlessness in the female of our species."

"I suppose you don't give them the vote."

"It will come ... eventually."

"I had a feeling you'd say something like that."

"It is the natural order of things, you know."

"What is?"

"This ruthlessness. Take, for instance, this woman Marika, whose prowess you appear to have so much respect for. I imagine that spurning her would be tantamount to earning yourself a death sentence."

Gallagher could not see Nbwale's expression, and so could not tell whether the man was smiling.

Ruthlessness. Karin had had that, all right. Despite himself, Gallagher found his mind returning to the distant time of the affair. Part of him remained totally alert, his senses still tuned to the vibrations of the night. The other part searched for and found the memory of the shock of the break-up with Karin.

Motivations, Nbwale had said. Has the ending of the affair with Karin been the true reason he had volunteered for special duty and offered his body to the punishing régime of the training he had subsequently received? Had Karin been the reason he had played tag with death all those years? And here he was: another place, another night, a gun in his hands, waiting.

"Physician," came Nbwale's voice, as if with instinctive understanding, "know thyself." He seemed to have deliberately scrambled his quotations.

And Gallagher continued to think of the distant Karin, married now to a man with a "safe, steady" job, and with three children. What would happen to that man when she got bored? *Had Karin even been the reason O'Keefe had died?*

Gallagher did not want to look that far into himself, and he silently cursed Nbwale for starting the train of thought; but his mind, once hooked on to it, would not leave him be. The part of him that was alert to the night remained so. The other dug remorselessly into a memory he hated....

They had been avoiding the pursuit patrol all day. The jungle clearing was not far. There lay safety in the shape of the unmarked helicopter that had been flown in by Gallagher himself. The female member of the ministerial guard in the African republic had materialized before him.

Oh, God, I can't! he had thought as he felt his hands bringing up the Ingram with practised swiftness.

The sweat-polished, sculpted black face had been nothing like Karin's, yet he had felt a minute hesitation. He had forced his hands to obey the training they had been given. The Ingram had kept rising, to point at the target.

Then a shot had sped past him. The woman's eyes had opened wide with the shock of the bullet striking home, but she had still found time to fire before she died, a long burst from her AK. Gallagher had felt nothing, but a grunt had come from behind him. He's spun quickly, dreading what he would find. O'Keefe was down on his knees, one hand pressed uselessly against a terrible wound in his side.

193

"*O'Keefe!*" Christ, Christ, Christ.

Gallagher had bent down to help him up. O'Keefe had pushed him away.

"Go on, sir! You can't do anything. We'll both be caught if you stay. I'm ... I'm no use to them now...." The words had died in a gasp.

"O'Keefe!" *Oh, God. I've finally done it. I've killed him.*

O'Keefe had said: "You think ... it was your fault ... don't you? Give me ... the Ingram. Come ... on ... give it to me."

Reluctantly, Gallagher had done so. O'Keefe had pointed the weapon at himself, pulled the trigger before Gallagher had known what was happening.

Nothing.

"See?" O'Keefe had said tiredly, letting the Ingram drop. "Jammed. Bloody thing jammed on you." He had breathed harshly a few times, and had stopped Gallagher from trying to dress the wound. "No. No, no. I've told you, sir. It's no good. I know where I'm headed. Now ... now you've got to ... get *out* of here." He'd stared at the Ingram. "Bloody thing."

It was all very well for O'Keefe to say the weapon had jammed, but Gallagher even now could not persuade himself that he had squeezed the trigger in time, if at all.

"Go on, for the love of God!" O'Keefe had said with all the strength he could muster. "Get to the chopper ... before her mates come. I'll hold them back long enough."

"For God's sake, O'Keefe! You can't expect me to do that!"

"This is not ... a bloody nursery. Piss off! Stop making ... me ... talk."

Gallagher had picked up the Ingram, stood up slowly. "All right, you miserable bastard," he said chokingly. "You're going to miss me." He turned to go.

"Sir."

He had looked back at O'Keefe.

"I've never told you," O'Keefe had said, "but you are the best. I always asked them to send me out with you. Trust no one else with my life, I told them. You're still the best."

"O'Keefe...."

"Now piss off, like I said."

"All right, you old sod," Gallagher had said gently. He had stopped briefly to grip O'Keefe's unbloodied hand. "Thanks for everything you've taught me. Don't let them take you alive."

"I won't."

And Gallagher had sped off down the track without a backward glance, the moisture in his eyes partially blurring his vision. He was nearly at the helicopter when he heard the shots, followed by a long, terrible scream; and he knew they had used the machetes on O'Keefe.

Choking with anger, self-disgust and a sense of loss, he had run on. He had unjammed the Ingram, and as he approached the clearing, two men had suddenly risen out of the long grass that bordered it. He had sneezed.

The Ingram had taken off, spewing .45s like confetti. It was a testimony to his training and the speed of his control that not one bullet had gone astray. The men, themselves startled by the unexpected sneeze, had died before they had even taken aim.

He had made it to the helicopter and had taken off without further trouble.

He would never forget O'Keefe....

"I believe Miss Tanner believes she loves you," Nbwale was saying.

Both parts of Gallagher were again with the Australian night. Less than a minute had passed.

"In situations like these," he replied, "emotions are heightened. She thinks she may die. Once she makes it back to the real world, she'll come to her senses and return to her social circle."

"What about yourself?"

"I, of all people, ought to know better."

"Cynicism?" Nbwale was definitely smiling. "Is that what your trip into your memories has brought back with it?"

Gallagher made no reply.

"There are certain people," Nbwale finally began softly into the long silence, "who would pay handsomely for your skills."

So that was it. That was what Nbwale had really come up the dune for.

"No."

"I don't understand," Nbwale said after another long silence. "You know what I'm talking about."

"Yes. I know. But I'm still turning you down."

"Don't you care what happens over there?"

"I care about what happens in a lot of places. I can't fight in all of them. If I intended to work with the people you've mentioned, I would not do it for money; at least, not the kind of payments you're thinking about. Expenses. That'll all I would want. But I've had it with guns. I've done my bit."

"You need them now."

"Yes, and it's my own stupid fault that I'm here."

"Is that your last word on the matter?"

"Absolutely."

The rest of the watch passed in total silence between them; and when it was time for Gallagher to leave, no words were spoken.

At the base of the dune, he met Villiger. "Isn't anyone sleeping tonight?" he asked with an edge of testiness to his voice.

Villiger said: "So you turned him down."

"What makes you think he asked me anything?"

"It was obvious that he would at some time."

"It's not a victory for you," Gallagher said evenly. "I detest what's going on in your country." He walked away, leaving the South African to stare after his receding shape in the gloom.

He went up to the Range Rover, put the M16 in. Lauren was still awake but Smallson appeared to be sleeping peacefully.

"I heard that dog," she said, as if to explain her wakefulness.

"He was no trouble. Probably trying to find his pack."

"It sounded kind of eerie."

Gallagher said: "I'm starving." The dog's behaviour still mystified.

"Here. I've got yours."

"Thanks." He took the can from her. Prawns again. "We'll be looking like these things before we get to Cook."

"There wasn't much time to choose a better selection." He was still standing outside, so she leaned across to kiss him, but missed in the dark. She got the corner of his mouth, then corrected her aim. "Perhaps we should go back and try again."

He smiled. "Feel free; but you go without me."

She got out to join him. They had spoken quietly so as not to wake the old man. Now they walked a little distance away from the vehicle. Gallagher began eating out of the can, using his hand to scoop.

"Do you think we'll have any trouble tonight?" she asked.

"I doubt it, but you never can tell."

"I'll stand a watch, if you like. Without Parguineau, you need an extra hand. I can shoot at least as good as Sumner."

"We've gone over than before. Your job is taking care of the old man. This is not chauvinistic nonsense. You're simply the most practical choice. OK?"

"Yes, boss." She put her arm about his waist. "I won't hurt you the way she did," she said without warning.

He stopped so abruptly, she was jerked to a halt. "You don't know what she did."

"It hurt. That's all I do know." She paused, watching him. He was not looking at her. "We've both been hurt," she went on, "and neither of us likes doing it to others. I think we have a good basis for a relationship."

"You don't mess about, do you, once you get going?"

"As Gramps would say, you'd better believe it."

They began walking again. She kept her arm about his waist while he finished his meal.

He hung on to the empty tin and put his free hand – the one he had not used to eat with – around her. "I won't be able to keep you in the style to which you are accustomed. No estates in Scotland; no grouse shooting; no chalets in Switzerland; and your parents will disown you. Are you sure you want this?"

"Don't try to put me off. It won't work. I can take a job."

"Determined."

"I'm Jake Smallson's granddaughter; a pretty tough cookie when I want to be." Suddenly, her boldness wavered. "Hey, just look at me, throwing myself at you."

He stopped and pulled her against him. He sought and found her mouth with his. She relaxed against him with a sigh, as if she had finally satisfied herself about something.

He shut his eyes in the darkness. *Dear God*, he pleaded, *just let me get it right this time. Please.*

Day Six

I

THE NIGHT had passed without incident; Gallagher took the last shift and Sumner went on before him. Gallagher had the feeling that Nbwale had stayed awake to watch them both.

Beginning early with the new day, they were about to set off when they discovered that Villiger's Range Rover had been standing in soft sand. It was bogged down. Villiger swore richly in Afrikaans.

They quickly off-loaded everything that could be moved, and began digging with their hands and the empty food tins. As they dug round each wheel, they saw why even the stalwart Range Rover had been unable to cope. There appeared to be very little solidity beneath the surface carpet of sand. Then the sand became damp.

"There's water down there!" Paula Browne cried, astonished.

"About a metre and a half down," Nbwale said. "But very salty."

"Well, it's no use to us," Gallagher said, "even if we had the time to dig for it." The sand had become more solid, though still damp. "Stones, rocks, dead wood ... anything you can find to fill these holes. That should give the wheels enough purchase."

They hurried about the space between the dunes where they had spent the night, gathering the sparsely scattered pieces of rock and weathered stones. Sometimes they had to dig around embedded pieces that at first appeared small, only to find there was more beneath the surface. Some turned out to be subterranean boulders whose eventual size could only be guessed. Much time was wasted like this.

At last, they had collected enough to form a reasonably firm surface for all four wheels. By then it was nearly nine a.m. The Range Rover came free at the first try. They gave a ragged cheer and began to load it swiftly, tired and hot though they were.

Then disaster struck a second time, with more ominous implications.

Gallagher had poked his hand into a recess in the vehicle, to store an empty can, when a sharp pain surged up a finger. He yelled with the savagery of it and snatched his hand away. Something scrabbled out of the recess and on to the tailgate. His finger hurting abominably, Gallagher picked up a full can and slammed it viciously on the creature. Everyone came to stare.

His finger was now numb, and the pain was beginning to shoot up his arm. The finger was swelling too. Gallagher began to sweat and felt dizzy.

Villiger took the hand, looked at it and immediately put the finger to his mouth. He sucked, while Gallagher yelled in pain. Villiger spat.

"I'm not sure whether this will do any good, but that thing was highly venomous. I may have got some out." He looked at Lauren. "Take him to some shade and stay with him. Give him water."

Nbwale had been looking at the thing Gallagher had squashed. It was a spider, not very big, considering the damage it had done. It was black, with a broad red stripe down its back.

"Redback," Nbwale said. "That's like a black widow."

Paula Browne looked green and haggard. "Does that mean he's going to die?" Her voice was weak with dread.

Nbwale decided to put the facts bluntly. "It is possible. We are too far from any medical help for it to be of any use to think about it. Gallagher has just one chance. His own strength, and possibly the age and condition of this spider."

"What do you mean?" Smallson asked.

"It may have been very old and weak – I have no way of telling – in which case its toxicity will be low. That's Gallagher's best hope, apart from his own strength, as I've said. He'll have a bad day or two of it, if that's the case, then he should be all right."

"A day or two!" From Sumner.

"Possibly three. If it's a bad bite, it will take more than a week, without medical attention, if he's going to recover at all."

"Jesus! A week! And what do you think is going to happen out there while we wait for a week? What about food and water?"

Nbwale looked at Villiger. "Are we waiting?"

The South African had already made his decision. "We'll see how he is in two days. We should not travel with him just yet. We may get into a firefight, and, apart from the fact that we need his expertise, he could get killed."

"What difference does that make if he's going to die, anyway?" Sumner said truculently. "Do we have to sit here until that goddam gunship comes looking?"

"We're safe here for the moment," Villiger said evenly. He surveyed Sumner with open distaste. "Gallagher picked well. We can't be seen."

"Except from the air."

"Sumner," the Afrikaner began with heavy warning, "I'm now in charge of this crazy little expedition. I say we wait here until we see how Gallagher's doing. That's the end of the argument." He looked at the others. "Does anyone else disapprove?" There was no disapproval. "Good."

He went to where Lauren was sitting on the ground in the shade of the Range Rover, with the recumbent Gallagher's head on her lap.

"You heard most of that?"

She turned a tear-streaked face up to him. "Yes."

He was made uncomfortable by her tears. "I'm sorry you had to," he said gruffly.

"The ungrateful bastard."

"Don't worry. We're going nowhere. I'll see to it."

"Thank you."

"How is he?" Villiger looked closely.

"He said he was feeling nauseous a short while ago, but he hasn't been sick."

Gallagher was lying perfectly still and seemed totally unaware of their conversation. His skin was taut across his face and was shiny with sweat. His eyes were closed.

"Have you given him water?"

"Yes, but he didn't take much."

Villiger felt helpless. "We'll just have to wait and see." He gave her an encouraging pat on the shoulder. "Take good care of him. He's a good man."

"I will," she said softly. "I will." She kissed Gallagher's hot forehead.

Villiger left to organize the defence of the camp, if the need should arise. Sumner was useless, so effectively that meant himself and Nbwale, the man he'd come to kill.

"How did that thing get in there?" he asked Nbwale.

"Their natural habitat is near buildings, among all the nooks and crannies they can find. We probably brought it with us from the complex. There's some rope in there. The spider got cosy."

Villiger stared at him. "Do you believe *they*...."

The big African shook his head. "Most unlikely. They would not handle one of those things if they had any sense. No. I think it simply crawled in and we took it for a ride." He paused. "Do you want him to die?"

"No."

"Neither do I. Now we who are enemies must fight together to defend him, if need be." Nbwale chuckled hugely. "A fitting irony."

Singapore. Colombo. Karachi. Tel Aviv. Rome. Gatwick.

Crofton saw the Outer Marker indicator come on, and was pleased to be coming to the end of his long flight, despite the pleasure he always got out of flying the Cessna. Most of the flight had been at fifty thousand; peaceful, smooth, relaxed, notwithstanding the fact that he had not slept for twenty-four hours. Benzies had kept him going; benzies and orange juice. What a combination.

Middle Marker.

It was a smooth let down and a feather-light touchdown. Whatever else he might be, Crofton knew he was a pretty good pilot.

As he taxied off the runway, he decided to refuel, despite his chronic need of sleep now that he'd finished the journey. Harding would want to take off as soon as possible, after he'd heard the news.

It was midnight, London time, on the same day he'd left Australia.

Once he'd finished at the airport, he took a taxi to his St John's Wood flat. The cab company had a contract with Harding International so he did not have to pay. He went straight to his bedroom and went to sleep fully clothed.

He was up at eight, feeling hungry but refreshed. He decided to have breakfast cooked for him, so after a long, slow bath, he dressed carefully, taking his time about everything, went down to the garage and got out the red Porsche. He drove to his favourite coffee shop in Hampstead.

Throughout breakfast, he marshalled his thoughts, preparing himself for the momentous thing he was about to do. He ordered another pot of tea, and while it was being prepared he went out to buy writing paper and envelopes from the newsagent's a few doors away. He then wrote a very long letter, addressed and sealed it. He put the letter in his jacket pocket and went out, leaving the remaining paper and envelopes on the table. He was gone by the time the waitress had realized it.

The red Porsche surged down Park Lane, heading for Harding International's offices in Knightsbridge. It was very cold, bright, and dry; the third day of December, and almost a week since the hijack.

Crofton hummed tunelessly. The letter made him feel much more relaxed.

When he was in town, Harding always went to the office early; which for him meant ten o'clock. One of the lights on the elaborate communications unit on his vast desk blinked. It was blue.

He pressed a button. "Yes, Jenny?" Jenny was his secretary, with whom Crofton had been to bed with at least twice.

"Mr Crofton is here to see you."

It was a tribute to Harding's self-control that he made no sound of astonishment. Crofton's presence could only mean very serious trouble, and an ill omen that could rock the very foundations of Harding International. Crofton would not have flown the Cessna single-handedly all the way from Australia just for the fun of it.

"Send him in." Harding was ice-cold.

Crofton entered and launched into his story without preamble. Harding listened, his face whitening; but that was the only outward sign of the mounting fury within him.

"Right," he said when Crofton had finished. "Is the Cessna ready for flight?"

"Yes, Sir Alex."

"Good. You've done well coming to London."

"I'm only sorry I didn't inform you earlier."

"I can hardly blame you. He fooled both Marika and me, after all." Harding's black eyes were like chips of obsidian, and as lifeless. "Wait for me at the airport. I have some checking to do before I join you. Are you fit for the return flight? I shall take spells at the yoke."

"I am ready when you are, Sir Alex."

"Good. I'll see you there."

As Crofton left, Harding pressed the button with the blue light. "Yes, Sir Alex?"

"Have the Camargue brought round, will you, please? And tell Porter I'll be driving."

"Very good, sir."

"I also want you to cancel all appointments for a few days ... let's say a week. Anyone wants to know, I'll be abroad."

"Yes, sir," Jenny acknowledged. She did not ask where abroad. It was well-known that Sir Alex took secret trips when concluding fat business deals. It was his way of staying ahead of the competition. Obviously Crofton had brought news of an important deal; a very big one apparently, because Crofton had not given her his usual squeeze before going in to see Harding. She'd been hoping to visit that fantastic flat of his again. Well, she'd have to wait till they returned.

It never occurred to her that she'd never be seeing Crofton again.

The 79,000-pound gunmetal Rolls-Royce Camargue cruised into Hyde Park and stopped. Its number plates said: HI 1A. Harding got out and began walking. He did not even bother to lock it, such was his disdain for car thieves. No thief would have got very far with it; a few yards, perhaps, should one be so stupid, before all the alarms started screaming and the car became totally immobilized, the thief trapped inside.

Harding went for a walk along a path he knew someone always walked at this time of the day. A few minutes later, he saw the person he was looking for. A smile totally lacking in humour twisted his lips. He caught up with his quarry.

"Hullo, Pimple."

Boyle turned round with a great smile of pleasure. Only one person called him by that name.

"Alex!" He stuck out a hand which Harding shook warmly. "This is a surprise. Didn't realise you were back. Staying long, or popping off again?"

"Popping off, I'm afraid, Pimple."

"Ah, the life of a tycoon! By the way, thanks for the use of the old yacht last summer. Haven't seen you since then, have I?"

"No." Harding looked suitably apologetic. "Awfully busy."

"What did I just say about the life of a tycoon?"

Harding smiled. "People usually think we lead such sybaritic lives."

"People."

They laughed heartily at silly people.

"How's the old job coming along?" Harding asked when the laughter had subsided. "Still like it?"

"Yes, by God. Awfully nice of you to have put in a word for me."

"Think nothing of it. If one can't do for one's own cousin...." Harding left the rest out.

"Quite," Boyle said. He hero-worshipped Harding. A senior at his old school and an absolutely clever bat. One could also tell Alex one's problems. He was such a good listener.

Boyle decided to tell Harding about a problem that had been nagging him for days.

"Have you brought that amazing Rolls of yours?"

"Yes."

"Let's go to it. There's something I'd like to talk over with you."

In the Camargue, Boyle went on: "It's this hijack thing. Got us absolutely stumped. Can't make head or tail of it, and we've got the Americans breathing down our necks because of...." Boyle stopped, suddenly remembering. "Good Lord! Of course! The yacht. The *Lauren*. Lauren Tanner. She's one of the victims. You two were pretty thick once, weren't you?"

"Yes, but that's all history now."

"Still, it must be pretty awful."

"It is. I've been putting out a few feelers here and there ... just to help, you understand. The family."

"Of course. You tycoons usually have your ... other channels. And ...?"

"Nothing. Absolutely nothing."

"We can't understand it either. No demands of any kind. Simply odd. The form is that terrorists always want something in exchange; money, or people, or some recognition for some idiotic cause." Boyle's mouth turned down. "Cause" in his mind was synonymous with anarchy. "We've got just about everyone looking." Boyle shook his head slowly. "Simply can't understand it. But," he went on, "we do have a curious anomaly; sort of nigger in the woodpile, so to speak." He smiled at his joke.

Harding waited, a spider with his trap set, knowing all he had to do was be patient until the fly fell in.

"Gallagher," Boyle continued. "The anomaly. He is among the victims; but he's no one of any importance. I wondered about that until I realized what had happened. The poor sod had blundered into it. Running from wife trouble. She'd been putting it about, apparently.

Well, this Gallagher used to be one of ours."

"Curious."

"Yes. Isn't it? Darkies in the mob. Whatever next? Still, the old man seems to think he's some sort of wonder boy."

Harding, with no trouble at all, got the full story on Gallagher. He came to a decision about Boyle. He opened the lid of the specially built central console.

"Care for a small one, Pimple?"

Boyle knew all about Harding's special drinks console. "One of your legendary brandies? It's a bit early, but I won't pass it up."

Harding got out a miniature balloon glass and filled it.

"Do you mind if I abstain?" he said apologetically. "When Porter's not driving, I prefer to err on the side of caution."

"I understand, Alex." Boyle was magnanimous in his sympathy for a man who had to abide by silly laws about drinking. What was a small snifter for someone who had earned so much revenue for his country? He thought Alex was being absolutely noble. He took the drink gratefully. Alex was like a big brother to him. Alex had always looked after him; even at school.

Boyle drank the rare brandy with relish. There really wasn't anyone like Alex.

"Alex?"

"Yes, Pimple."

"I don't suppose you could do anything about the old man."

"What on earth for?"

"He is rather of the common herd. Likes darkies and things."

Boyle's family, once rich before his time, were now comparatively impoverished. It therefore gave him an intense pleasure to be thus patronized by Harding, who was light years away from him in wealth and social standing. Alex could do anything. All one had to do was ask. Alex knew so many important people.

"I could look into it, I suppose," Harding said doubtfully.

"I'd appreciate it, dear cousin. The man's a pain in the neck. The Minister's on my side, I fancy."

"We shall see, Pimple. Now can I drop you off at your office?"

"Would you? Awfully kind."

Harding put Boyle's glass away and started the Rolls-Royce.

Boyle settled back in the seat as the car began to move. He shut his eyes. Within seconds, he was dead.

Harding reclined the seat slightly so that Boyle's head wouldn't loll. He drove through town and out into the country with Boyle's corpse looking for all the world like a sleeping passenger. Harding found a lonely spot where he dumped the body, taking care not to drive the car on to any surface that would leave tracks. He even wore a pair of cheap shoes he'd bought that day, for just that purpose.

204

Back inside the car, he changed them for his normal shoes, and put the others in a bag. He'd be taking them on the Cessna, to be buried later, somewhere in the vastness of the Australian Outback.

As he sped back into town, he called his office on the car-phone.

"Yes, Sir Alex?" came Jenny's voice.

"I'll be back within half an hour. Tell Porter I want him to drive me to Gatwick."

"Yes, Sir Alex. Oh...."

"Yes?"

"You had a call from America, from Miss Tanner's father. He wanted to know if your enquiries have come up with anything. He says he thinks the police forces have gone to sleep on this one."

"Call him back and tell him you've spoken to me. Tell him that the people I'm using are doing all they can, and that I must wait for them to contact me, as their identities cannot be compromised. I'm sure he'll understand."

"Yes, sir."

"Anything else worth mentioning?"

"Just two telexes from Australia. One's from Perth: the Jarrahdale investment is going ahead. And the other's from Adelaide. There was a temporary shut-down of the HA3600 computer at Kintore. They thought you'd like to know since you've some scientific guests up there, and asked whether you wanted them to send a man up to check it out."

The computer at Kintore. That would have been Gallagher's doing, Harding was sure. His lips tightened into a thin line before he spoke again.

"Telex Perth," he said calmly, "and say well done; then tell Adelaide there will be no need to send a man. My guests know all about the HA3600."

"Very good, sir. Will you be coming up to the office?"

"No. I'll simply be collecting Porter."

"Then have a good flight, Sir Alex."

"Thank you, Jenny." He hung up.

At about the time that Gallagher had been bitten by the Redback and Crofton had landed at Gatwick, the new day's hunt had been going on for over four hours.

Marika had wakened earlier than the others and had studiously spent the time putting her long blonde hair into a single plait which she had then coiled about her head in the German fashion. She then jammed her sunhat on. This had given the beautiful face a determined, and rather frightening look. She had promised herself she would catch Gallagher that day.

But the day had passed fruitlessly. It was now well after nine, and the sun, long gone behind the dunes, stained the sky faintly in the west with a purply-orange smear; but the dark of the sky was inexorably squeezing it out.

She sat on the ground, leaning against a wheel of her Landrover. Ngoma's vehicle had also rejoined, after an equally disappointing day. Between them, they had covered hundreds of kilometres of track, and Ngoma had even gone down to Waldana Well. Marika had pushed them at a punishing pace. Now they were grouped together, talking quietly in the darkness. They were warily alert to her mood, for she had not spoken to anyone for over two hours.

She continued to sit where she was, wondering why she had seen no sign of the fugitives all day. Was it possible that they were still in the dunefield, after all, and had not even yet reached the junction? Were they already out of fuel and water, and hopelessly lost in the sea of dunes?

Soon, the landrovers themselves would be needing fresh fuel supplies. She would either be forced to return to Kintore or wait for the gunship and the fuel truck. Going back was out of the question. Waiting for the gunship was humiliating.

She cursed frustratedly in Rumanian. She would make sure Gallagher begged for death, just as Serge had. No one used her with impunity.

She picked up the M16 which never left her side. Rising, she went up to the others.

"We start early in the morning," was all she said.

She placed her M16 in the Landrover, removed the sunhat, and slowly began to uncoil the long plait; then took her time about unplaiting it. When her golden tresses were hanging free in the dark, she reached in behind the driver's seat and took out the hairbrush she'd brought with her. She began to brush patiently at her hair. The action soothed and calmed her. She did that for a very long time.

She could not know that barely ten kilometres south of her position, Gallagher lay incapacitated; and vulnerable.

At Villiger's instigation, they had built him a makeshift shelter using the framework of steel tubes that had embraced the Range Rover from cab to rear and the men's discarded jackets, tied and stretched across it. They had removed the framework in its entirety, using the Range Rover's tools to unbolt it, after which the whole thing had come off smoothly, backwards. Throughout the day, they had also manoeuvred both vehicles in order to keep as much shade as was possible upon him.

With great care, they had hunted for but not found any more spiders. In a similar recess in Gallagher's vehicle, however, they had found another length of rope. Villiger had put the two lengths together in Gallagher's Range Rover, so that they would be close to hand in case of need.

Lauren had spent the whole day with his head on her lap. She had taken only sips of the water offered to her by Paula Browne, but had refused food. She had barely spoken to anyone, content to sit with Gallagher and cool his burning forehead from time to time with a damp cloth. He had complained at one time of burning and itching and of stomach cramps; but mainly, he had spent the day almost comatose. Lauren had refused any help with him, even from Smallson.

In the darkness, Paula Browne came up to her and sat down.

"Aren't you afraid of the snakes any more?" Lauren asked listlessly.

Paula tried to make a joke of it. "If one's going to get me, it's going to get me. So who cares?" That was not strictly true. She was still very frightened. "Here, kid. Let me help. You've been sitting like that all day. You need to stretch yourself."

"No. He might die. I want to be holding him if that happens."

Paula Browne silently fought that piece of logic for a while before saying, softly: "He's a pretty tough cookie. He's fighting the poison. C'mon, kid. Give. And get yourself some food."

"I'm not hungry."

"Of course you are."

Lauren remained silent.

Paula refused to give up: "You haven't eaten since morning. You're going to need your strength. We all do. You're not helping him or yourself by becoming weak for lack of food. God knows we need to keep going in this climate."

After a long pause, Lauren said reluctantly: "All right ... but only for a short while. I'm coming right back."

Gently, they exchanged places, Lauren with the hesitation of someone handing over a prized possession. Paula Browne smiled wistfully in the darkness. She had once cared as deeply for someone, a long, long time ago.

As Lauren stood up, she found her grandfather waiting with an opened can.

"Peaches, again," he said apologetically, passing it to her. "But healthy."

She took it gratefully. "Did you two plan this?" she accused the old man gently as she put a segment of fruit into her mouth.

"We thought we should try."

"I am hungry," she admitted sheepishly.

"So we were right."

She continued eating. "He's not going to die," she announced suddenly and firmly, as if just discovering the certainty of it.

A little distance away, Nbwale and Villiger were talking. Sumner was up a dune, on guard.

"What if he dies?" Nbwale asked.

"He won't." Villiger was positive.

Nbwale stared at the solid shape for a long while. The Afrikaner was not facing him.

"I can scarcely believe it," Nbwale said at last, wonderingly. "You really have taken to him, haven't you?"

"Haven't you?" Villiger countered without looking round. He was listening to the night, particularly to hear if Sumner did anything panicky up there. A couple of times during the day, they had heard the faint sound of motors, brought to them upon a light breeze.

"We do share the same colour," Nbwale said after a while. "Well, almost."

"That's a bullshitting excuse if I ever heard one," the Afrikaner remarked calmly. He continued to listen for Sumner.

He was in the hole again, and the water was coming down, and his face was looking down at him drowning, and more water was coming down and....

He screamed!

"Oh, Gordon, Gordon," Lauren was saying over and over again, softly, as she cradled his head. He was particularly hot, and she squeezed the newly-wet cloth over his brow.

Sumner, up on the dune and startled by the sudden scream, had fired his Uzi into the darkness. The measured, metallic barks sounded as if they would rouse the entire world.

Villiger ran to the base of the dune, risking Sumner spraying panicky shots at him. "Stop firing, you idiot!" he bawled.

"What happened?" Sumner's edgy voice came down.

"Gallagher had a nightmare. Now do your job properly." Villiger was furious.

Sumner said reproachfully: "Well, he shouldn't have screamed like that. I thought you were all being murdered down there."

Villiger walked away in disgust.

"How is he?" he asked Lauren as he came up to her.

Everyone crowded round, barely able to see each other in the dark of the hollow.

"He's very hot," she replied. He could hear the tears in her voice. "Oh, Gordon, don't die. Please...."

Marika sat up suddenly. She had not been asleep. Next to her Selini lay, completely out to the world. Marika went to where Giannetta and Charlie stood guard.

"Did either of you hear anything?"

"No," Giannetta answered, surprised. "What did you hear?"

"Shots. I am certain of it."

"From which direction?" Charlie asked.

"They were echoes, and at night it is impossible to tell. It was a very short burst."

All three listened keenly, but heard nothing further remotely resembling gunfire that night.

Giannetta and Charlie both surmised that Marika, obsessed by the need to catch Gallagher, had been dreaming.

Days Seven and Eight

I

HIGH ABOVE the Mediterranean, the Citation III drew snowy contrails across the December sky.

From the co-pilot's seat, Harding said: "It's a curious thing about Gallagher. He spoke the truth most of the time. He was running away from wife trouble, and he did get on the plane by accident." It was the first time during the four and a half hours since they'd left London that the subject had been raised. "We actually brought this problem on ourselves. Now this one man threatens the entire existence of Harding International." Harding shook his head slowly. "Incredible."

Crofton did not tell him that it was his murderous hobby, and not Gallagher, that had been the real cause.

"I did warn Marika," Harding went on, "but she allowed her sexual urges to get the better of her. You would think she would have learned, after her experience with the Frenchman she shot." Then he relented, remembering how thoroughly he too had been fooled. "Still, they did give him a watertight cover. Not even my best people had managed to penetrate it. So in a way, Crofton, we all owe you a rather special vote of thanks. The survival of all of us may have been due to your timely intervention."

Crofton smiled his gratitude, and got on with flying the Cessna. There were other things on his mind.

"Just let me know when you want me to take over," Harding said. "Don't tire yourself."

"I'm fine," Crofton said. It was the truth. He felt strangely refreshed, perhaps because of the knowledge of what he intended to do when they landed in Australia. He did not think Harding was going to come out of this affair unscathed. He believed that Gallagher had already done too much damage, and he had made his decision on that basis.

Some time later, Harding glanced at the colour radar on the instrument panel.

"This is where we keep a sharp look-out for Russian-flown Libyan MiG-25s, Israeli F-15 Eagles and American Sixth Fleet F-14 Tomcats. We would not relish a tangle with these trigger-happy gentlemen." He smiled ruefully. "The sky is so hostile these days, it's becoming safer to cross the road."

210

They were flying at almost maximum ceiling and cruising very close to the Cessna's limit.

Crofton said, lightly: "They wouldn't relish the idea of having shot us down, after they found out who you were ... even the Russians."

"That would not do us much good, would it," Harding said with a slight edge of testiness to his voice, "while we're spiralling down fifty-one thousand feet?" He briefly thought of the cousin he had murdered. Pimple had outlived his usefulness.

They were challenged by radio a few times, but, satisfied with their transponder code, their challengers sent no one up to investigate.

Crofton thought about the letter he was going to post in Darwin.

In the London office overlooking the sleepy square, the man pressed his intercom switch. "Any news of Boyle, Mrs Arundel?"

"No, sir."

"I see. Thank you." He switched off. He didn't like it. Something was itching at him.

He pressed the switch again. "Ask Mr Fowler to come and see me, will you?"

"Yes, sir."

Adrian Fowler was tall, thin as a rake, and fifty-eight years old. In his youth, he had been a daring pilot on the Berlin Airlift. He ambled into the man's office within two minutes of having been called.

"What's up, Greg?"

"It's Boyle," the man called Greg answered. "He's gone missing."

Fowler smiled blissfully. " 'Rid me of this turbulent Boyle, O Providence,' I once heard you pun. I should think you'd be pleased."

"Yes, well, Providence appears to have answered me in a way I'd rather not have had."

Fowler was immediately serious. "How long has he been missing?"

"About five hours. It could be anything."

"But your instincts tell you he's been hit?"

The man nodded. "Yes. I can feel it. Boyle is stupid, but one thing he never is, or should I say was ... and that's late. He enjoys playing his role of secret agent too much. He's always in the office, monitoring every message that comes in to us. I sometimes used to wonder if he slept here too. I'm certain he would have been in contact."

"No need to ask if you've checked his recent movements?"

"Even his customary walk in the park has been checked. Nothing. You'd think someone would have seen something."

"People *ignore* things these days. It's all no see, no hear, no speak. Assuming Boyle has been hit ... why?"

"That's what I'm asking *you*. The computer's only given us what any machine working from limited data would. I don't want logical answers. They've got us nowhere. Put that celebrated eccentric brain of yours to work. I don't care how outlandish your theories. I want to hear them all."

"They could have found out about Gallagher," Fowler said.

"Even so – God help him if they have ... it still doesn't explain Boyle. He did not even know Boyle. We have had no indications of suspected terrorists, agitators, what-have-you, entering the country...."

"*Suspected* terrorists. What about the unsuspected ones? Those could be anybody. Even your Aunt Clara."

"I don't have an Aunt Clara."

"No; but somebody has."

Fowler was scraping at the surface, but he was a long, long way from working it out. "I'll see what I come up with," he said, and left the man Greg to his worrying thoughts.

A full search was mounted for Boyle, but by the time his body would be found, his death would be of purely academic interest.

Gallagher had a quiet night, but at eight the next morning he was violently sick, bringing up everything he'd eaten the previous day. Dizziness came at him, leaving him light-headed. Through it all, Lauren held on to him, wiping gently at his mouth with a piece of cloth she'd torn from her blouse.

Watching her, Paula Browne said to Nbwale: "Think he's going to live?"

"He didn't die in the night. I think there's a pretty good chance. Pleased?"

"Yeah. I am. Too bad the spider didn't bite that sonofabitch Sumner."

They both looked up to where Sumner, on another spell of guard duty, was lying face down on the crest of the dune. Nbwale had the distinct impression that, after his display of abject panic during the night, Sumner rather wanted to be on his own.

"Sometimes, Mrs Browne," he said thoughtfully, still looking up at Sumner, "we don't always get what we wish for." He turned his attention once more to where Lauren sat with Gallagher's head on her lap. "And sometimes," he went on softly, "we get lucky, as you Americans say, and find the very thing. Of course, when it happens, we don't want to believe it."

Together they walked to the shelter and sat beneath it.

"How's he doing?" Paula Browne asked Lauren.

The grey eyes were red-rimmed from lack of sleep. "He's got a kind of rash on one arm."

Nbwale said: "Let me see." He examined the arm carefully.

Villiger came in at that moment. "Trouble?"

212

Nbwale moved aside for the South African to look. "I don't know what it is."

"Probably a reaction. We'll have to wait and see how it develops; which isn't saying much, I suppose. Anything else?" he asked Lauren. He'd been on a scouting patrol three dunes away and didn't know Gallagher had been sick, though the smell lingered slightly, despite Lauren having covered the mess with sand. Villiger sniffed.

"He's been sick," Lauren said.

"Perhaps it's a good reaction. Has he taken anything? Water? Food?"

"Water. He doesn't want food."

Gallagher ignored the conversation going on above him. His eyes were closed and he appeared to be asleep.

Nbwale asked Villiger: "Did you see anything?"

Everyone waited for the reply. "No. Not a sign of them."

"Maybe they're out of fuel. If they've been looking for us all this time, thinking we've gone to the wells, they will have covered great distances. They haven't got unlimited supplies."

Then Gallagher spoke for the first time since he'd been bitten. "They'll wait for the gunship." The voice was weak but very clear.

Suddenly everyone was beaming, and Lauren was shedding quiet tears.

"Hey, man," Villiger said, "how are you?"

"Wretched, and hungry."

"I'll get the food," Paula Browne said, and quickly went to do so.

"You were very lucky," Nbwale said. "That spider must have been very old and in poor condition. The venom was extremely weak, apparently."

Gallagher managed a wry smile. "Then I hope I never meet one in prime condition. Believe me, this is no fun."

"Your health must be pretty good too. You've only been down for twenty-four hours."

"I'm still down. You can take it from me. I'm down." He shut his eyes again.

Villiger motioned to Nbwale and they left the shelter. They met Paula returning with an opened can.

"Forget it for the moment," Villiger said. "He's still too weak. Perhaps later." He looked into Gallagher's Range Rover where Jake Smallson appeared to be sleeping. "Best way to conserve strength," he murmured, turning away.

Smallson seemed to have aged. Villiger hoped they would not have two incapacitated people to deal with.

He said to Paula Browne: "Keep an eye on the old man. The heat's getting to him."

She nodded. She wasn't looking too good herself.

"We'll see how Gallagher is tonight," Villiger went on. "Perhaps we'll be able to move in the morning. Keep under cover. No point in taking more sun than you have to."

She nodded again, and entered the Range Rover.

Villiger said to Nbwale: "The water?"

"Still bubbling."

They walked to the hole they had spent the previous day digging. They had removed the stones from one of the depressions in which Villiger's Range Rover had been stuck, and had decided to dig further, almost as a means of passing the time. Just before the depth that Nbwale had predicted, water had come bubbling up even as they dug. It was not fit to drink, being salty and very metallic in taste. But they had used it to wash themselves, and Lauren had been glad of it to dampen the cloths she had used on Gallagher's head.

Standing watching the little bubbling pool, Villiger said: "I saw them."

Nbwale stared at him. "But you said —"

"I know what I said. What was the point of creating panic?"

"Where are they now?"

"Gone. They came within three kilometres of us but obviously didn't know where we were, or we'd know about it. They're searching the dunefields further north. I followed their progress with the binoculars."

"Do you think they'll come this way again?"

"I doubt it. As you said, they must be running out of fuel by now. They'll have to wait for the gunship. I agree with Gallagher on that. We can really afford to spend only one more night here. Once the gunship gets in on the act, we've had it. We'll move in the morning, no matter how he is." Villiger looked up the dune. "We'd better get Sumner down. He's been up there nearly three hours. We don't want a sunstroke case on our hands. He's already peeling like a lobster as it is."

"What do you expect? He is just a fat white slob, as the Americans say."

"And you?"

Nbwale grinned. "I'm a large black slob; but I don't peel." He left Villiger, to climb the dune and relieve Sumner.

Villiger stared after him expressionlessly, watching as Nbwale took over, and Sumner came slithering and sliding down the sandy slope.

The first thing Sumner said was: "How much longer are we going to stay like rats in this hole?"

"We leave tomorrow morning," Villiger answered him.

"Well, hallalujah. His majesty is ready to travel, is he? Two goddam days we've wasted. You know, I don't understand you at all, Villiger. We could have left him here and saved ourselves. Anyone else wanting to stay with him, it's their choice. But what do you do? You keep us here two days to play nursemaid, while all the time those crazies may be getting their goddam helicopter ready to hunt us down."

The Afrikaner stared into Sumner's fat, red, peeling face. "We need him," he said flatly, and turned away, leaving Sumner to gaze after him.

II

Marika hated what she had to do but she knew she could not put the moment off any longer. It was past midday, and her fuel was running too close to the safety margin. She stopped and radioed Ngoma.

"Have you had luck?"

"No," came the unwanted response.

"Join me," Marika ordered. She terminated transmission, forestalling any questions; and when Ngoma's Landrover, driven with the usual panache by Giannetta, pulled up an hour later, she said to them all: "We shall have to wait for the fuel truck."

"We remain here?" Giannetta asked, surprised. "The day is only halfway. We have enough fuel to do another sweep."

"And if you still do not find them? You will be stuck out there, and we shall waste more time coming to you."

"But the gunship ..." Charlie began.

"I know all about the gunship!" Marika interrupted tightly. The green eyes seemed to roar her fury at him, and Charlie actually found himself taking a step backwards, although she had made no move towards him. "Do you think it is what I want?" She tossed her sunhat angrily into her landrover, walked away from them and up a nearby dune.

She had again plaited her hair that morning, now she was furiously unplaiting it as she moved upwards. By the time she had reached the crest, the golden blonde hair was freely swirling about her face in a moderate breeze that had sprung up. There were binoculars slung about her neck. She stood upright, the wind blowing the hair from her face now, and put the glasses to her eyes.

She searched the dunes patiently. She stayed up there for an hour. Once, she thought she had seen something, but when she had looked again, there was nothing. She rubbed her eyes, and tried again. Nothing. She went back down the dune. The breeze had lessened, and her hair framed the beautiful face in a golden shower that gleamed in the sun.

Villiger slid back down the slope. Had she seen him?

The powerful binoculars he had borrowed from Gallagher had first shown him the flash of light and he had centred upon it quickly. He had caught her in the act of turning, and had swiftly ducked behind the crest.

What to do? he wondered as he hurried. There was a slight breeze blowing away from the camp. To start the engines would be to give an unmistakable advertisement of their presence. The best policy would be to remain put. It was quite possible that they were running too short of fuel to do anything further for the time being. If, as Gallagher had suggested, they would be forced to wait for the gunship and the fuel truck, then the fugitives would hopefully be in better shape, and the pursuers would be unable to follow for the moment.

As these thoughts ran through his mind, Villiger hoped he had judged the situation correctly. He would have to tell the others, and he knew he was going to have trouble with Sumner.

He was right.

"Are you crazy?" Sumner yelled in disbelief. "You *saw* them and you want us to remain here? What the hell are you waiting for, for Chrissake? You want to see them on that dune there before you do something?" He pointed to the nearest one.

Villiger said: "I've already told you. They'll hear our motors. We cannot fight properly as yet."

"Well, goddammit, leave him here. Why the hell should I risk my life for him?"

"Could it be because he risked his for yours, you worthless shit?" Paula Browne snarled.

"For *me*?" Sumner began to scream. "*For me*? You know goddammed well who...."

"*Shut up!*" Villiger roared, and, when Sumner had complied, went on in a quiet, firm voice: "We shall have no more discussions, no more arguments about it. The decision has been made. You wish to leave, Sumner? Then go ahead. No one is stopping you."

Sumner looked at the faces about him. "You expect me to walk?"

"We certainly do not expect you to take one of the Range Rovers," Nbwale told him mildly.

Sumner strode away angrily. "Bastards," they heard him mutter.

At five o'clock, Gallagher opened his eyes and said: "I could eat."

Lauren looked down at him happily. "Are you sure?"

He nodded. "The stomach cramps are gone. So's the dizziness." His voice was much stronger.

"Can you sit up?"

"I can but try." He found he was able to, though the strange weakness of his body was still there.

"Gramps!" Lauren called excitedly. "Gramps!"

216

Smallson urged his overheated body down from the Range Rover where he had spent most of the day. He entered the shelter.

"Well," he said to Gallagher, beaming. "You are back with us."

"Only just," Gallagher said, smiling weakly.

Paula Browne had come in to find out what all the excitement was. Her life-ravaged face looked unashamedly happy when she saw Gallagher.

"You ready to eat now?" she asked him eagerly.

"As ready as I'll ever be. Let's have the lobster and the caviare please."

"Coming right up."

He was eating strongly of nearly half a kilo of the tinned ham, when Villiger and Nbwale joined the crowd.

"We've got problems," Villiger said without preamble.

"I should have stayed asleep," Gallagher said drily. "Tell me."

"They're about five kilometres from here."

Gallagher paused in his eating. "When did you see them?"

"About four hours ago."

Gallagher felt himself growing alert. "And they're still there?"

"Yes. I sneaked up for a look. They're parked."

"Well, we know they don't know we're here, because they would have been upon us like a ton of bricks. That means they're short of fuel. Good news for us."

Gallagher continued his meal, pleased to find that it was staying down. He was also trying to gauge how long it would take the gunship to join the act. Harding would have been warned by now; but Harding had to come all the way from England. Allow three days since the breakout. The gunship would not fly at night....

"We ought to move," he said to Villiger, "right away. You don't seem happy with that idea."

Villiger said: "They'll hear our engines, and you're not strong enough."

"I'll be fine. Nbwale can drive for the time being. As for our noise, check the wind direction. It may have changed. That will help. We've got to take the chance. If they're really short of petrol, they won't follow."

"And if they do?" Nbwale asked.

"We can outrun them. They're five kilometres away in a straight line. It may be a lot further by track. First, they'll have to catch up. I don't think they'll even try, unless they want to get stranded. They'll be running out of fuel even as they chase us. We can still make it to Muckera Rockhole."

"And then what?" Nbwale queried. "We'll be out of fuel by then. It will still be eighty kilometres to Cook."

"We'll have to fight it out. We'll need one of their Landrovers. So we've got to take it from them."

"And the gunship?" Villiger asked quietly.

"That's a nasty thought, but I have an idea."

"It will have to be something special."

"It is." But Gallagher did not tell them. If what he had in mind scared them half as much as it did him, it was best that they didn't know.

He continued to wolf down the ham. He was feeling better by the second. When he'd finished, he said to Paula Browne: "Thanks. And you, Villiger, thanks for waiting. I appreciate it."

"It was a group decision," Villiger said and went out quickly to start preparing for the move.

Nbwale followed him out.

Smallson said shrewdly: "He is like you in many ways. He does not like to be thanked. It was his decision. Of course, we all agreed...."

"All?" Gallagher stressed knowingly.

"I would not count Sumner among the sensible. We all agreed," the old man repeated firmly. "But I believe Villiger would have put his gun to our heads had we not done so." He smiled briefly. "A man of strange integrity."

"Yes," Gallagher agreed thoughtfully. He heaved himself up suddenly, swayed and gasped. "Christ!" He had to bend low because of the shelter.

Lauren had stood up quickly to hold on to him. "Gordon! You shouldn't...."

"Give me a few seconds. This thing in my system is still potent." He breathed deeply. "The heat's not helping either. God." He breathed deeply again. "Right. That's better. Let's try walking."

Together they moved out into the naked sun. Gallagher swayed again. Helped by Lauren and Paula Browne, he climbed into the passenger seat of the Range Rover and relaxed thankfully. He felt his head swimming somewhere above his body.

There was frantic activity as everyone worked to clear the camp; even Smallson, who really should have been out of the sun. Now and then, in passing, Sumner cast guilty looks in Gallagher's direction.

Gallagher ignored him.

In half an hour, they were ready to leave. They left the metal frame of the shelter, but took the jackets with them.

"Right," Gallagher said to Nbwale.

They set off and, three kilometres later, they regained the track. Nbwale put his foot down. Villiger followed close behind.

"Engines!" Marika shouted. She sprang up while the others were still trying to understand, and ran up the dune. At the crest, she put the binoculars to her eyes. She could see nothing.

She searched what she could see of the track as it wound its way in the distance. Nothing. Nothing. The sound of motors came to her strongly on the light wind. They were on the track, she knew, and heading west. She smiled grimly. *That was a clever try, Gallagher, but you won't be escaping me.* So close too.

She hurried back down the dune, leapt into her Landrover, blonde hair flying. "Let's go!"

They were all piling into their respective vehicles and Marika was moving before Selini had properly settled herself in her seat.

"Won't we be out of fuel before we catch them?" Selini shouted above the roar of the engine.

"We're not going to try," Marika shouted back, her face animated by the thought of having found her quarry. "We'll track them, but wait for the gunship."

"They can outrun us, especially if they have got more fuel than we think. They must have found out about the cans."

"It does not matter. They would not have saved much. What is important is that we know where they are and where they're going. I can wait another night now."

The Landrovers roared and bounced along the track, almost nose to tail.

Behind Marika's vehicle, Giannetta was in her element. She played a dangerous game, trying to see how close she could stay with Marika, her slim arms and legs handling the tough vehicle expertly.

In the back, Max shut his eyes and thought about women drivers.

The Cessna landed at six-thirty, Darwin time. Crofton got out to supervise the re-fuelling. Customs was a mere formality. While he was attending to that, he found time to post the letter he had written. It was addressed to the Ministry of Defence in London.

Half an hour later, they were back in the air and heading for the Kintore airstrip.

Crofton radioed ahead to get Flyboy to put the portable landing lights along the strip and to turn on the Kintore beacon. It would be night when they arrived, and Crofton wanted no accidents.

They landed just before nine, in typical Crofton style. Perfectly.

Flyboy gave them the full story as they walked to the complex. Harding listened without interrupting, his face grim in the darkness. He intended to go straight to bed, to neutralize the effects of jet-lag. He wanted to be in perfect condition for the day to come.

"When do we fly?" Flyboy wanted to know, as they entered the hangar.

"Is the Minigun ready?" Harding put a question of his own.

"All loaded."

"Good. We start early."

"That suits me just fine." Flyboy had his own grudge to settle.

"Crofton," Harding went on, "you'll wait here till it's all over. Inge will stay with you. Get some sleep. You need it."

And Crofton knew, as he looked into Inge's mean eyes, that getting away was not going to be so easy. He was a survivor, but he should have known by now that Harding, being the surpreme predator that he was, was the possessor of exceptionally acute instincts.

Crofton looked again at the mean mouth that went with Inge's mean eyes, and wondered whether Harding would later give her orders to kill him. He had not considered that possibility when he had posted the letter.

In London, Adrian Fowler walked into the office of the man he called Greg.

The man looked up eagerly. "You've got something!" Boyle had still not been found.

"An idea. Nothing concerete."

"Let's hear it."

"Suppose," Fowler began with the deceptive mildness that came into his voice whenever he knew he was on to something, "we have been looking at this all wrongly. Suppose, for instance, this is not a political kidnapping, but one carried out for specific criminal purposes?"

"You have seen the list. Nbwale is a well-known ANC sympathizer. We know who Villiger is, and...."

"I don't think it has anything to do with those two. They were just random fish, like most of the others."

"Then who was the target?"

"I have a vague idea, but it's too vague, too outlandish. It's beginning to look like the natural answer, because it's so unreal."

"Then tell me! Damn this suspense."

"No. I want to be absolutely certain; because if I am right ... hold on to your hat. Squalls are predicted, and when the Minister hears, he'll want our guts unless we are absolutely right. He'd love to have your head."

Fowler went out.

The man called Greg felt a strange tingle along his spine. Fowler did not make his statements lightly.

III

Marika said reluctantly: "We'll have to stop."

The fuel gauge was a tyrant that could not be ignored. They had been following the lights they had seen flickering between the dunes for over two hours now, and still the lights were on the move.

She stopped the Landrover and waited for Giannetta to ram her, promising mentally to make the Italian girl regret it. Giannetta's reactions were swift. She stopped with aplomb only inches from Marika's vehicle, lights blazing, engine running.

Marika felt disappointed. She wanted to vent the feelings that were choking her, upon someone. Anyone would do.

Selini said, cautiously: "He knew we would be running short of fuel, that is why he does not care if we see his lights. They will get very far tonight."

Marika wanted to pound the wheel in frustration. Why did Selini have to state the obvious?

She reached for the radio. "Hunter to station. Hunter to station. Hunter to station."

"Station to Hunter," came Harding's voice.

If she were surprised or discomfited, Marika gave no indication. "Hunter to station. You were quick."

Harding knew what she meant. "Didn't want to miss the hunt."

She said emotionlessly: "We need fuel."

"The truck will be on its way. Should be with you by morning. Are you on the route?"

"Yes."

"Good. See you tomorrow."

They ended transmission.

Marika said: "Well ... he is back. The gunship is in the game now." She gave in to her frustration and pounded the wheel. "*Gallagher!*" she screamed. "*Gallagher!*"

In Ngoma's vehicle, they heard Marika baying for blood.

Lauren was holding on to him from behind. "How do you feel?" she asked gently.

"Getting better all the time." His voice was back to its normal strength now. "The rash is itching like mad, though. Apart from a slight queasiness, I seem to be OK. The ham stayed down, so I must be improving."

At the wheel, Nbwale shook his head in wonder. "You have had phenomenal luck."

"You call being bitten by that little monster *luck*?"

"It was very lucky you survived so far from medical attention, after a Redback bite. As I said, it must have been ancient. They're supposed to live for a long time. The one that bit you may have been in that hole for...." He shrugged. "It's anybody's guess."

"Well, there are other things waiting to kill us." Gallagher felt Lauren's arms tighten about his shoulders as he said that. He wondered whether the lights they had seen following far behind them were still coming. "Slow down," he said to Nbwale, "then flash to warn Villiger we're stopping."

"We're not spending the night here, I hope," Nbwale said as he flashed the lights.

"No. Just checking pursuit."

They came to a halt and switched off all light. Villiger did not climb out of his Range Rover. The two vehicles remained darkened and silent for five agonizing minutes while all eyes searched rearwards. They saw nothing. No intermittent glows or flashes.

"That's it," Gallagher said in triumph. "They're out of juice. They'll have to wait for the truck. We'll make it to Muckera."

"And then?" Nbwale asked.

"We show our teeth. Isn't that what cornered rats do? Let's go."

Nbwale started up again, and the Range Rover moved off, with Villiger, as usual, right on its tail.

"Can you drive all night?" Gallagher asked Nbwale.

"I can do it," Nbwale answered.

Day Eight

I

THEY MADE Muckera Rockhole by morning, tired but kept alert by the grim knowledge that death was still stalking them. Gallagher found to his relief that his rash was almost gone and that, to all intents and purposes, he was feeling well enough for battle.

"Pythons lurk in places like this," Nbwale said to everyone as they filled all available receptacles with the muddy-looking water. "So be careful. They grow big enough to squeeze kangaroos to death. That's why they wait here, for the animals to come to drink."

"Thanks," Paula Browne said, and shuddered. She hurried back to the safety of the Range Rover.

Nbwale watched her go with a brief smile.

Villiger said: "We can't stay here." He was looking at Gallagher. "This is the first place they'd look, and it's wide open to the gunship."

"We're not staying," Gallagher told him. "How much petrol do you think you've got left?"

"We drove fairly slowly last night, so we may have squeezed some extra mileage out of what we have; but still no more than thirty kilometres."

"I think we're roughly the same, but it should be enough. We're going out there." He pointed to the west, across the shallowly undulating expanse of the Nullarbor Plain. They had left the packed dunefields and were now fifty kilometres into the northern border of the featureless plain.

"There's nothing out there," Villiger said, not understanding. "No cover." He looked to the east. "Over there the dunefield comes this far. At least we'll have cover of some kind."

Gallagher went to the Range Rover and got out the binoculars. "Take a look," he said, handing them over.

The South African put them to his eyes. "A group of isolated low dunes. That's all."

"Right. With wide open spaces all around. We'll see them coming for miles. Here, we wouldn't. Out there is our fort, and that's where we'll get our Landrover to get us to Cook."

Villiger was not sure, but he trusted Gallagher's instincts. "All right, man," he said at last. "But I hope you're right."

"So do I."

They climbed aboard the vehicles and charged across the empty plain. Gallagher had once again taken the wheel.

The helicopter's main blades churned up a funnel of red dust. Flyboy had a humourless grin stamped upon his face as he held the machine at the hover, two feet above the ground.

Harding was busy strapping himself to a special seat they had installed that morning, behind the Minigun.

"Right!" he called. "I'm ready."

Flyboy yanked the gunship up, banked it almost through ninety degrees and clattered round in a turn at no more than sixty feet, before righting the machine to go skimming across the red earth. His grin widened. This was going to be the best hit-mission he ever pulled.

Harding checked the Minigun to make sure everything would work when he wanted it to. Somewhere out there were people who could bring down his empire. To think that all he had wanted was to kill just one man; one man who had dared to take on Harding International.

One stupid old man.

Marika saw the open Landrover first.

"The truck is here!" She stood in the middle of the track, waiting for it.

The truck drew up, stopped, while everybody crowded round and began taking the cans off.

The Belgian driver climbed stiffly out. He stretched.

"What did Harding say?" Marika asked him immediately.

He knew what she meant. "Nothing. Not a thing."

"No word of blame?"

"No."

"I see. And where will you be giving him the fuel?"

"Wyola Lake. About a hundred and fifty kilometres from here." The Belgian gave a chuckle. "When I saw it on the map, I say to myself: 'He wants us to go into a lake?' And he sees by my face what I am thinking. It is then that he tells us that all those big lakes on the map are dry; salt, clay, mud, sand. This is a crazy place." He shook his head, smiled at the thought of all those lakes pretending to be water.

Marika said: "It will take you four hours to get there. You must go as soon as we are finished. Eat and drink while you wait."

"We would like to sleep a little...."

"Sleep when you get to Wyola." Marika made it clear that he had no choice.

The refuelling was soon finished, and the Landrovers sped away. At a more sedate pace, the fuel truck followed. Before long, with Giannetta in the lead in best rallying form, they had left it far behind.

Crofton's letter had caught a post within an hour of his putting it through the letter box. Someone, because of the address, decided to process it quickly and sent it by special bag. At about the time that Marika had been impressing upon the Belgian who was boss, the letter was thirty thousand feet above India, on its way to London.

Gallagher's "Fort", as Villiger instantly dubbed it in his mind, was made up of six dunes that had somehow arranged themselves about each other in a series of battlements, instead of the usual parallel lines that followed the wind direction. They varied from between five to ten metres high and from the tallest it was possible to see the flat, open land in all directions. No hardy stunted trees, no shrubs grew upon their flanks; but enclosed within their "centre" was an open space about fifty metres across, dotted here and there with salt-bush and other shrubs. It was in the centre of this space, however, that the real surprise awaited them.

Someone, years, decades before, had decided to sink a bore there; for what purpose, it was hard to guess. There was no rusting machinery to give a clue. The wide hole was open to the sky, its crumbled earthen rim looking very precarious, its sides precipitous. It widened perceptibly, the deeper it went. The surface of the water within it glinted from several feet down, with all sorts of things floating down there, including the bodies of small birds that had made the dive for a precious drink only to be overwhelmed by the weight of several hundred of their fellow-creatures swooping down with the same object in mind.

Spreading concentrically from the hole was a wild profusion of grass, shrubs and desert flowers, all clinging with deeply-probing roots to their little oasis before thinning out abruptly as the search for moisture became more competitive.

Paula Browne climbed down slowly from the Range Rover, and stared at the mingled clusters of yellowtops, clumps of creamy-white, globule-like mulla mulla and fragile-looking pink parakeelya among the hardier grasses that surrounded the hole.

"Well, will you look at that?" she said wonderingly as she approached the hole.

"Be careful," Nbwale, who had already inspected it, called to her.

She stopped. "Snakes?" Her mouth twisted nervously.

"There will be plenty of animal life here," he answered in his best schoolmasterly manner. "Minute life, possibly a few lizards; snakes too, though I doubt it. But that's not what I called out for. The edge of the hole is not safe. I don't think you would like to fall in."

"I'll be careful," she promised, and went forward more cautiously to look. Lauren went with her.

Gallagher and Villiger were standing apart from the others, looking about them with less aesthetic thoughts in mind.

"As usual," the South African began approvingly, "you pick your spots well. It's a good position."

"I have a feeling it picked me," Gallagher said thoughtfully. "I could not have wished for a better place in this no-man's-land. Luck. That's all I can call it."

"Call it what you like. If anything can help us, this will. Difficult for the gunship too."

"I was thinking the same thing; but Flyboy can do things with a helicopter that those machines were never designed for, so don't build up too much hope."

"But you still intend to take it on?"

Gallagher gave a wry smile. "Not much of a choice."

"How?"

"I wouldn't dare tell you. I'm trying not to remind myself."

"That bad?"

"Worse. I'll tell you when the time comes. I'll be needing you ... if you're still around."

The meaning of Gallagher's last words showed in Villiger's eyes. He said evenly: "You don't expect all of us to come out of it, if any do survive."

"No." No point beating about the bush. "But we must do our best."

The South African nodded slowly. He looked round at the others. Who would still be alive tomorrow? he wondered.

"We'd better take a closer look at the dunes," Gallagher suggested.

"Yes."

Nbwale was left in charge of the camp.

It took them nearly two hours. Though the curving dunes were smaller than average, the longest was still nearly a kilometre from end to sloping end. They found that the base of each was no further than ten metres from the other, and that some were considerably closer, almost touching. The dunes had arranged themselves so that they completely encircled the waterhole. The outer dunes were the lowest.

By the time Gallagher and Villiger returned from their scouting mission, the sky appeared to have darkened.

Villiger glanced up. "Another dust storm?" he wondered aloud, as they walked up to the vehicles.

"At least it would stop the gunship," Gallagher said.

"For a while."

Nbwale met them, a strange look on his face.

"What's up?" Gallagher asked, hoping nothing had already gone wrong.

"The old man wants to see both of you. Privately." Nbwale's eyes were oddly trouble. "He doesn't think he'll survive."

Thinking of Lauren, Gallagher said quickly: "Has he told the others?"

Nbwale was ahead of him. "She doesn't know. He spoke only to me."

"Thanks," he said to the African in gratitude for his understanding.

Nbwale asked: "Is anything happening out there?"

"Nothing. It will take them some time, so make the most of it. Rest. We'll all be glad of it later."

"We have been very lucky with casualties so far," Nbwale began. "Will be continue to be lucky?"

Villiger said mildly: "It was more than luck. Gallagher knows what he is doing."

Nbwale smiled. "The staunch disciple. An asset under such conditions. Now you're back, I think I'll go up that dune and keep watch."

As he left, Gallagher said: "You didn't have to stick up for me."

"I wasn't sticking up for you. I spoke the truth."

Gallagher fought back the smile he felt coming. "Let's hear what the old man has to say."

II

Flyboy dune-hopped the gunship with a skill that would have left Harding vastly impressed, had his mind not been determinedly concentrating on just one thing: the destruction of the people who were a threat to everything he possessed; to his very existence. It was far too much to lose, especially because of someone of such material unimportance as Gallagher.

Just to ease his frustration and anger, he squeezed the trigger of the Minigun. The monstrous sewing-machine chatter lived for a brief second. The gunship, as if taken unexpectedly, shied from the recoil, nearly clipping a dune.

Flyboy corrected smoothly. "Save it for the real thing!" he bawled. Nobody was going to waste his gunship on a dune. He always considered the Huey "his" ship, though it was owned by Harding.

Harding said nothing, but he did not fire again. His eyes searched the dunes in the distance.

Flyboy was doing a square search, because the fuel truck had radioed to say Marika had still found nothing.

Harding swore mentally. He would find Gallagher, if he had to fly the helicopter himself. Gallagher was not going to come out of the desert alive.

The gunship continued its angry searching, a hundred and fifty kilometres north of Wyola Lake.

Giannetta was keeping up an astonishing pace in the lead Landrover and, for once, Marika was glad of the Italian girl's crazy driving. It forced her to push her own vehicle to keep up; and every kilometre meant that Gallagher was being drawn nearer.

Despite everything, she could not help the twinge of remembrance that her body gave, betraying her once again with an invidious pulsing need. She bit her lip to stem the shudder that threatened to go through her.

Jake Smallson was lying across the back seat of Gallagher's Range Rover, looking very tired. Gallagher and the South African were standing by an opened door, listening to him. Lauren and Paula Browne, seemingly still fascinated by the rare sight of flowers in the middle of the desert, were on the far side of the hole. Nbwale was visible lying atop the dune, while Sumner sat on his own in Villiger's Rover, loading and reloading his Uzi.

Smallson had said, as soon as they arrived: "I don't think I'm going to make it."

"Nonsense," Gallagher had retorted. "Of course you will."

The old man had smiled sadly. "I feel it is only right that I tell you what this whole hijack is really about."

And they listened wide-eyed to the incredible, unfolding tale, not wanting to believe that one man's vendetta had been responsible for dragging them halfway across the world, possibly to die in a baking desert.

"I knew Harding had killed his own father," Smallson was saying, "because one day he told Lauren about a wonderful drug the company was experimenting with, and how people could be killed in such a way that would leave the forensic officials guessing for the rest of their lives. Lauren thought nothing more of it; but already I did not like that young man. I have my own eyes and ears in the business world and I knew he had been pressing his chemists to make the drug usable. When I heard about the horse ... I knew.

"But I did not care. Harding's father was the worst kind of person. The world was well rid of him. What better way than by the hand of his own son? I think it was his destiny. But is is not my knowledge of that which has sent Harding after my blood. You see, worse than that to him, I cost Harding International many millions of pounds. Hundreds.

"I told you his father was a dirty man. He used to sell defective machinery, dangerous drugs and bad foodstuffs to places that are now

228

called Third World countries." Smallson chuckled without humour. "Third World. Always, we must have something, someone to look down on.

"Many, many people died. Some with great suffering. So ... one day, I decided to do something. I have the money, the power, the connections.... I used these tools, as I will call them. The next time Harding's father made one of his deals, I acted. The intermediary company he used was controlled by me, although he did not know this. Before the money was paid, the ship carrying the consignment ... er ... sank. All the consignment was lost but the crew saved. It was very well done.

"The insurance people suspected sabotage and did not pay up; which was what I wanted. But who was responsible? Big question." Smallson permitted himself a brief smile. "Harding International's loss was very, very great. No consignment, no money paid, no insurance paid. To make matters worse, the clients got new material, good material, at a very fair price."

"Which you, of course, supplied," Gallagher said, stunned by the story.

Again, the smile. "I did not supply it personally, but I had a hand. Yes."

"Then what happened?" From Villiger.

"Then Harding's father died." Smallson made a face at his employment of the euphemism. "Alex Harding was a different creature. His father was too stupid a man to look beyond the obvious. Alex Harding is so successful in everything because to him the not-so-obvious is normal. He checked every single deal his father had ever made. He found the one I had interfered with, and somehow he was able to trace it to me. I had covered everything extremely well; but he still found out. It took him two years, and only God knows how much money."

"Why didn't he report you to the authorities?" Gallagher asked.

"And admit that Harding International was selling bad consignments to other countries? In the States we call that dumping. No, he wanted to handle it his way. I could have killed his father and he probably would have done nothing, except perhaps to thank me. But to attack Harding International? Ah, *that* is personal! He has killed other people before, for trying to expose the company. I know of one man who was trying to bring a drug case against him. He disappeared. Probably out here somewhere. Another died very mysteriously in Sicily."

Villiger finally got out what he had been storing up. "Do you mean to say that Harding hijacked the bloody plane, using those lunatics, just to get to *you*?"

"Yes."

"And we all had to die, just to cover him?"

"I am sorry, but I must say yes."

"Well, bloody, bloody *hell!*" Villiger was furious. His eyes seemed to disappear into his head in his anger. He switched to Afrikaans for choicer expressions of his fury. "Jesus, man!" he then went on. "Look at where we are! Look at what has happened – the people that crazy bitch has murdered...."

Smallson interrupted mildly: "You are here to kill someone."

Villiger closed his mouth, bit upon what he had been about to say, and glared. He regained enough control to say tightly: "I am fighting a war."

"So was I," Smallson said with the old steeliness.

Gallagher was fighting to keep his own anger under control. All that had happened to him had been due to this war between Harding and Smallson. He could still feel the slight itching of the rash from the spider bite which, though fast going, was there to remind him of what he had suffered. Yet part of him appreciated what Smallson had done.

And there was Lauren. Whatever he thought would always be affected by his growing feelings for her.

"We'd better not tell the others," was the first thing he said to Villiger. "Nbwale would certainly not like it, and as for Sumner...." He left the rest unsaid.

Villiger looked at him silently, still riding high on fury; then the South African turned away and marched towards the dune where Nbwale lay. For one tense moment, Gallagher wondered whether Villiger was about to carry out his assassination of the big African. Then he saw that Villiger was walking along the base of the dune and was showing no intention of climbing it.

Smallson said: "And you, Gordon? Are you also angry?"

"Anyone would be. We've all walked into a deadly little game between two people very few of us knew, even if we may have heard of them. It's bad enough walking into a fight between people you know. When they play the kind of games you do ... well! The stakes are our lives, Jake."

The old man sighed. "Don't you think I know? If it wasn't for Lauren, and if I thought giving myself to him would have saved your lives, don't you think I would have done it?" He sighed again. "You must promise me," he went on after a while, "promise me that if I should ... no, no. Let me finish. If anything should happen to me, you must promise that you will take care of my Lauren. I do not mean just take her to safety. I mean for always."

"Jake...."

"Are you not strong enough?"

"Of course I'm strong enough," Gallagher began to object furiously, "but her life, her family...."

"What has that got to do with it? She loves you. Or are you so blind ...?" The old man stopped, considered. "You believe that because of what has been happening she feels an attraction for you that is not real; like people in wartime. Yes?" It was almost a bark.

"Yes," Gallagher admitted reluctantly. "I have tried not to think about it like that."

"And you believe that when she is safe again she will forget all about you."

Gallagher nodded.

"Fool. You would think so little of her? Do you believe she would have told you about how Harding tried to use her to get to me if you were not important to her? *Eh*?" Smallson was looking angry. "Idiot!" He had risen from his lying position to make his point, now he fell back, as if exhausted by the effort.

"Jake!"

"I am all right," the old man said, a trifle impatiently. His eyes were closed. "Go and find Lauren and tell her what you truly feel before it is too late for both of you." The eyes remained firmly shut, precluding further conversation.

Gallagher turned away, to look for Lauren. She was no longer near the waterhole with Paula Browne. She was nowhere to be seen. Paula Browne was herself chatting with Nbwale near Villiger's Range Rover.

Gallagher looked up the dune. Villiger was there. Gallagher also noticed that Sumner was missing. That disturbed him.

He went up to Paula Browne and Nbwale. "Any of you seen Lauren?"

Paula Browne said: "Gone to what passes for the ladies' room out here." She looked at him solicitously. "How do you feel now?"

"As good as new, practically. There's still the rash, but it's going. Doesn't itch so much."

"Hey, I'm really glad you made it. You want to thank that girl of yours. I hope you appreciate her."

"I do," he said simply, admitting it for the first time without reservation. He was worried about her now, for some indefinable reason.

"What was up with the old man?"

"Pardon? Oh. Nothing. He just wanted to talk." He saw Nbwale looking at him shrewdly, but his mind was not really on it. Where was she? "Excuse me," he said to them and went towards the dune where Villiger was keeping watch. He climbed up the slope.

Villiger heard him but did not turn.

"Nothing on the horizon," Villiger said. He passed the binoculars to Gallagher who lay down and took them for a quick scan.

Gallagher passed them back. "Seen Lauren?"

"No. Anything to worry about?"

"I don't know. I can't find Sumner either." He glanced up. The sky was definitely getting darker, but there was no dust cloud on the horizon. Rain, perhaps?

Villiger was looking at him. "He may have just gone for a walk."

"Possibly." Gallagher knew that neither of them was thinking that Sumner may have run into trouble. "I'm going to look for her." He stood up, and went over the other side of the dune.

Lauren was on her way back when she heard a voice:

"That was pretty. Real pretty." Sumner.

She looked behind her, to see him coming down the slope of one of the outer dunes.

"You were looking at me?" she asked furiously.

"All the time. You've got real nice legs. Thighs too."

"You dirty bastard!"

He had reached her now, his fat face sweating from whatever lusts were churning about within him. "You watch whom you call dirty. I'm not the one getting ready to give it all to a goddam nigger. You saving those legs and those thighs for him? Is that it?"

She moved a couple of steps back. She knew if she turned to run, he would pounce on her. Her mind called for Gallagher.

"You keep away from me, Sumner."

" 'You keep away from me, Sumner'," he mimicked. His eyes were hard as he came closer, his sweaty face red. "Or what?" he snarled. "You'll set your buck on me? *Will you?*"

The Uzi was slung across his back, now he reached for her with his left hand, while his right dived for her skirt. Instead of moving backwards as he would have expected, she moved in closer, which momentarily confused him. Her knee came up viciously.

He wheezed and fell back gasping. He staggered a few paces before collapsing on to the hot sand. His hands clasped at his crotch.

"You ... you bitch! I'll ... I'll...." He started fumbling for the Uzi.

She ran.

A sharp click sounded above them. "Please give me the excuse, Sumner," Gallagher's voice said. It was tense with a murderous anger.

"Oh, Gordon!" Lauren ran up the dune towards him, her face happy with relief.

Gallagher's eyes did not leave Sumner for a second. "Take the Uzi off," he ordered. "*Take it off!*"

"Jesus Christ I'll be unarmed when they come!"

Gallagher lifted the M16 and sighted on Sumner's head.

"All right, all right!" Sumner threw the Uzi away from him as if it had suddenly turned into a snake.

"Now move away from it."

Sumner did as he was told.

"Go and get it, Lauren."

She placed her head shyly against his shoulder. "Thank you for saying it."

He smiled at her. "I need not have bothered. You handled him pretty well."

She smiled weakly. She was shaking. "He was going to shoot me! My God!"

He put his arm about her. "He would have been dead before he'd pointed the gun," he told her.

He kissed her in full view of Sumner. "I love you," he said.

She placed her head shyly against his shoulder. "Thank you for saying it."

They went down the slope with his arm about her, leaving Sumner on the other side, to his own devices.

They approached Villiger's dune, and climbed. They said nothing to him, but the Afrikaner looked pointedly at the Uzi.

"That yours?" he asked Lauren.

"No. I left it in the Range Rover. It's...."

"I know whose it is," Villiger interrupted. "Never travel without your own. You ought to tell her that, Gallagher."

"I'll remember next time."

"This one may have been the last."

Gallagher knew the South African was right. He took his arm away from Lauren. "Go and see how your grandfather is."

"What do I tell the others?"

"The truth. They'll be wondering about the gun anyway. Tell Nbwale not to let Sumner have another."

She nodded, and went down towards the camp.

Gallagher lay down next to the South African, "Still nothing?"

"Nothing. They're probably wondering where the hell we've got to. There's nothing out here, according to the map."

"Unless it was doctored."

"Do you believe that?"

"No. I don't think anyone knows this place exists."

Gallagher looked up at the sky again. A gentle breeze had begun to flirt with the top of the dune, and it felt cool on his face, but he could not see a rain cloud anywhere. On the distant horizon, to the east, a bank of bright white cumulus stood poised; but no nimbus, threatening rain, darkened their cotton-like luminosity. Would the wind strengthen and bring them over?

High up overhead, strato-cirrus wisped haughtily. It made little difference to the sun which was now winding up to its late morning intensity, as a prelude to what it would do with the rest of the day. In half an hour, it would be midday.

Villiger said: "Rain?"

"Better than dust in all sorts of ways ... but dust would screw up the helicopter engine."

"Unless they've proofed it."

"Which they probably would, in country like this. You can go down to eat, if you like," Gallagher went on. "I'll take over."

"I will in a while."

"Are you still fuming over what Smallson told us?"

Villiger took his time replying. "It's a hell of a thing, man, to find you have wandered into somebody else's war."

"Hijack or no hijack, we would have wandered into yours. You're out to kill Nbwale, remember?"

"He is actively supporting the Communists in my country. It is such people who ... ah, what do you know? What do you know about people who were struck on the Cape; people doing all the dirty jobs for the bosses in Europe; people going out of their own into the...."

"*Trekboers*," Gallagher said.

Villiger was genuinely and even pleasantly surprised. "You know of this? You know our history?"

Gallagher said: "When a people seem determined to destroy themselves, I like to know why. The Afrikaner, I would have thought, would know what it is like to be oppressed; but the history of the oppressed, it seems, is to become even worse than their former oppressors. The historical inevitable, as Nbwale would say. You're not an idiot, Villiger. You can't make me believe you really swallow that Communism bullshit. South Africa as it stands today is the biggest ally the Soviets have. If you really want communism out of Africa itself, all you have to do is wake up."

A silence fell between them, broken by the very gentle whisper of the breeze which seemed to have perceptibly strengthened.

Finally, Villiger said: "I'm going down." He handed Gallagher the binoculars and left without another word.

Gallagher stared out across the arid, limestone plain.

III

The helicopter was at Wyola Lake, taking on fuel. Harding was quietly fuming at having so far drawn a blank. They had not seen Marika's Landrovers either. Radio communication had been kept to a minimum so as not to make any eavesdroppers suspicious.

He waited with a patience he did not feel inside the gunship, while Flyboy and the two who had crewed the truck refuelled the machine. It was a long process.

Giannetta stamped on the brakes and skidded to a halt at the rockhole. Marika pulled up less spectacularly behind her. A stiffish breeze was playing along the ground, whipping up the dust and sand. It had been doing that for some time, and there was nothing to show in which direction any vehicle had left it.

Marika looked at the ground, seeing faint tyre marks on the powdery track. She looked about her. The wind played with her gold hair.

"I cannot understand it," she said at last. "They have not the fuel. They cannot be far." There was nothing on the empty plain to the west, and to the east the dunefield was at least forty kilometres away. No cover for forty kilometres. They certainly could not be further than that. They just didn't have the fuel.

She took the binoculars out of the Landrover and focused on the distant dunes. She wished she had the really powerful pair, but Gallagher had taken those, damn him. She searched along the ground. No tracks; but that meant nothing. Winds lived and died here all the time, with no regard for regularity. She turned west. Far in the distance, an isolated group of low dunes. Hopeless. Exposed. Nowhere for them to run. Nowhere in the dunefield either; but the dunefield would give a false sense of security. Fugitives were like that. It was a psychological thing.

She'd had plenty of experience in gauging the psychological deterioration of her victims over the years. Gallagher was different, of course, but he still had to persuade six very different people to agree with him. It would have been seven, had she not got the Frenchman. She smiled to herself. Not a bad shot in failing light.

She kept looking at the low dunes, seeming to float in the distance on what had once been the bed of a Miocene sea. If she'd had the time or inclination to dig, she would find sea shells, still perfect, where they had been deposited for tens of millions of years; but her quarry were not fossils. They were living creatures she must destroy to enable her to survive.

She took the binoculars from her eyes. Nothing out there; but it should be checked all the same. She glanced at the sky. The clouds seemed heavier, a little darker.

"Giannetta," she began, "I want you to take Selini and Charlie with you and have a look at those dunes." She pointed to the west.

"What dunes? I see nothing."

"They are very low. You need the glasses. Here."

Giannetta looked. "Ah, yes. They could not be there, I don't think," she said, getting in a tangle over her negatives.

"By now," Marika said coldly, "you should know that Gallagher does not do what is expected of him. Do as I say, please."

Giannetta knew that Marika in her present mood, was even more dangerous than normal; and that was saying something.

"Yes, Marika." Giannetta waited for Charlie to get in, then took her place behind the wheel as Selini got into the passenger seat.

"Don't take anything for granted," Marika cautioned. "It may look a hopeless place for cover from here, but you never know. I shall be going into the dunes to the east. If you find anything, do *not* engage. Keep out of range and call me. We shall attack together. Do you understand?" The green eyes burned into Giannetta's.

Giannetta nodded, and started the engine. She wiped at her forehead with the back of her hand, stroked an itch on her nose.

Marika slapped the bonnet. "All right."

Giannetta let in the clutch and the landrover took off in a manner its makers had never seriously expected, though they had been prudent enough to incorporate into the design the tolerance with which to withstand such treatment.

Marika watched the vehicle bouncing across the plain, trailing its wake of limestone dust. She would never get over Giannetta's driving.

"Come on," she said to Max and Ngoma, and got in.

It was two o'clock.

At Kintore, Crofton felt afraid but hoped he wasn't showing it. Everywhere he had gone, the mean-mouthed Inge had followed like a faithful puppy; except that no puppy he'd ever seen walked around with a fully cocked AK-47. She had even followed him around the Cessna while he checked it, and she had sat in the co-pilot's seat while he'd carried out some unneeded calibration checks. The way she had held the AK had dispelled any thoughts he might have entertained about overpowering her.

Now they were sitting in the Mess and he was pretending to enjoy a meal she had made him prepare for them both. They ate in silence and, every now and then, the mean eyes would pass over his face with feral curiosity.

The AK stood upright on a chair next to her, like a third guest at their table.

Gallagher put the binoculars down. He had been watching for some minutes now, waiting to see whether the two distant Landrovers would go off together. He was pleased there were only two. Marika's professionalism had again made her cautious, but her shortage of forces had compelled her to divide her strength once more. She had to check every possibility. There was no choice.

"Here comes our Landrover," he murmured to himself. He had forty-five minutes within which to prepare, he guessed, at the outside.

He was not worried about the Range Rover tracks being seen. Throughout the time they'd been at the waterhole, light winds had tufted intermittently across the plain, whipping up billows of dust and depositing them elsewhere. He was satisfied that the tracks had long disappeared; except for very close to the cluster of dunes, where there had been no winds of any strength to speak of.

He hoped to have the Landrover before the people in it saw those.

He took another look, keeping well down on the hot sand, then he slid backwards and rushed down the slope. Villiger, who had been watching, came towards him, weapon ready.

"Our Landrover," he said quickly in answer to the question he saw in the South African's eyes. "They've split up. The other one went east. I saw it go."

"That's good. But which one?"

"I don't think it's Marika," Gallagher answered, including the others who had now come up, in the conversation. "The Landrover is being driven like a racing car. I think it's your favourite lady," he added to Villiger. "You've got a second chance." He gave a brief smile to show he meant no offence. Their little disagreement on the dune had taken a back seat.

Paula Browne said shakily: "What do we do?"

Briskly, Gallagher said: "Villiger and I will take them. Nbwale, the camp is your responsibility, if anyone should get past us. Paula, you take that Ingram, point it at anyone who doesn't belong here, and squeeze. Don't worry about aiming. It will make the person think twice long enough for Nbwale to get him. I hope. Lauren, you watch your grandfather. Use the Uzi the way I showed you. And...."

"I can look after myself," Smallson interrupted. He was carrying Sumner's Uzi.

"What about me?" Sumner cried, outraged. "You going to leave me without a gun to defend myself?"

Gallagher ignored the outburst. He no longer trusted Sumner enough. "Nbwale," he said evenly, "if Sumner does anything stupid ... shoot him."

"*What*?" Sumner yelled. "Why you goddammed coon! Who the hell...."

Villiger lifted his AK. "Shut up, or I'll save Nbwale the trouble. You're a menace to us all, Sumner. Behave yourself, and you just might live to get out of here."

Sumner's eyes grew round with sudden fear. Up to that moment, he had not believed it. He stared at Villiger as one would a traitor.

"I'll remember all of you," he whispered. "I'll remember."

He moved away from them. Gallagher went to his Range Rover, now useless as transport for lack of fuel, and took out the blooker. He slung it across his back. He took a few rounds. He also kept the M16 and took more ammunition for it. He left the binoculars.

Villiger had followed him. Nbwale was already setting up defensive positions.

"I thought you wanted to take the Landrover, not destroy it," Villiger said.

"I don't intend to. But there is a use I can put the blooker to. Besides, I don't want to leave any weapon that Sumner can get his hands on, while the others may be occupied." He turned to the others. "No noise if you can possibly help it. Right," he said to Villiger. "Let's go."

As they ran towards the dune, Villiger said: "You OK? Can you handle it?"

Gallagher knew he was talking about the lingering effects of the spider bite. "As long as I don't have to do any hand-to-hand wrestling, I'll be fine."

Villiger gave one of his rare, brief smiles and patted Gallagher on the shoulder. They were a team again.

They ran up the dune, rolled over the top and slid down the other side. Gallagher hoped he hadn't got sand in the booker as they ran along the natural trench created by the close separation of the inner and outer dunes.

Seen from the air, the waterhole and its attendant dunes looked like a flattened view of a spiral galaxy, with the hole at its centre, surrounded haphazardly, yet completely, by the six mounds of sand. The ends of the dunes curved inwards, maze-like, so that no direct line of entry or exit was possible, except by crossing them. There were two dunes facing westwards. The inner, and highest, upon which Gallagher and the others had stood guard, curved towards the waterhole in a great half-moon; while the outer and much lower one was smaller and shorter, with a less pronounced curve. It was along its base that Gallagher and the South African now hurried. They came to its northern end and stopped, backs against its flank. Gallagher inched round to have a look. The plume of dust was heading directly towards them. He ducked back, pleased he had judged correctly.

"They're coming. Right at us." He unslung the blooker, loaded it.

Villiger checked his AK. "Same as before?"

Gallagher nodded. "If we get the chance. But it may not be like that at all. We've got to get them without destroying the Landrover." He glanced up at the sky. The clouds were moving westwards. There was plenty of nimbus now, heavy with rain. He was sure it was already falling at the Muckera Rockhole. He could smell the wetness on the wind. "Hope we finish this before the rain gets here."

They could hear the racing engine of the vehicle as it came hurtling towards their position. Then the revs dropped suddenly and practically died. They knew it had stopped, engine idling, a cautious beast watching.

They waited.

By the waterhole, the others had heard it too. Paula Browne's eyes, mesmerized by fear, stared out of her ravaged face. The past days had

238

taken their unkind toll, and without the many expensive aids she normally had at her disposal with which to mask herself to face each day, her features stood bared with a nakedness that was so revealing she looked pitifully vulnerable, not at all like the hard case from the tough streets of New York.

Nbwale listened to the sound of the motor. Smallson patted his granddaughter's hand to give himself courage. It was a long time since he'd held a weapon. Sumner lay among the desert grasses, and prayed.

Aming the dunes, they all waited.

In the Landrover, Giannetta said: "Let us go round it, then come back here. Then, Charlie, you will get out to have a look. I will go in closer and wait for you."

Charlie nodded. If he had any foreboding about his being a possible sacrificial goat, he kept them to himself.

They heard the Landrover moving again, waited agonizingly as it did its slow circuit. Giannetta was careful, staying nearly three hundred metres out while she covered the four-kilometre distance. It was a punishing half-hour for the fugitives. Gallagher silently prayed that the tyre tracks entering the dunes would not be discovered; but luck stayed with them. The playful winds scooped up dust sufficiently to hamper close scrutiny of the ground. The Landrover came back to its original position, stopped.

"Nothing so far," Giannetta said into the radio. "I am sending Charlie to look."

"Very well," Marika's voice said. "We are halfway to the dunes. Keep looking."

Giannetta cut transmission and began to move the Landrover closer to the dune behind which Gallagher and Villiger were hiding. For once she was driving with caution.

In the passenger seat, Selini thought of death.

IV

Gallagher said: "They're coming!" His ears strained for every cadence of the engine. "They've stopped again!"

They looked at each other, forcing their ears to pick up more than they could hear.

"Someone's coming!" Villiger hissed. He swung to cover the southern part of the dune. The inwards-curving end allowed him to see along its entire length.

Soon, they heard cautious footsteps approaching. Charlie came right up to the dune and stopped, listening. They held their breath.

Gallagher had put down the blooker to pick up the M16 which he now held ready.

Two more steps crunched on the sand; stopped again.

Come on. Come on!

Charlie chose to come round, rather than go over the dune.

Shit, Gallagher thought as he realized it. *He'll block my field of fire, and that will warn them.* There was only one thing to do.

"*Get him!*" he bawled at Villiger as he dropped and rolled swiftly. When he stopped, the Landrover was squarely in his sights.

The suddenness of it all took Charlie completely by surprise, and he gaped long enough for Villiger to put two bullets into his chest at point-blank range. He did not hear the sharp, double-crack of the AK as he sailed backwards to cannon against the dune, leaking his redundant blood into the sand.

In the same instant, Gallagher had fired three rapid shots. One shattered the front left tyre on the Landrover; the second went through the windscreen, entered Selini's head directly above the nosebridge and out messily through the crown, spraying Giannetta with blood and shattered bone. The third missed because Giannetta, with the reflexes of a cat, was already moving the Landrover. She did not use the radio and even if she'd had the time, she would not have been able to. The bullet that had missed her had come through the door and had ploughed into it, shattering it beyond repair.

She drove the crippled Landrover towards a dune that curved in a north-westerly direction and was the next one along from the one where Cahrlie had died. Selini's body rocked grotesquely to the *bump-bump-bump-bump* motion of the vehicle as it limped on its shattered tyre which was beginning to come off with the fury of Giannetta's driving. She took it right up to the dune and bailed out even before the Landrover had stopped. It tried to stagger up the dune and had gone nearly halfway up before its tyreless wheel finally baulked it and caused it to stall. It slid backwards all the way down to finally stop, hose on the slope, the right way up.

Selini lolled back against the seat in death, her shattered head emptying its contents to the floor behind the seats.

Giannetta had disappeared.

Marika said suddenly: "I hope Gianna does not go too close when she sends Charlie in." She grabbed the radio. "Gianna? Stay well out."

Silence.

"Gianna?" Tensely. "Gianna? *Gianna answer me!*" Marika broke transmission. "*Mon Dieu!*" she said in a low anxious voice. "He was out there all the time!" She gave Ngoma the mike. "Keep trying." She swung the wheel and headed back at a speed that would have had even Giannetta worried.

240

After a while, she told Ngoma to stop calling. Whatever had happened, it was too late now for little Gianna.

"Oh, God," she prayed aloud. "Let me kill him. *Let me kill him!*"

She glanced at the sky and saw that rain had come from the south and had veered westwards, directly towards where the cluster of dunes waited for her. She could actually see the belt of rain curving. She would arrive with the rain.

Giannetta had found herself a little promontory on the inner flank of the dune. She squeezed her neat little form behind it and waited.

On hearing the first shots, Lauren had tensed; now in the ensuing unnatural silence, she stood up.

Nbwale furiously motioned for her to get back down.

She shook her head at him, held the Uzi ready and began to move away.

"*Where are you going?*" he hissed at her from his hiding place among the grasses and desert flowers that barely covered his bulk. "*Stay where you are!*"

"He may need my help!" she hissed back and ran towards the dune. She was already running up the slope before he had moved.

He stayed where he was.

Paula Browne looked across to where Smallson was practically hidden by one of the big Range Rover wheels. "Your kid's got guts," she said softly. She was relatively close by, beneath the other Range Rover.

Nbwale had considered blocking the two entrances with each vehicle, then had decided against it. He opted to settle for concentrated fire on whichever entrance was chosen. He hoped they would not come from both at once. He sighed. What did that girl hope to do?

What could he himself hope to do if they did come all at once? Not much. Even with the added firepower of Lauren Tanner's Uzi, he doubted that there would be much hope against an assault by professionals, most of whom had seen combat, the few who had not being skilled assassins.

He sighed again and waited.

Giannetta was muttering quietly to herself in Italian: "I'll show you, Gallagher. I'll show you how to fight. This is little Gianna!"

She brushed off a tiny something that had alighted on a slim, shapely thigh. That was all the movement she made.

She could hear them moving, looking for her. *Come*, her mind said. *Come. Little Gianna is waiting.* Her thoughts were almost sensuous.

She saw him. The dark one. Gallagher. Where was the other? There were at least two, she was certain. Someone else had taken Charlie.

The big South African. He would be the other one.

She watched Gallagher, biding her time. He was careful, and very good; but little Gianna would get him. *Sorry, Marika. He is mine.*

Gallagher approached the promontory. He knew where Giannetta was. He had seen a tiny stream of dropping sand. He only hoped Villiger got into position in time, otherwise, as bait, he was finished.

He couldn't know that Villiger had missed his footing on the other side of the dune and had slid down a few metres, losing vital seconds which he was even now frantically trying to make up, though he would be much too late.

Giannetta watched Gallagher approaching. *Soon. Soon.*

Now!

She began to rise in a swift, feline motion, rifle coming up dead on target, tight grin of promised death on lips that could kiss with stunning passion. A different passion now coursed within her.

"*No!*" came a sudden scream.

Both Gallagher and Giannetta were startled. Giannetta lost her aim as Gallagher dived for the ground. She tried to swing round to this new threat. She was too late.

The Uzi chattered its full magazine of forty, nine-millimetre rounds at her. Nearly half of them missed, because Lauren, unaccustomed to the weapon, had merely pointed it in the direction of the target and sprayed.

But twenty-two entered Giannetta's lovely body, stitching across it from right hip to left shoulder, tearing at her flesh like a can-opener. The body danced like a frantic puppet before collapsing upon itself to slide down the dune and land near Gallagher's feet. Neither the lovely, plump face nor the equally lovely slim legs were touched. It was as if the Uzi had decided that would have been sacrilege.

Gallagher stood up slowly, wonderingly, just as Villiger came over the top of the dune.

"Look, man ... " he began abjectly, but Gallagher was now staring up at the other dune.

Lauren had dropped the Uzi and was sitting halfway up, vomiting between her legs. Gallagher scrambled up to her. He slung his M16 and held her by the shoulders. Her body shook violently with each retch. Tears were streaming down her face.

Finally, it was over. She lifted her blouse and wiped her lips with it.

"Oh, God, oh, God," she cried, crying and sniffing at the same time. "I just killed somebody. I just killed somebody. Oh, Gordon ... but I couldn't let her...."

"Shhh...." He helped her up gently, stooped to pick up the empty Uzi. He knew what it must have cost her. He held her tightly to him with one hand, while he signalled with the other to Villiger.

242

The Afrikaner picked up Giannetta's weapon and raced up the slope.

"Take her back, will you, please?" Gallagher told him. "Can you handle this Uzi too?"

"Sure. Look. I'm sorry. I lost my footing, and...."

Gallagher could see the terrible regret in Villiger's eyes. He knew the man was thinking about what would have happened had Lauren not been there; of the effect of the killing on Lauren; of what he, Gallagher, was thinking.

It was Gallagher's turn to be generous. "It happens," he said. "Forget it. I'm going to check the state of the Landrover." He went back down the slope, ran to where he'd left the blooker with its rounds, slung that across his back to join the M16, then picked up the AK of the dead man whose name he did not know.

He went to find the Landrover.

By the waterhole, they had all heard Lauren's scream, followed by the four-second chatter of the Uzi; followed by the unnatural silence. Everyone had leapt up, including Sumner, to stare up the slope of the dune; then they stared questioningly at each other.

At last, Nbwale said: "That was an Uzi, fired by someone who doesn't know how to use it properly. There were no answering shots, so we can assume that Miss Tanner is all right."

"We can assume no such thing," Paula Browne said nervously. "Don't forget where these guns came from. It could have been one of the terrorists and Lauren maybe lying dead out there."

"And Gallagher and the South African?"

She didn't want to say what they were all thinking. She glanced at Smallson, who had suddenly become very old.

Then Villiger appeared on the crest of the dune with Lauren. Smallson brightened considerably, relief showing plainly on his face as he rushed to meet her. Paula Browne also went forward to take her by the arm and lead her towards Gallagher's Range Rover. Sumner stood a little way from everyone, his face without expression.

Then they realized that Gallagher had not come down.

"He's all right," Villiger told them as he read their anxious looks. "He's checking the Landrover."

"You mean we got one?" Paula Browne asked eagerly as she helped a white-faced Lauren into the vehicle.

"We're not sure of its condition. That's what Gallagher is checking. I'm going back out there to help him. The rest of them will know something's gone wrong and will be on their way here. We were very lucky Miss Tanner turned up when she did."

"What happened?" Smallson wanted to know. He glanced at Lauren who sat in the passenger seat, head back, eyes closed, and looking extremely pale.

Villiger told them all, not sparing himself. He was still feeling very guilty about his part in it. He left them quickly, hurrying back up the dune. They watched him go.

Nbwale said: "He is feeling very bad about it. Not only Gallagher, but your granddaughter could have been killed, Mr Smallson, if that woman had been just a little faster."

The old man said: "It could have happened to anybody."

"Yes ... but to men like Villiger, such a thing is a matter of professional honour. Men like that don't expect to miss their footing like a rank novice. It will take him a long time to forgive himself. He will be a harsher critic than Gallagher."

"I'm sure Gordon would not hold a grudge on this."

"So am I. But I know men like Villiger." Nbwale kept staring at the dune, long after the South African had disappeared. "White *and* black," he added softly.

The South African found Gallagher staring at Selini's corpse. "So in the end," he said, "you wound up shooting her." He remembered Selini from the time of their break-out.

Gallagher said nothing. There was a strange stillness about him as he continued to stare at the dead woman.

This one doesn't count, does it, O'Keefe? he was thinking. *I shot her through the windscreen, so I didn't see her face properly. She could easily have been a man.*

He knew Villiger was looking curiously at him, but he paid no attention.

"Apart from the wheel that needs changing," he began, "the steering's jammed. It may be nothing very serious, probably a rock just beneath the sand; but we don't have the time to try and find out. The rest of them will be here before we could fix it." He glanced up at the sky. The rain clouds were almost overhead, and a slaty greyness covered the day. At least it was appreciably cooler. "The rain will help us. The Landrover will be bait."

"How long have we got?" Villiger asked.

"About an hour, I'd guess. No more. We'll watch from the high dune."

They began to run back. The wind had risen appreciably and was tugging at their clothes as they climbed the slope. Just before they made it to the crest, they heard a long, echoing scream that ended in a distinct splash.

"Bloody hell!" Gallagher exclaimed. "Someone's fallen down the hole. Come on!"

They rushed over the top and hurried down the other slope in a series of slides and jumps.

"Who was it?" Gallagher yelled as they reached the base.

"The old man!" Nbwale shouted back.

"Get the ropes!" Gallagher ran to his Range Rover, dumped his weapons and climbed behind the wheel. He turned the ignition. Nothing. No fuel. Christ. He jumped out. "Try yours!" he told Villiger.

The South African had already been moving to do just that when he'd realized that Gallagher's wouldn't start. The big V8 rumbled smoothly into life.

Nbwale had tied the two lengths of rope together. Villiger, knowing what Gallagher was up to, began to inch the Range Rover across the desert garden, towards the hole. He stopped a few feet from the edge. Nbwale began to secure one end of the joined rope to the front towing bracket.

A distraught Lauren was trying to see down the hole. Faint splashing could be heard. Smallson was not calling out.

"What happened?" Gallagher asked her.

She put her hands to the sides of her face, shook her head. "I don't know! I was lying back in the Range Rover, when I heard Gramps scream. I jumped out and Paula said he'd fallen down the hole." Her eyes were wide, staring. She was still in a mild state of shock from the killing.

He looked at the others. Nbwale was letting the rope down carefully so as not to hit the old man with the full length on the head and cause him to drown among the dead zebra finches.

"Did any of you see it?" Gallagher asked them in turn. "Paula? Nbwale? Sumner?"

They all shook their heads.

"Hold on, Jake!" he called down the hole, hearing his voice boom and echo. "I'm coming down to you."

Villiger had climbed out of the Range Rover, leaving the engine running. "You handle the Rover," he said. "I'll do it. You may still be too weak from that spider bite."

Gallagher shook his head. "I need you up here, if that thing runs out of petrol. It would be easier for you two to pull me up." He peered down. He could just make out Smallson's weak splashes in the gloom. He wondered if Villiger had noted his deliberate exclusion of Sumner.

Was the old man badly hurt? Was the rope long enough?

He gingerly inched over the edge and began to climb down. As he went, the vision of Lauren's grey eyes, staring anxiously for both of them now, remained with him all the way down to the water.

The rope, he found, barely reached it. Smallson would never have made it on his own.

V

"That rain's not going to help," Flyboy said, pointing ahead to the rain cloud in the distance. "It's low down. Ceiling's about a thousand feet. We won't be able to see anything." He'd had to shout to make himself heard.

They had been searching for about an hour since the refuelling, and were approaching Muckera Rockhole at about a hundred feet, coming from the east.

Harding chewed at his lower lip in frustration. His hands itched to use the Minigun. "Go round again," he called.

They hadn't seen anything and Flyboy doubted whether they would; but he obediently swung the helicopter round for another circuitous search. He had dune-hopped, flown at zero feet between the narrow troughs where the dunes had been closely packed, gone high for a wider view; he'd done it all already. The track receded westwards in the rain as the gunship again headed towards the dunes.

Then Flyboy suddenly frowned. He swung the helicopter back towards the west, banking it so steeply to the left that Harding found himself staring directly at the ground.

"*I said ...*" he began to shout.

"I think I saw something!" Flyboy interrupted as he levelled out on the new heading.

Harding was immediately alert. "Where?"

Flyboy pointed to the squall. "Something just went into that."

He flew towards the rain. He had seen Marika's Landrover.

Marika had heard the helicopter for some time, above the noise of the rain on the roof, but she had chosen not to radio Harding. She wanted Gallagher for herself. Her sensitive hands held the wheel firmly as she peered through the windscreen. The rain made it difficult to see the low dunes clearly, so she had slowed down, not wanting to drive right past them. Now and then, they became totally invisible and she had to drive by memory and by an accurate sense of direction.

The wind that accompanied the rain gusted and lifted a section of it like a coquette raising a corner of her skirt to show a leg. For a few seconds, the cluster of dunes showed clearly, then the dark skirt hid them again.

There were still a few kilometres to go.

It was eight a.m. in London. Adrian Fowler stared calmly at the man he called Greg.

"You're mad!" the man said. "You're a raving lunatic!" he

exploded, going one better.

Fowler was unmoved. "You asked for something eccentric; outlandish, I think you said."

"Don't throw my words back at me! This is monstrous, Adrian. Alex *Harding*? *Sir* Alexander Harding of Harding International?"

"Hear me out before you have me committed," Fowler said calmly. "The whole thing assumes a crazy logic of its own. Let us start with the actual landing of the hijacked aircraft. A fact that should have been noticed, but wasn't, was the proximity to the 747 of a Fokker F28 belonging to Harding International. I'm still guessing, of course, but it would not have been all that difficult to transfer thirteen drugged people under cover of night, while the whole airport was in a panic about bombs on the aircraft. Then the empty vans, probably driven by members of the gang who would fit in with the local fauna, so to speak."

"Africans?"

Fowler nodded. "There were never any hostages in them. They were simply diversions. The drivers would have simply melted away in the ... I was going to say darkness." Fowler gave one of his wicked smiles. "Then let's jump and take Boyle. Who influenced his appointment? And which famous young industrialist has the ear of the Minister as well as other well-known figures in politics?"

"Oh, come now, Adrian."

"Who?" Fowler insisted.

"Alex Harding," the man admitted, reluctantly.

"Let's return to Boyle. He may have been a little weak in the intellectual department, but even you must admit that in combat he was reasonably competent. All his tests show this. He was also carrying that cannon of his. That American monstrosity, the .357. I suggest that Boyle was approached by someone he not only knew but held in high esteem. I have proof of that at least."

"*What?*"

"People still do notice things. It took some doing, but we found a young couple who noticed Harding's Rolls Royce Camargue in the park. The young man had been trying to impress the girl and was promising her he would one day own one of them."

"That's no proof of anything." Sceptically.

"It wouldn't be ... if there hadn't been an F28 near the hijacked aircraft, and if Harding were not a cousin of Boyle's who had virtually fed him into the system, and if Harding had not left suddenly a couple of days ago for ... Australia — and in quite a hurry."

The man rose slowly from behind his desk. "How did you get this?"

"In my usual inimitable way." Fowler went on to tell him about Crofton's urgent flight. He had simply sent one of his younger operatives to chat up one of the lower-echelon secretaries in the

Harding International building. She, in turn, had found out about Crofton from Harding's own secretary, who had once visited Crofton's flat.

"But why, Adrian. Why? You haven't given me a motive. We can't go to the Minister with suppositions and coincidences. We need the proof. Solid proof. Alexander Harding.... My God!"

"I'm working on that. I'll let you have it." Fowler left him.

Unknown to either of them, Crofton's letter was just arriving at Heathrow.

Gallagher felt the water close coldly about his waist, then his shoulders, then he was swimming. The water stank with the combined smells of rotting vegetation, damp earth, dead birds and other flotsam that swam in it. Smallson looked almost out, eyes seeming glazed.

Treading water, Gallagher reached for the weakly thrashing old man. His hand closed on an arm.

"Aaarrrhhh!" Smallson cried. "It's ... it's broken, I think."

Gallagher quickly shifted to the torso, moving his right arm so that he wound up grasping the old man across the chest from behind.

"What happened, Jake?" Some foul-tasting water had got into his mouth. He spat it out.

"Sumner," the old man replied weakly.

"How?"

"I had left Lauren to sleep, or rest, and was standing by the hole. Sumner ... came up behind me ... pushed...." Smallson's speech was punctuated by quick gasps. "He ... he got ... the gun. I'm sorry, Gordon. I should ... have been ... more careful."

"All right, Jake. Don't fret. Here's the rope. Just keep hold of yourself for a while longer."

Gallagher saw that Smallson was never going to hang on to the rope long enough to be pulled up. It would have to be tied about him. The rope itself was barely touching the water.

"Bring the Rover closer!" he shouted.

They heard the voice floating up. Nbwale, who was the closest to the edge, motioned to Villiger to drive forward. The Range Rover cautiously inched across the beautiful flowers. Nbwale, watching the wheels, held up a hand. Villiger stopped.

"That's as far as we can go without bringing the Range Rover down on your heads!" Nbwale called down.

The thought terrified Gallagher. He did not dare imagine what it would be like to have the heavy vehicle blocking the hole while they slowly drowned among the drowned creatures. He glanced up at the rope. The end had disappeared beneath the surface. It would just have to be enough. He spat out some more water. His clothes were becoming waterlogged and Smallson's had already made him abnormally heavy.

248

Gallagher got hold of the rope, passed it round the injured old man while trying to keep him supported at the same time.

"Just a bit longer, Jake, and we're there."

The rope was long enough for a knot to be tied. Just. He tested it. It held. Then he saw that Smallson had fainted.

"All right!" he shouted. "Pull! He's passed out!"

He heard the Rover's engine increase in revs and the rope tautened; then Smallson was lifted out of the water. All manner of dead things clung to his clothes briefly before dropping off. Water cascaded. Two of the dead finches landed upon Gallagher's upturned face and he brushed them off with revulsion. Smallson's body cannoned now and then against the wall of the hole, dislodging loose earth that plunked down into the water. Once, a good-sized stone missed Gallagher's head by inches.

Then the rain came down. It poured with an astonishing and sudden ferocity. Watching Smallson's limp body as it rose through the deluge, Gallagher tried to fight off his nightmare. He began to imagine all sorts of things lurking in the water beneath his feat. How deep was this hole? Was it part of an underground river? Did water snakes live here? Were there underground currents?

He trod water with a calm that belied the raving thoughts in his head. Smallson's body had disappeared. Now the entire rim of the hole appeared to be pouring water down upon him. *O God, O God. No! Not here! Don't let it happen! Don't make that dream come true....*

What was keeping them? Were they going to leave him here to drown. There was a Landrover waiting, and Sumner had a gun.

Gallagher looked up at his nightmare and tried not to scream.

VI

Sumner had waited until the old man was pulled well out of the hole and everyone was crowding around him.

"All right!" he said.

They turned to look at him, stared at the Uzi he pointed at them. The rain hammered down angrily, having already drenched them to the skin within seconds of its arrival. Lauren's thin blouse clung to her like a new skin, while her skirt pressed itself against her hips, buttocks and thighs, leaving very little to the imagination.

Sumner noted all this, squinting and grinning at the same time. "I'm taking the Landrover," he said, "and I'm taking her with me." He jerked his chin at Lauren. "That's just to stop any foolish ideas. I'll shoot her if anyone comes after me." His eyes showed he would do something else, too, once time and opportunity afforded itself.

Villiger said quietly: "The Landrover has to be fixed." He stared unblinkingly at Sumner, despite the rain.

"I'll fix it!" Sumner's lips stretched across his teeth. "But first, you take off that rope and drop it into the goddam hole."

"*No!*" Lauren cried. "He'll drown!"

"That's the idea," Sumner snarled. "Go on, Villiger, you goddam traitor! Do it!"

"I won't let you!" Lauren began to run towards Sumner, fully intending to attack him.

Villiger blocked her with a massive arm, never taking his eyes off Sumner. "You're going to have to shoot me, man. But let me warn you. I'll take you with me." And his hand began to move towards the Browning High Power at his hip.

"*Don't do it!*" Sumner screamed, and pulled the trigger.

Nothing happened. Villiger's hand froze while Sumner tried again and again to make the Uzi fire. He had not checked the weapon. It was the one that Lauren had emptied and Smallson had picked it up by mistake. Villiger walked up to him, yanked the Uzi from him and punched him hard in the face. Sumner fell but was not knocked out. He scrabbled about among the wet flowers and the grass, weeping in rage and pain. Villiger tossed the gun into the Range Rover.

"Use the Ingram if he moves from there," he told Paula Browne. "Get that rope back down, Nbwale. Fast!" He jumped into the Range Rover while Nbwale frantically untied Smallson.

Then the Range Rover ran out of petrol.

Marika saw the crippled Landrover just as Ngoma said: "I think the gunship is coming back."

Marika pulled up next to the Landrover and stopped. They listened. The beat of the helicopter came faintly to them. She stared at the crippled vehicle, knowing that Gianna, Selini and Charlie were dead, although she could not see them. Then she peered harder and made out a slack shape. She climbed out into the rain to look at Selini. She looked for a long time, oblivious to the pounding rain and the perceptibly increasing sound of the approaching machine.

Gallagher had decimated her team. There was only one way to repay him. She bitterly regretted the fact that he had only one life for her to take.

She climbed back into her own Landrover. "Selini," she said emotionlessly to the others. "The back of her head is gone."

Ngoma swallowed.

Max said: "They may be watching us."

"They cannot see in this rain. We will go after them." The beautiful face was coldly set, the golden hair plastered against her scalp. She

reached for her M16 and a good supply of ammunition. "Come."
They followed her into the pouring rain.

Flyboy poled the gunship through the rain unworriedly. He kept it at a
height of twenty metres, just above sixty-five feet, knowing there was
nothing higher in his path for him to hit. He had briefly seen the
cluster of dunes and knew that was where Marika was heading,
despite his not having seen the Landrover for some time now. There
was no need for him to see the dunes any more. His instruments had
already told him where they were. In six minutes, he'd be there.

Gallagher stared up at the deluge that descended upon him, knowing
his nightmare had at last become reality. He would drown in this
terrible hole and no one would find his bones for thousands of years.
They had gone. They had left him. Even Lauren? He focused his mind
upon her and trod water, trying to forget the flood descending upon
him. He could not even hope that the hole would fill up, taking him to
the rim. The rain would make no difference to the water level. It was
probably swallowed, even as it fell, by a subterranean lake. He
thought of Lauren and held on to his sanity.

A face appeared. *His face!* Just as in the nightmares! O God. Then
something coiled menacingly downwards. *Python!* Pythons lurked near
waterholes, Nbwale had said. A scream rose in his throat. Then
reason took hold of him again. The python turned into a rope; blessed
rope. And the face ... the face was Villiger's.

"You all right?" the South African called.

"Yes." Gallagher was astonished to hear how calm he sounded.

"Right. Grab the rope! We're going to pull you up. The Range Rover
conked out, and we had a slight problem with Sumner."

Gallagher needed no second bidding, and soon Nbwale and Villiger
were pulling him up; slowly, agonizingly. He was halfway there when
he heard, above the rain, a sound he dreaded. *The gunship.* The
pulling became more frantic and he tried to help by putting his feet
against the wall of the hole and "walking" up; but his feet slipped
repeatedly and made things worse. He forced himself to stop, while the
sound of the helicopter grew stronger.

Then he was gratefully being dragged over the rim. There was mud
plastered all over him, but the heavy rain was washing it off quickly.

He grinned his thanks at Villiger and Nbwale, and Lauren came to
fling herself against him, her wet body pressed hard to his. It aroused
him. He wanted to hold her like this and kiss her until they both
collapsed with exhaustion. Instead, he pushed her away.

He took her face in his hands, kissed her once more and said: "Get
your gun and find some cover!" The others had already scattered.

"*What about you?*"

"Never mind me! Where's Jake?"

"He's in the back of our Range Rover. We put the back seat down. Paula and I did the best we could with the arm."

"All right. Stay with him." Gallagher ran to the Rover, hoping Harding would not use it as a target for the terrible Minigun. He saw Smallson lying there, apparently still out. He picked up the blooker, the M16 and as much ammunition as he could carry. He hoped the Walther at his hip would still work if he had to use it. God alone knew how it had fared after being immersed for so long in the muddy water.

He looked at Lauren as she settled herself down on the soaked ground, beside a wheel. He wanted to stay with her but knew he couldn't.

She seemed to be shivering. The Range Rover gave her some shelter from the rain, but not much. He stooped briefly to kiss her again.

"I don't want to lose you," he said. "Look after yourself."

Her eyes were frightened.

What are we doing here? he thought

The gunship told him. It swooped through the rain and raked the clearing. Flowers were decapitated and grasses cascaded into the air. No one was hurt, although Paula Browne screamed in terror.

The rain was spoiling Harding's aim. The gunship disappeared into the murk. Gallagher took one last look at Lauren's terrified face and ran, blooker slung across his back, M16 in his hands.

"I love you!" she called after him, the wind and rain taking her voice with them.

He did not look back. He wondered if they would see each other again. He passed Nbwale. "Watch her," he said. Nbwale understood.

He ran up the dune. He could not see Villiger. Water streamed down the sandy slope, but, oddly, it was easier going than when the sand was dry. It had become hard-packed, so that his feet made steps in it. He crawled over the crest and slid down. He knew that Marika and her remaining cohorts would have arrived by now. He had to find them. The gunship, which he could hear up there in the rain, a huge angry wasp, would have to wait for now. As long as no one exposed themselves, Harding would have to wait until after the rain for targets.

Just keep him away from the Range Rover, please God. Just give me the time.

By the waterhole, Nbwale lay against the flank of the big dune, trying to keep his eyes on three possible avenues of attack at the same time and attempting to keep the rain from blurring his vision.

He could see Paula Browne lying among the grasses and flowers, the patterns of her now-tattered clothing, covered as they were by mud, blending perfectly with her surroundings. If she did not move, she would be virtually invisible. He hoped she realised that.

He could not see Sumner. Sumner did not have a gun, he knew.

Nbwale would have shot the man had he seen him trying to get another.

He looked at a terrified Lauren Tanner. He admired her. Despite her fear, she had killed to protect Gallagher. Gallagher was a lucky man, he thought. He thought also of Villiger, the Afrikaner who had been chosen to be his assassin. He had a strange feeling about Villiger....

I have learned many things, he thought. *Here I am, protecting two white women and an old white man. Willingly! A week ago, I would have found nothing of value in these rich, privileged people. Today, here in this rain-soaked trap, they may die with me. And I admire them.*

He was strangely glad that Sumner had turned out to be as foul as he had at first thought him to be. There was nothing of value in Sumner.

VII

Gallagher ran just above the base of the outer dune. The trench was covered by a film of running water, and he didn't want to make splashing noises. He came to where the crippled Landrover was. He saw Marika's and knew without looking that it was empty.

Suddenly, three rapid shots cut across the sound of the rain. He ducked behind Marika's vehicle. The shots had not been for him, he decided.

He looked to his right. On the third dune, barely discernible in the bad light, something was moving.

A body; a man's body, and it was rolling slowly, now quickly, now slowly again, until it reached the bottom. Not Villiger's.

Gallagher waited. All the time, the gunship buzzed angrily above, frustrated by the driving rain. Nothing.

He moved, running at a crouch to where the body was. Marika's man. So that had been Villiger. How many more? Including Marika, three? Four.

He moved cautiously over the dune. No one. He began working his way back to the waterhole. He came to the big inner dune and, instead of going over it, decided to go around it. Its northern section was curved right round, so that its end pointed due west. He was quite close to it. Cautiously, he moved forward. He reached the end of the dune, moved round.

And Marika was standing before him, her M16 pointed at his chest.

He froze. His own M16 was pointing back at her.

They stood there, staring at each other, the rain drenching their faces. Marika's green eyes were wide, and the rain made it appear as if she were crying. Maybe she was. The beautiful face was composed but the cheeks were white with an inner pain. There was anger, too, in the eyes; but none of the earlier fury.

She had promised herself she would shoot him on sight, but now she had him at the end of the M16, her body began to betray her. She cursed herself for needing him. Why didn't he shoot?

"I would have given you anything," she told him in the rain. "Anything." Her voice was soft, almost detached from her, as if her mouth spoke but her mind were elsewhere. "Why, Gordon? Why? You have destroyed everything for me."

He said nothing, waiting for the moment when, he knew, she would pull the trigger.

"I loved you," she said, and he knew it was coming.

He watched her eyes.

She looked at him, remembering too many things that brought warm stirrings within her. She had arrived at the top of the big dune just in time to see the way he kissed the American girl; and then the gunship had attacked. She had wanted to shoot him then, but had held back, wanting him to know when the time came; wanting to see his face.

But she would have shot the girl if only his body had not been blocking the target. Then the moment had passed, because she had seen the fleeting movement of the South African out of the corner of her eye and had been forced to move quickly. She had heard the girl call, "I love you!" even as she had moved.

Marika burned, and the fire began to show in the green eyes. Gallagher saw that the moment had come.

Are you watching O'Keefe? It's happened again.

Marika's eyes widened just a fraction as she realized that he was not going to shoot, and not understanding why. He was hers to love, and to kill. Her finger began to tighten on the trigger.

The two shots tore through the rain, the reports sharp punctuations within the sounds of the wind and the downpour.

Marika's eyes widened to their limit, and blood, richly red, bubbled out of the mouth that had once kissed him with such urgency.

Lungs gone, Gallagher's mind observed detachedly.

Her body was wrenched backwards, the M16 flying out of already slackening hands. There was a terrible, flat sound as she hit the water-cloaked earth. Her legs moved towards her stomach, as if to contain an unbearable pain, then they relaxed, straightening once more.

He saw that her eyes were upon him, and that the blood was spreading from the wounds in her chest, and that the rain was patiently washing away the redness from her mouth; a redness that flowed continuingly. The mouth moved, trying to speak to him; but only more blood came out. She made a soft bubbling sound.

The eyes continued to look at him, questioning. She knew he hadn't shot her. Then the astonishing green eyes began to film over in the rain. Soon, the rain fell unheeded upon them.

He squatted to reach over and gently shut them. The magnificent body was just another dead thing in the desert. He picked up the rifle. Villiger was with him as he stood up.

"That was a lucky shot," he said. "I was afraid I'd miss." He looked at Gallagher with the same curious look he'd had when he'd found him standing by the abandoned Landrover with the dead Selini inside. "I thought there wasn't going to be time. I saw you two run into each other, and didn't wait to see who would fire first."

"Did you see her speak?"

"No," Villiger answered, surprised by the question. "There wasn't time for speeches. Man, a fraction of a second. That was all."

To Gallagher, it had seemed like years.

"She actually talked?"

"No," Gallagher answered. "She didn't say anything. Let's find what's left of them."

They left Marika's body to the rain and hurried round the dune. As soon as they entered the enclosure, Gallagher saw a sight that would stay with him for the rest of his life. Ngoma was on one knee, taking a bead on Lauren who, oblivious, was lying where he had left her, beneath the Range Rover. Nbwale had seen the danger and was already rising, bringing up his AK. He yelled something.

Ngoma was incredibly swift. She simply changed her aim to the more immediate danger, pumped four shots into Nbwale, and was re-aligning her sights on Lauren as the huge African toppled backwards like a massive tree, his face totally destroyed by the four heavy bullets striking home.

Gallagher had known that Villiger would not be able to do anything in time, and had dropped Marika's rifle to allow him to use his own M16, while Ngoma was still firing at Nbwale. By the time she'd got Lauren in her sights again, he was ready.

His actions were smooth, unhurried, yet with the deadly, swift precision that had once brought a sense of wonder to O'Keefe. He fired six rapid shots at Ngoma. Every one found its target. They were all head shots.

Then Gallagher realized what he had done. His stomach heaved, but he was not sick. That was worse.

O'Keefe! his mind screamed. *Leave me now! It's done. I've paid.*

But it didn't help. It never would.

Villiger was staring at him, then he saw Lauren, on her feet and rushing towards him.

"Stay down!" he shouted. He saw her drop flat as the gunship leapt over the crest of the high dune to come sweeping in.

255

The rain had slackened considerably, with an abruptness that left him feeling naked. Visibility was rapidly becoming too good for Harding. He heard Villiger dive for cover, as he too flung himself down. Then he saw, with horror, that Paula Browne had stood up. Dear God, she was trying to run away.

Although he knew exactly what was going to happen, it was still shocking when it occurred. The Minigun chewed Paula Browne's running figure to mincemeat, and Gallagher had a horrific vision of the dingoes being blasted into flying fur, chopped meat and shattered bones. Paula Browne simply came apart.

Lauren saw it happen. "*Paula!*" she screamed. "*Paula!*"

"*Stay down!*" Gallaghed yelled at her frantically. "*Stay down! She's dead!*"

With vast relief, he saw that she stayed down; but her head was buried in her arms and he knew she was weeping. He dearly wished he could go to her, but instead he watched as the gunship flung itself into the rapidly lightening sky to do a half-loop and a half-roll and come streaking back, nose down.

The Minigun chattered madly again, but Harding only got already dead bodies, and Villiger's Range Rover. The bullets marched up its side, turned the windows into shrapnel, chewed up the roof, before marching across the sand and over Nbwale's huge body. Then the machine was climbing into the sky again. Flyboy was really having a good time at the pole.

"We've got to stop it!" Gallagher shouted at Villiger. Quickly, he unslung the blooker, loaded it. He would have just the one chance. "Come on!" he said to the South African, and ran at the crouch to Nbwale's body.

After only the briefest of hesitations, Villiger followed.

"*Gordon!*" Lauren was looking fearfully at him.

"Don't move from there!"

She stayed, but did not take her eyes away from him.

He said to Villiger: "Smear my back with Nbwale's blood!"

"*What?*"

"Do it, for God's sake!"

Suddenly, Villiger seemed to understand. He reached down quickly to put his hand to Nbwale's shattered face and rub the blood liberally on Gallagher's shirt. Then Gallagher lay down in full view, his limbs at a grotesque angle, with the exception of one hand which hid the blooker beneath his body.

"It's crazy," Villiger said. "Bloody dangerous. You don't know if they'll go for it, and even if they do, you've got to be fast enough to beat that bloody gun."

"It's our one chance," Gallagher said. "I thought this place would give Flyboy problems, but he's too good. He could probably take that

256

gunship sideways through a door if he put his mind to it."

"Gordon! *What are you doing*?" It had just dawned on Lauren. "You'll be killed!"

"What will happen if I don't do it?" he asked, partly of himself. "Villiger, whatever happens, make her stay down."

"I will."

"Thanks. Now leave me. The chopper's coming back."

The South African hesitated.

"You're supposed to be a pro, Villiger. Go!"

Villiger went. He dropped to the ground, next to Lauren. The rain had stopped completely now. The sun was already drying out the ground. It was becoming hot again.

"He told me," Villiger began quietly, "not to allow you to move, no matter what."

She stared across to Gallagher's spread-eagled form. "If he doesn't make it," she said softly, "that's it, isn't it?"

"More or less. *Ja*."

"I see." She said nothing more. The grey eyes stared at the man she loved so strongly, offering himself as bait once again. He had done so much, she felt, it would be unfair if he failed now. She prayed that whoever made the rules of life would rule in his favour. She was no longer surprised by the intensity of her feelings. Today, she had killed to save him and knew that, had she not been incredibly lucky, she would probably have died for him; but it was still hard to believe that a week before, she had not known of his existence.

The gunship was high up, directly above the dunes.

"Head down!" Villiger told her. "And don't move it for anything!"

They pressed themselves tightly to the ground, letting the flowers and shrubs cover them as much as possible. Lauren made her hands into fists, and prayed.

VIII

Flyboy brought the gunship down like a stone, spiralling and side-slipping to the desert below, a huge bird of prey descending upon a rabit.

He grinned. This was just like the time he'd dropped out of the sky on to that Cong village, leading the other three gunships of the air cav troop in. The Cong never knew what hit them. That had been a good one. He grinned again, remembering.

"Lovely, lovely, my beauty," he cooed at the Huey.

Just when it appeared he was certain to crash, the gunship halted abruptly, a mere ten feet above the ground.

He held the ship to one side as he peered out. "Looks like someone got Gallagher."

Harding, his stomach queasy from the rapid descent, said: "Marika, no doubt. She had marked him down." He didn't sound so interested now. It was obvious no one was going to get away. With Gallagher dead, any other survivors were finished. Harding International was safe. "Let's find the others."

"I can only see dead bodies."

"I don't see Smallson. Let's look!"

"You got it." The helicopter began to rise; then Flyboy paused to peer down at Gallagher. "Hey! No bullet holes...."

But it was already too late.

Gallagher heard the machine begin to rise and knew it was now or never. He rolled, blooker tracking for the gunship. Harding's startled face as he frantically tried to bring the Minigun to bear. Flyboy, with highly sharpened instincts, already jinking the ship out of the way.

Gallagher fired.

What keeps a helicopter from rotating about itself and disappearing up its own behind is the little rotor in the tail, put there to prevent just such a thing from happening. Because of Flyboy's superb speed of reaction and expert skills, within the split-second that he had seen his danger, the gunship had escaped getting a blooker round in its cabin. However, Gallagher had his own skills too, and it had required only a minute adjustment of his aim with allowance for deflection, for him to hit the tail, where the blooker round exploded. It blew the tail section away and the rotor with it.

The helicopter subsequently behaved exactly as it was meant to. It began to rotate, spun by the torque of its main rotor shaft. Flyboy did his best, which was considerable; but even Flyboy was not proof against the laws of physics.

The gunship slammed, in full rotation, against the upper flank of the big dune, bounced sickeningly and tore like a maddened thing along its length, gouging a great scar as it went, bounding, rolling like some gigantic, mortally wounded insect. Pieces flew off it. Spars, braces, supports snapped; glass shattered with the sound of machine guns. Once, the Huey seemed to pivot on its main blades.

At last, it came to rest at the far, curving southern end of the dune, propped on its side by the bent and twisted mountings of the Minigun. Miraculously, it did not explode.

Gallagher was on his feet and running, tugging the Walther out of its holster. He reached the gunship just as Flyboy climbed, incredibly unhurt, out of the wreck. Flyboy had his big Army Colt out, and was trying to sight on Gallagher. He rocked a little.

Gallagher stopped, raised the Walther two-handedly and fired rapidly. The four nine-millimetre bullets took Flyboy in a close group in the chest. His arm was flung outwards as the force of the four bullets striking home in rapid succession hurled him against the wrecked gunship. His finger squeezed the trigger of the .45in a dying spasm. A single shot went harmlessly into the air. Flyboy was already dead. Every bullet had gone through his heart, each doing more damage than the one before. The first had already done the job.

Gallagher moved cautiously forward, pistol ready for a new target. He reached the gunship, peered in. Harding was there, impaled by a support that had come loose from the Minigun. Harding had reached the end of everything.

The black eyes flickered open even as Gallagher looked.

"Well," Harding said weakly, though with the same cynicism that Gallagher had come to recognise. "Mr Gallagher. Or ... may I still ... call you Gordon? Humour a dying man. Well, Gordon. You have managed to bring down an empire. No ... no small feat ... that. Marika ... I take it ... is dead?"

"Yes."

Harding tried to nod, but that caused too much pain. He grimaced. "So you bested even her. Remarkable. She ... was unique. Such incredible ... talent. Do you know what ... what has survived us? Mediocrity." Harding tried to laugh, but failed. His blood sloshed about in his throat. "You may take Lauren. I give her to ... you."

"I don't need your bloody permission, you bastard!" Gallagher said angrily. But Harding was dead. "Trust the sod to have the last word." Gallagher felt cheated, and was furious with the dead man.

He heard a sound behind him and whirled, the Walther tracking round like the head of a snake; but it was Lauren and Villiger running towards him. They paused momentarily, seeing something terrible in his eyes; then came on as he relaxed, and the weapon dropped to point at the ground.

She came slowly to him, her eyes searching his face. His arms enfolded her, and she pressed herself to him, squeezing him with a strength he would not have thought possible. Her body seemed to demand possession of him. She still managed to smell fresh, and his nostrils savoured the scent of her.

Villiger stared at Flyboy's body, then moved up to peer into the gunship. "O'Keefe was right," he said calmly. "You are something special."

Gallagher was stunned, but the South African was not looking at him. "*O'Keefe*? How do *you* know O'Keefe?"

Villiger ignored the question. "It wasn't until I saw you pull that trick with the gunship that I was sure," Villiger continued as if Gallagher hadn't spoken. "He never told me your name, of course. No description, either. But that gunship trick was his. He taught you. I

259

heard he died. Were you with him?" His eyes at last turned to Gallagher.

Gallagher was shattered. O'Keefe worked for *South Africa*? "Yes." Reluctantly.

Villiger read his expression. "No. He didn't work for us. He worked *with* me. Once. They way you and I have."

"This is different ... oh, what the hell. What does it matter?" Gallagher walked slowly back to the undamaged Range Rover with Lauren. The sun was blazing again, and the thin layer of mud that had caked itself to their ragged clothes began to crumble off like dust. "Well," he went on to Lauren, "we seem to have made it ... what's left of us."

Out of the original thirteen people in the room, only four were now left still alive. Thirteen people. The price Harding had wanted for one man. Poor Lamoutiers, poor von Dietlingers, poor Bannion, poor Paula Browne, poor....

Sumner!

Gallagher suddenly smelled danger. "*Down!*" he yelled, dragging her with him and not knowing where the threat was coming from.

They heard a single shot and a choked cry. They looked. Sumner's body was rolling down the slope of the big dune. A rifle had stayed near the crest. By the gunship, Villiger was just lowering his AK. He slung it on his shoulder and came towards them.

"Go and see how Jake is," Gallagher said to Lauren. She seemed reluctant to leave him so he added, giving her a brief squeeze. "No, no. It's all right. Go on."

She went away as Villiger came up.

Villiger said, mildly: "I'd been watching him for some time. I knew he had picked up a gun from somewhere."

"You set him up?"

"Of course. It was the only answer. I've worked for people like Sumner for as long as I can remember," the South African went on, as if just stumbling upon a revelation. He paused. "I would not have killed him, you know."

Gallagher was puzzled. "Sumner?"

"Nbwale. He was a good man." Villiger began to move away.

"Villiger," Gallagher called. "Piet."

Villiger stopped, turned around.

Gallagher said: "You've saved my life three times...."

"I didn't know what I was doing with that spider bite."

"Whatever. Thanks. It's not enough, I know, just bald thanks...."

Villiger was clearly uncomfortable. "Special people should not go to waste," he interrupted again, gruffly, and for the first time that Gallagher could remember, the piggy eyes actually seemed to smile.

"I'll get that other Landrover so we can get out of here." He started up the dune.

Gallagher walked on to the Range Rover.

Adrian Fowler hurried into the office of the man he called Greg. "I've got your proof!" He stopped. The man had not looked up from his desk, but was reading a many-paged letter, his face pale. Fowler walked slowly to the desk, sat down, and waited.

At last, the man looked up. "It's all here, Adrian. In this letter. It matches everything you said. The F28 took them to Australia, via various refuelling points. No one anywhere bothered to check the consignment of perforated crates." His mouth twisted with disgust as he thought of it. "Vital equipment for the research station at Kintore. Who would doubt Harding? Crofton blew the whistle. He gave his former RAF rank and number. It's genuine."

"Why did he do it?"

The man gave a brief smile of genuine pleasure. "Gallagher." He passed Fowler the letter. "It went to MOD, MOD sent it to us."

Fowler took the letter, began to read. At one stage, he simply said, "Ah, ha," softly. When he was at last finished, he returned the letter. "Gallagher seems to have got over that O'Keefe thing. Looks as if he'll bring down the whole organization."

"He's not out of the woods yet, but I think he will. I've alerted my people to mount a rescue."

For a moment, Fowler was puzzled, until he realized what was meant. Greg Kingston-Wyatt was a first-generation Australian who had joined the RAF just before Korea and had stayed. Aussies were his people, even after all those years.

Then Fowler told him about Jake Smallson. It was still just nine a.m.

Crofton stared at Inge. If he had to get off before dark, he'd have to do something soon. The German girl was looking very worried. There had been no radio communication for some time.

She stared at the radio, but her gun was pointed at Crofton. She would shoot if he did anything threatening, and she would not miss. Then suddenly, the radio came alive. A voice was calling from Adelaide. Inge tried to do two things at once. She instinctively reached for the radio, and tried to keep Crofton under guard. For a brief instant, she failed to achieve both objectives.

Crofton, in a desperation born of the need for survival, lashed out. Inge fell. It was an inexpert blow and she was only stunned. Crofton ran out, heading for the Cessna, while the radio continued to call fruitlessly.

261

Crofton ran as if the Devil himself were on his heels. He wasn't too wrong about that. He made it to the Citation, skipped his checks and started the Garretts. They whirred into life and he was rolling the Cessna forward while Inge, swearing luridly in German, was pounding along the corridors.

He lifted the sleek jet cleanly, heading for Darwin, as Inge charged on to the airstrip, the dust of the jet's passage settling down upon her. She fired uslessly at it, emptying her magazine and screaming obscenities into the reddening sky.

No one stopped Crofton at Darwin. No one stopped him when he took a passage out on an airliner.

They had made Jake Smallson as comfortable as possible in the back of Marika's Landrover. The makeshift sling that Lauren and Paula Browne had rigged up, using an Uzi, worked surprisingly well. But the old man needed a doctor, and soon. Cook was still over a hundred kilometres away and it would be well into the night before they made it there. For some reason, Marika's radio hadn't worked.

Then they heard a sound; heavy, powerful.

"Sounds like a big jet flying low," Villiger said.

They looked up. It was not a big jet but four Aardvarks, their eight engines thundering across the plain as they swept above, at what Gallagher had judged to be about five thousand feet, even as he ran frantically towards the crashed gunship.

God God God, please let the radio be still workable. He reached in, forcing his body through the wreckage, and ignoring Harding's staring black eyes. He found the headphones and hurriedly selected 121.5, the international distress frequency.

"Mayday! Mayday! Aardvarks Mayday! Mayday! *Anyone* Mayday! Mayday!"

Was the bloody thing still working? Did it have the range? Would the Aardvarks hear?

"Mayday! Mayday! Aardvarks Mayday! Mayday!" *Work, you bloody thing*! Work work *work.*

All four F-111Cs heard him. In the leading aircraft, the pilot said in surprise: "He knows what we are."

The Weapons Systems Operator, in the right-hand seat, said even as he made to reply to the Mayday: "Probably a downed pilot who flew one of these once."

The captain of the aircraft doubted it.

The WSO called: "This is Aardvark. Select one-three-oh-decimal-seven, and state your position."

Heart bursting with joy at his success, Gallagher cleared the distress frequency, selected the suggested frequency and hoped that would work. "Hello Aardvark. We are twenty-five kilometres almost due west of Muckera Rockhole. Do you read?"

"We read. Twenty-five kilometres west of Muckera."

"Right. We need medical attention urgently, and there are a lot of dead people down here."

In all four aircraft, the crews were stunned. The leader had already given the order to turn, and with beautiful precision, they turned together, angling down towards the desert, their variable wings sweeping forward to a sixteen-degree spread so that they came down like a flight of huge birds of prey getting ready to pluck a scuttling creature from the ground.

In the lead aircraft, the WSO said: "Sounds like a Pom. What's a Pom doing down there with dead people?" Then a new message came through his headphones. His eyes stared.

Gallagher watched the F-111Cs as they approached.

"Are you Gallagher?" came the Australian voice on the radio.

Startled, Gallagher answered: "Yes."

"You've got powerful friends. Rescue and medical attention are on their way. Stay put."

"We shall. Thanks."

"Any time." The Aardvarks circled once. "Have you poled one of these?"

"No. But I had a Phantom. Once."

"Ah! We must leave you now, Phantom." The Aardvarks swept their wings and climbed on afterburners, shaking the desert with their sound. It was a beautiful sight.

"Show off!" Gallagher said. He couldn't resist it.

Laughter came over the air as the Aardvarks disappeared. "Out," someone said.

Then rescue came; and there was the press, and the photographers, and the shock and the awe and the amazement, and the need to believe the unbelievable, and the horror, and the questions, questions, questions. Then blessed peace, and a clean bed.

Day Ten

JAKE SMALLSON came out of it very well. He saw Gallagher alone, the next day, in his Adelaide hospital room where he was being kept for further observation.

"There's nothing wrong with me," was the first thing he said, then he went straight to the point: "Your wife called, Lauren says."

"Yes."

"And?"

"I told her no."

"Good. Now you can marry Lauren. Don't worry about her stupid father. I have enough money —"

"Jake. I don't want money from you."

The old man stared at him. "You would begrudge my granddaughter a wedding present? You would begrudge my giving you a wedding present?"

Gallagher sighed. "No, Jake."

Later that day he saw Villiger. The South African had come to say goodbye. Gallagher hadn't seen him since the rescue. He wondered whom Villiger had reported to.

"If things were different," Villiger said, "I'd ask you for a drink, up Table Mountain."

"If things were different, I'd accept."

They stared at each other, not saying the things they would have liked to.

Villiger stuck out his hand. "Look after yourself, Gordon."

"You too, Piet."

They shook hands once, and parted. Neither looked back.

Fowler said to Kingston-Wyatt: "Our Gallagher is still quite formidable." They had been studying the reports. "Harding International rocked to its foundations, and that incredible gang of assassins wiped out."

"With a little help from Villiger." But Kingston-Wyatt was smiling. Villiger's report, of which he'd received a copy by devious means, had been full of praise for Gallagher, as much as O'Keefe's reports had once been. What would Villiger's superiors have thought about that? He smiled again, at the thought.

The two men with the truck had been caught, but the German woman was still missing; and so was Crofton. He was not too bothered about Crofton, who was no danger to anyone, except maybe to those who employed him.

Kingston-Wyatt's mouth twisted briefly. His cynicism had been born of long years of observing his fellow men.

Fowler said: "Are you going to ask him back?"

Kingston-Wyatt stared blissfully at nothing. "Did he ever leave?"

"He thinks he did."

"Oh." Kingston-Wyatt went over to the window. The square was empty. "Adrian, how many Alexander Hardings do you think there are?"

"How long is a piece of string?"

"Lovely world."

"I never said it was."

The January wind came off Zürich See, hurled itself over Quaibrücke, headed north along the Limmat, threading its way over and under the next three bridges until it came to the Bahnhofbrücke where it veered right, to whistle up Weinbergstrasse. It was a cold wind, yet oddly benevolent. A covering of night-old snow lay on the streets. On this Sunday morning, Zürich felt quiet and empty.

Crofton walked along the Limmat Quai, his feet crunching rhythmically across the snow. He liked his Sunday morning walks before finishing up at the café in the Rössligasse, where he had his breakfast. For the past two months, he had been leading a comparatively simple life, keeping a low profile, as the Americans liked to call it. He smiled to himself. What was a low profile? No one had come after him.

A friend had sold the Porsche Turbo in a slightly shady deal to someone in the Middle East, and the money had found its way to him in Switzerland, less the friend's commission, of course. He now drove an unobtrusive VW. The same friend had rented out the flat lucratively, to a Japanese businessman. That money, too, found its way to Switzerland. But Crofton did not really need the money, he'd already had plenty stashed away in Swiss banks. He had decided to take it easy for some months before putting himself on the market again. There were plenty of places were pilots were needed, with no awkward questions being asked. He no longer called himself Crofton.

He entered the café, and as usual, was practically the first customer of the day. The usual young waitress served him with a smile. They had already shared a bed. He ate his breakfast, went back along the Limmat Quai, turned right into Königengasse, then left into Niederdorfstrasse, where he had a modest flat. He went up the narrow stairs to the first floor and entered the flat, shutting the door firmly behind him. It was only then that he saw the silenced pistol looking at him; and behind it, Inge's mean eyes.

Epilogue

SHE CAME to him in the night, her body bringing to him that wonderfully fresh scent that had first captivated him. She was warm and soft and all-enveloping, her beautiful legs holding him, caressing him, squeezing him. They made love slowly, gently, as if in a dream, their bodies worshipping each other.

The top sheet was off the bed, and their entwining, enfolding bodies slid and sighed against each other, using the whole bed as if in ecstatic celebration of this glorious freedom.

They had the whole night, and the rest of their lives.

He was on the beach. The sun beat down, but it did not seem to bother him. He saw her in the distance, coming towards him; beautiful, naked. He waited for her.

She reached him, hand outstretched. He took her hand and together they walked to the water's edge. They put their free hands together and scooped up some water.

She smiled.

They walked back to the hole. Not a drop was spilt.

They poured the water into the hole. It drank, and was full.